20/10/15
29/9/16

Doncaster
Metropolitan Borough Council

DONCASTER LIBRARY AND INFORMATION SERVICES

Please return/renew this item by the last date shown.
Thank you for using your library.

D1363164

Painting by John Freeman
© Studio of John Freeman
9 Market Place Whitby YO22 3DD
www.johnfreemanstudio.co.uk

Matador
9 Priory Business Park
Kibworth Beauchamp
Leicestershire LE8 0RX, UK
Tel: (+44) 116 279 2299
Fax: (+44) 116 279 2277
Email: books@troubador.co.uk
Web: www.troubador.co.uk/matador

ISBN 978 1783060 344

British Library Cataloguing in Publication Data.
A catalogue record for this book is available from the British Library.

Typeset in Aldine by Troubador Publishing Ltd
Printed and bound in the UK by TJ International, Padstow, Cornwall

Matador is an imprint of Troubador Publishing Ltd

Thank you to my son, William for his greatly appreciated support and assistance,

Thank you also to Ian for the many journeys to and around Whitby.

and

Thank you to Charis for being the first person to read through my work.

Prologue

The prince and his guest were sitting at ease in tall-backed chairs, partaking of pipes before a blazing hearth after a hearty meal. A large white dog and a big mastiff lay at their feet. The two men seldom met in such convivial circumstances. Both were exceptional men, and commanders whose respective lack of years belied their experience.

The prince was enjoying the far-ranging discussion. He was keen to hear his guest's well-informed opinions on a variety of matters. He did not delve beyond them. A part of him remained wary of his guest.

When the man seemed preoccupied suddenly, he exercised caution. 'Is there aught amiss?'

His guest got to his feet. The man's left hand rose to his throat. He appeared now to be oblivious of the prince's presence. In the next moment, he quit the chamber in haste, the mastiff at his heels, leaving the prince to stare after him, bewildered and astonished.

PART ONE

EARLY SPRING

"Sow an act, and you reap a habit,
Sow a habit, and you reap a character."

CHAPTER ONE

Catch the Wind, Hold the Moon

They were strangers in a strange land. They were fugitives in their own country.

Stretched like a good-wife's pristine cloth, the snowy, star silent bleakness surrounded the cliff top tavern. A lowly structure on the outskirts of a fishing hamlet, it was situated in a wilderness that would be forever haunted by rugged isolation. The constant sighing of the North Sea escaped the black void beyond the ragged lip of the snowbound North Yorkshire moorland and slithered on the frozen air to where breath hung suspended around the tavern.

Sanctuary was being given to exhausted men within its rough walls. The crackling flames spread warmth through chilled bones and brought the blessed oblivion of slumber. But soon dreams were infected by the horror of discovery, the frenzy of defence, the terror of defeat and the guilt of flight.

The sharpened instinct for self-preservation registered a half-stifled cough.

Upon waking, Sir Alan Malbury discovered that sleep was not the only thing to have crept up upon him. Sitting bolt upright in the rickety fireside chair he stared at the stocky, grey-haired stranger kneeling beside the benches that had been pushed together to form a makeshift bed for his wounded companion. With growing alarm, he looked to where two well-armed men were lounging at the door of the tavern. Abe Pearson, the plump landlord of the Wheel and Anchor, stood between them, a smug grin on his coarse features. Earlier in the evening, he had welcomed the elderly gentlemen. They had been iced by the frigid climate. One of their number had been also begrimed with blood.

Another stranger was sitting astride a narrow bench. A large, inscribed bow and quiver rested close to his slender hands on the rough table. Despite what he considered a lowly weapon, Sir Alan found no common traits in its apparent owner, which set him apart from his companions. The young man's cloak, breeches and boots were of good quality. He was long-legged and lean. His long fair hair was drawn back in a tidy knot. Refined upon maturing youth, the handsome contours of his thin, pale face were not unfriendly. Nor did they reflect sympathy.

Firelight and candlelight conspired to thrust ominous silhouettes upon the crude walls and low ceiling.

Sir Alan felt impelled to ask, "Be you friend or foe?"

The nervous question roused Sir Alan's other lifelong friend. Sir Cuthbert Mainworth woke to find a mastiff sitting close by. The last dregs of sleep left him as he registered the ominous presence of the newcomers. Startled, he heaved his bulk upwards in the inadequate chair. Shooting a fearful glance across the hearth at Sir Alan, he sought reassurance. It was not forthcoming.

"Ain't much life left in 'im," observed the grey-haired stranger, without interrupting his gentle examination of the wounded man.

"The physician?" mumbled Sir Cuthbert. "What of him?" He rose gingerly, keeping a wary eye on the huge grey dog, and shuffled away from whatever was vague and unmoving in the dark corner behind his seat.

Abe Pearson snorted. "Mark Wood be aways in Whitby."

"But…" spluttered Sir Cuthbert, holding onto Sir Alan's chair. "You dispatched a messenger?"

"Aye, that I did," responded the landlord, his triumphant gaze sweeping over those men he had ushered into the common-room while the old knights slept.

Sir Alan's concern for his wounded companion briefly outstripped his fear of the present situation. He got to his feet, his aristocratic features indignant. "Are we to sit here whilst Roger succumbs to his wounds?"

The grey-haired man kneeling beside Sir Roger Verity spared him a cool glance. "Y' were all fer sleepin' while y'r friend went."

"What brings you to these remote parts, especially at this time of year, sir?" asked the youngest, fair-haired stranger. He coughed, then cleared his throat before hoarsely continuing, "Better you explain to us, for, rest assured, we are not your foe. I am Richard Massone. Allow me to introduce Tom Wright, attending to the wounded member of your party. At the door, with the good landlord, are Bill Todd and Danny Murphy." He glanced towards the dark corner behind the chair vacated by Sir Cuthbert, but said nothing further.

"You must forgive me, young man," responded Sir Alan. "Recent events have made us circumspect. How are we to trust your words?"

Richard Massone smiled. "We are here, sir, armed only with a desire to understand your plight, and, hopefully, to assist you."

Reassured that his initial impression of the well bred young man was not erroneous, Sir Alan, a little heady from euphoria, resumed his seat. "In that case, I shall endeavour to explain the predicament in which we find ourselves. We were making our way to Whitby. My wife, Joan, and myself. Cuthbert and his wife. And dear, poor Roger and his sixteen-year-old daughter, Catherine.

"Roger has an acquaintance thereabouts who will, he assured us, secure for us a passage to the Low Countries. Our loyalty to King Charles has seen our homes around Driffield become prime targets. Roger had several very nasty encounters with the Parliamentarians prior to our departure.

"We had journeyed beyond Pickering when we fell foul of a Parliamentarian patrol. Roger urged us to make haste. Alas, the older ladies were soon taken prisoner. After a rigorous chase, Catherine was surrounded. Roger battled against the troopers around his daughter. When he received those ghastly wounds, Cuthbert and I realised we must take flight if we were to stand any chance of assisting the ladies. By following at a prudent distance, I witnessed the troopers take our loved ones to a military encampment close to a substantial Hall.

"Upon informing Roger of our predicament, he insisted, despite the serious nature of his wounds, that we should press on

5

and locate his acquaintance. His deteriorating condition, our fatigue and the worsening weather forced us to pause at this tavern.

"Mayhap, you gentlemen know of the man we seek? For I understand he has quite a reputation. His name is Shadiz? I believe he is also known as the Master?"

It was the turn of the armed men to be taken aback. With one accord, they looked towards the dark corner where the mastiff sat beside the empty chair. Sir Alan got the impression that their surprise was mixed with caution.

"You know the wounded fellow?" exclaimed Richard Massone.

The expectant pause finally ended. The mastiff rose, wagging its spiky tail.

The impact of the leisurely emergence from the concealing corner on the elderly gentlemen was immediate and profound. They had struggled for survival in winter's cruel landscape, dogged by puritanical aggression, only to be confronted by this towering, dark creature.

His tremendous height was partnered by a powerful physique. Unlike the other men, he wore a black leather coat instead of a cloak. A mighty broadsword was slung across his back. A scimitar, curving wickedly at his slender hip, hung from the thick belt that secured his long outer garment.

Falling halfway down his broad back, his wild hair was the colour of deepest midnight. A single gold earring glinted in the draught-prone candlelight. Having a vague slant to them, his jet-black eyes dominated his barbarous, tribal dark features. Scarred across one high cheekbone, they arrogantly projected an indeterminable age.

His silent movements possessed a warrior's assurance. An air of intelligent authority established beyond doubt that this charismatic man was a leader.

The fearful knights might have taken heart had it not been for the menacing aura, which engendered caution. Or should have.

"*You* are Shadiz?" exclaimed Sir Cuthbert.

The aged knight quailed beneath a brief sidelong glance from chilling black eyes.

"Alan...."

Sir Alan, startled rigid for a second time in a remarkably short time, provided a tardy response thus also attracting the attention of the black glare. He hastened to the laden benches and knelt beside Tom Wright. "I am here, Roger."

The mortally wounded man struggled to speak, "Have ... have you located ... him?"

Sir Alan hesitated.

Not so Sir Cuthbert, "We have, indeed."

"Shadiz?"

"Aye," came the low-pitched response. He went down onto one knee at the other side of Tom Wright to Sir Alan.

The knight was surprised by the absence of an accent. Shadiz appeared alien to English shores. Then the truth dawned on him.

The Gypsy was answering Sir Roger in a deep, distinct voice, strangely muted, "Y'r friends've explained y'r troubles."

A haunted expression vied with the agony remorselessly pinching Sir Roger's countryman's face. It was with sick determination that he succeeded in clutching Shadiz's arm. Tom Wright glanced sideward at Shadiz.

"Find her. I ... I beg you."

"She'll be rescued."

"'Tis ... the future ... Catherine ..."

"She'll be protected. I give my oath." There was no discernible expression yet the whispery pledge remained a powerful one nonetheless.

Relief seeped into every deep line etched into Sir Roger Verity's face. In the next moment, agony reasserted itself. At length, when the cruel spasm had diminished, a shrewdness entered his heavy-lidded eyes.

The two very different men regarded each other.

★ ★ ★

"Have no fear. She will not awaken, especially while she continues to regain her strength in sleep."

Still the tall man hesitated in the gathering gloom of a balmy August evening.

"Please," urged the older man. "She cannot remain in the arbour, however sweet the scent of the roses. And tis a pity to wake her."

With great care, the tall man picked up the twelve-year-old girl and carried her in his arms into the elegant white chateau. In one of the upstairs chambers, he gently laid the girl on the bed. She stirred in her sleep. He took a hasty step backwards, then another. Then he stopped, looking down at her.

"I would raise no mountains. Nor even molehills," said the girl's father. Seeing the other man's expression, he said no more.

★ ★ ★

Shadiz gave an imperceptible nod.

Pain engulfed Sir Roger for the final time. "Hold the moon ...."

Smeared with blood, the hand on Shadiz's arm grew limp. He shook himself free of lifeless fingers and straightened.

"He was a good and brave gentleman," sighed Sir Alan, sadly.

"'e were a bloody fool," rasped Shadiz. The mastiff followed him to the door of the tavern, where his two men stood at either side of the cringing landlord. "Todd, Murphy, get body to Tockwith. Tell 'im I don't give a damn 'ow 'ard ground be, get the old man in it. Wi' a proper marker."

Sir Alan was outraged. "I cannot conceive how Roger became acquainted with you, but I do not think."

"That's a bloody good start," sneered Shadiz, softly. He wrenched open the tavern door, inviting butterfly snowflakes into the common room.

"Indeed, the ladies will be rescued?" queried Sir Cuthbert.

"Develesko Mush," growled Shadiz. He slewed round. "D'you old bastards imagine I give an oath t' a dyin' man just t' smooth 'is passage into the unknown?"

Tom Wright's footsteps were magnified in the tense silence. He positioned himself between the alarmed knights and the intimidating Master, murmuring, "Lad."

Shadiz thrust him a venomous look. Tom remained outwardly unaffected.

"Bring 'em," commanded Shadiz. He spun on his heels and disappeared into the snowy night.

★ ★ ★

"Approach me again and, so help me, I'll re-route you."

Thickset and panting, the soldier stood angrily arrested in the middle of the small, dingy tent. To make matters worse, he was obliged to squint down the business end of his own pistol.

"Oh, do take care, my dearest," wailed Lady Mary Mainworth.

Captain Cranwell glared at the tall girl holding him at bay. Her blue eyes were ablaze with hostility. Her unflinching silence was a blatant challenge. Self-preservation encroached upon his feeling of superiority. His gaze strayed over her flushed, delicate face, slithered down her cascade of fair-white hair and crept down her slender, ripe figure in the dirty green riding habit. Those same emotions that had led him into the absurd situation returned. This time they were coupled with a soldier's caution.

"I shall call for assistance," snapped Lady Joan Malbury.

Cranwell gave an unpleasant laugh. "An' who d' y' reckon's gonna cum runnin'?"

"Sir Nip-A-Long, mayhaps?" suggested the girl, "Patron saint of interrupted travellers." The pistol was growing heavy.

When the soldier pounced with bear-like logic, Lady Joan shouted a warning. Lady Mary screamed.

Catherine Verity fired the pistol.

★ ★ ★

While Colonel Thomas Page waited beside the warmth of the smoky brazier in his canvas field tent, his watery gaze came to rest on the summons from Fylingdales Hall. One did not keep Francois Lynette waiting. Ordinarily, he took care not to do so. It was in one's best interests to comply with the wishes of the custodian of the huge Fylingdales Estate, brother of the Dowager, Lady Hellena. A guilty qualm ruffled his wilful decision. His audacity made his insides turn momentarily cold as winter upon the moorland he detested. A carbuncle upon the parkland sculptured over generations from the wilderness, the large Parliamentarian encampment he commanded was close to a bare-branched wood. It kept the iron clad humanity within his domain out of sight of the ancestral Hall, an impressive structure, starkly appropriate for the rugged highlands of Yorkshire.

The first feeble rays of dawn escorted a soldier into the tent. It was not Cranwell bringing the youngest prisoner to him. He was eager to see her again. She was exquisite. No shrinking violet was she. He had watched at a prudent distance as she had struggled with his troopers, while they had followed orders and inflicted the wounds upon her father that would take his life after he had served his purpose.

"Sir, there be gypsy yonder," the soldier informed him, looking pale. "Wants t' speak wi' y' about Shadiz an' whereabouts o' 'is camp."

"Gypsy, you say?"

"Aye," confirmed a deep, distinct voice, strangely muted.

Corpulent and pompous, Page shot up straight and rigid in his leather chair. He stared at the stranger. The shivering light of the candle lantern suspended from a tent pole revealed a formidable presence. "You ... you possess details of Shadiz's camp?" he asked, struggling for normality. It was with a disquieting pang that he realised the soldier had dismissed himself.

"Place be but a day's march away," came the curt reply.

The command tent had suddenly become ridiculously small, threatening to suffocate the colonel. "Why would...."

"There be score t' settle." The interruption was edged with icy impatience. "Do I go instead t' Lynette?"

"No," protested Page. The word seemed to spring forth of its own accord.

Too late the floodgates opened and he recalled what had been recently described to him. The revelation meant the lofty, dark strangeness was a reminder that death was a shape-shifting entity on life's precarious highway. The soulless fury smouldering in those hypnotic jet eyes made him sharply conscious of his precious mortality. He shrank from the enormity of rising to the challenge. Far better to feign inglorious ignorance and to follow the contrivance of trying to reap the rewards for the capture of Shadiz, the Master. That elusive creature of havoc, made terrifyingly substantial.

It was rumoured the Master had entered the northern war arena after he had been recruited a year ago by King Charles's foreign nephew, Prince Rupert. Within weeks, he had proved himself to be a past master at covert raids and deadly ambushes. A great fear of him had been quickly established amongst the Crop-Ears. They never knew where he would strike next between the Humber and the Tyne. Shockingly sudden. Lightning swift. Always vicious. The least amount of disciplined men-at-arms were used to inflict the maximum amount of damage upon Parliamentarian strongholds, supply depots and military cavalcades.

Not surprisingly, an already colourful reputation had been significantly enhanced. Rumours were rife. Although many had tried, no one had so far managed to locate the Master's lair.

"You'll need most o' y'r men." Page's early morning visitor informed him.

The summons from Fylingdales Hall lay buried beneath several maps of the district. Page thought wistfully of its dismissed import.

The hanging tent flap was flung upwards. The Gypsy looked up from the maps spread over the crude desk several seconds before Page. The colonel was relieved to see his newest captain was absorbed with his bleeding ear.

Catherine Verity's footsteps faltered. A painful soul jolt. An odd spine tingle. In less than a missed heartbeat, a fresh reality.

Ashen-faced, she received a brutal push from Cranwell, which sent her careering across the smoky interior of the command tent. The Gypsy watched as she sprawled head first over the colonel's laden desk.

"Delightful," commented Page, trying to sound cheerful.

"Spirited, too," he added, with real conviction. He sighed regretfully. For he regretted everything about the present situation. "I'm afraid we must postpone our little chat, my dear."

Catherine straightened, having only vaguely registered the colonel's words. She stumbled away from the Gypsy, shaken beyond understanding. He remained motionless. She endured his weird jet scrutiny with none of the defiance she had shown Cranwell.

There was an odd pause.

Worried, Colonel Page looked at his captain. The fellow had been recently foisted on him because it was hoped he could assist with the latest design. His uncharitable heart sank as he viewed the soldier's belated reaction.

"*Shadiz*!" Cranwell recalled, shrilly.

He started to back away but never reached the tent flap. The flickering light of the lantern hung from a thick pole glinted upon honed metal. Catherine and the colonel were stunned witnesses to the quick, deft kill. Shadiz had moved at last.

"*Shadiz*?" whispered Catherine, staring at the man.

He turned on Page. The blood-stained dagger pricked the colonel's flabby, scarlet neck. "Go. Tell 'em out yonder t' get ready t' march," he commanded in a whispery tone that brooked no opposition.

To Page, shaking from head to toe, Cranwell's death vindicated his self-seeking conduct.

Shadiz went to the entrance of the tent with the colonel, kicking the body of the dead soldier out of the way. A tall, threatening shadow, he stood with the ready dagger just out of sight of the sentry stationed outside the opening. Afterwards, he tossed the fearful colonel his thick winter cloak, saying, "We're off for a ramble."

Quick to realise his intention, Catherine was shocked into saying, "Have you a death wish?"

Shadiz slowly turned his head and looked at her with a queer intensity. At length, he commanded, "Go back t' tother women an' wait for my men t' come for y'."

The misty greyness of an icy dawn made her return to the older women no great hardship. Once ensconced in the comparative safety of the prison tent, still trembling, Catherine explained about their forthcoming rescue.

Not long afterwards, peering cautiously out of the ragged opening of the tent, she watched the long column of sullen infantry, punctuated at both ends by skittish cavalry, strike out across the snow covered rise and fall of the surrounding moorland. For as long as possible, fascinated by the sheer audacity, she watched the man mounted on a black stallion, riding with apparent ease alongside the stiff, portly figure of the colonel.

When men and horses had been swallowed up by the bleak, undulating landscape, she found it hard to settle down to wait with the anxious women. Impatient to have tidings of her wounded father, in an attempt to occupy her mind, she reviewed his reticent explanation. On reflection, there had been about the entire, amazing piece, the ring of careful confession.

Sixteen years ago, at Scarborough, her father had saved a wild, young vagabond from the wrath of an ugly mob. One kind act had led to another. He had taken the gypsy youth back with him to his manor, Nafferton Garth near Driffield, and provided honest employment. Two days later, half of his beloved horses had disappeared along with the gypsy youth.

At the time having been more concerned with the recent birth of his only child, her father had put the episode down to experience. He had never expected to be recompensed for his loss. Yet that was what had happened several years later, when the youth as a man had grown notorious. It seemed the somewhat inebriated gesture had amused her father. He had accepted the marvellous horseflesh without asking too many questions. Against all the odds, a friendship had developed between the two very different men. Unbeknown to Catherine.

Interrupting thoughts, Richard Massone stepped into the little prison tent and peered through the cold gloom he encountered within. "Ladies, fear not, for we have come to escort you to safety." His gallant reassurance deserted him. He knew he was staring like a witless oaf.

"Young man," snapped Lady Joan.

"She means," said Catherine, grinning. "Keep to the plan."

The women found that the sprawling Parliamentarian camp now appeared to be occupied solely by Shadiz's men. A number were ransacking the makeshift huts with quiet efficiency while others stood guard, holding muskets and loaded crossbows. Several men closed about the women as Richard escorted them through the grubby, trampled snow to where the steaming horses were tethered. On the way, they passed two large piles, one of food and the other of weapons.

Anxiety tarnished breath hung freedom. Amongst the gabble of questions, one stood out.

"How fares my father? Sir Roger Verity?"

Tom Wright knew at once who she was. Shadiz had insisted that he be the one to break the news of her father's death. He took a deep breath. "I'm sorry, luv," he said, gently. "Y'r da died o' 'is wounds last night."

The bolt from the blue threatened to cleave her wildly beating heart. She did not register the consoling clinging of the two older women. "Where ... where is he?" she managed, her blue eyes quite desperate.

Greatly relieved that he could do so, Tom told her.

Concern grew when she demanded to be taken to her father's grave. It became clear if they did not relent they would be obliged to gag her and strap her to one of the spare horses they had brought with them on the rescue mission, which had caused a whirlwind of activity in the past few hours. Tom had a feeling such an action wouldn't go down well with Shadiz. Conscious of his leader's uncharacteristic attitude, he finally succumbed. "Danny, take five o' lads an' get women t' their menfolk at Lodge." He turned to Richard. "We take rest wi' us." The younger man's disapproval was obvious. "Think, lad. 'e wanted 'er da buried in the churchyard at Mercy Cove for 'er." He hoped Bill Todd had been successful in getting the dead knight into the ground. To Catherine, he said, "We'll need t' be quick, lass. We've no notion o' where lad's leadin' Crop-Ears. 'e's backed by 'is pack o' gypsies but...." He shrugged.

14

Giving further vent to his worries, he added, "An', o' course, we don't know who else be about." He glanced at the wood bordering the Crop-Ears' camp, made sparse by winter's killer frost, "We're too flamin' close to Fylingdales 'all."

"They are aware of his identity. At least the colonel is."

All the men engaged in various tasks stopped and stared at Catherine. Their mute alarm prompted her to supply yet another swift explanation. For a second time, she omitted certain details.

"We must go after him," declared Richard.

"Nay, lad," responded Tom.

Catherine's mind was in turmoil. She longed to go to her father's grave. She also found herself wanting the anxious men to gallop off in swift pursuit of their leader. Why had he taken such a suicidal risk? It didn't make any sense. Surely a better way could have been found to rescue Joan, Mary and herself?

When Tom remained unmoved by any of his arguments, Richard shrugged. "Alley cat luck," he muttered, sourly.

"Alley cat?" queried Catherine, as they mounted. A sudden image of black eyes, staring oddly, sprang to mind.

"Aye, lass," murmured Tom, without illusion.

★ ★ ★

The old, blind Romany woman had sat in silence beside the open air hearth throughout the hours of his agitated pacing and his thoughtful stillness. Now she deemed it to be the correct moment to demand in her sharp manner, "Thy decision, Posh-Rat?"

He answered in their language. "I ain't much choice."

★ ★ ★

"Y' ain't t' come after me."

With the notable exception of the Master, everyone who hailed from the Lodge had been against the audacious deception.

It had begun outside the Wheel and Anchor, in the crisp snow blanketing the fishing hamlet of Mercy Cove. Shadiz had made it plain that speedy action was essential. Therefore, instead of accompanying Bill Todd to the cliff top graveyard with the body of the dead knight, Danny Murphy had been dispatched to the Lodge, the Master's headquarters, to collect the bulk of his men. Sir Alan and Sir Cuthbert had been obliged to keep pace with Murphy as best they could across difficult terrain.

By the following morning, the women had been reunited with their menfolk at the Lodge. By dawn of the next day, the Master had still not put in an appearance. His men were beginning to contemplate the unthinkable.

The grey-stoned Lodge dominated the large clearing in which it had stood since Norman times; an abandoned gem deep within Stillingfleet Forest. Drystone walls smothered in ivy and moss, ruined in places by the work of ages, still sought to enclose a broad, cobbled courtyard. To the rear of the square, two-storey edifice, stables and outbuildings were ranged around a wide pasture. All of the buildings had been disfigured by creeping decay; weed infested homes for forest creatures and industrious spiders. Then the Master had arrived and instigated a patchy, habitable rejuvenation, permeated by an atmosphere of genial mustiness.

Having occupied for overlong in his opinion a chamber given the grandiose title of library because of the empty, worm-eaten shelves lining the high stone walls, Richard Massone exhaled with fervent gusto. "There can be little doubt as to what has transpired." When Tom Wright, grappling with his own morbid thoughts, did not respond, Richard flung away towards the large carved hearth.

Like a cankerous slug, the thought crossed Tom's mind that Richard ought to be pleased with the ominous turn of events. Sighing, he shunned the sour reflection. He started to speak and then broke off, listening. Hoping with bated breath against wishful thinking, he glanced at Richard and saw at once from the younger man's tense stance that he, too, had heard the remote disturbance within the forest's frosty stillness.

The heavy oak door creaked open. Keeble swung jauntily on the rusty latch he could barely reach, declaring happily, "Master's back."

Tom got stiffly to his feet, grinning at the man whose crooked height was no more than that of a child of eight.

Immediately, as if released from a tightly wound spring, Richard left the chamber, muttering to himself about the incredible survival of alley cats.

A few minutes later, Tom caught up with him at the front of the Lodge. They stood side by side beneath the rickety porch, overhung with snow trimmed ivy. Both men were taken aback by the sight of horses capped by empty saddles. Tom laughed. Richard coughed in the crisp early morning air, delaying his sarcastic remark.

Several amused guards from the permanent sentry posts throughout the forest were busy shepherding the steaming herd across the torch lit courtyard towards the pen in the rear pasture. The commotion of barking dogs, another form of guard, vied with the slithering clatter of many hooves on the icy cobbles. After hours of silent waiting, the Lodge was alive again.

The two men glimpsed at roughly the same time the mounted shadow beneath the courtyard's lop-sided stone entrance. The Master was unmistakable. Together they circumvented the jostle of horses, men and dogs. They came to a halt close to where the mastiff stood. Like the huge, grey dog, they kept a wary eye on the black stallion.

Standing uncloaked beneath the petrified foliage on the uneven archway, Tom kept his heartfelt relief to himself. "Cavalry's in fer a long walk, then."

"Foot should be pleased," commented Richard. His initial reaction to his leader's eventual return had been replaced by a caution acquired over recent, difficult months.

When it became clear there would be no response from the mounted shadow, Tom explained, "We got women away. They be in our chambers wi' their menfolk." He realised one of Shadiz's will-o'-the-wisp scouts would have enlightened him.

"Verity's daughter?"

As ever, Richard found the unnaturally quiet, curt tone irritating. He said, "Catherine had no idea her father had been mortally wounded."

The half-wild stallion moved restively.

"And?"

Tom forestalled Richard. "We took poor lass to 'is grave."

They had feared despairing hysterics. What they witnessed had given them both pause for thought. She had knelt in the thin layer of snow covering the grave, freshly chiselled out of the frigid earth. While the silent tears fell, she had caressed the simple, wooden cross, roughly inscribed with her father's name.

"Quite a young lady," remarked Richard, pensively.

The stallion pranced forwards, tossing its noble head, its long, flowing mane rippling down the length of its elegant neck. Tom and Richard took prudent steps backwards. The mastiff had already done so.

"*Eagle*'ll be off Ravenscar tonight."

"Bob's takin' 'em all across t' Ijuimden, then?" assumed Tom.

"I'm sailin' wi' 'em."

Tom grimaced. "Van Helter needs quick kick up arse," he observed, grimly. "Last two consignments o' powder flamin' Dutchman sent were both rotten t' core." Yet he had never expected Shadiz to go himself to the Dutch port.

"May I accompany you?" asked Richard, bracing himself. His busy mind conjured up an all-knowing smirk on the barbarous face, concealed in the shadow of the archway.

"I want y' wi' me now. Shift y'rsen."

Richard was pleased, nettled and rattled all in the same instance. "Yes, sir," he retorted, swinging away.

Tom watched him go. "Y' ain't no trouble, then?" he asked, for want of anything better to say.

He received no answer. And felt all the more troubled by the lack of communication. Of late, he had dared to hope he was making progress with the lad. Everyone at the Lodge was aware of the certain leeway he had with the aloof, forbidding Master. With the notable exception of Richard Massone, they no doubt wondered how such a thing had come about. Yet, at the moment, he did not feel he were treading on safe ground.

Minutes passed while horse and rider remained in the shelter of the timeworn archway.

Tom gazed upwards. "Lad?" he found himself murmuring.

"She's t' stay 'ere when rest o' 'em leave t' board *Eagle*."

"What?" Tom was unsure he had heard correctly. "Catherine, y' mean?"

Turning his back on the Lodge's illuminated, ramshackle façade, Shadiz swung the stallion with expert ease despite the great beast's mutinous desire to return to the stables. Low-pitched, he said, "She's headstrong an' clever. Don't underestimate 'er. Tonight, from now on, she stays 'ere."

Shocked, Tom Wright struggled for words of persuasion. "True, old 'uns won't be much use t' lass. But, lad, think. Every Crop-Ear in North's after you an' whereabouts o' this 'ere place. Then, o' course, there's allus might o' Fylingdales, used against y' by Lynette, prodded on by 'is sister, 'er flamin' high an' mighty *Ladyship*." Tom shook his head. "Catherine Verity is nowt but a bairn whose known best o' everythin' an' lost it overnight. Tis wrong, lad, t' keep 'er 'ere wi' us."

Mounted and cloaked, his longbow wrapped in canvas and slung across his back, a cloth bag of arrows hanging from his saddle, Richard came up behind his leader at the same time as Shadiz bent towards Tom in a threatening manner. Curious suddenly, he failed to catch his leader's words.

"I mean what I say. You'll keep 'er 'ere. Understand me?"

Tom swallowed convulsively. He was bathed in a coldness deeper than winter's breath. He nodded his inevitable acquiescence.

CHAPTER TWO

By Water

Richard Massone stifled a groan. What did escape his compressed lips as he lay on the bunk would, he knew, alert Captain Bob Andrew to his plight.

"Thump, lad. What possessed y' t' sail wi' us?" asked the robust, bearded captain, glancing with amusement across his lantern lit cabin. "Y' don't normally."

Richard closed his eyes. In his present condition his self-conscious request at the old Lodge was overlooked. In vivid contrast, he recalled the old knights and their wives bursting to impart the tidings they could scarcely believe themselves.

Shadiz had kept Catherine Verity at the Lodge within Stillingfleet Forest.

Richard's subsequent change of heart about boarding the *Eagle* on the frosty January night had not been an option. He was therefore of a mind to blame the black-hearted bastard circumstances forced him to call leader for maliciously press-ganging him.

The passengers, willing or otherwise, had been rowed out from Old Peak, the headland close to Ravenscar. Struck down by the wretched malady soon after the merchantman had sailed from Mercy Cove, he had been in no condition to locate his leader, let alone tackle him about the unexpected development.

Anger lingered. Richard groaned.

Bob Andrew's grin broadened. He reached for his leather flagon. It had pride of place on his hopelessly untidy desk. "Get a slurp o' m' brandy down y'r laughin' gilpos, lad?"

Before Richard could offer up a feeble refusal there was a sharp knock on the door of the cabin. Unlike the captain, he took no interest in the short-lived scuffle out in the gloomy companionway. The door drifted a leisurely crack. It then burst open slamming against the captain's bunk. Two burly seamen bundled a squirming ragamuffin into the cabin.

"We've got oursens a stowaway," gasped Sam Todd, bo's'un of the Eagle.

"Get your great paws off me!"

Bob almost dropped the leather flagon.

Upon hearing the feminine voice, Richard decided he had taken a turn for the worst and had begun to hallucinate. He lifted his throbbing head too quickly. The cabin spun around him.

The struggle between the trio ended when, resourceful to the last, the stowaway bit the bo's'un's hand. The fingers of the other seaman were twisted in a particularly nasty way. Upon her release, ignoring agonised growls, Catherine Verity gave Richard Massone a shrewd appraisal as he struggled off the bunk. "I see I'm not the only one adrift."

Contrary to popular belief, she was not at the Lodge with Tom Wright. Richard collapsed onto a convenient stool.

Although tall, the thick woollen jacket and grey breeches she had cunningly acquired smothered her willowy figure. She pulled off the leather cap allowing her fair-white hair to cascade in glossy, lantern lit waves down to her waist. Something other than the sea-sickness affected Richard's guts. He managed to give her ethereal beauty a gimlet eye. In doing so, he discerned dark shadows of hardship, dominated by sapphire spirit.

"Is this lass you've been jawin' about?" asked Bob, flabbergasted. "Why, thump, lad, she's nowt but a bairn."

"I much prefer, an old head on young shoulders," put in Catherine, brittle and bright. "Or, put another way. I may have been dumped into Lord Hade's lap, but why on earth should l take up residence. You get the gist?"

"Lord, who?" asked Bob, slack-jawed.

"Our divine leadership," croaked Richard.

"Who does not have divine rights over me," insisted Catherine with glowing defiance made grubby by her furtiveness.

"*Almighty*," muttered Bob Andrew, as the full implication of her appearance on board his ship hit him with cannon force. "'e'll 'it roof."

Catherine glanced up at the cabin's low, shadowy ceiling. "Well, he won't have far to go, will he?"

Her bravado masked inner qualms. She recalled weird black eyes piercing her. And the savage expression when movement had been so unexpected, so incredibly fast and lethal. Fear welled up in her, not least because she could sense the feeling was prevalent in the cabin.

"Y' ain't t' start wi' 'im," Bob Andrew warned Richard Massone. "Leave it t' me."

"You are a match for him, are you?" retorted the younger man.

Catherine had a shrewd idea why Shadiz wanted to keep her at his decrepit headquarters buried deep within the forest. It was the hideous suspicion that had prompted her flight.

Sam Todd and his shipmate, still smarting from her unladylike defence, looked glad to be leaving the problem to their captain, especially when Shadiz made a sudden appearance. He ducked through the low doorway. Upon catching sight of Catherine, he halted, as if an apparition had sprung up before him.

Richard took great delight in the undisguised shock. Seldom did events conspire to confound the Master so utterly.

No one spoke. No one moved. Only the ship, making good progress through the North Sea, gave creaking comment to the impact of the moment.

Shadiz began to back away from Catherine.

Neither Richard nor Bob could believe their eyes.

Shadiz came up hard against the doorframe, his complex black gaze riveted on Catherine's young, pale face. He had almost made good his escape, for that was all it could be viewed as, when she detained him by her resolute statement. "I wish to remain with Joan and Alan."

Reality only served to reinforce the fantastic image burnt into her mind's eye. She had been unable to escape it since their devastating meeting in Colonel Page's tent. Her heart was hammering against her ribs. She was having difficulty breathing.

22

Yet she stood her ground, painfully aware that everything to which she had previously laid claim was gone; the sweet music of the past. All that remained in the discordant present was a birthday gift from her dead father. She gained comfort from the jet pendant beneath the coarse woollen jacket, feeling the warmth of its silver rim, inscribed with curious symbols. The unusual pendant also gave courage. For she was desperate to stay within the caring familiarity of those people who were the precious link with her old way of life. Without them, the future was too bleak to contemplate. Therefore, however galling, she must appeal to the towering, dark creature who stood immobile halfway in shadow, halfway in light.

"Please. Permit me to go with them to The Hague." The plaintive note was purely involuntary.

Immured in animal-like stillness, Shadiz continued to stare at her.

"What gives you the right to hold me ... a prisoner?" she challenged, exasperated by his peculiar manner. "What must I do to make you understand?"

Finally, he answered her in a low-pitched voice, "Y' ain't dun bad. Passin' y'rsen off as fog in a charity suit." In an even quieter tone, he demanded, "Did Tom Wright've owt to do wi' this?"

"Absolutely nothing." She was quick to assure. "I regret the circumstances which forced me to deceive him. I found these clothes in the chamber I was given at the Lodge. It proved remarkably easy to join the company that left for the night rendezvous with the ship. Once on board, I found a corner below decks." She ended her brief explanation with a rebellious shrug. Nothing would induce her to admit she was stiff in every joint, almost hung with icicles and ravenously hungry.

"D' y' understand risk y' took?"

"I understand I had nothing to lose," she retorted. The lantern hanging from the ceiling of Bob's cabin danced to the seagoing rhythm of the *Eagle*. Its flickering light gave an unwanted glimpse. The realisation hit her like a slap across the face. Despite all the risks, she had gained absolutely nothing. "You are going to make me go back," she said, flatly, "aren't you?"

Shadiz slowly, guardedly, nodded.

A madness took hold of Catherine. There was an overwhelming need to strike out at the cruel vagaries of fate, personified in the strange, intransient Gypsy. "So," she began, brightly. "Presumably, I start upon our return to your headquarters?"

"Start what?" muttered Shadiz.

His scowling perplexity fired up Richard and Bob with even more fascination. However, they did not lose sight of the fact that their unpredictable leader was dangerously at bay. Their mutual concern was for the young girl who was having such an extraordinary affect upon him.

"In the kitchen, of course."

"Y' ain't goin' back t' labour in kitchen," snapped Shadiz, clearly taken aback.

"Ah," murmured Catherine, blue eyes innocently expanded. She cast a significant glance at the captain's bunk. "Must be the other thing," She lifted her shoulders apologetically. "I've no experience...."

"*Develesko Mush*," rasped Shadiz.

Catherine pressed on regardless. "Oh, I see." She feigned relief. "You would have me prevail on the souls of your devoted followers."

Richard laughed outright. Bob could not suppress a fleeting grin.

"I've told y'. I ain't takin' y' back t' Lodge t' labour, dammit"

Abruptly serious, Catherine demanded, "What is your reason?"

Shadiz took a deep, repressive breath. "I give me oath t' y'r father." He gestured to Richard, tensely hunched on the stool. "Ask 'im, 'e were there."

"You believe that entitles you to separate me from the only kind of family I now possess? I've witnessed your expertise at slitting a throat. It makes me doubt your death-bed repertoire."

Bob's astounded gasp filled the deep pause. Fighting the nausea, Richard almost choked. The two men were prepared to defend her. Yet again an unexpected reaction took them by surprise.

Shadiz met her hostile glare with an unmasked plea. "Kore. Stop this."

24

She stared at him, all at once feeling truly adrift.

Shadiz swung on his heels and disappeared.

Richard was sick. Afterwards, he managed, "What did he call you?"

"Catherine Kore Verity," she murmured, still staring at the empty doorway.

CHAPTER THREE

By Fire

Catherine stood in a pool of despair. A forlorn figure, she watched from the head of the *Eagle's* gangway as the elderly group were led away from Ijuimden's bitterly cold quayside by the two-man escort provided by the Master. Unlike her, they were bound for The Hague, a place of safety and impoverished living for Royalist refugees.

All too soon, she lost sight of her surrogate uncles and aunts. Thereafter, she moved in a very different world, occupied by strangers.

No. That was not entirely true.

Now that the merchantman had berthed at the modest Dutch port, the sea-sickness which had afflicted Richard throughout the voyage from England had abated, leaving him gaunt but attentive. The captain treated her like one of his daughters, of whom he spoke fondly. And his crew behaved like gentlemen whenever they were around her.

Of Shadiz, she had seen nothing since the evening of her discovery aboard the *Eagle*.

It was while Richard was guiding her through the winter defying cluster of stalls within a small square carpeted by grimy snow that he appeared, causing the raucous, persuasive calls of the foot-stamping stallholders to falter. Up until then, Richard and Catherine had been passed by with barely a second glance. The inhabitants of Ijuimden were accustomed to newcomers, their home being a port, albeit connected to the North Sea by a narrow channel. However, they were plainly finding the presence of Shadiz in their lanes something of a disquieting rarity.

Catherine could not resist a surreptitious look. It had not been careful enough. He met her gaze with black directness. The impact caused her to henceforth keep her eyes averted. Yet she was conscious of his dark, protective shadow.

Aware their progress was now being viewed with suspicion and apprehension because of his leader's intimidating presence, cursing inwardly, Richard led Catherine away from the market day bustle and down a narrow lane in which the convivially close houses almost met above their heads. Halfway down the lane, he steered her into a shop next to a busy tavern.

Catherine was glad to escape the upsurge of attention. The shop was cluttered with diverse merchandise. Narrow aisles meandered through haphazardly stacked sacks and barrels. The abundant shelves were crammed with a thousand and one items in no particular order. The top most levels were covered in a thick layer of dust. Come fresh and rosy from a cold, lively world, the place seemed to her oddly still and airless.

His welcoming smile blooming automatically at the fairy tinkle of the door bell, the shopkeeper turned. He saw Shadiz. Like dirty ditch water freezing over, his expression told its own tale.

"D' y' sell women's attire?" demanded Shadiz.

It was clearly not the opening shot Van Helter had expected. The bald, podgy shopkeeper darted a nervous glance at Catherine, taking in Bob's seagoing cloak in which she was swathed, as much to conceal her outlandish, stowaway garb as to keep her warm. The Dutchman mumbled something in broken English about his wife.

"Get 'er."

Stout, plum-cheeked, wiping her large hands on an embroidered apron, Rose Van Helter appeared. Upon catching sight of Shadiz, she halted abruptly behind her husband, sharing his trepidation.

Gesturing at Catherine, Shadiz demanded, "D' y' 'ave owt t' clothe 'er?"

"Er ... well, sir," the woman began, timidly. "There's them things I've made up that ain't been collected, sir," she answered in plain Yorkshire tones.

"Find summat suitable."

Suffering from the after affects of the sea-sickness, Richard lowered his weakened body down onto a chair of sacks. His relief was piqued by his leader's sharp command.

"An' while y' at it, don't let 'er out o' y'r sight."

Curtseying obediently, Rose ushered her newest customer into a cosy parlour at the rear of the shop, closing the door behind them. Seconds later, the door was opened by Shadiz. He thrust Catherine a meaningful look, then disappeared. Spurred on by furious impulse, she shot across the small parlour and slammed the door shut. Barely had she turned away than the door was wrenched open again.

Shadiz filled the disputed doorway. "Y' leave door open. Or y' change in shop. Y'r choice."

Inclined to be awkward, Catherine took up the challenge. His quick-handed grip on both of her arms brought her impetuous march to a jarring halt. Cast into a pit entirely of her own making, the knowledge that he, too, was breathing hard and not rock steady had its compensations.

Coming up behind his leader, Richard uttered a forceful reminder. "You are not in the company of wh ... low life now."

Meanwhile, Van Helter appeared ready to make a break for freedom. Unfortunately for him, the opportunity sped away on silver wings about the same time Shadiz released Catherine and turned away from her without another word. His barbarous countenance darker than midnight, he pushed past Richard, slamming him against the door, and seized the terrified Dutchman.

Richard lingered in the doorway, an arm around his tender middle. Catherine gave him a resigned nod in response to his questioning look. When he had gone, leaving the door half open, she tried to keep her mind occupied with the assortment of clothes Rose Van Helter provided for her inspection.

From being very young, she had possessed the ability to sense the emotions of others, even in some cases the texture of their thoughts. With ease, she could discern the atmosphere within the shop. Whatever was wrong had to do with the Master's dissatisfaction with his Dutch supplier, Van Helter. That much she had gleaned from Richard's sketchy explanation. She heard Van Helter's anguished denials. So did Rose. The Dutchman's wife was more than happy to follow her back into the shop. They found Shadiz towering menacingly over her quivering husband. Blood oozed from the corner of Van Helter's mouth.

Reclining on the sacks, Richard's expression of pallid repugnance altered upon catching sight of Catherine. His appraisal of her new attire, a blue velvet gown, trimmed with delicate lace at the neck, and a matching cloak, was being copied to a less open degree by his leader. Without doubt, Rose Van Helter was a dab hand with needle and thread. There was a well made attractiveness about her work, even if the garments she produced were left of style.

"An admirable transformation," Richard commented, gallantly, getting to his feet.

No one glimpsed the fire that lit the jet blackness before it was ruthlessly suppressed.

Her colour high, Catherine laughingly bobbed a quick curtsey. "The magic is entirely due to Rose."

"You are too modest," countered Richard, smiling.

"'e fair shines on dry land, don't y' reckon?" Shadiz's disparaging whisper, chased away their smiles. "'ave y' left place intact fer maids an' their mistresses?"

"And you owing for this lot. To be paid within the month or the underwear has to go back," retaliated Catherine, sweetly. She hoisted an ironic eyebrow. "Tis all part of being a guardian."

She was taken aback by his lazy grin.

"I could allus set y' t' work," he pointed out, arms crossed loosely over his chest. "Back at Lodge."

Catherine felt her own mouth twitch despite her best efforts. "Should I prove too costly."

Watching them, Richard felt excluded. The bitter bile of loathing rose in his gullet.

In the next moment armed men invaded the shop.

Catherine had barely registered their presence before Shadiz was pushing her down behind the sacks Richard had used as a seat. Not one to be nonplussed for long, she saw Rose Van Helter was stiff with fear. Bobbing up, she yanked the plump woman down beside her.

Having drawn their swords, Shadiz and Richard positioned themselves between the sacks and the eight burly thugs. Both men watched in grim readiness while their unknown assailants spread out, insofar as the highly cluttered place would allow, behind what was obviously their leader, a great, bearded bear of a man.

Attempting to capitalise on their determined intrusion, the thugs rushed their two victims without preamble, certainly without finesse, but with the gruff-edged silence that had accompanied their arrival into the shop.

Shadiz and Richard met the vicious onslaught with ruthless expertise.

Knelt in her new finery behind the barrier of sacks, Rose almost crushing the bones of her right hand, Catherine watched and understood that the two men were fighting for their lives. And her own. Swallowing panic, it occurred to her that proximity to Shadiz lent a dangerous unpredictability to life.

Both sides were being restricted by Van Helter's comprehensive stock, piled around the shop. Instead of using the big sword upon his back, Shadiz was wielding a curved sword, the like of which Catherine had never seen before. Yet swords alone were not enough to deter a flight of cudgels, jabbing swords, daggers and slicing axes. Both Shadiz and Richard found it expedient to employ well-placed kicks and whatever came easiest to left-handed swipes, from bags of flour to bundles of firewood.

Two of the thugs found they had placed far too much faith in their cudgels, bristling with rusty nails. Shadiz and Richard dealt with one apiece. Another went down, screaming in agony, sending barrels spinning. Indeed, the attackers were going down with what was for them alarming regularity. Expertise was winning the day.

Richard stumbled.

Forced into the rigours of combat soon after the draining bout of sea-sickness, he had nonetheless fought with remarkable fortitude. Now he was visibly tiring. His ashen face was bathed in sweat. His chest was heaving. Like wolves scenting weakness, two of the thugs exerted their collective advantage. Richard was forced to give ground, and in doing so he tumbled backwards over ruined sacks. Aggressive glee pursued his hapless descent.

Catherine jumped up, shaking off Rose's detaining grip. A quick scan of the immediate area located the perfect weapon. She snatched up a large copper pan from the splintered remains of the counter. Following the movement through with as much force as she could muster, she caught one of Richard's attackers on the side of the head with a blow that laid him out cold.

The jarring pain in her arms made her grit her teeth. It did not stop her from wielding the bloodstained pan against the next thug along, who made the mistake of looking up to see what had befallen his friend. The mean edge of the pan struck him full in the face. Catherine winced. More at the sickening crunch of breaking bones than the return of pain in her arms. Blood splattered but exhilarated, she was relieved to see that Richard had regained his feet.

She was looking about for another victim upon whom she could use the handy pan when an iron limb encircled her from behind. Lifted off her feet with startling ease, she began to struggle.

"Dammit, Kore," growled Shadiz into her hair. "Stay put."

Relief flowed through her. The pan slipped from her grasp. She relaxed against his powerful chest, engulfed in his masculine warmth. His arm tightened about her.

While holding her, he was challenged. Her position against him was tantamount to a shield. She was therefore spun away to the safe place next to Rose Van Helter.

Preoccupied with disturbed emotions while watching Shadiz guard against Richard's weakness, Catherine failed to notice movement behind her. By the time Rose shrieked, the foul threat was unavoidable. She was wrenched upwards by her hair. Her arms were crushed against her sides.

"Shadiz, y' 'od it reet now. Or y'r fancy whore gets cut."

A glinting blade rested with cold malice against Catherine's throat.

The cacophony of an armed struggle melted away into heavy breathing silence. Having gained the upper hand by their leader's action, the two remaining thugs disarmed Richard, taking advantage of his dismay. No one approached Shadiz.

Afraid to swallow or barely to breathe lest she aggravate the ready dagger, Catherine appealed to Shadiz with enormous, soulful eyes. He remained motionless, darkly tall and inscrutable in formidable isolation.

In marked contrast, Richard's flushed features were alight with sweaty urgency. The sight of the girl, who had made such a tremendous impact upon him, being held hostage by the unknown English brute made him desperate to remedy the situation with prompt, effective action. He cast a questioning look at his leader. "Defend her!" he hissed, giving breathless vent to his feelings.

"Do owt, gypsy," rumbled the thug's leader through his shaggy brown beard, "an' I'll slit y'r sweet darlin' from ear t' ear."

Sinking cruel fingers deeper into Catherine's dishevelled hair, he jerked her head back against his stained tunic. Grinning, his malicious gaze fastened on Shadiz, he slid the dagger's shiny blade the length of her stretched throat, managing to infuse the movement with crude suggestion. "'eard tell y' likes 'em young."

It was Richard who, powerless, cursed the gibe.

"I … I am not his mistress," whispered Catherine, cautiously, "I … I am a liability he aquire."

"Kore," said Shadiz, softly, without heat. "Shut up."

"'appen bastards share 'er," suggested the weasel-faced thug standing next to Richard.

"'appen we could," put in his toothless comrade, hopefully.

Catherine's burly captor laughed approvingly, engulfing her in pungent odours.

"First off," warned weasel face, studying Shadiz. "We get out o' 'ere."

For the first time, Catherine wished she was at the Lodge with Tom Wright. Or, better still, at Nafferton Garth, ideally with her father. In vain, from an awkward angle, she searched for ransom. It dawned on her that here was the perfect opportunity for Shadiz to

32

rid himself of unwanted baggage. Propelled roughly forwards, she caught a brief glimpse of Richard's tormented face. Loud threats rang in her ears.

Ignoring Richard's frantic pleas, his cold, soulless attention fixed on the thugs' leader, as it had been throughout, Shadiz lowered the scimitar. Emitting every appearance of acquiescence, he went down onto one knee. Bowing his head, his enigmatic face was curtained by his long black hair.

Everyone in the wrecked shop stared at his submissive posture. Breaking the incredulous spell, Richard resumed his demand, "For pity's sake, you bastard! You cannot allow them to have their way with her?"

Weasel-face struck him on the back of his head. Too engrossed in Catherine's plight, Richard had failed to anticipate the blow from the hilt of his own sword. Stunned, he slumped down onto his hands and knees.

Catherine felt terribly alone, deserted by guardianship. As the door of the shop came within easy reach, her captor growled, "Fire bleedin' place."

Van Helter shot up from his bolt hole. "*No! Plea ... No!*"

Whatever else he was about to blurt out was cut short. The thug to whom he had appealed sank his dagger into the Dutchman's chest.

Rose Van Helter screamed. Scurrying from behind the sacks, she headed towards her ominously still husband. When thuggish weapons were rattled at her, she veered away and fled up the narrow staircase leading to the second floor of the shop.

Recovering slowly from the blow on the head, Richard discovered what was causing his coughing spasm. The place where he was kneeling was being surrounded by smoke and flames. He was trying to make sense of the burgeoning blaze when his muzzy head was subjected to the painful stab of a primitive wail. Both he and the thugs sought its origins.

Shadiz used his dagger to dispatch two of the remaining thugs before Richard realised his leader had moved a muscle. Lethal speed did not entertain any margin to ward off the strike designed to alleviate pressure. Roaring at the sudden pain in his shoulder, Catherine's captor released her. Finding herself abruptly free, she tottered backwards. Her giddy progress was intercepted by Shadiz. He swept her into a rough embrace. Seeking sanctuary, she buried herself within his fierce strength. Thus, she failed to realise she was being prevented from witnessing how, in one dextrous stroke, he cut the throat of the man who had dared to hold her captive.

Richard saw the expert kill; saw the repulsive lustre in his leader's black eyes.

Wordlessly, Shadiz picked up Catherine and carried her out of the shop. Coughing, Richard followed his lead into the lane, retreating from the growing heat within the devastation.

Her teeth would not stop their ridiculous chatter. Nor would the betraying tremors cease. Dampened regrettably by tears of relief, her face was pressed against the front of Shadiz's long coat. The smell of warm leather was overwhelmingly comforting. The cold wind ruffled her hair. She became aware of the affect it was having on the fire that was sending shockwaves down the lane. Yet she was only vaguely aware of the shouts of alarm.

Resilience overcame reaction. Catherine lifted her head, to discover Shadiz's barbarously sculptured face too close for rational thought. Neither of them spoke. He stood statute-like, holding her with the greatest of care in his arms.

Standing beside them, Richard experienced that unnerving exclusion again.

"A lost opportunity?" Catherine could not stem the tell-tale quiver. Then all was forgotten as she marvelled at the way his smile spread day through night.

"Roger would've come a-'auntin'," he murmured.

"I would sincerely hope so." His one gold earring held a condensed image of someone struggling to regain composure. "You possess a rare talent for splitting eardrums?"

"I am a Rom Posh-Rat," he told her, soft-voice.

"Is that what you are?" she responded, attempting flippancy. "Does this sort of thing happen often?"

"Only when I complain."

His quiet observation reminded her of the Dutch shopkeeper's tragic demise. This in turn prompted her to recall the poor man's terrified widow. Gazing over Shadiz's left shoulder, she saw for the first time how the tall, narrow shop was already well alight. "Is Rose still in there?" she exclaimed, her horrified gaze darting back to Shadiz.

"I believe so." It was Richard who answered her, his thoughtful gaze on his leader.

"You must help her," pleaded Catherine, unconsciously intensifying her hold on Shadiz.

He drew a long breath and then exhaled slowly. "First off, promise me you'll return t' *Eagle* wi' Joyous Gallant."

"I want."

"Promise."

Their eyes locked. Giving into his undeniable authority with bad grace, and some urgency for Rose's sake, Catherine muttered, "I promise."

He set her down on her feet. Wraithlike, his hands slipped away from her.

Turning briskly to Richard, he commanded, "Get down that alley. It'll lead y' into Van Helter's yard. Get wagon you'll find there back t' ship an' unloaded."

"That load does not belong to you," pointed out Richard. Nevertheless, he was already leading Catherine in the direction of the alley.

"Does now," came the sardonic retort.

★ ★ ★

The mundane activities toiling the length of the winter-blasted quayside were rudely split into two equally startled halves by the recklessly trundling wagon. The team of white-eyed nags were hauled to a shuddering halt alongside the *Eagle*.

Bob Andrew lumbered down the narrow gangway. The closer he drew to where Richard was swinging Catherine down onto the

35

slippery flagstones, the more it became apparent to him that the younger man was uncharacteristically dishevelled. His chesty cough was even more pronounced than usual. Bob looked at Catherine. Although now attired in feminine garb, he was shocked to see there were bloodstains on her gown and cloak. Frowning, he asked the obvious question. And received two conflicting answers.

Richard slewed round, speaking sharply to Catherine, "He has no intention of saving Rose Van Helter." When she opened her mouth on a rejoinder, in a more restrained manner, he pointed out, "He simply employed the most expedient measure to speed you back to the *Eagle*." Then, switching back to the captain, feeding the older man's confusion, he went on, "The bas ... he is, as usual, not letting his left hand know what his right one is doing. I intend to return and discover exactly what made him embark on this excursion." He jerked a thumb at the barrels on the wagon he had driven from the yard behind Van Helter's burning shop. "He wants those loaded."

"I'm going back with you," declared Catherine. She had promised Shadiz that she would return to the *Eagle*. She had not promised to stay on the merchantman. In an attempt to thwart disapproval, she hitched up the heavy velvet skirt of her new gown and started to run. Her tall, slender figure had been attracting the attention of every male within squinting distance. Now, those same admirers stopped what they were doing to watch her hair-flying bolt away from the quayside.

"Come back!" shouted Richard. He dashed after her, and was himself pursued by ribald cheers and advice.

Secure in the knowledge she held the record for the half mile dash from Millhouse Beck to Loftsome Bridge, Catherine sped through the eerily deserted market place. The jet pendant beneath her gown felt strangely warm against her skin. A sharp foreboding snapping at her heels, she made a hasty return to the lane she had entered earlier with Shadiz and Richard.

Glimpses of grey smoke billowing upwards into a snow laden sky had not prepared her for the tunnelled chaos within the narrow lane. On a winter's day, torrid heat radiated around the glowing buildings. Regular flurries of sparks instead of the more seasonal snowflakes kept bombarding the lane.

A crowd of anxious townsfolk hindered Catherine's path. She was surrounded by their foreign jabbering. Although the soul deep urgency had increased, pounding in both head and heart, her pace had, of necessity, slowed frustratingly. This gave Richard the opportunity to catch up with her. His breathing laboured, a hand upon his chest, he grasped her arm, hoping to detain her. Catherine won the short-lived tussle. Dragging him with her, she wove her way to the ragged fringe of the on-lookers. Once there, they both tried to make sense of the calamitous scene before them.

Two begrimed groups were hard at work tearing down the buildings at either side of the ravenous blaze, frantically attempting to create firebreaks. They had no time to listen to the entreaties of the owners, who were trapped between the flames and ruin. Elsewhere, crazily angled, slopping bucket-lines were making little impression, mainly because the furnace was being fuelled by the combustible kindling within shops and houses.

Catherine was curious about the soggy black stuff which had evidently spewed out of smashed barrels strewn across the lane. Richard took one look at the littered ground and swore. He prevented her from moving forwards to take a closer look. This proved providential. For, without warning, a fat barrel fell to earth, splitting open on impact, demonstrating what had happened to its predecessors.

Having bowed to self-preservation, the bucket-lines were quick to resume their back breaking labour, particularly the bendy one closest to the fresh influx of black stuff.

"More damned gunpowder," wheezed Richard. "Where ... the ... hell?"

In order to discover its source, both he and Catherine had to gauge the angle of descent of the last barrel. It was not easy. The smoke stung their eyes and made both of them cough. The hot brightness dazzled their narrowed, questing gazes. Together, they peered upwards into the fiery monster, whose rampage had all but devoured Van Helter's shop.

Utter disbelief and horror followed hard on the heels of their mutual discovery.

Shadiz was up there. Hung upon a funeral pyre. Weighed down by a half-glimpsed form.

"Shadiz," whispered Catherine, between the barrier of her cold fingers.

Having undergone a significant change of heart, Richard did not hear her. They knew they were cursed by helplessness. Catherine prayed for a dubious existence to prevail. Richard simply held his breath.

His leader was trapped within the incandescent weaving of the flames that had gleefully infected Van Helter's hapless neighbours. He was being held prisoner in their recreation of Hell, where the air could only be a searing insult to the lungs and every action boiled in multi-hued heat.

The problem of how to cheat the cage of fire soon resolved itself in the most appalling manner.

The last few remnants of Van Helter's shop shuddered. They disintegrated in a spectacular display of leaping orange flames and colourful, flying sparks. Roasting life within its heathen heart was plunged downwards into the chaotic lane.

Richard and Catherine were swept by grey smoke, intensive heat and sheer panic as the Dutch down tools and fled.

In the midst of the fearful retreat, an inexplicable knowledge held Catherine fast. Of its own accord, her hand sought her pendant. All around her, the world existed in the mortal anguish of ordinary time, unheeded by her. Drawn like an iron file to a magnet, her left hand clutched burning jet and silver. She was connected with hot space; with suffering. And being so, guided the stumbling phoenix to safety.

Much later Richard would come to realise that it was his recent association with the demanding Master which endowed him with the necessary edge of authority. Bellowing himself nearly hoarse in passable Dutch, he rallied the less faint-hearted of the bucket-line brigades and set them to work.

Bombarded by inconvenient sparks, the gunpowder on the wet

ground sizzled fitfully in places but fortunately did little else. Watery attention was being directed elsewhere. So enthusiastic was the merciful deluge on the consuming heat upon him and his inert burden, there was a real danger of impeding Shadiz's progress in Catherine's direction.

The determined rescuers eventually laid hands upon him and the unconscious woman he was clutching.

Having relinquished his cloak prior to the armed conflict in Van Helter's shop, Richard now tore off his doublet and used it to smother the last of the flames upon his leader, trying his best to control a coughing spasm. At Catherine's instigation, more water was poured over raw flesh. She had suddenly experienced a vivid image of how the blind old Romany woman, the White Witch, had dealt with the casualties when a barn at Holme Farm had caught fire.

Because of their proximity to the fire, Richard dragged his semi-conscious leader to his feet. Catherine sped to the other side of Shadiz. Both of them were aware that wherever they touched grimy, raw flesh they would inflict pain. That they could touch him at all seemed like a miracle.

Having perceived they were in no immediate danger, the Dutch crowd had curbed their stampede and reformed into an apprehensive flock. A clutch of women gathered around the spot where Rose Van Helter had been laid, unconscious, ragged and burnt, but alive.

Along with the Master's long coat and weapons, someone handed Richard a mug of water. More shaken than he cared to admit to himself, he knelt beside Catherine on the waterlogged ground. "A drink. Shadiz?" he offered, awkwardly. When there was no response from the place where he had lain his leader, he gave her an anxious sidelong glance.

"Please, have a drink of water," she urged, her voice unsteady.

Laying prone, dripping wet from head to toe, Shadiz's breathing was shallow and rapid. The remnants of his shirt and jerkin had been sealed to his upper body by skin-ravishing burns. Deep grooves across his back, weeping gore, had every appearance of damage inflicted by red-hot debris.

With a trembling hand, Catherine gently brushed soaked strands of his hair away from his face. She inhaled sharply. It was as if a flaming brand had tortured his left cheek beneath the old scar across his high cheekbone.

"Told ... y' t'... go ... back," came an almost indecipherable whisper.

"I should have told you to have a care for yourself," retorted Catherine, almost choking on the upsurge of guilt. If she had not implored him to do the impossible.

Very, very slowly, he turned his head. He opened his red-rimmed eyes and with obvious difficulty focused upon her. Within the black depths, she saw pain and an incomprehensible, haunted weariness. After a moment, he closed his eyes, mumbling, *"Forget ... not yet ... the ... tried intent."*

She clamped down on her inner turmoil. And ignored Latin riddles. Becoming supremely practical, she told him, "You must drink. And you must move."

Yet movement proved almost beyond him. Catherine would have given assistance, but Richard lay a restraining hand on her arm.

When Shadiz had managed, by laborious stages, to drag himself up and onto his knees, Richard held out the brimming mug. Half of its contents sloshed out as his wrist was seized.

"Next time ... y' ain't t' let 'er ... wrap ... bloody rings ... round y'." The rebuke was no less harsh because of the lack of breath and a smoke damaged throat.

A hostile look passed between the two men.

"Drink," demanded Catherine, through gritted teeth.

Richard wrenched himself free of Shadiz's weakening grip. He straightened, watching in tight-lipped silence while his leader drank the mug's remaining contents in one long, shaky pull.

When Bob Andrew drew up alongside of them on the wagon, it was like the answer to a prayer. For, though he was clearly preparing to try, Catherine and Richard were aware that Shadiz could not possibly return to the *Eagle* unaided.

Isolated on the deserted quayside, having watched as smoke whirled steadily thicker over Ijuimden's jumble of rooftops, turning the snow laid upon them a sooty grey, the captain had realised eventually he had the perfect excuse, the wagon, which he now saw was badly needed. He sat upon the inadequate seat with an expression of riveted astonishment on his bearded, weatherbeaten face while Shadiz managed to get himself into the rear of the empty wagon. The effort terminated in a dead faint.

"Wait!" cried Catherine. She dashed across the hot, smoky lane.

What the apothecary bellowed at her upon following her into his shop to find her ransacking the crowded shelves was lost on Catherine, in much the same way her hasty explanation was upon the tall, thin man.

When Richard arrived, she prevailed upon him to pay for the armful of herbs and salves she had snatched up. Less than his usual respectable self, he was tempted to communicate with his sword. Instead, loathed to emulate Shadiz, he produced a bag of coins and thrust it at the apothecary before the irate fellow could have her detained for looting. He then whisked her back to the ponderously moving wagon, still smarting from the husky reprimand delivered by its senseless occupant.

All of them were very aware of Shadiz's condition upon leaving the lane to its fate.

It had seemed as if the entire population of Ijuimden was presently engrossed in the catastrophic fire within the heart of their close knit community. Therefore it was a surprise to discover that the crew of the *Eagle* was not alone on the quayside. To describe the gaggle of figures brandishing cudgels, ancient swords and pikes as an unruly mob would have been insulting. To call them a disciplined militia would have been highly complimentary.

What immediately incensed the captain upon pulling hard on the reins of the nervous horses to bring them to a halt alongside the merchantman was the way the Dutchmen were rough-housing his crew. "What devil's goin' on 'ere?" he roared, skating on the irregular flag-stones, polished by frost, in his haste to leave the wagon.

A short, plump man of well-to-do appearance moved pompously in the shadow of his large, well-armed protector. "You be captain?"

"Aye," snapped Bob, his glare raking over the rowdy scene. He was grimly satisfied with the tough response of his seamen to foreign provocation. "Tell 'em t' quit that. Me lads've done nowt."

"Gypsy had," declared Johannes Steen. "He reason for fair."

Startled, both Bob and Richard turned to him.

"For the fire? What nonsense is this?" demanded Richard. Slower off the wagon than the captain, he had identified members of the militia as being mostly fishermen and shopkeepers, presumably those whose premises were not threatened by the fire. "Shadiz saved Rose Van Helter. What is more, had it not been for his efforts, Ijuimden would have been blasted apart by the amount of gunpowder Van Helter was storing in his shop. You, sir, seek a scapegoat."

Steen viewed Richard with disdain from the security of his guarded leadership. Thus, the argument flourished. Richard refrained from mentioning that the subject of the discord was sprawled unconscious in the wagon. Or so he thought.

So did Catherine. She sat as if alone in the wagon, in spite of having Shadiz's head resting in her lap. His vulnerability prompted her to cast a casual glance downwards. She found black eyes studying her.

Her stretched nerves vibrated painfully. As heady wine fills a dirty pitcher, colour gushed hotly into her cheeks. Nevertheless, she strove with a semblance of calm to meet his intent look, as much for his sake as her own. At last, beneath her hand, his chest moved. He gestured for her to look upwards. Complying jerkily, she caught Richard's curious eye. At the same time, she felt the telltale weight leave her lap.

With growing alarm, she watched Steen's inexorable advance. Due to his leading citizen's rhetoric, the little Dutchman failed to see the apparition rise up out of the wagon. Too late he realised the dagger threatened his flabby neck.

English and Dutch alike gaped at the bedraggled, mangled appearance of the Master.

His husky, guttural conversation with Steen's thwarted protector was lost on Catherine. Not so the checked fury with which the stalwart's ancient weapons were flung onto the cobbles. She could sympathise with Steen. He was paralysed by terror, just as she had been a short time earlier.

"Such fierce defence," Shadiz whispered, flicking a sardonic glance at Richard.

He got out of the wagon slowly while still managing to keep Steen facing his fidgeting compatriots. "Tell y'r playmates t' drop their toys. Don't be shy. *Allah obligeth no man t' more than 'e 'ath given 'im ability t' perform.*"

Members of Bob's crew took great delight in kicking the grudgingly relinquished weapons into the murky harbour water slapping at the *Eagle's* portside. The Dutch stood in frustrated silence and watched while their leader was marched up the gangway of the English ship.

Shadiz's steps lacked their usual animalistic vigour. On a bitterly cold January day, sweat was pouring down his burnt face, as if he alone moved cautiously through summer's midday heat.

Several skiffs were commandeered at the captain's bidding. The combined tow took the merchantman, still fully loaded, out into mid-harbour, whereupon the strong north-easterly wind filled the loosened canvas, taking over from straining muscles.

Seeing his home port begin to disappear behind the *Eagle's* stern, Johannes Steen plucked up the courage to beg for his release. He was interrupted by Bob's young nephew, who arrived topside with dramatic tidings. "Barrels've cum loose!"

Everyone swung towards Will. They then, on another man's vessel, looked towards the battered Master. "Massone," he commanded, ignoring the captain's distress. "Get below." That he did not feel inclined to investigate the problem personally was a good indication of his present condition.

Already beginning to feel queasy, cold without the benefit of either cloak or doublet, Richard would much rather have retired to Bob's cabin instead of having to deal with one of the worst occurrences to befall a ship under sail. "What of them?" he asked, pointing aft.

His leader cast an indifferent glance at the armed ketch being

43

sailed in pursuit of the Eagle. "They won't bother us," he dismissed.

Passing Catherine, Richard hoisted a sceptical eyebrow before grimly disappearing below decks with young Will and Sam Todd.

"So, little man. Y' want t' leave?"

Steen swallowed convulsively. He nodded, believing he had heard Shadiz's barely discernable, rusty words correctly. Once aboard the merchantman, his bizarre looking captor had perched him on the starboard rail.

Malevolence worked the faint grin. "If that's what y' want." With the minimum of effort, Shadiz pushed Steen off the ship's rail.

Incredulity expanded Catherine's blue eyes. She caught a glimpse of the terror on Steen's chubby face as he fell backwards over the side of the *Eagle*, arms wildly flapping. Leaning over the rail, slick with ice, she released her pent up breath the moment the Dutchman broke the ruffled surface of the incoming tide. Anxiously, she watched as he started to bob along in a frantic dog-paddle, too absorbed in keeping afloat to splutter for a saviour.

"No doubt, y' would've presented 'im wi' a gilded barge pulled by bejewelled nereids," remarked Shadiz, laconically.

"I would have viewed his request with sympathy," retorted Catherine. Looking sideward, she saw how tightly he was gripping the vacated ship's rail, his scorched knuckles working white.

"An' miss fun?" Wicked mischief swirled with pain in those incredible black eyes.

She was still watching the hapless victim of a cruel wit when Richard reappeared topside.

"The rope securing several of the barrels had been cut," he informed his leader's black, bowed head, "allowing the damned things to roam."

"By a two-legged rat wi' mean intentions," Shadiz muttered, without looking up.

He was resting on his haunches, his blackened hands braced on the deck. The burns across his half-naked back were the worst, the rest were less serious, including the one in his left cheek, but nonetheless raw, open sores in need of attention. Catherine had urged him to allow her to attend them. He had given her an odd, searching look immersed in a fierceness she had taken as a rebuff. She felt responsible for his injuries; prey to an instinctive feeling he had saved Rose Van Helter from the fire because she had beg him to.

"Anyway," added Richard, "they have been secured." He watched with interest as Steen, a difficult, soggy catch, was hauled aboard the ketch being sailed by the infuriated Dutch militia in the *Eagle*'s wake.

"He went via the Grand Canal," supplied Catherine.

"Develsko Mush," came the hoarse exclamation from down below. "Don't set 'im off."

"I'd much prefer to be a canting preacher than the Devil's advocate," snapped Richard, glaring downwards.

The *Eagle* entered the narrow channel connecting Ijuimden's sheltered harbour with the North Sea. Gulls drifted overhead on grey flecked wings. At either side of the channel, the snowbound landscape was flat and featureless. Swept by the salty breath of the sea, the district was devoid of habitation except for a few huddled sheep and the signalman in his thatched hut.

"What d' y' reckon t' that lot?" asked Bob, looking apprehensively astern. It was clear to him, as it was to everyone on board the *Eagle*, that the Dutch militia was seeking revenge for their humiliation by the Master. Now that their leader was safe, albeit half-drowned, they were busying themselves with the small cannon lodged cleverly in the prow of their determined little warship. "Almighty! That rotten gun o' theirs could do us some damage, th' knows."

Upright again, Shadiz cast another indifferent glance over his shoulder. "They'll not 'urt us," he muttered.

"They are about to have…." began Richard.

There was a sudden, tremendous explosion.

It caused the gulls riding the waves to shoot skywards to tangle with their equally startled fellows. Feathers flew when they were all scattered by thick chunks of incandescent wood flying through the vibrant air. In stark contrast, all movement across the decks of the *Eagle* had frozen. All aboard stared in horrified disbelief when fiery debris descended around the stern of the merchantman. Shooting stars in the dismal day. The final one for those aboard the militia's flagship. The subsequent, thunderous echo rumbled out of the channel and proceeded to sweep away across the harbour to play upon an empty quayside; a fanfare for premature death. Steep, foaming grey waves hit the *Eagle* astern and then, in disruptive haste, rolled the length of her cargo heavy hull.

Richard fell victim to the rough backlash. He was sick over the starboard rail.

The bitter wind stirred narrow avenues in the ominous black smoke billowing around the entrance of the channel. By grudging degrees, the grotesque mixture of blazing wreckage and drifting carnage was revealed. The glimpsed reality of murderous death chilled the silent onlookers far more than any pitiless winter ever could. The more so because of the suspicion that the merciless perpetrator stood amongst them.

Richard and Bob found themselves turning towards the Master. He was standing motionless against the supportive rail, his savage, injured face impassive, his black eyes coldly brooding.

"You were so damned adamant that the Dutch posed no threat?" pointed out Richard, appalled.

"*I'll thrust thee from this earthly tenement. And thou shalt to another world be sent,*" Shadiz's whispery, mocking tone left no leeway for doubt.

Outraged, Richard opened his mouth, but it was Catherine's condemning voice that rang out over the *Eagle*'s inactive decks.

"*You are a killer!*"

True enough. Yet no one in their right mind uttered the unequivocal fact in the flawed presence.

Shocked beyond measure by the callous act, which her father would have recognized, she shunned Bob's restraining arm. "You are, indeed, the Master. Master of the Underworld. Hades come amongst mortals to prey upon unsuspecting souls." With each emphasised word, Catherine had taken a decisive step towards Shadiz. When she came to a passionate halt within two short feet of him, the incessant drumming of fate went on regardless of his fixed black stare.

"Uncle! Uncle! There be a sail up yonder. *Uncle!*"

Dispatched with something akin to panic from the merchantman's bows, yet again the lanky youth was the bearer of unpleasant tidings. The fresh threat stirred Bob. Richard also hurried away, unable to suppress the sickness. That left Shadiz and Catherine momentarily facing one another.

Fortified by a strangely despairing anger, she was prepared for a brutal retaliation. When Shadiz began to stiffly move, she resisted the backward step. He paused alongside of her, a fire damaged figure impossibly tall.

"I am what I am."

The whispered statement would have driven Richard to distraction. But it was not aimed at Richard. Therefore, instead of being whipped by sinister arrogance, Catherine was left alone to feel like some poor, baffled fool who had stumbled upon a dangerous secret.

Standing braced and stricken at the bows of his ship, Bob realised the reek of smoke emanated from Shadiz. "What now, d' y' reckon?"

His silence intimidating, Shadiz studied the oncoming Dutch fluit. She was much smaller than the *Eagle* and therefore far more vulnerable. Her workhorse lines were low in the choppy tidal flow of the North Sea into the channel. Aboard such a two-mast vessel, the crew was usually small and the hold large and crammed full of merchandise, destined on this occasion for ruined shopkeepers.

There was no comfortable margin within the channel for the two trading ships to pass. They seemed destined to be unequal partners in an encounter that had every potential for disaster. The fluit's disbelieving crew soon sprouted irate gestures. When they had no affect, they tried pigeon English, inspired by the name of the oncoming merchantman. In the end, they began to bellow across the rapidly diminishing gap between the two ships with an urgent sentiment anyone of any race could understand.

On board the *Eagle*, the feeling of going home the hard way was building to fever pitch.

"*Almighty!*" muttered Bob, glaring at the smoke rising lazily from the hole in the thatched roof of the lonely hut. "That signal fella likes 'is 'earth too rotten much." He wondered whether Shadiz would have complied with an inconvenient order. In vehement silence, he wished the Master was anywhere but aboard the *Eagle*. Yet that did not stop him from handing over command of his ship. He did so, he knew, to no ordinary man.

Commerce frequently took the captain into the Mediterranean. And in sailing into the inland sea, he had become well acquainted with the Master's notoriety. A Sea Gypsy, he was a devastatingly successful predator.

Bob had heard, and passed them onto Tom Wright, the old tales often repeated in the quayside taverns from Malaga to Marseilles how the Bey of Algeria had taken a gypsy galley slave and instructed him in the skills of the sea after the gypsy galley slave had, by some unknown means, turned certain defeat at the hands of the Knights of St John, patrolling out of Malta, into victory for the Moor. Whoever had been responsible, their expertise had helped to draw forth a natural aptitude for seamanship.

Feeling vindicated, Bob recognised a man in his element. The challenge of attaining the open sea worked like a tonic.

With an alacrity borne out of confidence in the Master, no matter what his condition, the seamen climbed the ratlines. They toiled on the yardarms high above the *Eagle*'s decks, responding to his hoarse commands, some of which Bob had to relay. However, their enthusiasm began to flag along with their captain's when it became apparent that the unorthodox combination of sails they had been called upon to unfurl ensured that the merchantman tacked alarmingly close to the south bank of the channel, where slabs of ragged stone waited with reptilian patience. The diligent leadsman in the chains sang out the ever-decreasing mark. Everyone, no matter how they were occupied, cocked an ear to his gloomy tidings.

Given no option but to alter course, the captain of the Dutch fluit sailed his long, trim vessel away from the deepest part of the channel. Unfortunately, he was a man of mundane nerve. His laborious tack to port did not take the fluit close enough to the north bank. Upon their inevitable meeting within the channel, the distance between the two trading ships was insufficient. Starboard timbers thudded against starboard timbers in water made turbulent by their close proximity. They proceeded to jostle and grate ominously in passing, making for a shaky experience that had everyone aboard both ships holding their breaths and their balance, and praying to whichever saint they revered.

In the midst of the hazardous encounter, Catherine responded to the sensation of being watched. She looked sideward down the main deck and found Shadiz's gaze resting upon her. For a long second, his veiled attention unsettled her more than the passage of the ships.

Elongated by dread, at last the perilous clash, which could so very easily have scuppered both ships, came to a shuddering end. Making tedious headway, they parted company. Life began anew, to be relished. Being the bigger of the two, the *Eagle* had taken the shockwaves of the unwanted meeting in her watery stride. Cheers rose from her decks and yardarms. Futile threats reared up from the fluit before the Dutch crowded on sail and headed for the second unpleasant surprise awaiting them in Ijuimden's wreckage strewn harbour.

The Master moved decisively. The merchantman was sailed away from the south bank of the channel with the same expertise that had kept her safe during the sluggish trickle of the sandglass.

He had managed to get her within sight of the North Sea. He could do no more.

Having just recovered from heaving his guts up over the ship's rail, Richard ignored Bob's efforts to keep the peace. Intent upon confronting Shadiz about the unforgivable slaughter of the Dutch militia before he was overtaken altogether by the sea-sickness, he seized his leader's raw arm. What Richard had not anticipated was the complete lack of resistance as he spun Shadiz around. In the next moment, his rough grip become a timely restraint.

Shadiz swayed. His knees buckled under him.

Bob lumbered forwards to help Richard prevent a headlong collapse.

Catherine made anxious haste to join them. Shadiz seized her arm. He dragged her down with him as the captain and Richard lowered his senseless weight onto the wet deck.

CHAPTER FOUR

Upon a Painted Sea

After Shadiz had been carried below decks, Catherine surveyed the damage done to him by the fire with a healer's eye, as she had been taught by Mamma Petra, the White Witch. She knew she must shut out all other responses to his appalling condition. After braiding her long hair, she set to work, determined to bring a measure of relief as quickly as possible.

The only satisfactory linen aboard the *Eagle* was her petticoats. She tore them into strips and used them to cleanse the fire-wounds in his big body that overhung Bob's inadequate bunk. With painstaking care, she eased the remnants of his shrivelled shirt and jerkin away from the clinging morass of flesh on his back.

She was grateful for small mercies. While she worked, bent over him, Shadiz kept slipping in and out of consciousness. She always sensed when he was with her. Although he made no sound, not even a stifled moan, his battered body would grow tense beneath her gentle fingers. Every shallow breath was taken in an attempt to guard against the pain. When it overwhelmed him, there would be merciful oblivion. Whereupon she would breath a small sigh of relief.

★ ★ ★

It was during one of the lucid moments, when he fought against the torture crushing him, that a detached part of his mind viewed his present situation. He was half-mad already. Weary beyond measure. Yet the Maiden's tender touch was preventing the other half from slipping away.

Bob stayed with Catherine as much as possible, leaving Sam Todd, his capable bo's'un, in command. Those times he did feel the need to reassure himself that all was well aboard his ship, he reminded her that a seaman was on duty at the cabin door, if she had need of help.

He returned to his cabin after one such foray topside to find her straightening stiffly. She arched her back, giving him a tired smile.

"'ow's lad doin'?"

Catherine looked down at her senseless patient. "The herbal salvers will hopefully ease the pain and begin the healing," she said, sending up yet another silent prayer for having had the presence of mind to visit the apothecary in Ijuimden. Taking a shaky breath, she switched from the occupied bunk to the improvised bed on the floor of the cabin, where Richard lay having succumbed to the debilitating sea-sickness less than two nautical leagues out of Ijuimden. "And Richard is sleeping finally. From pure exhaustion."

Bob put an arm around her drooping shoulders. "Thump, luv. Y've got y' 'ands full, alright." Catherine leant against him, taking comfort from his fatherly concern. She was so tired her legs were trembling. "Come on, luv. They're both at rest, one way or tother. Sit y'rsen down for a bit."

She was about to take his advice when she caught sight of fresh blood on Shadiz's injured cheek.

Emitting a tender-hearted sigh, Bob watched her dab gently at the left side of the Gypsy's dark-skinned face. "Where'd y' learn t' see t' folk?" he asked, not for the first time marvelling at her skill, even more remarkable for one so young.

Catherine continued to carefully stem the trickle of blood in Shadiz's ravished cheek. "When I was twelve my father invited a Romany tribe to winter at Nafferton Garth, our home near Driffield. After that they came every year. The matriarch, Mamma Petra, the White Witch to us Gorgios, taught me, first how to look after my animals when they were sick or injured. She then moved onto humans."

Shadiz suddenly gripped her wrist.

Believing him to be insensible, he startled her. He was staring at her in such a hot-eyed manner, Bob moved quickly to her side. Ignoring the captain's concern, she knelt beside the bunk. "Rest," she soothed, smiling down at the gaunt mask holding in the excruciating pain she could easily sense. "You need to rest, to heal." She stroked his damp, wild hair, gently brushing it away from his heated brow. Riveted on her, slanted jet burnt with agony and that odd, searching look he kept bestowing upon her. For the first time since being carried to the captain's cabin he made a sound. It was a cross between a moan deep in his throat and a frustrated hiss.

"You are safe. I will watch over you," Catherine told him softly.

She continued to meet his furrowed gaze, willing him to give into healing sleep. Gradually, the brutal grip on her wrist grew slack. His lids flickered and closed. His incredibly long lashes rested upon his cheeks, including the one she felt she had branded with her plea to salvage life.

★ ★ ★

Shadiz's last thought before he was dragged back down into a nebulous realm was that his mind had been turned completely by the agony raging upon his body. The Maiden was there beside him. She was touching him. Smiling at him. Caring for him.

He prowled the south bank of the river. The great wolfhound trotted at his heels. Devoid of pity, he surveyed the throng. They awaited the ferryman, coins at the ready.

Irritated by the unbroken heat, he spoke in the Romi, English, Arabic, French, Spanish, Italian and Dutch to those souls who tried to conquer their fear of him.

On the far side of the river, he glimpsed the woman. He spat pure hate at her.

★ ★ ★

Confounded enough to doubt the quality of his own hearing, Bob

53

Andrew stared down in utter disbelief at the delirious man. Seeking confirmation, he switched from his occupied bunk to where Richard Massone lay on blankets on the floor of the cabin. Although ailing himself, Richard appeared equally taken aback.

Preoccupied with her patient, Catherine missed the exchange between the two men, muted by astonishment.

When she paid her hasty visit to the Dutch apothecary, she had striven hard to remember all that the White Witch had taught her about herbal potions used in the treatment of burns. Her choice of agrimony and betony had proved invaluable for combating the burns upon Shadiz's face, chest and particularly his back. No matter how hard she tried, the remedy to mitigate his fever was proving frustratingly elusive.

The captain was having to sail the *Eagle* on a tortuous course. He was terrorised by the spectre of an inauspicious encounter. If the merchantman were to be intercepted by a patrolling Parliamentarian warship, no corner would adequately conceal the Master in his present fever-agitated state. Unfortunately, the longer Richard remained in the middle of the winter heaving North Sea, the worse his malady became.

By the sixth day at sea, the situation was verging on desperate.

The atmosphere in the captain's cabin was rank with illness. Bob had wedged the door open but by the time the draught that flowed down the companionway from the cold decks reached the cabin, it barely stirred the sickly cauldron.

Sitting down with a ponderous sigh in the chair behind his cluttered desk, Bob wiped a hand over his sweaty features. Absently scratching his grey beard, he looked across his cabin, lit by the constant, swaying candle lantern. Catherine was sitting on the floor, littered with herbal paraphernalia, between his occupied bunk and the makeshift sickbed. In their present, respective conditions, neither leader nor lieutenant were aware of her weary presence. She was gazing down, owl-eyed, at her hands. They rested limply against the stained blue velvet skirt of her gown.

"I reckon we ought t' make for a Dutch port, th' knows, luv," he suggested, reluctantly. Catherine lifted her head. Seeing her expression, he quickly added, "Not Ijuimden. T' be sure." He tried to look enthusiastic. "There be plenty o' others. Richard needs t' be off watter." He hesitated, before adding quietly, "I know you've done y'r best for 'im, luv, but tother's...." His regretful voice trailed off into a difficult silence.

Steeped in wretched thoughts, their respective gazes were drawn to the bunk. Shadiz persisted in thrashing about and muttering incoherently. If he became still for any length of time, they both grew perturbed.

The persistency of the fever had begun to frighten Catherine. Her throat tight and aching, she said, "He will ... depart ... before we reach any port. If only I could find the means by which to break the fever. If only the White Witch were here. I have done all she has taught me. But it would seem not to be enough. I am proving an inadequate pupil. And, of course, you are correct about Richard. His constitution strikes me as not being overly strong at the best of times. Right now, he is in dire need of dry land."

Her quiet despair penetrated the captain's tired preoccupation with their dilemma. He was immediately contrite. It was with an ashamed jolt that he realised just how much he had come to rely upon her.

Studying her while she remained focused on her patients, he decided she appeared for all the world like a grubby, exhausted angel, haloed by fair-white hair; vexed by the capricious absence of miracles. Beneath the witty maturity, the unflappable commonsense and the unwavering determination, was a sixteen-year-old girl, only one year older than his oldest daughter, who had just lost her father and her home.

It now seemed highly likely, because of his uncharacteristic deed, she was about to lose her improbable guardian.

Bob could not help wondering whether that was necessarily a bad thing. He even toyed with the idea of welcoming her into his own family, such was the impression she had made upon him. Then reality smote the good captain. Although she never flaunted her good breeding, he had to admit that such an inherent quality established her on a loftier rung of life's ladder than the one occupied by his family and himself. She occupied Richard Massone's aristocratic level. Bob knew that he was smitten with her. He knew also that at present the young man's options were limited.

He wondered what Tom Wright would make of it all. Tom and him went way back to simpler times. Knowing him as he did, Bob was sure Tom would agree with him that the Lodge was no place for the young lass. But his old friend would disagree vehemently with his thoughts regarding Shadiz's fate. He was fully aware that Tom would be devastated should anything happen to the lad. Moreover, he was quite convinced many folk in and around Whitby, throughout the North-East of Yorkshire, would be vulnerable without the Master's formidable protection. In just one year, since making an unexpected entry into the Civil War, the charismatic Gypsy had established a firm grip on life in general.

Too weary to continue with his difficult speculations, Bob commended all of their fates into the hands of the same compassionate deity which thus far had kept them safe upon a sea stirred by winter's ladle.

He heaved himself up onto his feet and reached for the leather flagon atop of scattered paperwork. The mug he filled boasted a series of dents which told of heavy seas. Walking around his desk, instinctively matching his stride to the pitch and roll of his ship, he urged, "'e, luv. Get this down y'r laughin' gilpos."

The French brandy was a product of smuggling practices restructured by the Master, apparently using his many contacts throughout the Mediterranean. Having been introduced to the potent liquor after she had been found, a half-frozen stowaway, Catherine was wary of the well-meaning offer. Her eventual acceptance was a half-hearted attempt to rejuvenate spirits which had plummeted down a well of despair.

In the next few moments, emotional needs were suspended by the abrupt, overwhelming need to breathe. While she made a variety of unladylike noises, Bob gave a satisfied chuckle.

In no time at all, the brandy spread blessed ease throughout her aching body. Gazing bereft of thought into its depths, she lost herself in the golden liquid. The drone of Bob's voice. Shadiz's fevered ramblings. Richard's low-pitched moans. They all became background murmurs in her shrunken world within the battered mug.

Gradually, an image formed. It was of the blind, old Romany woman, the White Witch, who had ignored the strict Romany code and, at Nafferton Garth, made Catherine her apprentice. A memory stirred. Within the gentle ripple of the brandy, Catherine saw her mentor walk waist high into the River Derwent to immerse a fever-ridden child in the cold water.

All at once, ignoring the tremor caused by the vision, Catherine knew what had to be done. She scrambled to her feet. "We must take him up onto the deck."

"What? Shadiz?" exclaimed Bob, astounded. "*Almighty*, lass. Y'd kill lad for sure."

"If he remains here, in this condition," she retorted, flinging out an expressive hand, "he will expire in his own heat. Either that, or he will drown in his own sweat. We must get him to the deck."

A sceptical frown drew Bob's bushy brows together. He made his way to where she stood beside his bunk. "Luv, 'tis middle o' night, th' knows. Almighty, 'tis middle o' rotten winter. An' we be in…."

"The middle of the North Sea," interrupted Catherine, twisting around to him. An odd urgency had invaded her. "That is what will save him!"

Bob stared down at Shadiz. The sharp angles and deep hollows of his tribal-dark, unforgettable features, shrivelled on the left side by the fire, were bathed in sweat and contorted by hot ramblings. The memory of another, earlier voyage came to mind. On that occasion, it had been Tom Wright who had striven to aid the strange Gypsy, who both fascinated and frightened him.

★ ★ ★

" *Almighty*. If we ain't careful lad'll wreck me rotten ship."

"What d' y' want me t' do? Chain 'im up, like 'e 'as been?"

57

The quiver in Tom Wright's voice brought Bob Andrew up sharply. He sighed regretfully, and placed a comforting hand on his old friend's shoulder. "I just meant…." He shrugged helplessly.

The two men were standing at the *Eagle's* starboard rail. Bob could see that Tom was appreciating the cool north-easterly breeze on his warm cheeks, but that he could not enjoy the respite. At length, gazing across the placid North Sea, Tom said, "Junno is wi' 'im."

Bob nodded. "Fer 'owever long it tak's, eh," he murmured.

★ ★ ★

The captain knew what Tom would want him to do. He sighed. "Oh, thump," he muttered by way of reluctant agreement to Catherine's bizarre course of action.

Several members of the *Eagle's* crew, having exchanged surprised looks, obeyed their captain's succinct command and carried Shadiz topside. They laid him, wrapped in a blanket, in the rearing shadow of the poop deck. Wearing one of Bob's thick cloaks, Catherine knelt beside him.

Overhead, an abundance of diamond stars jewelled the velvet sweep of midnight sky. Armed with the frosty spears of winter, the northerly wind swept across the decks of the merchantman. Ghostly white sails, taut and majestically lofty, determined the ship's swift passage to nowhere through an inky landscape.

Bob hovered at the edge of the light shining valiantly from the three candle lanterns he had placed around the prone Gypsy and Catherine. Uncertain how to proceed, he glanced around his ship. Despite the wintry nature of the night, the seamen had coalesced into indistinct, speculative groups in the pale light of the quarter moon. Set upon its age-old path through the dark-time heavens, the sliver of silver marked the passage of time.

Had willpower alone been the main requisite for ensuring Shadiz's emergence from the stubborn fever, Catherine would have succeeded in much the same way her use of the herbs was beginning to heal his burns. She had followed the blind, old

Romany's use of the coldness of nature to mitigate fever. Indeed, she had felt strangely compelled to do so. Yet all she had managed to achieve by the time dawn lurked in the east was an unnatural stillness. Baffled by her lack of success, she knew it did not bode well for the man laying upon the cold wet deck.

"You are a killer."

Catherine's words to Shadiz skimmed the broken surface of the rustling sea, ominous as a wounded albatross. Yet, she sought to mitigate the truth by championing a selfless act, performed in the jaws of death. For, she thought defiantly, was life defined in black and white or in shades of grey? When another thought came skulking, she cried out aloud, "No!" She would not influence her own destiny.

Bob heard her. Fearing the worst, he hurried to her side and rested a comforting hand on her shoulder. Looking down at Shadiz, he fully expected death. What he saw was its ghastly hovering, ready to snatch another victim. That it should be the Master was unbelievable. "Luv," he said, with genuine regret, "you've done all y' can."

Catherine ignored him. She dashed away the tears. She would not relinquish the fight.

Countless times during the past few days, she had found herself staring at the pendant Shadiz wore on a silver chain. It was a delicate, white moonstone. There were rune-like symbols around the broad silver border, very similar to those inscribed upon her own jet pendant. She reached out a trembling hand to the moonstone. Amazingly, it had been untouched by the hot tentacles of the fire at Ijuimden. It had been while they were at the Dutch port, after Shadiz had escaped the fierce blaze, that she had first seen him wearing it; after her own pendant had become inexplicably warm against her skin.

A remarkable possibility revealed itself to her. She bid the weird concept welcome and trod the path taken on one other notable occasion.

The moment had come to dispense with a healer's patience. She could no longer suffer the arduous helplessness that lurked beneath. Instead, in an attempt to reach a fading spirit, she would concentrate on the unspoken connection. On the incredible silver link, she instinctively felt existed.

Catherine bent over Shadiz taking his right hand in hers. It lay limp and icy as she gazed briefly at the scarlet, ruptured skin and the ripped fingernails, revealed in the dwindling light of the candle lanterns. Then she closed his unresisting fingers around her own dangling jet pendant, which she was beginning to believe was a very odd gift from her father on her twelfth birthday. Next she rested her left hand over his moonstone pendant, laid upon discoloured flesh, stirred by shallow breathing.

"I shall not permit you to slink away like a thief in the night," she announced in a firm voice. Without thought, she became the channel. "Mithral Bel cayel nay lay tarna."

She could feel the moonstone and its silver rim grow warm within her hand. Gradually, as if answering her call, the symbols became more defined against her palm. They were unknown to her, but still the words they inspired sprang forth from her.

"Canast fay nay par."

Remarkably, as before at Ijuimden, her own jet pendant grew increasingly warm through her grip on his slack fingers.

"Canast fay nay par."

★ ★ ★

He stood on the gloomy, subterranean river bank and watched the ferry glide away. On board was a familiar, respected figure. The Countryman stood amongst the summoned throng leaving with the ferryman. The Countryman turned one last time. He smiled his forgiveness and slowly nodded his approval.

It was growing cold. He looked down at his right hand. The tangible link rested within it. She was calling to him. He had stumbled upon her, aeons ago. The Daughter. The moon within his jet-darkness.

Shadiz gradually opened his eyes. His cracked lips formed his unique name for her.

"*Kore.*"

CHAPTER FIVE

Upon a Hostile Sea

An elusive disturbance tapped against the periphery of sleep, a persistent breeze against a darkened window. She was reluctant to draw back the veil to investigate, content to remain cocooned in the drowsy state between sleep and wakefulness.

"Let 'er wake up, dammit."

Catherine came fully awake with nerve-jarring suddenness.

She barely noticed Bob hovering over her or Richard struggling to prop himself up on one elbow close by upon his makeshift bed on the floor of the cabin or Bob's young nephew standing in the open doorway, all agog. She simply looked upwards into deep jet pools.

She had never given up hope. Her reward for clinging to the precious silver strand was to view the miracle above her. Her young face lit up with gladness.

Shadiz lay on his stomach upon the inadequate bunk above her. His roughly bearded chin was resting upon his pillowed arms. "Mornin'."

"Is it?" Catherine answered, preoccupied with his existence.

"It were mornin' when gates o' 'ell were slammed shut in me face." His barely audible words held the rusty notes of a very sore throat. "So Bob tells me. Your doin'."

"I considered the Devil's request to be presumptuous," she replied, happily.

"The Devil takes care of his own," Richard muttered.

The only indication that Shadiz had heard the feeble barb was in his next few words, again directed at Catherine. "Devil came garb as an angel."

She gave a breathless laugh. "My father always maintained I was a little devil in skirts."

A heart-stopping smile creased his scarred gauntness. It almost proved the undoing of Catherine. She retreated before she drowned in his potent darkness. Attempting to sit up, she discovered she was as stiff as one of the boards upon which she lay. "How long have I been asleep?" she asked, struggling to peel herself off the floor of the cabin. Someone had covered her with a thick blanket. It smelt of lavender and chicken stew.

"A day an' 'alf. Or thereabouts," Bob told her, his manner edgy.

Only when she had been quite certain that Shadiz was truly out of danger had she allowed her vigil beside him to be overtaken by the kind of deep sleep pure exhaustion demanded.

Bob was about to help her win her battle upwards when Shadiz cautiously shifted his position on the bunk in order to extend a hand down to her. She decided the tremor was due to his fragile state of health. She attributed her own shakiness to her rude awakening. When she hesitated, not wishing to inflict further suffering, his expression compelled her to accept the gesture.

"Accordin' t' Bob, wet-nurse's been busy."

Pulled up into a sitting position by strength she had underestimated, Catherine flushed guiltily. "It was my fault you were hurt. Had I not pressed you to go to the aid of Rose."

"Y' weren't responsible for what went on at Ijuimden," came the hoarse response.

"Who was?" asked Richard, weakly. The herbs Catherine had given him, which by some miracle he was managing to keep down most of the time, were beginning to have an affect on the sea-sickness.

Shadiz let go of her hand. His manner altered upon his gaze switching from her to Richard. Despite his malady, the bleak, obsidian impact was not lost on Richard.

Not for the first time, Catherine wondered why Shadiz and Richard were constantly at loggerheads. A reason lurked beneath the obvious chasm of personalities. Whatever that might be, Bob was only too aware of it, she felt sure. Why else would she sense he rested on a knife edge when Shadiz belittled his lieutenant and Richard was quick to counter the malicious baiting with righteous anger?

"Well, who was responsible?" repeated Richard, a brusque edge to his tremulous voice.

A queasy shade of white, his flesh was drawn tightly over the illness sharpened bones of his handsome face. He possessed barely enough strength to keep himself sitting upright. Because his leader did not seem inclined to supply an explanation, he answered his own question in an irritable manner, "A certain party wished to lure you to Ijuimden. Presumably, Van Helter accepted a hefty bribe to reduce the quality of your consignments." He frowned. "Even so, there was no guaranteed way of getting you to make the voyage to the Dutch port."

Shadiz tried to raise a sardonic eyebrow but clearly found the small movement painful. "No?" he snapped.

Richard emitted a breathless growl, "How the devil am I supposed to know?"

"Y' ain't kept informed?" came the whispered mockery.

"How many times do I have to make matters plain?" What should have been passionate emphasis was instead a limp appeal.

"Y' could swear oath on any archbishop's pate an' I'd still not believe y'."

"Someone," retaliated Richard, laying back upon the threadbare blanket acting as his pillow, "possessed advanced knowledge of the *Eagle*'s voyage to Ijuimden."

"Aye," put in Bob, " 'alf o' Whitby." He gave the low, shadowy ceiling of his cabin an exasperated glance.

Precious time was being wantonly squandered while the sleek, deadly threat bore down on them. Even if his young nephew, who seemed to have become the harbinger of ill-tidings, had forgotten the reason for his hasty entry into the stuffy cabin, Bob had not. Both half-alive, Shadiz and Richard were still at each other's throats, still pursuing a bitter quarrel that could easily sink all of them.

Catherine's untidy fair-white hair swept the floor as she turned to Shadiz. She found his disconcerting gaze resting on her. "What

Richard means, I believe. Your presence on board the *Eagle* was not common knowledge."

"Or y'rs," came the forthright answer.

"Me?" she exclaimed, startled.

Richard's attempt to pour fragile scorn on such an observation was interrupted by Shadiz. He spoke so low, the rest of the people in the captain's cabin had to strain to catch his words. "Let me instruct, bitti chavi a chavo. Van Helter was bribed by Lynette's men we met in 'is shop."

"Who is Lynette?" asked Catherine.

" 'e presently controls Fylingdales Estate," Shadiz informed her, black eyes fixed on Richard. "The encampment y' were 'eld in was on Fylingdales land."

"He is for Parliament?"

Shadiz attempted to shrug. Then winced. "Suits 'is purpose."

Richard snorted with sour humour. The sickness rose up into his gullet, preventing any comment.

"When I was seen to've swallowed bait, a member o' *Eagle*'s crew relayed Lynette's next set o' orders t' men already in the Dutch port."

"The orders?" managed Richard, swallowing hard.

"T' eliminate yours truly, what the 'ell else?" Shadiz exhaled. "Tis gettin' bloody predictable."

"You were aware of these facts when we quit the Lodge?"

Shadiz nodded slowly. "Y' weren't?" he murmured, with an unpleasant grin.

Bob's voice clashed with Richard's. The healthy, indignant captain won out. "There be no traitor aboard me ship."

"Y' reckon barrels cut theirsen loose?" came the derisive, rusty retort.

Bob opened his mouth but did not voice his loyal rejection. He had caught sight of his usually unflappable bo's'un pushing past young Will in the doorway. Sam Todd's weatherworn countenance showed his heightened worries. "They be gainin' on us," he declared with some urgency. "Wi' cannons run out an' aimed at us."

"Who are?" asked Catherine, puzzled. She automatically turned back to Shadiz.

Again the eyes of leader and lieutenant locked.

How, thought Richard, was the Master going to extricate himself from what was an inevitable development? Only Catherine's presence on board the merchantman, known for the past year to be at the beck and call of the Master, stopped him from gloating.

"Who are?" she repeated.

"Lynette's blockader's about t' intercept *Eagle*," said Shadiz, switching from Richard to her.

"Tried tellin' y', lad," pointed out Bob in a tight neutral tone.

The revelation hit Catherine in a blinding flash. "*Ye gods and little fishes*," she exploded, scrambling to her feet. "Bob did his utmost to preserve your safety. The *Eagle* sailed about the North Sea like a ... a blue-arsed fly. Then what happens? You calmly lay there while whatever-his-name's ship catches up with us."

Unaware of the anxious reaction her outburst had caused in the silent cabin, Catherine continued to glare at Shadiz. Nor was she receptive to the collective disbelief when Shadiz bent his head. Although his long singed hair curtained his face, his broad fire-marked shoulders could be seen to be carefully shaking. Catherine could have cheerfully hit him where it hurt the most.

"Y' ought t' move a bit sharpish, lad. Into 'old?" said the captain, wanting the Master to be gone, for all their sakes.

There was no response from the bunk. The lack of movement only served to feed the tension within the cabin.

Eventually, the gypsy black head lifted. All traces of humour had vanished. "What y' done wi' y'r own clothes?" Shadiz asked, surveying Catherine with a hooded gaze.

Being above average height for a sixteen-year-old maid, Will Andrew's spare set of clothes fitted Catherine far better than the odd creation she had worn when a stowaway. Glancing down at the serviceable breeches and homespun shirt she wore with unconscious, tomboy grace, she explained, "Rose's gown became fit only for the fishes."

"Y' salvage nowt else?"

"Only the herbs I have been treating your injuries with. And those to combat Richard's sickness," she answered, catching a glimpse of his clenched fists.

"Y' best collect 'em up. An' owt else that shouldn't be in 'ere."

His hard mouth compressed into a tight line when, by laborious degrees, he pushed himself up and onto his knees.

As the coarse blanket slipped away, uncovering his nakedness, Catherine hurriedly terminated her study of his ravaged back and turned away from the bunk. For the moment, she was content to do his bidding, her annoyance at his reckless tardiness notwithstanding. It had been a nightmarish experience to have him so utterly dependant upon what she considered her small skill. The last thing she had done before exhaustion had claimed her was to apply further soothing salve in an effort to continue the healing process upon the slowly fading rawness and shrivelling blisters .

By the time she had filled the small sack provided by Will, Shadiz was sitting on the edge of the narrow bunk. Elbows on knees, head bent, the effort of pulling on borrowed breeches and his own boots showed in every slumped line of his big body.

"Will, lad," said Bob, during another period of apprehensive stillness in the cabin. "Get topside an' see what's goin' on."

Shadiz got slowly to his feet. He swayed alarmingly. Reaching out to the cabin wall for support, he muttered, "You'll need t' come wi' me." He did not look in Catherine's direction but it was obvious to whom he was speaking.

"Why the devil should she?" gasped Richard. He had just gone through a bout of painful retching, followed by an agonising fit of coughing.

" 'ell's teeth. 'as the bloody sickness addled y'r brain," rasped Shadiz, his sweat-bathed face thunderous. "Why the bleedin' 'ell d' y' reckon she were on Fylingdales in first place?"

In the process of wiping the sleeve of his dirty shirt across his mouth, having long since forgone the niceties of his upbringing, Richard stopped and stared at Shadiz.

"Could I pass lass off as me daughter? Me niece?" pondered Bob, doubtfully.

"No," said Shadiz and Richard together.

Bob nodded, resigned to the truth. Shot through Catherine's friendly, casual simplicity, like golden threads, were all the unconscious hallmarks of good breeding. Little wonder Richard was so taken with her.

"Right now, I would happily be a relation of yours, Bob. However, I believe it would prove too much of a coincidence for the men from Fylingdales. Therefore, not to arouse inconvenient suspicion, I have collected everything else that could be deemed out of place in your cabin, I may as well tuck myself away, also." She was conscious as she spoke of Shadiz's piercing attention. Her mind occupied with other worries, the question of her own safety had not occurred to her. Trying to hide the turmoil within, she added, "If it will avert disaster, so be it." A thought struck her. Looking his way, she asked Richard, "What of you? Surely, it would be wiser for you to accompany us?"

"Oh, I reckon Joyous Gallant'll be safe enough 'ere," observed Shadiz, sneering in the direction of his lieutenant's pale hostility. His gait stiff and tentative, he advanced unaided upon Richard. "Uncle's bloodhounds daren't be too rough wi' 'im."

"*Uncle?*" exclaimed Catherine. "This Lynette is your uncle?"

It was left to the agitated captain to supply a grim affirmative.

Shadiz gradually sank down onto his haunches beside the makeshift bed on the floor of the cabin. As he spoke, beneath the range of the curious onlookers, Richard's drawn face began to resemble ash caught in a vice. Sweat had plastered his lank fair hair darkly to his temples. An unhealthy moisture glistened on his parchment skin. He shot a quick glance at Catherine. And then surveyed his nearby leader, pure loathing giving his hollow cheeks spots of hectic colour. His low-pitched words drew an unfortunate response.

Catherine intervened with a timely reminder. "We must be away."

It was his dire weakness that mastered Shadiz's dangerous temper. Straightening unsteadily, he put a hand out to the cabin wall for support.

Richard glared up at him. "I will supply the necessary cloak. For

Catherine's sake. I would not condemn her to Francois's hospitality."

Following a brief cold appraisal of Richard, without another word, Shadiz pushed himself away from the wall, and very nearly collapsed. Only the timely, combined efforts of Bob and Sam Todd prevented him from falling to his knees. Between them, they propelled Shadiz out of the cabin and down the gloomy companionway. Both men shared the impression of gingerly helping an injured wild cat.

Catherine followed the men, dependant on their expert lead. Little could be discerned beyond the small pool of floating light being emitted by the candle lantern held aloft by Bob. Clutching the sack containing the precious herbs, she tried hard to avoid the unseen obstacles awaiting her blind passage through the pitching darkness. Becoming increasingly disorientated by their tortuous route through the rumbling belly of the merchantman, before long she caught hold of Bob's jacket.

By the time he and Sam came to a halt, her concern for Shadiz was paramount. The two seamen lowered him down onto a convenient barrel, and there he meekly remained, breathing heavily. Though the lantern revealed little of their surroundings, Catherine realised they were in the main hold. The cargo Bob had been unable to discharge at Ijuimden stretch away into the concealing darkness. Neatly secured barrels and sacks were making an unexpected return to their port of origin.

The cold, damp atmosphere within the hold was seeping into her bones. Having grown accustomed to the summer-like warmth within Bob's cabin, she was grateful to Sam Todd for his chivalrous gesture. She pulled the bo's'un's thick woollen jacket tightly about herself, not knowing whether her shivering was due entirely to the frigid conditions.

His worries illuminated briefly, Bob passed the candle lantern onto Shadiz. He left them at the Master's curt bidding to go topside and meet the *Endeavour*'s dangerous boarding party.

Casting weird shadows around them, the candle lantern highlighted the toll their urgent passage had taken upon Shadiz. It also showered weak light on the deft movements of the muscular bo's'un as he shifted around barrels and sacks. Before very long, he had uncovered the side of a large crate. To Catherine's surprise, he heaved aside the deceptive wooden square to reveal a deep niche.

Each of his slow movements accomplished with caution, Shadiz bent in order for the lantern he held to shed light into the secret hold. Sam ducked inside and swiftly rearranged the barrels stored within, presumably those Richard and herself had transported from behind Van Helter's blazing shop.

So that was it. She was going to be shut up with barrels of gunpowder and a volatile, hurting Gypsy. In utter darkness. For any kind of light would act like a deadly beacon.

Catherine was gripped by a terrible panic. "I cannot do this."

The two men looked at her.

"I ... I am sorry. I just ... cannot."

Her heart was racing. Goaded by an irrational dread, she was having difficulty breathing. She shook her head, staring fearfully into the box-like space.

The bo's'un looked dismayed.

Shadiz handed the lantern to him. He seemed not to be surprised by her reaction. His left hand rose, palm open. "Kore, trust me."

Sam blinked at him, clearly amazed by his considerate manner.

"I ... I," Catherine stammered, frantically, "cannot...."

"Y'r fears're understandable. But this ain't the cellar at Nafferton Garth. Trust me."

It took a couple of moments for her to grasp the significance of Shadiz's barely audible words. He waited, black eyes gently compelling. Trembling, she found herself responding to his proffered hand. Hers was gloved in clammy fear.

The small area cleared by the seaman allowed just enough room for Shadiz to sit down in some kind of comfort. A quivering prey to her forebodings, Catherine knelt beside him. At a nod from him, Sam sealed them into an unrelieved void. Whereupon, she clung unashamedly to her guardian's left arm, heedless for once of his tender flesh.

"Shut y'r eyes," he said.

"It makes no difference," she cried. Panic threatened to engulf her.

"Shut y'r eyes. Do it."

"Would to God, I had been sensible and remained at the Lodge," she bemoaned, obeying him. Deprived of one sense, the reek within the dank cargo hold and the interminable seagoing whispers compensated.

"This time, 'tis nowt t' do wi' a thirteen-year-old's prank that went awry," Shadiz told her.

"It was not my fault."

"I know."

Her anxiety faltered. "You know?"

"Twas me who released y' from the bloody cellar."

Thankfully lost in the all-encompassing darkness, a hot flush of embarrassment replaced the icy sweat of terror. "How on earth?"

"Them times I visited y'r father, I'd take ... unconventional routes. It were one such time when I 'eard y'r 'ollerin' an' 'ammerin'. Cellar door'd warped an' jammed shut. I'd just got bloody thing open when Roger arrived."

Catherine had always been under the impression her father had released her from the frightening experience of being trapped in the pitch blackness of the cellar beneath Nafferton Garth. He had never said anything to the contrary.

" 'e ain't enlightened y'?"

"Only when we were having to flee our home did he mention you. When the attention of the Parliamentarians became too unpleasant. Even then, only with the thumbscrews applied. I had heard of your ... er ... reputation. But until then, I had no idea my father was acquainted with you. From him, I learned you were a random cross between a flippant scholar and a hard-bitten mercenary."

"*O opportunity: thy guilt is great!*" Amusement spiced the quote.

"My father is ... was ... a great believer in looking beyond notoriety. What does?"

"*Though all my wares be trash.* Y'r mare, Twilight. She's at Lodge."

Catherine was overjoyed to hear that, like herself, her beloved mare had been rescued from the Crop-Ears. That he should even be aware of Twilight's existence astounded her. "How?"

"Does it matter?"

"Not unless you have sprained your crystal ball."

"Develesko Mush."

There was a deep pause. The impenetrable darkness was once again closing in around her, whether or not her eyes were shut. Struggling against the cruel grip of terror, her hold on his arm intensified.

"I'm truly sorry about Roger's death. 'e possessed rare qualities." Catherine heard Shadiz's faint exhale of breath. "Ain't I livin' proof?" And, almost to himself, " 'e shouldn't 'ave died."

"Why did he?" she asked. Recalling his harsh words to Richard, she added, "I don't understand why my presence on the Fylingdales Estate mattered so much?"

He was silent for so long Catherine thought he was not going to answer her.

Then, at last, he gave a resigned sigh, as if a decision had been made. "Afore word was got t' me, Roger bolted wi' y'. I'd drummed it into 'im, if 'e ever 'ad need o' me, I'd get t' 'im. Only Page made a bloody good job o' puttin' 'oly fear o' any sod's god into 'im."

"Colonel Page?"

"Aye."

"I still don't understand." He must think her a witless fool.

Shadiz said nothing for several moments. When he did continue, his husky, whispery tone was without emotion. "When Page an' 'is troopers followed 'im from Nafferton Garth an' moved in on 'im, Roger was left just enough alive to find me an' inform me about bait in Lynette's trap."

Catherine came to a startling conclusion. "*Me*?" she exclaimed.

"Aye."

"Are you telling me ... Oh, no. Are you telling me, my father ... he was ... used ... killed ... murdered ... simply as a means to ensnare you?" The pressure of blackness was mitigated by the burden of disbelieving grief. "He died because of ... *you*?" Hot tears were burning her eyes and spilling down her cold cheeks. The honed spear of truth pierced her soul. Her nails dug into his burnt flesh. "You could have saved him." Her voice was shrill with the rage erupting within her. "I've heard what people say about you. How clever you are. Devious. How you can achieve whatever you set your mind to. Why didn't you save him?"

Hitherto suppressed beneath a sequence of fast moving events, her sorrow now burst from all restraints. "His death is your fault." She released his arm and began to beat her fists upon his chest, heedless of his injuries. "You are to blame!"

Shadiz made no move to stop her. He said nothing. In the concealing darkness, he became the rock upon which her misery pounded.

When the storm of tears finally abated. When the husk of her grief had been shed and only the heartbroken kernel remained. Only then did he draw her into his arms. Sobbing against his bleeding chest, Catherine was unaware of what demons the darkness held.

★ ★ ★

The two ships were ill-matched participants in the high seas encounter. Cannons bristled the length of the *Endeavour's* portside. With each hoisting wave and deep, dipping trough their aim never strayed from the inferior trader.

A skiff soon came bobbing alongside the *Eagle*. In a remarkably short time, well-armed men took root upon the main deck. Concealing his misgivings, Bob Andrew greeted their two superiors with what he fervently hoped was the correct measure of innocence and righteous annoyance.

Henry Potter was squat and grizzled, impatient to proceed with the business at hand. As chalk is to cheese, Gerald Carey was slender and elegant.

The captain was acquainted with both men. He had long since realised that Francois Lynette, custodian of the great Fylingdales Estate, chose his men with care in order to benefit from their various talents.

His manner crisp and direct, Potter demanded, "Do you submit peacefully to our dealings?"

"O' course," affirmed Bob, "I've nowt t' 'ide."

★ ★ ★

It took time, but, eventually, Catherine was sufficiently in control of herself to mumble, "I'm sorry. As a rule, my behaviour veers sharply from hysterical brat."

"Y' bein' too 'ard on y'rsen."

In sensible retrospect, despite all she had seen him commit in the short time she had known him, she had to accept that his regret at the death of her father was sincere and that her accusation had been unfair. "I'm sure you did everything within your power to help my father." A sob escaped her struggling control. "No one is infallible."

"That's a relief."

The ironic inflection in Shadiz's habitual quiet and presently hoarse tone of voice caused her to give the darkness a sad half-smile. She remained within the circle of his arms. Her right hand came away from his chest wet. "Oh, no!" she exclaimed. "Your bleeding." He halted her attempt to move away from the damage she had done to him.

" Tis nowt. Be still, Kore."

His gentle understanding brought tears to her eyes. "I'm sorry."

"Enough o' that," he murmured.

She gave a shuddering sigh. "I ... I just find it so difficult to believe he has ... gone."

His response to her loss was a tender caress upon her arm that first surprised and then comforted her. He felt warm in the wintry void. Thankfully not with the unnatural heat of fever, but with the steadily breathing strength of masculine presence. A sensation arose within her. She swallowed, putting down the reaction to proximity in dangerous circumstances.

"Presumably, my presence in here means I can't go back to Nafferton Garth? That I still qualify as bait?"

73

"Y're Roger's daughter," came the neutral response.

Catherine possessed no insight into the ceaseless movements of the merchantman. Ending the silence which had developed between them, as if he had read her mind, Shadiz informed her, "Bob's reduced sail. 'e's runnin' *Eagle* off *Endeavour's* port bow." After a moment, he added, "They've boarded be now. Lynette's men."

Absorbed in morbid imaginings, she was unaware of the soul-deep hesitation. And probably would have remained in ignorance in the full light of day.

Shadiz began to speak to her about her life.

Following his solicitous lead, holding onto his deep distinct voice as she would a compassionate hand, Catherine's thoughts were shepherded away from the ominous darkness within the cramped space they were being forced to share. He became her surprise companion with whom she traversed the years, reviewing childish pranks, youthful achievements and the few disappointments. Fascinated by his knowledge, her thrusts of curiosity were parried by his skill in leading her through another eventful year.

There could be only one conclusion to the journey through memories. An alert warrior aware of what was to come, Shadiz placed gentle fingers over her mouth.

Catherine was immediately flung back into the black hole of dread. She felt sure the sudden tension she could feel within Shadiz due to their closeness meant that his curved sword, which had been deposited in the secret hold as well as his larger one and his long coat, was at the ready to defend. Yet following his recent injuries and fever, she was aware his aggressive prowess had been greatly weakened. Her worries were all for him.

Barely daring to breath, with mounting horror she heard the muffled voices. Shadiz's hold on her tightened protectively. Without hesitation, she turned into the refuge of his hard chest, regretting the blood, but finding the calm beat of his heart reassuring. Her own heart was pounding so hard the blood was swirling around her eardrums, sending her dizzy where she sat huddled against him.

The disembodied voices rose and fell against the background of thuds that sent chills down her spine and dragging noises that frayed her already ragged nerves. She was persecuted by the devilish knowledge that the man she clung to in the tormented darkness, though he remained an enigma to her, would shield her no matter what his condition. Trembling in an eternity of fear, the beat of vast imagination marked the passage of time.

Snatches of words, impatient curses and brief glimpses of light drifted through the narrow cracks in the rough wooden niche. Heavy footfalls were drawing ever closer to their place of concealment. Discovery seemed inevitable

Shadiz's long hair fell across Catherine's face. Distracted by terror, she thought she had imagined the brush of his lips upon her forehead.

A great hammering on what was in reality the roof of the secret niche, masquerading as a large crate, made her jump violently within Shadiz's possessive embrace. Two more heart-stopping bangs followed in quick succession, moving methodically along the wooden top. Through their physical contact, she felt Shadiz's reaction. Her fears for him rose tenfold. Only when the footsteps moved away, presumably to another part of the ship's hold did she realise she had been holding her breath.

All nightmares lose their grip in time. And, in time, the voices, the noises and the random flashes of light grew increasingly distant. How long Catherine and Shadiz waited, on guard against discovery, she could not be sure, for judgement had vanished.

At length the prolonged absence of sound other than the mundane, sea-rhythmic pattern within the hold of the merchantman heralded the unmistakable conclusion of the dangerous search. Even so, Catherine found it hard to accept Dame Fortune's precious gift. Only when the silence, filled perversely with the echoes of the disturbance, got the better of her did she slowly lift her head.

The atmosphere of tension had subtly altered. No longer did the cause originate from outside the secret niche.

The critical situation had drawn them together. With the retreat of immediate danger, they were left vulnerable to their closeness. Sanctuary desperately sought and unstintingly given had resulted in a new dimension to their concealed intimacy.

His head was still bent towards her. His long hair continued to lay upon her face. His breath was feather light upon her cheek. Neither of them spoke.

Catherine sensed his inner struggle. She dare not stir, willing him with all her young heart into a natural conclusion to the quandary. But when his hesitation continued, she found herself being drawn even closer to him by an irresistible impulse. Only when she felt him draw back from her did she curtail her artless movement.

He was trembling. His breathing rapid. Another burdened moment eroded the last of willpower. Shadiz was undone by an age-old reaction to a long cherished dream. In the darkness, infinitely gentle, his mouth found hers.

CHAPTER SIX

Upon a Deceptive Sea

Neither Henry Potter nor Gerald Carey displayed any great surprise upon discovering Richard, if nothing else, on board the *Eagle*.

A thorough, at times aggressive search of the merchantman had left the efficient boarding party frustrated by their lack of success. The crew of the *Eagle* were grimly satisfied with their good fortune. Their captain's relief knew no bounds. Nonetheless, he sought to maintain a neutral attitude while Potter and Carey settled themselves in his cabin and, much to his hidden chagrin, partook of his brandy.

Sitting in the chair behind the desk, strewn with documents, Potter sniffed suspiciously. "What's that smell?" he demanded.

Flustered, Bob hesitated.

"The good captain has been playing physician with his sister's herbal remedy," said Richard, speaking for the first time since the three men had entered the cabin.

"Aye," said Bob, hastily, trying not to look relieved. "Ain't worked, though."

"Clearly," observed Carey, flicking a lace kerchief like an over-perfumed nosegay beneath his pert nose. "You find it more accommodating down there than here?" he added, indicating with an airy gesture to the neatly made up bunk on which he was sprawled, swinging an elegant leg.

Richard swallowed the upsurge of nausea. "I'm not beyond the pail down here," he answered, glancing at the leather bucket that was his constant companion.

Potter gave an impatient grunt. Henceforth his stern attention was directed downwards to bills of lading. He tolerated the captain's polite peering like someone balancing a nosy parrot on his shoulder. Before long, he asked, "Why was your cargo not discharged at Ijuimden?"

Once more Bob struggled for an answer. "I … er … I'd trouble wi' me agents." There had been little time for him to concoct a plausible alibi.

Richard groaned inwardly at Bob's ineptitude. He muttered, "The good captain deemed it prudent to quit the Dutch port without unloading."

"You don't say," murmured Carey, displaying elaborate interest. "Do tell?"

"There was a fire."

"A fire?" snapped Potter, scowling in Richard's direction.

"Aye," muttered Bob. He was beginning to feel like an nonentity on his own ship.

There was a brief pause.

"We want a word with his lordship," stated Potter, curtly. "Captain."

Bob had half-expected the request. It amounted to a dismissal. He was loathed to leave Richard alone with Lynette's men. Although he sympathised with the lad's situation, like Tom Wright, he didn't trust Richard Massone, the rightful Lord of Fylingdales. However, given the circumstances, there was little he could do but comply. On his way out of his cabin, he shot Richard a pointed look, which the younger man chose to ignore.

"You must convince them. For her sake."

Shadiz's words echoed in Richard's pounding head. In uttering them, Shadiz had come the closest yet to admitting that Catherine Verity was, for some reason he could not fathom, a valuable pawn in the deadly rivalry that existed between his leader and his uncle beneath the trappings of civil strife .

"Where is he?" demanded Potter.

"Even the devil he is, the gypsy cannot disappear without a trace in the middle of the North Sea," remarked Carey.

The irony was not lost on Richard. He had spent the last few months trying to bring the combined scheming of his mother and his uncle to fruition. And now, when success was within his grasp, when Shadiz was unbelievably at his mercy and he was in a position to exact the retribution he craved, he was prevented from capitalising on the amazing piece of luck by the overriding need to safeguard Catherine.

"Well?" demanded Potter, impatiently.

Richard swallowed and licked his cracked lips. If only the ghastly sea-sickness was not clouding his mind. The feeling of being adrift in nauseous aspic was unremitting in spite of Catherine's natural medicine. If only he could think of a way to disclose the damn gypsy's whereabouts without her coming to harm. She had suffered enough having lost her father and her home, not to mention coming under Shadiz's highly dubious protection. He could not risk exposing her to the cold hatred lurking at Fylingdales. Life, as usual, possessed an unfair sting. The old bitterness laced the sour bile.

"Take your time, sweetheart," drawled Gerald Carey, studying his long fingernails.

The honey sarcasm proved a spur to Richard's pledge. "The men Francois sent to the Dutch port put torch to Van Helter's shop. Shadiz was there at the time. He was preparing to transport the gunpowder the Dutchman had stored above his shop. His notorious luck deserted him. The damn stuff blew before he could escape."

The second irony was his inability to tell the truth of what had actually happened at the Dutch port, and cite that as the cause of the gypsy's death. Not in a million years would either Potter or Carey believe Shadiz had battled the fire to save Rose Van Helter. He could hardly believe it himself.

He glanced at Carey and then looked back at Potter. Neither man was renowned for their gullibility. Beneath their sceptical gazes, Richard sighed irritably. He felt as if he were scaling a mountain that would not remain still long enough for him to catch his breath. "Why would I lie to you? Especially about that bastard?"

"Well, of late, my dear Richard, you have become a trifle, shall we say, unreliable," pointed out Carey, a spiteful smirk on his perfect mouth.

Richard was obliged to control those emotions Carey, a fair-haired creature of malicious wit and sly ways, invariably aroused in him. "I was given no opportunity to warn anyone before the damn gypsy paid his early morning visit to Page," he muttered. "Or that he would sail so soon to Ijuimden." The familiar nausea was rising from his contracted guts. "Besides, you have not discovered the bastard aboard the *Eagle*, have you? The *Eagle* in no way attempted to avoid the *Endeavour*, did she? Therefore, the conclusion has to be…." Yet again the sickness gripped him. For the next few minutes, he was unable to continue. After retching convulsively, all he could do was slump exhausted on his makeshift bed.

Potter got up and carried a mug of water to where he lay. Richard managed a feeble shake of his head, which made the cabin spin around his problem. Potter grimaced. "What foul impulse caused you to set sail?" he demanded, not unkindly.

Carey rose gracefully from the bunk. He sauntered forwards to stand tall and slender beside Potter's thickset figure.

"I sailed by the decree of that damn devil," mumbled Richard, rubbing at the sweat on his furrowed brow. "Remember," he continued in a sickly passionate voice, "I wanted his demise just as badly as anyone else. More." He recognised the opportunity and weakly seized upon it. "If I were not speaking the truth, wouldn't the converted member of Andrew's crew, whose identity is unknown to me, have alerted you?"

The shot in the dark failed to hit its mark.

"What of Catherine Verity?" queried Potter, wearing his habitual, bushy-browed scowl. "Have you knowledge of her whereabouts?"

The question reinforced the need for caution. Finally, Richard understood. It did all amount to the protection of Catherine. Now was not the time for revenge. He tried unsuccessfully to close his mind to where she was at the present.

"What the bleedin' 'ell d' y' reckon she were doin' on Fylingdales?"

Shadiz's brutal words rattled around Richard's mind as he sought a plausible explanation. "She stowed away on the *Eagle's* outward voyage in an effort to remain with the knights and their wives from Driffield. After the gypsy's death, I deemed it pointless, indeed heartless, to drag her back to England. I allowed her to continue to The Hague with her elderly companions."

He would have loved, even in his feeble condition, to probe the tricky subject, but dare not. Instead, stifling a cough, he regarded both of his uncle's men in turn, awaiting the outcome of his fabricated account of Shadiz's death.

Gerald Carey was waiting, too. It was clear from his foppish demeanour that he wanted none of the ponderous responsibility associated with the decision which had to be made. Francois Lynette was waiting at Fylingdales Hall.

At last. "Very well," said Henry Potter, curtly, "I see no reason why you would deceive your uncle and your mother. I take it you don't feel up to transferring to the *Endeavour*?"

"No," Richard responded with genuine feeling. "Thank you." His relief made him feel dizzy.

Heading for the door, Potter caught sight of Richard's longbow, abandoned in a corner of Bob's cabin. "You should've used that on him," he commented.

"We'll inform your uncle you will return to Fylingdales ere long," Carey told him as he floated after Potter. "Rejoice, dear heart. Your task would appear complete."

"I'll rejoice," muttered Richard when he was alone in the cabin, "When Catherine is out of that hole and away from that murdering bastard."

★ ★ ★

"Forgive me?" Shadiz's low-pitched voice possessed a deeper huskiness.

The darkness within the secret niche had gained a heady spin. Liquid fire had spread throughout Catherine's entire body.

"For giving into curiosity," she responded, shakily. Had she not done the same, with devastating consequences

"Was that what it was?" he murmured.

"You are nothing like the stable lads who hang around the

81

kitchen door at home hoping to take the maids to Driffield fair. The sentiment remains the same."

Heard for the first time, Shadiz's soft laughter caused gooseflesh to ripple along her arms, throwing her further off balance. He gave no indication of wanting to relinquish their closeness. They remained entwined in a creaking darkness they seemed to have all to themselves.

" 'as anyone else been curious about you?" The merriment had vanished.

"A couple of our neighbours' sons kept squinting in my direction. My father advised me to stick to four-pawed creatures. He maintained I would stunt the growth of any young two-footer."

His laughter came again. Consumed by its deep texture, her next few words slipped out. "You are the first." Leant against his chest, she felt Shadiz's momentary stillness. Then she heard his slow exhale of breath.

"Who is Gianca?"

Catherine had never meant to voice that particular question. The darkness remained ominously silent. Disconcerted, she furnished a hasty explanation. "You spoke her name repeatedly, as well as mine, when you were ill."

"I did?" Shadiz sounded surprised.

There were several thumps and bangs outside the secret niche. Catherine jumped violently and was suddenly afraid again.

"Master?"

"Sam," Shadiz said, quick to reassure her. "*Endeavour* must be makin' sail away from *Eagle*." He quoted, "*We read that we ought to forgive our enemies, but we do not read that we ought to forgive our friends.*"

There was the sound of barrels being shifted and a muffled oath and then the bo's'un heaved away the deceptive side. Trying to be helpful, young Will swung a lantern into the confined space, blinding the occupants with its madly flickering light. Moments before they had been revealed, Shadiz had put Catherine away from himself.

She was the first to emerge from the deceptive crate, helped by Sam. Behind her, Shadiz made painstakingly slow progress into the

82

main cargo hold. Although Sam and Will looked questioningly in his direction, both seemed unsure whether or not they should offer support to the Master. Both had glanced at the blood smears on his chest.

"It be Walt Smithson, sir," exclaimed Sam Todd. " 'e be the treacherous bastard. Beggin' y' pardon, m'lady."

Shadiz had straightened with difficulty. "Where's Smithson, now," he demanded. His narrowed gaze flicked to Catherine for a second before returning to Sam.

"Caught 'im tryin' t' signal skiff while it were pullin' away from *Eagle*," Sam explained, with gruff disgust. "Lads sat on bas … 'im. Cap'n sent me down fer y', sir."

Catherine stood hugging the sack of herbs, enjoying the lantern's soft glow, unlike Shadiz. Having shunned the light, he was a looming shadow, bowed by the limited headroom in the full cargo hold, which conveniently masked his fragile condition, she suspected.

"Get the lady back t' y'r uncle's cabin, lad," Shadiz commanded. "Go wi' Will," he added in Catherine's direction.

Bristling at his dismissal, she allowed the shy youth to guide her out of the cargo hold. For awhile they followed Shadiz's shadowy, laborious progress topside, supported awkwardly by Sam's bowed shoulder. At the door of his uncle's cabin, Will escaped his duty, unable to conceal his desire to be elsewhere.

Following his hasty departure, long, thoughtful seconds passed while Catherine stood and stared at the indistinct door in the cold gloom of the companionway passage.

Why hadn't she tried to question Shadiz about the extraordinary pendants, moonstone and jet? Why they bore identical symbols around their silver borders? Why hadn't she asked him about the half-remembered words, which had spilt from her the night he had lain close to death on the *Eagle*'s deck? Why hadn't she probed more deeply what made her a useful hostage? Her father was dead, beyond mortal hurt. And why hadn't she asked him why he had constantly uttered her name? Kore. In feverish desperation. With a feverish plea. Or like a feverish caress.

Why, instead, had she questioned him about the other name, Gianca, he had uttered while in the throes of fever; exhibiting all the traits of jealousy?

Jealousy? She'd never been jealous in her life.

The realisation came as a soul-deep, shuddering shock. It went a long way to explaining the thunderbolt that had struck without warning in Colonel Page's tent. The powerful blast that had swept over her in a lane consumed with fire. And the unbearable despair she had experienced on a night strewn deck. It explained the tight knot which was fast becoming lodged between her head and her heart.

Her blue eyes expanding, she slapped a trembling hand over her mouth. And then found herself tracing her lips where his had touched hers. The only soft part of him.

She needed no special sense to realise he possessed killer instincts. He was a predator, who even now was stalking his prey. He was dangerous; lethal.

Was that why her father had not mentioned his friendship with Shadiz to her? Had he known what manner of man he was? Had he been protecting her? Until death had forced him to place her into Shadiz's safe-keeping?

The healer in her, assisted by the White Witch, should have been repulsed by her strange guardian. She should hate him for what had happened to her father. Resented him for not allowing her to return to Nafferton Garth. And yet....

Her insides were cringing. Her commonsense was screaming at her. Nevertheless, Catherine placed the small sack containing the herbs on the floor of the companionway to one side of the closed door.

★ ★ ★

Illness had not diminished the Master's charismatic presence. Upon his approach, the mob-like anger of the seamen faltered. They drew back from the figure squirming on the weathered planks of the main deck, leaving just a couple of their burly comrades to maintain a detaining grip. Forewarned by the tenor of his former shipmates' silence, Walt Smithson made a frantic effort to take advantage of his partial release. To no avail. In the next moment a deadly weight descended upon him. Face-down on the deck, he tried to resist. Sitting astride the small, wiry seaman, the Master brought vicious pressure to bear with his knees.

Fearing discovery, the captain wrenched his condemning gaze upwards. He was relieved to see that the *Endeavour* was continuing to sail away from the *Eagle,* superiority prevalent in her full blown sails. Those outraged on the merchantman had taken the precaution of dragging Smithson out of sight of the keenest eyes, when he had been first spotted trying to catch the attention of the retreating skiff, conveying Potter and Carey back to Lynette's high seas hunter.

"Y' left it a might too late, rat. *Why should a dog, a 'orse, a rat, 'ave life?*" Shadiz's low-pitched voice was sinister rust. His haggard features were carved out of soulless granite.

"Go t' devil. Bleedin' gypsy," spat out Smithson, over loud in his defiance.

The seaman's left arm was trapped beneath him. His right one was seized by Shadiz and twisted up towards his shoulder at a crippling angle. Overwhelmed by searing pain shooting through his limb, made muscular by years of trimming sails, Smithson let out a piercing scream that drowned out the grisly collapse of his right shoulder.

"Who were it o' Lynette's lot that got to y'?"

Gasping in agony, Smithson shook his head.

When Shadiz grasped a vicious handful of his short brown hair, yanked his upper body off the deck and seized his left arm, the brutalised seaman groaned. "No, y' bastard."

Prey to mixed emotions, Bob stirred the watchful stillness across the *Eagle*'s icy decks.

"Keep out o' this, Captain," rasped Shadiz, his black eyes intimidating jet.

Bob's hesitant footsteps halted. Experiencing the bitterness of betrayal, his troubled gaze switched from the Master and the disloyal member of his crew to the rest of the ship's company. Come raw to weatherbeaten faces, a thunderous lack of pity meant that none were about to challenge the Master's right to meter out rough justice. The captain understood he too was simply an observer, with a vested interest in the punishment.

Theirs was a solid community, whose links with the sea went back generations. It was unthinkable that one of their own kind should wilfully cut a hole in the tightly woven net. Yet Smithson had done just that by his traitorous deed. Many among his brethren had no liking for his furtive, carping ways. Although known since childhood, he was not one to whom confidences had been given easily, if at all. Nonetheless, being a useful cog in the tireless, often dangerous workings of an isolated seaport such as Whitby meant he had come under the all-encompassing blanket of belonging. Not anymore. By his betrayal, he had made himself a pariah; a loose, frayed ratline worthy only of contempt.

Moreover, Smithson had crossed the Master. The extraordinary, forbidding man, whose reputation loomed large among them, hailed from the sea; they had all recognised that in him. They had come to appreciate his other qualities. He was fast becoming master of the land, North East Yorkshire, as unique and powerful as himself, which would crush anyone fool enough to challenge its natural influence.

"All right. All right," cried Smithson, desperate to alleviate the torture.

The cruel grip on his splintering left shoulder relented fractionally.

"Y' were chaipani who carried Lynette's orders t' 'is ratvalo drabaneysapa at Ijuimden?"

"What? Aye," Smithson muttered.

"It were y' who cut that bloody barrel loose?"

"Aye. Oh, God, aye. Damn y'."

The Master rewarded painful honesty with unrestrained brutality. In one deft twist, he shattered the seaman's left shoulder. Smithson's scream penetrated the fog of grim silence blanketing the merchantman. He continued to cry out shrilly fearing further punishment, but was given a respite when his tormentor was unable to continue.

Shadiz had bowed his head. His long black hair curtained his face. The entire ship's company could see how his cruel fists were pressing down upon Smithson's back, supporting his crumpled weight. His struggle to regulate his ragged breathing showed in his heaving sides.

Sam Todd answered his captain's sharp gesture. He and another seaman began to move cautiously towards the Master. When Shadiz raised his head, the ferocious expression on his moist face warned the seamen to stay back.

"Who got t' y', rat?" There was an involuntary breathless note within the Master's demand.

Smithson was either in too much pain to answer or simply taking perverse satisfaction in heavy breathing silence. Whatever the reason, the Master was savagely impatient with the lack of response, probably because he himself was suffering from imperfect health. He gripped Smithson's hair with one hand and his unshaven jaw with his other and then twisted the seaman's head around until the ominous creaking of neck bones could be heard. He repeated his demand.

Smithson knew he could not expect mercy, even if he were to sing like a song thrush. Instead, his thin face contorted, he managed to fire a poisonous barb.

"Wouldn't y' like ... t' know .... about maggot ... reet under ... y'r nose."

The Master knew men; knew the futility of further probing. His weird grin sent a chill through all watching. The battle of wills was a poor contest. "So be it," he acknowledge, in barely a whisper. "Go t' 'ell, rat."

Retribution came with swift expertise. Cast to his fate by his own actions, the seaman's head lay on the deck at a murderous angle. His sightless eyes gazed up with vague surprise at a leaden sky.

Something akin to a collective sigh wafted over the *Eagle*'s decks. Her crew lingered a few minutes about the slack-helmed merchantman. Then they dispersed to carry out the commands of their grim-faced captain. They were glad to delve back into familiar tasks. Their nimble feet on the yardarms and disciplined hands on the heavy canvas sails set the *Eagle*'s bows slicing a deep certain furrow homewards through the North Sea.

Meanwhile, in gradual stages, Shadiz hauled himself up from the mutilated body of the dead traitor. The January day was bitterly cold. A stiff northerly breeze carried feather-light snowflakes between the scudding clouds. Yet sweat glistened on the slowly mending flesh of his shirtless upper body. His barbarous, freshly scarred face reflected only the brutal determination keeping him upright.

"You foul bastard!"

Though fragile, the exclamation had sufficient potency to turn heads and cause a certain distraction to infiltrate tasks.

A sore, white-knuckled hand gripping the starboard rail, Shadiz viewed Richard's staggering attempt to approach him across the main deck.

"You piece of corrupt filth," added Richard, managing to hurl a second insult at his unimpressed leader.

"Friend o' y'rs, were 'e?" remarked Shadiz, flashing a wolfish grin.

Richard could go no further. Arms wrapped tightly around his shrunken middle, his white, drawn face drained of the nervous energy which had got him thus far, he fell to his knees beneath his leader's scornful regard. It had taken an enormous effort to crawl up on deck. He had been driven to such desperate lengths by the need to discover Catherine's whereabouts. For he had waited, and waited, but she had not returned to the captain's cabin. "You had no right, no right at all, to seek your vengeance before her. God damn your lust for inflicting pain and death."

Shadiz's stance altered immediately. He scanned the decks.

When his questing gaze settled upon her, Catherine watched with bated breath as his eyes widened in surprise and then narrowed in black fury. If she was not to appear a coward, ashamed of having yet again defied his wishes, she must take the step. And so, bracing herself, she left the soaring shadow of the mainmast.

It was bad timing on young Will's part that he should be passing, with uncontained fascination, when the Master was in need of support. The youth was waylaid and his shoulder imprisoned in a vicelike grip.

Catching sight of his nephew's wide-eyed appeal from the other end of the main deck, the dread of Shadiz's viciousness lent wings to the captain's lumbering haste. He had recognised in an instant the danger not only to Will and Catherine but also to those members of his crew who appeared ready to impede Shadiz's unsteady advance. Family men mostly, the seamen had welcomed into their midst the well bred, young girl who had the skill to save the Master and the spirit to challenge him. Bob knew all too well, as they did, his capacity for feral cruelty.

As for Richard, stuck out on the fringe of the defensive crowd, he was consumed with self-condemning rage at the way in which he had inadvertently placed Catherine in the path of his fierce leader.

She was conscious of the courageous protection being offered by the seamen gathering around her. For their sake, she knew she had to abandon their good intentions. She did not want them suffering from the same wild malevolence she had witnessed from her place of concealment. While her heart persisted in marking out the beat of Shadiz's approach, she stepped away from the defence the seamen would give to the detriment of themselves. At the same time, she held up a warning hand to curb the captain's anxious charge.

Glaring down at her, Shadiz came to an abrupt halt a mere pace away from her. Cursing, he roughly hauled Will back. The terrified youth stood quaking beneath his callous grasp, staring piteously at Catherine. In response, she gave him a reassuring smile. For she was experiencing fear only for those around her, because of what they might attempt on her behalf. She did not understand how or why, but she instinctively felt herself to be safe from her guardian's dark violence.

"Cease this bloody capriciousness, Kore. Nowadays, you are well beyond the boundaries of Nafferton Garth. It's not safe to do what you previously considered acceptable. Fate's chewed you up and spit you out into bleeding mire of a callous world, ready and eager to crush you. You're under my protection. Your father, who I held in high esteem, placed you there. And I mean to honour his trust. I sought to keep you safe at the Lodge. Well guarded. You, it was, who saw fit things went otherwise."

Shadiz had spoken in French, confident of Catherine's understanding. His hoarse voice had been pitched customarily low. Despite all appearances to the contrary, his constraint made her feel guilty. She had flushed scarlet beneath his oddly earnest glare. If she could turn back time, she would have taken that step into the captain's cabin.

A response, couched in defensive terms and set within the same foreign framework he had used, never left her lips. Richard's unexpected appearance between Shadiz and herself filled her with sudden alarm.

He had mistaken the inaudible words of his leader for a despicable reproach. As a yardstick, he had used the fearful expression on Will's full moon face. It had not occurred to him that the detained youth was putting his own interpretation on the words he could not comprehend.

Catherine was quick to lend support to Richard while at the same time trying to curb his incoherent agitation. Dizzy and weak, he ignored her and the logic of the situation and seized his leader's fire-damaged left arm. Only, on this occasion, his leader was not on the verge of collapse. Shadiz immediately broke free. He then drove his fist into Richard's stomach.

Dragging a cowering Will with him, he loomed menacingly over where Richard had crumbled onto the deck, retching convulsively. "Convincin' were y'?" he rasped, malice etched in his moist face. "Y' wouldn't find it too bleedin' 'ard," he added, striking out with the toe of his boot at Richard's vulnerable middle.

"No!" cried Catherine, aghast. "For pity's sake. *Shadiz!*"

She positioned herself between the two men. For a fleeting

second, she recalled the man who had been sealed with her in the secret hold. Within darkness there had been light. Now, in daylight, there was only rampant darkness. "No more," she urged.

To the astonishment of those watching in difficult stillness, Shadiz checked his fury.

"Get it out o' me sight," he growled, gesturing with contempt at Richard, who lay in an agonised heap at his feet. "Minister t' bastard wi' y'r damned pattriensis so when we make landfall 'e'll be fit t' show off 'is ratvalo perfect manners."

"He seeks only to uphold decency," Catherine retorted, her young face angrily flushed.

"Develesko Mush. Decency is a bleedin' rod that's been stuck up 'is arse by the vengeful bitch who whelped 'im."

"And you," she flung up at him, "have a tendency to be bloody-minded wherever you happen to be."

Judging by Shadiz's threatening scowl, this time Bob felt justified in fearing the violent temper was about to be turned on Catherine. Despite her preoccupied warning, he moved closer to her, continuing to be greatly concerned about his tearful nephew.

"Release Will," Catherine snapped. Not for a moment did she take her unflinching gaze from Shadiz's forbidding countenance. "That is, if you can stand alone?"

"Duvvel dammit. I've allus stood alone. Whereas you pick up any flawed thread an' bind it t' y'."

Despite Shadiz's irate response, the captain and crew of the *Eagle* once again marvelled at his compliance as he shoved Will away. Caught off balance, upon his rough release the youth fell sideward. In an instant, he scrambled to his feet and made stumbling haste to get away from the Master.

Left without support, blighted by weakness, Shadiz swayed. "Who were it taught y' t' meddle?" he demanded.

Catherine frowned. "Meddle?"

"Who taught y' about pattriensis? 'erbs, dammit."

"The White Witch, the matriarch of the Romanies who are ... were welcomed by my father each wintertime at Nafferton Garth," she answered, coldly, "Mamma Petra."

Shadiz gave a short, nasty laugh. "As if I didn't bleedin' know."

She saw how his black eyes, always strangely dense, were dilated and half closed. He was looking down at her almost as if, on a bleak winter's day, she was standing within the full glare of a summer sun. Her anger was diminished by fear of the fever that had blighted his recovery making a possible return.

He ploughed a trembling hand through his long, black hair. The vicious action disturbed his precarious balance. When he swayed towards her, she reached out to him. Immediately upon touching him, she felt her jet pendant spring to life. It grew warm beneath Will's homespun shirt.

Daylight vanished. At first the darkness was profound, in much the same way it had been in the clandestine hold. Afraid, clutching at the immobile man in much the same way she had done when they had been secreted together, she tried to make sense of the bizarre transformation. In the next moment, the darkness became filled with brightly coloured lights. They whirled and sparkled causing her to feel sick and dizzy. Her temples felt as if they were about to split asunder.

Images began to appear. Spiteful imps, they shimmered and darted in the rapidly changing hues of the cruel light. With devilish glee, they pulled her inexorably downwards. She found no succour at the end of the terrifying vortex. For the conclusion was upon a stony shore beside a sluggish river. Its width and the thick, grey clouds overhanging its murky surface foiled any glimpse of the opposite bank. Nonetheless, what prowled there in that otherworld caused terror to abound in her soul. The more so because she sensed the man's irrational longing to be in that mysterious realm.

There was a boat moored beside a decaying wooden wharf. Maidenly shades drifted through the dismal mist swirling about the ancient barque. Catherine sensed their humiliation. It clung to them while they waited at the rear of the passengers handing over their coins to the indistinct ferryman. The hood of his black cloak concealed his face. He turned momentarily and shook his head.

She experienced the towering, powerful closeness of the man; sensed the haunted weariness cast upon him by the ferryman's refusal. Thereafter, she became a bewildered witness to the drift through remote towers built on desolate plains.

In the next moment, the waking nightmare fled.

Catherine was doused once more in the light of an ordinary day. Although overcast, the January rawness made her blink. Dazed, she focused upwards on Shadiz. She was certain he had severed the horrendous conduit by wrenching free.

A long look passed between them. His expression, she realised, reflected her own deep shock. Briefly, so very briefly, she wondered if she had imagined the random spark, a plea seemed to flare in the mesmerising black eyes.

All she could do was stand and watch as he jerked away from her and made his shaky way to the *Eagle*'s rail. The traumatic experience had left her feeling thoroughly disorientated. Belatedly, she realised she was gripping her pendant. Hoping for some insight, she caressed the jet stone with cold trembling fingers. None was forthcoming. Instead, she was left with a feeling of heartsick frustration.

"Lass!"

Catherine came back to herself. She had the feeling it was not the first time Bob had appealed to her. Reluctantly, she switched from Shadiz to the worried captain. He was bending over Richard. Truth to tell, she had forgotten about his plight. She gave herself a mental shake, trying to concentrate on what Bob was saying to her.

"Lad needs y'r 'elp."

She knelt alongside Bob, and saw for herself the blood within the persistent bile. Yet he was at pains to point out the disturbing symptom of the Master's brutality.

Taking them both by surprise, Richard managed to grasp her hand which rested gently upon his agonised guts. He communicated his sense of urgency with an anguished stare as he lay in a tortured ball.

At first, Catherine found it impossible to discern his garbled words.

"Let's get y' back t' me cabin, lad, where y' can rest a bit easier," advised Bob, giving her a pointed look.

She readily agreed, and tried to soothe Richard while Bob sought help. Members of the Eagle's crew answered their captain's call, casting wary glances towards the place where the Master stood, hunched at the ship's rail.

Despite his painful condition, Richard exhibited a single-mindedness of purpose which delayed his departure below decks. Licking blood-stained lips, he made one last effort to voice the warning he was so desperate to give.

"Do ... do not defend me. He hates me ... for ... what ... I am. Half-brother."

★ ★ ★

Hence, loathed Melancholy,
Of Cerberus, and the blackest Midnight born,
In Stygian cave forlorn,
Mongst horrid shapes, and shrieks, and sights unholy.

The self-loathing, unuttered words crawled through Shadiz's mind. At the same time, the unending bitterness swilled around his mouth, caged by savage lips.

Grizzled by winter, the sea was hypnotic. Each of its ceaseless movements jostled beside a white-crested sibling in a never ending cycle of birth and death; paying homage to the unobtainable moon. The silver goddess of the darkness.

God help him, soon even the sanctuary of the waves would become vague and shrink away into mindless nothingness wherein all condemning rage was vented. For several long moments, he considered the cool darkness of the secret hold.

The throbbing within his temples had increased tenfold. Years had come and gone, each mundane span filled with meaningless trivia; each a separate eternity. He had begun to think himself rid of the curse. Only after he had allowed himself a rare glimpse, unable to resist the pull of the moon within his solitary darkness, had a suspicion of the familiar ache afflicted his flight back into Hadean exile.

Twice in an amazingly short time she had saved his worthless life. Because of her misplaced compassion, she had gone beyond the healing skills she had acquired erroneously. Pure innocence had existed the second time. For she had no idea his parody of a half-brother would have gleefully danced on his grave had it not been for her presence.

Jealousy raised its ugly head. The serpent deep within raged against her closeness to any other man. It took all of his willpower not to go below and drag her away from his loathsome sibling. The chains that kept the beast tethered were fashioned out of the iron knowledge that she could never be his.

The pendant had revealed to her his living nightmare. The silver link threatened to undermine his citadel. Her remarkable sensitivity was not the only threat.

"Wouldn't y' like t' know about maggot reet under y'r nose."

A dead man's defiant boast echoed in vibrant derision around the pain-wracked dome that was his head. Haunting him. Confirming his worst fears. For Kore. The Maiden. The damned Choviar should never have bid her enter into his divio world. She should never have used her as an instrument of her *ëdrukkerebema'*.

Stood at the ship's rail, Shadiz buried his head in his hands.

CHAPTER SEVEN

Requiem for Effort

To gaze upon Fylingdales Hall was to stand witness to history. And the history of Fylingdales Hall could be summed up in one word. Power.

Each wealthy dynasty has its roots in the foundations of civilization. Like so many prestige Houses, Fylingdales Hall was a gem forged and polished by the lofty aspirations of successive men.

The monkish clerics at Whitby Abbey and across the wild breadth of moorland at Rosedale Abbey were diligent in their recording of the arrival of a renowned warrior from the South in 1068.

Sift through the sands of time and one would discover that Flambard De Massone was an obscure knight who, due to his courage in the service of Count William of Normandy during the battle of Hastings, was rewarded with a slice of the defeated land.

"Let not your countenance take on a gloomy aspect, my son."

In truth, De Massone had been awarded a tract of land no one else wished to contemplate, as wild as the east of Lombardy from whence he had come seeking a noble fortune he could bequeath to his son.

Unfortunately, just like his biblical hero, he lived only long enough to glimpse what he considered to be the promised land before succumbing, on the threshold of the rugged moors, to the ironic wound he had received an hour after the battle heralding the Norman Conquest of England.

Philippe De Massone buried his father in the strange land. He was ready to ride south to diplomatically toss the parcel of land back at the newly crowned King William when he discovered

Stillingfleet Forest. The great, verdant swathe stretched from Whitby in the north to Pickering in the south. Few inroads had been made either by Bronze Age migrants and the farmers who were their descendants, or wandering Vikings ready to settle, certainly not enough to diminish the forest's dapple-leafed magnificence. It easily sustained De Massone's passion for the hunt.

He ruled his new domain only long enough to import a wife and impregnate her with his dynastic seed before his death in 1071.

Legend states he ignored a druidic warning and instigated the building of a hunting lodge in a wide clearing within Stillingfleet Forest, bounded by mighty oaks said to have stood for over a millennium. Before a second layer of stones had been laid, Philippe De Massone had died in agony after being impaled upon the tusks of a great boar reputed to be the Guardian of the Sacred Grove.

The progeny of the obligatory union between Philippe De Massone and Anne Rossier was, it seemed, left to his own devices at an early age when his mother returned to her native Normandy, apparently to nurse her elderly father.

Some years later the words of Guy De Massone were set down by an unknown scribe.

"You misinterpret my intention, sir. With your permission, I would make your daughter my wife. Do you not seek, like me, to unite our two communities and therefore make us strong against the raiders of our hearths from the cursed North?"

Shortly after his marriage to the Saxon chieftain's eldest daughter, Guy De Massone moved his household from the hunting lodge he had built in a more prudent clearing in Stillingfleet Forest. In so doing, he transferred the emphasis of his authority away from the ancient forest, and instead established his hopes for future generations upon the bold sweep of Fylingdales Moor overlooking Mercy Cove.

Some twenty years later, his son inherited the grey-stoned keep. Its stark, imposing appearance had been created to deter any marauder from land or sea.

Fylingdales prospered through the ages, especially in the reign of Henry VIII.

"By your actions on our behalf, Sir John, you have proved yourself to be one of our most loyal subjects."

"My desire is but to serve you, majesty."

"That you have done. By your efficient service, you have eradicated another nest of vipers disloyal to us. You shall be rewarded for your labours."

So it was that Henry received the riches of Whitby Abbey, in the same way he had profited from the dissolution of so many other religious houses. The newly created Marquis of Fylingdales was awarded the monastic lands in and around the port, adding to his already considerable slice of North East Yorkshire.

Due to shrewd management by successive generations of the Massone family, by the seventeenth century the Fylingdales Estate had become one of the largest in the North of England. Only the lands of the bishop princes of Northumberland rivalled the estate's far flung boundaries. The fishing port of Saltburn marked its northern boundary whilst the market town of Driffield was the southern one. To the west, the estate reached across the moors beyond Helmlsey. To the east, the North Sea defined the limit, and supplied food for a distinguished table.

Visitors to Fylingdales Hall, noble or humble, having traversed the well-trodden causey that skirted the fishing hamlet of Mercy Cove, were obliged to climb the steep rise known locally as Massone's Hag. Its summit broadened to give access to a well-defined stretch of parkland created from the grudging moorland.

Whether a salute to an inspired ancestor or simply a prudent defensive measure, Guy's Keep had been cleverly incorporated into the Hall built in the fourteenth century. At either side of the intimidating, slit-eyed old warrior there stretched the grandeur of regimented arched windows, set like glinting diamonds in the same gritty texture of grey stone as the keep, mined from the moors. Newcomers who passed through the guarded archway were seen to glance nervously upwards at the murder holes above their heads. To their relief, Guy's Keep gave a sloped, cobbled access to the elegance of the Inner Quadrangle, where cavorting fountains, rustic benches and classic marble figures lightened the mood.

In 1612, Richard Massone became the seventh Marquis of Fylingdales.

An exceptionally tall individual of great physical prowess, like all of his predecessors, he had been well-versed in the smooth management of the huge estate. He brought to the commanding position an intelligent, stern but fair-minded, hard working persona.

For the four years since he had taken up the reins of his inheritance, he had remained unwed but not unattached. Indeed, his attachment remained a source of speculation throughout the estate.

"Mother, I have every intention of marrying her."

"Do not utter such nonsense. She is a gypsy. Keeping her as your mistress at the Hall has already provoked much gossip. To contemplate making her your wife is beyond belief. Beyond all decency. You would make of yourself a laughing stock by such a ridiculous act."

"Recall, if you will, mother. Guy Massone wed a Saxon, thereby uniting two communities. What is more to the point. Gianca carries my heir."

★ ★ ★

An illustrious combination, the crackling blaze flickering upon the hearth of Dutch blue tiles and the shimmering beeswax candles in the silver candelabrums warmed and illuminated the elegant chamber. Velvet drapery had been drawn across the tall windows, shutting out the icy February night. A rich array of tapestries depicting various scenes of Diana hunting with her sleek hounds adorned the smooth white walls above the oak wainscot. Sumptuous Eastern rugs brightened the parquet floor with their intricately woven colours.

There was silence in the Dowager's Solar. The four occupants closeted within its feminine splendour were able to discern with little straining the conversations taking place beyond the ornate floral patterns carved on the closed door. The senior officers of Fylingdales were taking their ease in the company of loyal dignitaries. Within the grandeur of the main hall the atmosphere was far more amicable.

Grey-haired and solid, Henry Potter appeared uncomfortable sitting in a narrow, velvet chair. Nearby, Gerald Carey was reclining in a high-backed tapestry chair, a beautiful, youthful presence of exquisite frills and furbelows, smugly safe in the knowledge that he had succeeded in divorcing himself from the blame Potter was having to stoically shoulder.

Lady Hellena Massone was the only woman present. She was sitting on the satin cushioned settle opposite the two chairs. The high neckline of Gozo lace and the damask shawl draped about her thin shoulders relieved the bleakness of her black gown, which owed nothing to puritanical fashion. Her white hair, drawn back in a severe style, identified the passing of the years. Otherwise her smooth beauty confounded age. Small and straight-backed, all that existed beneath the austere, aristocratic perfection was dedicated to one objective.

Her condemning blue gaze rested briefly on Henry Potter and then switched with cool expectancy to where her younger brother was standing.

Francois Lynette was the suave, golden-haired French Catholic who served his own silver tongued version of loyalty to the English Protestant Parliament.

Shortly after Lady Hellena had been widowed in tragic circumstances, he had, at her behest, relinquished his post of special envoy for the Knights of St John. He had left Malta and arrived at Fylingdales Hall in order to assist his bereaved sister in ruling the vast estate. All he had learnt from the time he had been sent, the youngest son of a wealthy Normandy family, to the hotbed of priestly politics now stood him in good stead for negotiating the complexities of the English Civil War. And, more importantly as far as his sister was concerned, for combating the Royalists' mercenary leader in the North East of Yorkshire. In her unshakeable opinion, nothing more than a common criminal.

Lounging against the marble hearth, Lynette appeared the epitome of a perfect nobleman. The emerald velvet doublet and breeches he wore emphasised his slender elegance. To the casual observer, he gave every appearance of being a thoughtful scholar, a patient diplomat. Upon closer observation of his handsome face, framed by immaculate short fair hair, his vivid blue eyes betrayed traces of glittering steel beneath the flattering silk.

"Twice the net was flung wide with high expectations, mon ami," he commented in dulcet tones set within an attractive French accent. "And, behold, on both occasions the net was hauled in empty. It would appear we are poor fishermen."

"Page must have ignored your warning," observed Carey, "even when you sent him Cranwell."

Lynette gave an eloquent shrug. "Even if the good Colonel had taken heed of my warning, the outcome would have been the same, I fear. He would have succumb all too easily to the magic of the prowling black cat."

"He paid for his mistake," observed Henry Potter.

"He looked to have been ripped apart by a wild animal," put in Carey, suppressing a delicate shudder.

Lynette frowned, glancing at his sister.

She dismissed his concern with an impatient gesture. "By a wild animal, indeed."

"Richard was the reason why the second opportunity failed," pointed out Henry Potter, bluntly. "After Ijuimden, the gypsy must've been well nigh defeated. What with fire an' all." He cleared his throat, glancing at Lady Hellena. "Yet Richard...."

"Yet Richard tossed him an elaborate cloak," interrupted Gerald Carey in an indolent drawl, compounding Potter's discomfit.

Lynette gave a delicate sigh. He straightened and, with casual grace, strolled across the chamber. "Whatever shall we do with the dear boy?" he mused. Thin eyebrows arched quizzically, he paused beside the settle and looked down at his sister. "The fair seed planted in the forest has, of late, grown wayward."

"Leave him," snapped Richard's mother. Her French accent was slightly more pronounced than her brother's. "Leave him to brood. One thing he excels at."

"I would imagine, the dear boy is wondering who instructed the seaman."

As her brother spoke an emotion stirred Lady Helena's cold demeanour. "Let him bear the weight of suspicion. In that way, he maybe of use."

"What of Catherine Verity? There is little doubt she was tucked away with the gypsy when we boarded the *Eagle*. Fascinating, don't you consider?" Carey's voice was innocently smooth, yet his hooded eyes failed to approach his leader.

Lynette did not reply at once. He sat down next to his sister on the settle. For a couple of moments, he contemplated the rings on his long fingers, glittering in the firelight. Without looking up, he said, "How deliciously awkward must the outcome of our lamentable efforts be for him. He parried each thrust quite splendidly. Only to be left stranded in what he must be viewing as an impossible position."

"Richard could assist the fiend," remarked Lady Helena. "Again."

"Indeed, cheri," responded Lynette, giving her a smiling sidelong glance. He shrugged. "We must not overlook the possibility that he, too, may have become enamoured. It would go a goodly way towards explaining his deception aboard the merchantman."

"Let us keep such a thought in mind," suggested Lady Hellena, "and be ever vigilant to make capital out of such foolishness."

"To be sure, cheri," agreed Francois Lynette. His shrewd gaze swept over the chamber's occupants. "We shall be patient, mon ami. We shall bide our time until the weakness comes within our grasp again. As she surely will. If not through Richard's connivance, then by another, more reliable source. Then will the silver siren be held up to tempt the night." He was a born diplomat, possessing the insight to decipher the complexities of human nature. He went on to voice his suspicion. "I do believe there is more to be uncovered. I am convinced the gypsy has returned for a definite reason. That wild creature who roams the world. Why has he left his profitable enterprise in the Mediterranean in the hands of Nick Condor and come to England? He stalks a purpose. It is imperative we discover what that is. *We must bell the cat.*"

102

PART TWO

LATE SPRING

"Sow a character, and you reap a destiny."

CHAPTER ONE

Witch's Brew

Short of imploring Zeus for winged heels, his instinctive manner of approach, which foxed all other humanity, would be detected. Even then, if given the god's connivance, her phenomenal quality would probably catch the loathsome beat of his heart.

She was sitting beside her open-air hearth in the sheltered pasture. She appeared not to have moved since he had paid his last visit to Nafferton Garth, over a month ago. Scornful of shelter from the frosty night air, her drab garb was being illuminated by the colourful sprites dancing in the blaze of a cheerful fire, her only concession to the comforts her tribe attempted to press upon her, always with the greatest respect.

Come fresh and raw from the empty manor, his anger spiked, pricking his resolve. Fighting her damned '*drukkerebema*', he listened to the fast running River Derwent, swollen by snow melting off the tops of the Wolds. Its splashing transit over rocks was lost in the night. He turned his attention to the camp.

Prowling dogs were on guard, night and day, against the approach of the Gorgio. The tethered horses were statuesque shadows. The many fires cast a convivial glow about the camp. Their mingling smoke drifted up into the night sky and wove a gossamer veil between the cold earth and the myriad of stars strewn across lofty velvet. All was konyo, peaceful. Yet, knowing he had come, the Rom prals were alert. He could feel the thrust of their watchfulness.

The tents erected beside the large flat vardos, their framework constructed of stout wooden poles and covered by thick, cured hides, could withstand the fiercest of storms. All the well-travelled trappings of the Romany tribe were drawn up in a protective circle around the Puro Daia. Forced during the winter months to curtail their wanderings, the big, lusty families lived cheek by jowl awaiting the time when the highways were no longer blighted by frosty snow or mud. The Puro Daia and her tribe were fortunate. More enlightened than many of his contemporaries, Sir Roger Verity had welcomed them each year. And, it seemed, the practice would continue in spite of the Rai's death.

He sighed away his anger. Even before he had arrived at Roger's estate several miles north of Driffield on his self-imposed mission, she would be aware of his feelings. Isles within ice, all bridges torn down. While he never ceased to marvel at her mystical powers, there were times when he found them bloody irksome. By dint of her aloof insight, she plumbed the depths of a soul's foolhardiness and, thus, made provision for the mitigation of ultimate devastation or cowardly escape, depending on any random sod's point of view.

Time had been her ally. She had invested in formative years. However, the clay had not been of her choosing. Just as it had not been his. He realised that now. Patience had found its own reward. Her pupil had excelled.

In resigned silence, he stood directly behind her, a towering black shadow.

"So, Posh-Rat," said the blind old woman without turning. "Thou wilst show me."

He knew better than to argue. She understood far better than he ever would.

"Nam et ipsa scientia potestas est."

Kore would have known that he had quoted Francis Bacon, *'Knowledge itself is power.'* For Roger had taught her well, just as his all-knowing puri daia had done.

CHAPTER TWO

Home Comforts

Catherine awoke with a start. A shuddering sigh, an unshackled fugitive, accompanied her escape from haunted dreams.

By its very frugality, the square chamber had become familiar upon her awakening. It was her fifth in what was now considered to be her chamber at the dilapidated Lodge. The only spark of cheer in the stony bleakness was the smoky fire labouring in the small hearth, no more than a hole in the gritty wall. Mary must have coaxed last night's embers into early morning life while she slept. Pulling the coarse blankets about her shoulders, she delved deeper into the narrow bed, hoping the burgeoning flames would soon gain strength. Her sleepy smile bore gratitude for the girl's quiet concern.

Mary and her mother, Alice, were two of the gaggle of women from Glaisdale who tended to the needs of the Master's men. They were escorted daily along the twisting forest tracks from the remote moorland village tucked into the protective lee of Stillingfleet Forest. Tom Wright had plucked the thin, shy girl out of the medieval kitchen to become Catherine's maid and companion. She was beginning to approve of his choice. She was beginning to erode Mary's nervous deference.

The first thing she had been at pains to do upon her return to England was to apologise to Tom Wright for her thorough disappearance. While they had been aboard the *Eagle*, Richard had pointed out in an effort to appease her guilty conscience that Tom possessed an abundance of commonsense, and would have concluded that she must have stowed away on the merchantman in a reckless attempt to remain with her elderly friends from

Driffield. Yet, Tom's relief had been touchingly evident when the *Eagle* had berthed in her home port of Whitby.

Upon their arrival, they had been met not only by Tom but also by a strong contingent of the Master's men. It seemed a messenger had been dispatched to the Lodge the minute the *Eagle's* overdue sails had been sighted from the lofty cliff upon which stood the ruined glory of Whitby Abbey, a distinctive landmark for all sailors at journey's end.

Catherine saw little of the isolated port. She was given only the short time it took to load the barrels of gunpowder stowed in the merchantman's secret hold onto a suitable wagon in which to become acquainted with Bob Andrew's family. Laura, the captain's slim, attractive wife, some years younger than her husband, and his two daughters, serious Megan, just a year younger than herself, and Tessa, a twelve-year-old tomboy. All of whom, Catherine felt she knew well already because of how the captain had spoken about them during the *Eagle's* prolonged voyage. All too soon she had been called upon by a still-recovering Richard to depart their cosy cottage overlooking the harbour and embark upon the arduous trek across moorland, iced by the savage beauty of February's purity.

There had been no opportunity to study the interaction between Shadiz and Richard from the fresh perspective. Astounded by Richard's tormented revelation, Catherine had gained grim confirmation from Bob Andrew. The two vastly different men were indeed half-brothers. But since the vengeful demise of the traitor, Walt Smithson, there had been no contact between them. Well, none she had witnessed.

During the homeward voyage, she had learnt how a Romany could disappear thoroughly when he wished to, even whilst aboard an average sized merchantman. Concerned about half-healed injuries, she had found the captain not to be of much help. She suspected his lack of cooperation had had a lot to do with the demands of the Master. When he had put in an appearance upon their disembarkation at Whitby, fiercely remote, he had not spoken to either Richard or herself. Then, according to Tom, after closeting himself in the library to deal with the dispatches which had arrived during his absence, the Master had quit the Lodge with only his faithful mastiff.

The Master. Shadiz. Her guardian.

Being brutally honest with herself, she was still reeling from her introduction to the savage enigma. Little wonder her father had refrained from mentioning his friendship with the Master. Yet, he had not been one to keep secrets, especially from her. He always maintained he was too ridiculously honest to aspire to intrigue of any kind. Once again, the thought came unbidden, as it had aboard the *Eagle*. Had he been protecting her?

Memories plagued her.

Her father's freshly dug grave. A bitter farewell on a foreign quayside. A fire-assailed figure striving to salvage life. Unforgivable carnage in an unsuspecting harbour. A man laid on a night shrouded deck. The strange words she had spoken and still did not understand. The warm touch of the pendants, hers and his.

Drifting like precious cargo amongst all the flotsam and jetsam of ifs and buts was Shadiz's undoubted respect for her father. She was proud of her father. He had gone against the grain of society and shown his considerable measure by proffering an unfettered hand to the soul within a wayward character. All she could assume was that the respectful friendship the two men had enjoyed was what had prompted guardianship.

Knowledge of her childhood, exhibited by Shadiz during their time together in the secret hold, must have been acquired over time from the tedium of a doting father. It had been wielded to keep her quiet and docile during a critical period.

The thought hurt.

To define the kiss was just as embarrassingly easy. The startling intimacy was due simply to male curiosity. Nothing more. She must dismiss her stupid, adolescent reaction.

The thought hurt.

The memory of her struggle to keep him alive caused her stomach muscles to knot. She had fought panic and recalled everything the White Witch had taught her in an effort to heal him. And upon her eventual success, she had sensed his surprise that she should have sought to help him. Along with an inexplicable resignation.

A thought struck her. It seemed too preposterous to contemplate. And yet, Mamma Petra, the White Witch, was known to have the *'seeing eye'*. Or, as it was known to the Romanies, the *drukkerebema*.

She must know of the Master. His reputation was widespread. Had she foreseen his injuries? Was that why the blind, old Romany had given her lessons in the art of healing? She, who was a Gorgio, had been given access to Romany tradition by the White Witch. And due to her matriarchal position in the tribe, no one had dared to question the Puro Daia's actions, which went against the very fabric of her creed.

Shadiz had called himself a Rom Posh-Rat when they had been at Ijuimden. A half-breed. And knowing now he was half-brother to Richard Massone, it seemed highly likely he was a bastard. Names by which he could also be known. Amongst all of them, where was the truth of the man?

He disturbed her. Not in the way he did others. It was just that he made her prey to feelings she would rather not experience. He reminded her of *'Noble Savage'*. Half dog, half wolf, she had sensed the torment and loneliness in the great beast. Where others would have seen its demise with relief, she had gained her father's support and, by flooding the beast with kindness, had gained its trust and healed its physical pain. Thereafter, the half-breed had become her protector. Her father had known wherever she had roamed, she would be safe. She had cried bucketfuls when *'Noble Savage'* had succumb to an old age advanced by the hardships endured before coming under her auspices.

Thoughts of yester-years made her long to go home to Nafferton Garth despite everyone doing their utmost to make her feel welcome at the Lodge.

The rusty hinges of the door to Catherine's chamber complained shrilly as Mary scurried out of the cold darkness of the landing and into the weak firelight. "Tom wants y' t' go down t' 'im, missy," she blurted out, breathlessly.

Catherine was jerked out of her early morning reverie. Fearing bad tidings, she sat bolt upright in the narrow bed. "Whatever for?"

The rumble of wagons and the clatter of many hooves on the worn cobblestones in the courtyard could be heard in the chamber. Engrossed in troubled thoughts, she had previously dismissed the clamour of arrival, having already grown accustom to the constant comings and goings at the Master's headquarters, set deep within Stillingfleet Forest. "What is happening down there?" she asked, leaving the warmth of the bed to stand chilled in her shift, her only form of night attire.

"Tek a look," Mary twittered nervously, twisting her pinafore into a knot.

Snatching up a shawl, Catherine went to the glassless window. She pushed aside the stiff leather hide hung there in an effort to keep out winter's icy blasts. Pulling the shawl tightly about her shoulders, shivering nonetheless as the cold air swept over her poorly clad body, she peered down into the enclosed courtyard below with some trepidation. The flickering light of torches held aloft by several of the Master's men had banished the early morning greyness. Three wagons were drawn up before the rough stone face of the Lodge. Each team of two horses stood steaming in the still air. There seemed to be an abundance of horses in the courtyard, stamping, tossing their heads. Their breath and that of their riders floated on the frosty air. The cloaked riders, like the drivers of the wagons, were Romanies. From what she could discern from her vantage point, the men were not the type of nomads to be found at any fair or market. Surveying them, intrigued, it seemed to her that it would be beneath the dignity of the dark-skinned warriors to serve by benign means.

Wondering why Tom should summon her, she dressed in haste in the coarse woollen garments borrowed from Mary's older sister, over top of which she donned Bob Andrew's voluminous cloak, still in her possession in the absence of a suitable replacement.

There came a familiar rapping on the door. At Catherine's bidding, Keeble trotted into the chamber. The little man's large, ugly face was alight with merriment. "Come an' see, m'lady," he urged.

While Mary strove hard to be her maid, Keeble had taken on the role of page with aplomb. Both were her constant companions, giving her little time to ponder the future, as if they were obeying an edict. The conscientious pair were often joined by Tom. Richard had found little solace on land. He had been forced to take to his bed a couple of days after they had arrived at the Lodge, struck down in his weakened condition by a heavy cold.

Out in the bleak February morning, hurrying towards the place where Tom was standing beside the library's icicle-hung window, her small retinue in tow, Catherine was struck by his expression. Half-turning, he saw her and his welcoming smile chased away the thoughtful clouds from his craggy features.

An exclamation, in a voice familiar to her, made her switch instantly from one person of advanced years to another. In fact, she saw to her amazement two very familiar people approaching her. The youngest was assisting the older one across the slippery courtyard. Both were beaming conspiratorially.

Shadiz's overbearing height of four inches above six foot was unusual. Yet the bald-headed Romany approaching her would stand head and shoulders above any man, including Shadiz. Whereas his muscular, broad-shouldered physique compounded his feral, sinister spell, Mamma Petra's grandson, Junno, had an honest, berry-dark face that reflected his amiable nature in spite of his powerful size. Leaning heavily upon his solicitous arm was Catherine's old nursemaid, who had cared for her since her mother's death when she had been just two years of age.

The plump, grey-haired woman hobbled the last few strides unaided and, weeping copiously, fell upon Catherine as if she were her long lost daughter. "Oh, me sweetie," she wailed. "Be ye well, me luv? I've been beside mesen wi' worry."

"I am hale and hearty, dearest Bessie," Catherine reassured, trying to breathe within the thick arms clamped around her with maternal possessiveness. "How on earth do you come to be here?" She looked up at Junno, including him in her mystified inquiry.

"Tis good t' see y' again, Rauni," he said, smiling down at her.

It always seemed to Catherine as if he spoke from the bottom of his boots. Bowing over her welcoming hand she had managed to prise away from Bessie, he brushed her knuckles with a light kiss. Such a gesture was his customary greeting whenever he had accompanied his grandmother. Catherine squeezed his massive hand, always warm whatever the weather. She had known him since the age of twelve, shortly after her father had invited Mamma Petra and her tribe to establish a winter camp at Nafferton Garth. Dismissive of his size, if anything his size emphasised his goodness of character, she had always harboured much affection for the kind, patient Romany.

"I be sorry about y'r dadrus," he told her, his gaze overflowing with sincere emotion.

"So am I," replied Catherine. "If only your grandmother had been at hand. Perhaps, he would then have survived his wounds."

"Oh, y' dear, poor father. Oh, me sweetie," bemoaned Bessie. "Cut down so cruelly." Her grip on Catherine intensified. "Who would've thought such a fine upstandin' gentleman would've come t' such a terrible end."

Irritated by the old woman's clumsy comfort, both Tom and Junno attempted to steer the conversation away from Sir Roger's tragic death. But it was Catherine who persuaded her old nurse to dry her tears. "Now, before my curiosity devours me. You must tell me how all of you come to be here," she demanded, brightly.

"Aye, well. Gypsy come, didn't 'e."

Catherine glanced in Junno's lofty direction.

"Not 'im, me sweetie," dismissed Bessie. Her three-layered chin wobbled significantly. "I mean *the* Gypsy. The ... what y' m'call 'im ... Master." Her nose for gossip was put out of joint momentarily by a bout of sudden nervousness. Her sharp, beady gaze swept the busy courtyard in one long furtive glance, causing the others to follow suit. When it appeared that the person in question was nowhere to be seen, she added in a low-pitched voice, "An' Master 'e were, all right. Tellin' me t' pack this, that an' tother. Saw t' it 'issen. What came."

Catherine stared at her old nursemaid, dumbfounded.

"Junno's been tellin' me 'e intends keepin' y' safe 'ere for time bein'," continued Bessie. "I ain't sure that's...."

Catherine's delighted laughter interrupted her. She ran towards the wagons pulled up before the Lodge. Still mounted, the Romanies watched with polite indulgence as she began to lift a heavy leather cover, trying to see what lay beneath.

"There's y'r clothes," explained Junno, coming up behind her. He held up the cover for her. "Y'r books. Some furniture."

Leaning heavily on Tom's arm, Bessie reached the wagons, accompanied by Keeble and Mary. Upon turning to all of them with a happy smile, Catherine caught sight of the man and horse, motionless beneath the courtyard's lop-sided entrance.

Without taking her eyes away from the unmistakable shadow, she said, "Mary would you please escort Bessie indoors and attend to her needs."

"Fair chilled t' bone, I be," complained the old nursemaid, pulling her cloak about her small, ample figure while being led away towards the Lodge.

"Go careful, luv." Tom's quiet warning drifted behind Catherine.

He got the impression Junno was about to follow her to the arched entrance of the torchlit courtyard. But then the big Romany checked himself. He appeared troubled. The older man thought he understood. But he had no idea that Junno's first glimpse was being made all the more disturbing by the storm clouds which had gathered along the way from Nafferton Garth to the Lodge.

Catherine was drawn irresistibly to where the mastiff stood wagging its tail in greeting. Coming to a halt, it felt as if a burdensome hand had reached out from between the mighty tree trunks of the forest to rest like a lode-stone against her breathless chest. Bending, she stroked the large, grey dog, while its wraithlike master looked on. For she knew with absolute certainty that slivers of jet burned in the early morning's frosty greyness.

Flaring nostrils scenting warm stables filled with hay, the black stallion made a sudden entry into the tidal boundary of torchlight.

Crow blackness revealed Shadiz, reined in his restive mount a few feet away from Catherine, veiled eyes fixed upon her. She straightened, looking up. The moment of confusion had melted away into the need to evaluate him.

The rough beard seeded by illness had been harvested. There was now only careless stubble about his set jaw. The shadowy gauntness had gone, too, replaced by characteristic hardness. The deep burn in his left cheek had healed well, leaving the dark flesh pitted. The disfigurement had branded her, too.

She was determined not to be intimidated by him. Nor would she be churlish after his generous deed. After ransacking a sluggish brain, in the end only two words seemed appropriate. "Thank you."

When he eventually answered, she could barely hear his paraphrasing words.

"If mountain ain't able t' move, then ferry its stones t' trees."

Catherine grinned. "Or, if nuisance is plonked down, keep her quiet."

Humour wafted reluctantly over his chiselled, nomadic features. "Summat like that. At least y' still 'ere. I'd visions o' arrivin' wi' y'r stuff t' find y'd took t' y' 'eels. Again."

"Little chance of that," she retorted, wanting her annoyance to be known however well-meaning the obstruction to liberty, "I cannot get any further than a few cobbles before I am, oh so politely, but firmly detained."

When the stallion sidled her way with mane-tossing impatience, she reached out.

"Don't."

Catherine stilled the hand that would have soothed. She looked up questioningly.

"Brute'll tak y'r bloody 'and off."

"The horse, the hand. Its master, the head," she observed, dryly.

"Develesko Mush," he rasped, very quietly.

Now was possibly not the ideal time to attempt to stretch his unpredictable goodwill. Bracing herself, she said, "Tom has informed me, I must seek your permission to visit my father's grave." She did not prevent her tone from conveying her resentment. "I realise the prevailing conditions are not conducive to such a desire, yet I would very much like to go?"

A muscle flexed in his scarred cheek.

"I have every right. Surely, you must see that?" She seemed to be making no impression. Frustrated, she exclaimed, "Ye gods and little fishes! Do you wish me to beg?"

Shadiz sighed repressively. He raised a hand to stem any further arguments she was ready to fire at him. "So be it," he muttered, "I'll escort y' within 'our, dammit."

Despite the obvious reluctance on his part, she was delighted by his acquiescent. "You will want to break your fast," she said, pivoting on the balls of her feet, her long hair and outsize cloak swirling around her.

"Kore."

Her glad heart turned a queer, jolting somersault. Halting jerkily, she turned back to him, uncomfortably aware of her flushed cheeks.

Shadiz dismounted. Catherine saw that a fringed blanket made up of colourful patches was his only form of saddle for the stallion. Leading his querulous mount, he strolled up to her and stood in silence, his black gaze roaming over the rough stone features of the old Lodge. Standing in the tall shadow he cast, she waited for him to speak, trying to ignore the persistent thumping of her heart.

"Y' not t' worry about Nafferton Garth," he eventually informed her, low-pitched. "Roger's steward 'as all under control. I've left men there t' aid 'im. But nowt's 'appened since you an' Roger left." Still without looking her way, after a brief pause, he added, "I've got Junno 'ere t' stay close t' 'y."

"I am in no danger here at the Lodge. Surely?" she queried. The disquieting implication eclipsed her relief over the safety of Nafferton Garth and all living there, people she had known all her life. "Who on earth would defy your authority?"

He gave her a sidelong glance. "Who, indeed?"

The sardonic implication was not lost on her. "Oh, for goodness sake," she retorted. "Have you forgotten so soon Richard's assistance whilst we were on board the *Eagle*? Had it not been for him, both you and I would have been at the mercy of Lynette's men."

"What was done, was done for y'r benefit," he snapped.

"And you find that irksome?" She was skating on thin ice, she knew.

Although the black eyes flared, the volcano refrained from an explosive comment. Instead, after a moment of contemplating the stallion's reins, threaded tightly through his long fingers, in a clipped tone, he asked, "Does it still ail?"

Catherine could not allow the opportunity to pass unmarked. "Your half-brother is prostrate in a camphor haze." She got the impression she had failed to take him by surprise.

He gave a wicked grin. "Martyrdom can be a danger t' bloody 'ealth," he remarked, softly.

She compressed her lips to keep from uttering a scathing rejoinder lest he withdraw the lukewarm offer to escort her to her father's grave. Remaining silent, she watched as the wagons, having been emptied of her belongings, were driven around the side of the Lodge, presumably to the rear pasture, in which the long, low stable block was situated along with other outbuildings. The courtyard was now deserted, except for Tom and Junno. The two men were talking quietly together.

She thought of what Shadiz had done for her, at an inauspicious time of year. Turning back to him, Catherine said, "Thank you again. And for Bessie."

"It were either bring 'er along or get me 'ead split open by a bloody warmin' pan."

Soon after leaving the courtyard, Catherine found her old nursemaid thawing out beside the ingle-nook hearth in the cavernous kitchen. She was being fussed over by Mary while her mother and the other chattering women prepared thick broth and crusty bread and cheese for the Master's men and the recently arrived Romanies. Fortunately, they had grown accustomed to catering for fluid numbers.

Nibbling on a snatched oatcake, she made good her escape from Bessie's dismay at her crude surroundings and soft-cheeked delight at her former charge's good health. With eagerness giving wings to her heels, she dashed up the worn stone stairs, her fair-white hair swinging brightly in the gloom between the torches thrust into crooked sconces. On the landing, a pang of guilt caused her to pause by the shadowy, worm-eaten door of Richard's chamber. The only sound coming from within was thick, nasal snoring. The decision to leave him in ignorance was easily made.

The intriguing noises coming from further down the dim landing drew her towards her own chamber. Entry into the hive of activity slowed her expectant footsteps.

Open chests containing her clothes, bedding and other personal items stood in solid abundance, awaiting her inspection. Several of the Master's men and a couple of Romanies were setting up her own bed in place of the serviceable pallet. Keeble paused in directing the operation to grin at her.

Arrested in the doorway, her delighted gaze took in achingly familiar objects. A couple of tapestry-backed chairs, a pair of carved stools, several bright Eastern rugs, a small round table inlaid with mother-of-pearl, a walnut bookcase, her collection of books, most of which had been given to her by her father, tapestries to adorn the stone walls and heavy velvet drapes to be hung at the glassless window. Even her collection of herbs and the accompanying paraphernalia had been included.

Her attention was captured by the gilt-framed portrait, leaning against the wall.

Her joy dissolving, she walked across the chamber to the painting. She sank to her knees and gently caressed the canvas portraying her father. The artist had striven with consummate flair to capture in oils strong, rustic features, the subtleties of scholarly intelligence and the merry twinkle in steadfast blue eyes.

Here before her, conveyed astoundingly to her, was the enduring reminder. Tears blurred the beloved image.

At first, bound up in her grief, the gentle hand resting on her drooping shoulder went unnoticed. Only when that touch became stronger reassurance did she realise its presence and respond.

There was a feeling of inevitability about the moment. She had known without acknowledging the fact that he would appear, suddenly as was his animalistic way. The only conceivable link was her father. Cast in stony darkness, his remoteness possessed fissures of regret.

Shadiz's hand slipped away from her shoulder. He swung away from her young, upturned face, brimming with sorrow. His gaze held a black menace as it swept over his industrious men. With a sharp command, he emptied her chamber. Keeble closed the door quietly behind himself.

The abrupt silence grew loud in the stillness of the chamber.

Still on her knees before the portrait of her father, Catherine said, "He once remarked that the artist had possessed the keen eye of a hawk and the entertaining wit of a scholar." She sniffed and wiped her wet cheeks with the heels of both her hands. "He never did say who was the artist."

Turning back to Shadiz, she saw his hard, cruel mouth soften and twitch, as if he had been paid a rare compliment. After years, the true import of her father's words struck her. Her natural reaction was to dismiss the staggering suspicion. Frowning, her curious gaze switched back momentarily to the portrait and then returned to the fathomless man standing over her.

Catherine scrambled to her feet. "*You?*" she exclaimed, wide-eyed.

Shadiz had taken a step backwards. He shrugged. "As I recall," he said, softly, considering the portrait, "I'd t' play Chaucer t' stop Roger from twitchin' so bloody much." He grimaced. "Runs in family."

The flippant confirmation, while reinforcing her shock, went hand in hand with another equally disturbing discovery. Unsure what emotion to award the obvious discretion, Catherine asked, "Where was I?"

He seemed to flinch. Then, with the suppleness of a panther retreating from an impossible prey, he swung away from her.

Arriving at the closed door, the mastiff at his heels, he paused. The inscribed hilt of the great sword slung across his back glistened in the firelight. Without turning, Shadiz half-whispered, "*Over 'ills an' far away.*"

Three Cold Comforts

'*Over hills and far away.*'

The words spoken by Shadiz as he had left her chamber came to mind.

Catherine breathed in the crisp air upon the moors, refreshing a spirit that had been overlong restricted by well-meaning intentions. Although her qualms about living at the Master's headquarters had been mostly dispelled by the reception she had received from everyone at the ancient Lodge deep within Stillingfleet Forest, it felt good indeed to be riding out in the crystal morning. God's lantern, the winter-white sun, had risen over the vast, undulating land. She felt as if she could reach up and touch the few snowball clouds in a strikingly azure sky.

Unlike the largely domesticated Wolds around Nafferton Garth, pitfalls awaited the unsuspecting traveller within the wild landscape, overlaid by the season's frigid presence. But if Catherine lacked experience in negotiating the difficult terrain, her mount did not. For when she had emerged from the Lodge, attired in a blue riding habit beneath a velvet cloak from her own, newly-arrived wardrobe, she had found not her own mare wearing her side-saddle. A piebald pony had been standing in Twilight's stead.

It had been left to Junno to sing the praises of the shaggy little beast. Already mounted, his leader had made no comment, his distinctive aquiline profile set in lines of disapproval of the expedition he had reluctantly sanctioned.

Instead of leading the escort consisting entirely of Romanies, Shadiz rode halfway down the column, at the other side of Catherine to Junno. Thus, flanked protectively between his black stallion and Junno's huge Clydesdale, she felt safe on the sure-footed pony, if not a little ridiculous. She was almost on a level with the easy lope of the nearby mastiff. Short of being set upon by ingenious goblins, nothing would touch her while in such lofty company.

The strong, nomadic force made confident progress through the wilderness where primeval silence hovered over the glistening snow. So unlike the pastoral landscape she was accustomed to, her surroundings intrigued Catherine. She relished the atmosphere of savage freedom; that was until an unpleasant thought invaded her enjoyment.

"How close are we to Fylingdales Hall?"

"Too bloody close," Shadiz growled, ending his brooding silence.

Upon a surge of apprehension, she asked, "And Fylingdales Estate?" When it became clear she was not going to receive an answer from him, she turned to Junno.

Above her, the big man's round face showed his worries. "We be on it, Rauni."

She experienced a stab of guilt. Had her determination to see her father's resting place put the men in needless jeopardy? The fact that the strong breeze was charged with the alertness of experienced warriors was a comfort but did not entirely shore up her conscience.

Despite her presence with them and the wintry conditions, before too long the sweeping arc where moorland bowed down to the North Sea lay ahead of them. Henceforth, becoming steadily less brutal in its snowy aspect, the land inclined steeply downwards to the ragged cliffs and surf-laced waves of Mercy Cove.

Following a rough track made rock hard by successive frosts, they began to pass signs of habitation. A hardy shepherd cloistered with his shaggy flock in a wind-whistling barn. Farmhouses with canine sentinels. And, as the descent grew ever steeper, an increasing number of stone-built cottages, their chimneys emitting vertical, homely smoke into the still air.

Hitherto, there had been an unrestricted view of their

surroundings. But as they journeyed on, the keen surveillance of her escort became hampered by the close-knit trunks of leafless oaks and groves of skeletal ash and beech. Tall hedgerows posed an ever-present threat due to the intertwined ivy that never slept. As a consequence, Catherine perceived an upsurge in the protectiveness by which she was surrounded. She pitied any poor soul unlucky enough to stray into the path of the Master's tribal force.

The snow muffled their passing over last year's iced leaves and frozen ruts, only the jingle of harness and the snorting breath of horses gave away their presence as they skirted the cliff-hugging haven above a pebbly shore, where fishing boats were drawn up in a defensive huddle upon big slabs of rocks in the lee of ragged, sandy cliffs. Swinging south, headfirst into a strong wind that filled cold noses with the tang of sea-salt, they rode towards the drystone wall enclosing the graveyard, a pearl carpet around the sturdy, grey-stone church, built by fishermen with the hard won knowledge of how to withstand North Sea gales.

When the sun's glazing light was doused by a flotilla of shoreline clouds, the last shreds of Catherine's early morning exhilaration were extinguished by a growing dread. Yet, conversely, there was a need to continue to what awaited her.

She could not recall hearing the persistent, hissing murmur of the sea the first time she had been brought to the cliff top graveyard by Richard and Tom. On this occasion it was Shadiz and Junno who accompanied her, walking protectively at either side of her. She was guided by the two men, for she could not remember the whereabouts of her father's grave. All that remained clear from that first visit was those hideous words chiselled in the simple wooden cross.

And there it was.

The two men halted, allowing her to trudge alone the last few dragging footsteps. She felt as if her own cold breath would strangle her. Sinking down slowly into the deep snow, eyes smarting with hot tears, Catherine brushed the fine white powder away from the engraved marker. But she needed no telling who lay in the earth beneath her, and that she was her father's daughter.

Before long that strong hand once again came to rest upon her shoulder.

She found release in the conduit. In the secret hold of the *Eagle*, she had grieved for her father. On this occasion, she angrily bemoaned the unbearable emptiness his passing had left within her transformed world.

"Don't you touch me!" she exclaimed, springing to her feet, knocking Shadiz's hand away.

Immediately, he stepped away from her, his dark features splitting asunder. After the momentary lapse, he was once again in command of himself. He ground the snow beneath his boots as he turned and started to walk away.

"No! Wait!"

Junno stepped in front of Shadiz, hindering him. Cursing, Shadiz attempted to side-step the big man. But Junno used his superior bulk to block any retreat, something few men even of his stature would have attempted.

Catherine viewed the actions of the bald-headed Romany in frowning surprise. His sense of urgency was palpable. The bitter pain of her emotional outburst lessened as she witnessed the heated exchange, in their language, between the two tall men. The Romi was a secret language. In her time with the White Witch's tribe at Nafferton Garth, she had gleaned only a small store of words and therefore found it difficult to understand the source of their dispute.

Finally, the two men said no more. Featherlike snowflakes had begun to float silently around them and Catherine. Shadiz's face had grown brutally hard. Nonetheless, Junno stood regarding him with a pleading expression. Wordlessly Shadiz retraced the deep imprints of his footsteps in the snow. He passed Catherine and stood looking down at her father's marker, his right hand gripping the hilt of the curving scimitar at his hip. Though he had not glanced in her direction, she could easily sense the smouldering fury within him.

"I've got t' tell Rauni!" cried Junno, plainly.

Shadiz's lack of response seemed to increase the big man's desperation.

"Tell me what?" demanded Catherine, perturbed, looking from first one to the other of the men.

The relentless wind whipped up the thickening snowflakes. It seized upon the single Romi word that was grudgingly muttered. "*Arva.*"

Straightaway, Junno turned in Catherine's direction. Remorse an open sore, he explained, "I'm t' blame fer what 'appened t' y' dadrus. I failed 'im. I failed y' all. All this winter, afore the Rai took y' away, I were about in Mamma Petra's winter camp at Nafferton Garth t' guard you ... an' y' dadrus, o' course. It were me own fault. I knew Page an' 'is lot were about an' up t' no good. I'd gone out scoutin' when the Rai were made t' flee wi' y'." He cast a tortured glance at his leader's stubbornly turned back. "'e were away wi' t' prince down in Oxford. The Rai couldn't get 'od o' me. So ... So 'e took y' an', Devel 'elp me, 'e...."

"Ran," put in Catherine, flatly. "Ran to what he considered safety. Only what awaited him was...." She shook her head, unable to continue. It was clear that the two men had done their utmost to protect both her father and herself. It was equally clear that neither Shadiz nor Junno were accustomed to such horrendous failure. She cleared her throat, and told them, "I'm certain my father would not direct blame at either of you. Nor shall I."

As if jerked by invisible strings, Shadiz slewed round. She got the impression his anger was not directed at her or Junno. "What I told y' aboard *Eagle* remains."

"No, it does not," retorted Catherine.

"Develesko Mush," rasped Shadiz, "'ow bloody plain do I've t' make it? If Lynette an' that old bitch o' a sister o' 'is ain't been after me, none o' this would've 'appened. Roger'd be alive. You ... y' wouldn't be 'ere."

Standing her ground, Catherine told him, "Whatever you say, either of you. What's done is done. And nothing...." Her voice broke with emotion. Tearful, she managed, "No explanation, however well-meaning, will bring him back." She stumbled past Shadiz, drawn back to her father's grave. "Nothing," she murmured with despairing finality.

After an uncharacteristic hesitation, discerned only by Junno, Shadiz announced, "Enough. You've mourned enough. Roger'd not want this." Without further ado, he took Catherine up in his arms and returned to where the vigilant Romanies waited.

Junno lingered beside Sir Roger's grave. He was filled with a great sadness for the dead Rai, who had been a steadfast friend to his tribe. The ponderous emotion mingled with his burden of guilt, and terrible helplessness. Eventually, following his leader's snow disturb trail back to the horses, Junno muttered to himself. Had he been alive, Sir Roger would not have understood the words. He would have certainly understood the heartfelt sentiment.

Catherine's resentment deepened when Shadiz placed her atop of his own mount, speaking sharply to the capricious stallion. Did he now consider her incapable of riding by herself? She was furious at the high-handed way he had cut short her visit to her father's grave. Her tight-lipped anger kept her stiffly upright while he mounted behind her. Keeping in the midst of the column of Romanies, alongside Junno, he rode with his left arm loosely balancing her on his tall mount. She gave the snowy graveyard a lingering look as they were ushered away from the cliff top by the strengthening wind.

Turning their backs on Mercy Cove, they returned into the dense whiteness of the moors, made bleak by the sun's fickle disappearance. Soon the snow began to fall in earnest. The north-easterly wind infused the icy air whipping around the bowed riders and their horses with a blizzard of snowflakes. Visibility became increasingly reduced in hostile terrain.

Catherine's indignant mood was replaced by appreciation for the nearness of her guardian's warrior body. Bent against him, she had pulled her hood down as far as possible and wrapped her cloak tightly about herself. Yet, in spite of her efforts, the chilling tentacles of the worsening weather penetrated her garments, making her shiver.

Keeping his left arm around her, Shadiz swung the leather baldric over his head and handed the great sword he wore across his back to Junno. After a brief struggle, he managed to pull his long leather coat free of the thick belt upon which the scimitar at his hip was attached. He shook off the build up of snow upon Catherine's cloak as best he could in the prevailing conditions. Quickly, he wrapped her within his opened coat, giving her not only the benefit of a weatherproof covering but also complete access to himself. Without reservation, she embraced his muscular heat.

No one was aware of the tears Junno shed into the wind.

The stallion stumbled in one of the deep snowdrifts it was being urged through. Catherine, her fright short-lived, experienced through their intimate link Shadiz's expert control of the floundering animal. It was through her secondhand experience of the stallion's tiring efforts that she was aware of the battles up steep slopes and the slithering descents. Even when the land seemed fairly flat, the deep snow felt as if it were sucking the legs of the stallion down into an abyss. She wondered how the shaggy pony she had ridden from the Lodge was faring until she recalled how the Romanies valued their horses. And then she began to worry about the mastiff.

At length, she felt the deep vibration of Shadiz's words and caught Junno's faint response. Although huddled against her guardian, it was becoming clear to her by their snail's pace that progress across the moorland was getting beyond even the nomadic warriors.

She detected a laborious change of direction. After what seemed like an eternity, the gait of Shadiz's mount became easier. The constant shrieking of the wind, which had caused her to imagine a dozen banshees were pursuing them, had diminished into a weird, thwarted howl. The stallion came to a halt and thereafter stood quivering. She felt the strain of battling the fierce elements leave Shadiz in a grateful sigh.

With her own heartfelt sigh, Catherine emerged from the cocoon in her damp cloak and Shadiz's leather coat. Curious, she looked about her and discovered they were in a cavern large enough to shelter both snow-blasted horses and riders. The snowdrifts around the mouth of one of earth's stone churches had been trampled down by their entry, a sorry congregation in need of sanctuary. There was just enough daylight merging with the winter-white moorland at the entrance for her to see the discoloured lichen hanging from the craggy roof, petrified in curious forms by the season's cold breath. It had impregnated the cavern with a musty stench. Dead vegetation decorated the sloping walls. Having thickened over abundant summers, leafy tendrils had formed interwoven tapestries.

Not only nature had made her presence felt. A little peering brought into focus crude drawings of animals upon the nearest wall of the cavern. They gave a haunting glimpse of a hunt from a long-dead age. And, remarkable still, beneath the vital record of fleeing prey were handprints. Possibly of the figures hurling spears?

Upon reaching out over the centuries and touching the human marks, Catherine was comforted by an abiding sense of safety. She was left in no doubt that for over a millennium the cavern had served as a refuge.

Turning aside from ancient wonders, she marvelled at the nomadic instinct for survival in the present age. The continuation of tribal preservation. Surveying her recovering escort, relieved to see the mastiff jump down from Junno's Clydesdale, she saw that their darkness had become plastered with seasonal whiteness, proving how dangerous it was to be caught out on the moors in such foul conditions. The sight of them made her wonder why her guardian had consented, however reluctantly, to her request.

Looking up at him, the only answer she discovered was how he was no exception to the artistry of the weather. His devilish appearance had been given clinging purity. She raised a hand. And had no idea how Junno held his breath as he watched her touch Shadiz's snow-encrusted face and hair. The impulsive action had attracted not only Junno's attention. Realising this, and reassured by his leader's expression, the big Romany motioned his brethren to follow him into the inner sanctum of the cavern, with which they were all familiar.

Absorbed in dislodging the aftermath of the storm, Catherine was at first unaware of Shadiz's gaze. Only when she was moved to comment on the stubbornness of the crystal gems in his long hair, did she realise his black eyes rested intently on her. A hot scarlet hue crept into her cold face.

"How is your back feeling these days?" she asked in an awkward rush, her wet hand resting on his scarred cheek.

"About mended," he answered, softly. He covered her hand with his. "Don't fret."

"It's a habit of mine," she responded, taking his intertwined fingers with hers while caressing the ridges in his burnt cheek.

His smile became an amused grimace. He turned over her hand and brushed her palm with a gentle kiss. The gesture took no liberties.

Seeing its inferior fellows disappear into the gloom behind the only creature worthy of its respect, the stallion pranced forwards. Its preoccupied master cursed. Dislodged by the unexpected movement, Catherine began an abrupt, ungainly dismount from dangerous heights. Shadiz's deft action saved her from pitching downwards onto the frozen ground the mastiff had prudently vacated.

"*Ye gods and little fishes!*" she exclaimed, shaken, clutching her rescuer. Glancing up at him, she witnessed the shadow pass over his barbarous features. She sensed the change in him. The fleeting intimacy had dissolved and become elusive once more. He dismounted in one fluid movement, keeping strict control of his capricious mount.

She was left atop of the stallion believing she was a nuisance. Or worse.

However, Shadiz was glaring not at her but at the indistinct rear of the cavern. His stance full of hostility, he spoke in the Romi.

A moment later, Junno's huge figure emerged from out of the concealing gloom. The big man came to a halt a few paces away from the stallion.

All at once, it dawned on Catherine that she recognised one of the Romi words Shadiz had harshly uttered. "*Simensa.*" She had learnt it during her many visits to the encampment of interwoven families at Nafferton Garth. "Cousin?"

Shadiz gave a derisive snort.

"Aye, Rauni," confirmed the big man in a neutral tone.

His troubled gaze rested briefly on her. She got the impression he was accustomed to Shadiz's inclination to be viciously unkind and did not want her to be upset by it.

One revelation quickly followed another. "That means Mamma Petra is your...."

"Grandmother." Shadiz gave her a smouldering, sidelong glance. "Me all seein', all knowin' puri daia." He massaged his temples, as if he were trying to dislodge a painful irritant.

"I don't understand?"

"Develesko Mush," growled Shadiz. "Think, Kore."

She was trying to, but must appear terribly slow-witted. At that precise moment, having broken out in a cold sweat, all she could recall was the eerie sensation of being overlooked while she had battled to save his life. She had been armed with the traditional knowledge of a Romany healer. Now, it seemed, the White Witch who had taught her was his grandmother. Mamma Petra.

"D' y' 'onestly reckon Puro Daia'd impart any o' 'er bloody precious wisdom t' a Gorgio unless prompted by summat she ain't been able t' deny?"

His blunt words startled her. Frightened her.

Being honest, Mamma Petra frightened her. Since the age of twelve, when the Romany tribe had, by her father's invitation, arrived each autumn to set up winter quarters in pastures at Nafferton Garth, she had stood in awe of the blind, old woman. There was a powerful aura about her. Her strange mantle set her apart from everyone, be they Gorgio or Romany.

When Mamma Petra had started to encourage her efforts to heal the various ailments and injuries of those animals she had taken into her care, Catherine realised the old woman's behaviour had prompted surprise and unease amongst the Romanies. None had ever dared to voice their objections to the matriarch of their tribe. Such an action would have been a transgression and highly disrespectful. In time, Mamma Petra had led her to human needs. She had instructed her in the various healing properties of herbs and how to administer them. By which time, Catherine had come to realise she had acquired an exacting tutor. She had worked hard.

To be sufficiently skilled to care for the White Witch's equally strange grandson?

She looked at Shadiz, aware that the flow of her thoughts had registered on her features. Dense and narrowed, his black eyes retreated from her quizzical gaze as he swung her down from the fidgeting stallion.

Catherine and Junno followed Shadiz into the inner part of the cavern. The light from the fire started by the Romanies revealed a perfectly round, domed chamber. She became engrossed in her surroundings, and failed to notice after Shadiz had led his mount to where the other horses had been hobbled that he began to help the young Romany, much to Tomas's amazement, to attend to the animals as they stood gingerly sniffing the crisp plant life which thrived in the crevices of the rough walls.

By the time Shadiz had completed his self-imposed task, Catherine had been found a place close to the warmth of the fire, fed by the abundance of tinder dry vegetation, and given cheese and bread to stem any hunger pangs she might be experiencing. To wash down the meagre meal, she was offered the leather flagon that had been passed round her relaxing escort, with an apology for the absence of a drinking vessel.

"Let it warm y' insides," Junno urged her, "while fire warms rest o' y'."

"I pray it is not like Bob's mead," Catherine replied. The potency of the flagon's contents came very close, making her gasp for breath. She was quick to pass it on.

She noticed how Shadiz ignored the circulating liquor.

He wandered over to where Catherine and Junno were sitting on the floor of the cavern. Saying nothing, he squatted down on his haunches and stared into the fire, idly stroking the mastiff's wet coat.

Realising he was aware of her gaze on him, her attention turned to the intriguing handprints and the drawings on the smooth, fire-flickering wall, similar to those she had seen at the entrance of the cavern. The long-lasting hues were remarkably distinct.

"That be Eon," Junno said, seeing her interest in the spear-wielding figures grouped around a snakelike creature. "Legend 'as it Eon were a dragon. 'is lair was beneath moors. Its food were 'uman-kind. One day a storm put out fire in Eon's throat. Afore long the Onino were on their way t' bury their chief when they saw Eon. Tribe carried torches wi' 'em. Eon were too weak to fight so many 'umans. The Onino said they'd light its fire if it'd promise to guard their chief's burial place 'til 'e marched t' sky life. Eon agreed an' went wi' 'em. Its fire were lit. Eon turned on the 'ated 'umans, killin' 'em, except the brave 'uns y' see on wall. They pierced its eyes wi' their spears so it weren't able t' see their stabs in its 'eart. Afterwards, they drew their victory on wall o' Fargange. The cave that gives us shelter."

Catherine was fascinated by the big man's story. She looked anew at the cave drawing.

"O' course, there's tother version o' pattrimishi. Legend."

"There is?" asked Catherine and Junno in unison.

"Aye," answered Shadiz, low-pitched. Firelight glinted on his single gold-earring as he moved backwards and sat down at the other side of Junno from Catherine. Curious, they both turned in his direction. Drawing his knees up and circling them with his clasped hands, his hooded gaze dwelt on the fire.

"There was once a serpent named Want in days long gone. A great black beast existin' in bowels o' earth. No mortal could slay the vile one. Immortality was upon its shimmerin' scales. Its ragin' 'unger was sated by the taste o' young maidens. A slitherin' murderer in their unsuspectin' path, it coiled its slimy body around their innocent flesh an' throttled life out o' 'em.

"After centuries o' foul existence, one day it be'eld a maiden so fair, so pure. Settin' eyes upon 'er, Want's stinkin' juices were warmed by 'er beauty. For once, the serpent crawled away. It feared its own loathsome appetite. Restless in its deep, dank lair, its desire t' glimpse again the maiden eventually got better o' it. It returned t' see if its eyes'd deceived it. An' found 'er beauty'd increased tenfold.

"The maiden lived in a village borderin' the Great Sea. Men o' that village'd seen serpent lurkin' about an' sought t' protect their women. Want told them that if they let it take the Fair Maiden t' its lair it'd no longer prey on rest o' womenfolk in their village. None knew 'ow t' answer. If they agreed, they condemned maiden t' lifetime wi' foul serpent. An' yet not t' agree t' its demand meant all their women were at risk. It were only when the Fair Maiden spoke up an' said she'd go wi' Want that dilemma be resolved. Feelin' great guilt, the menfolk agreed t' let Want take 'er. That were when 'er mother cried out in despair. Attemptin' t' 'elp 'er daughter, she told serpent that bein' a widow an' crippled she needed 'er daughter t' be wi' 'er t' 'elp in season when fish were plentiful in shallows o' the Great Sea. Seein' the Fair Maiden's distress, Want said if she went wi' 'im for six months, the next six could be spent wi' 'er mother.

"Want kept its promise. After six months, it allowed 'er t' leave its lair. An old crone livin' in the village told menfolk she'd found 'ow t' unlock immortality within serpent's scales. Takin' 'eed, the menfolk awaited comin' o' Want at the end o' the six months 'e'd allowed the Fair Maiden t' stay wi' 'er mother. The serpent was lured t' edge o' the Great Sea. It were told that was where the Fair Maiden be, bringin' in the last catch o' fish for 'er mother afore goin' back wi' 'im. So great was its desire t' set eyes upon 'er, it slithered in the direction o' sea, careless o' threat water posed t' 'im. Busy in the shallows, the Fair Maiden looked up as the men o' the village were about t' strike. 'er mother was amazed t' 'ear 'er daughter cry out a warnin' t' the 'ideous monster. Want looked upon the Fair Maiden. Saw 'er standin' in all 'er beauty 'e'd tainted by 'is love for 'er. 'e knew then the cruelty o' returnin' 'er t' 'is lair. 'e let the menfolk drive 'im into the Great Sea. The Cleansing washed away 'is scales o' immortality. An arrow was shot straight an' true into serpent's 'eart. 'e died treasurin' the Fair Maiden's sorrow at 'is death."

"Oh, that is sad," murmured Catherine.

Shadiz scrutinized her young face. The fire glow highlighted a curious, bleak intensity. "Y'd feel summat for any misbegotten sod," he muttered in an odd, almost regretful tone. "Like 'im." He indicted his cousin with a hard thrust of his stubbly chin.

"Junno?"

The big man lifted his head and gave her a weak smile. Silently shed tears were running down his cheeks.

" 'e's nowt but a great, sentimental fool," remarked Shadiz, sardonically.

"I'm glad *you* are not made of stone," responded Catherine, moving closer to Junno. "Take heart, it was but a tall tale," she continued, tucking her arm into his thick, muscular one.

"Aye. A tall tale, Rauni," muttered Junno, squeezing her arm.

Resting against his accommodating bulk, lulled by the warmth of the fire and the Romany wine, before long Catherine drifted off to sleep. She therefore missed the vicious black glare to which Junno was subjected.

★ ★ ★

Grubby snow was falling like volcanic ash. Fire burned bright and hot. Its cleaved tongue licked the roof of the cavern. There were faces trapped in the walls of ice. Fair maidens drawn for the eyes of obsession, framed within bloodstained spears.

An indistinct shadow became first a serpent and then a tall, dark figure standing beyond the barrier of flames, inscribing with palette and brush in hand, slowly becoming covered with the discoloured snow.

Mamma Petra suddenly materialized. An old crone dressed in shimmering rags, she drifted through the flames as if they were sheaves of corn. Her gesture grew more and more demanding.

★ ★ ★

Catherine woke with a jolting start.

Startled out of his pensive reverie, Junno attempted to soothe her. "Y' be all right, Rauni." He held her stiff body in a reassuring embrace while she breathed raggedly against his massive chest. "It was horrible," she mumbled, still experiencing the dream.

The big man chuckled softly. "Gatta's brew got that effect sometimes. Y' be safe."

Safe, yes. Yet afraid. The jet pendant was burning her flesh. Looking about her, she asked, "Where is Shadiz?" She drew away from Junno, searching the inner cavern for him.

"Reckon 'e's gone t' check on weather."

Catherine caught the note of doubt in Junno's response. When one of the Romanies strode up to where they were sitting, speaking rapidly in their language, she knew at once that something was amiss. It was not just the sudden change of expression upon Junno's round face, but also the way the surrounding Romanies were getting to their feet, their fire lit swarthy faces reflecting concern.

"What is it?" she asked, rising at the same time as the big man.

"Stay 'ere, Rauni," he told her, hurrying away.

She watched him disappear into the gloom, heading for the outer part of the cavern with the young man who had spoken to him. She would have followed had it not been for two of the older Romanies politely but firmly blocking her way. Given no choice, she waited with ill-repressed frustration until Junno reappeared, if anything looking even more worried than before. Her guards stood back and let her run across the uneven floor of the cavern to him. "What is amiss? I know whatever concerns you has to do with Shadiz," she cried, catching hold of his arm.

Anxiety was etched into Junno's honest features. He gave a troubled sigh. "'e's gone, Rauni."

She stared at him. "What do you mean, gone?" She looked to where the stallion was tethered next to the Clydesdale. "His horse is…."

" 'e set a guard at cave entrance," explained Junno, "It were Manscal's turn. 'e said 'e just saw 'im … walk out."

"Is it still snowing?" asked Catherine, fearfully.

Junno nodded. "Though it looks like storm's eased off."

"Cold comfort," she muttered, aghast at Shadiz's inexplicable return into the atrocious weather upon the moors. "You must go after him," she declared.

Junno shook his bald head, looking very doleful. "I'm sworn to remain by y'r side."

"I'll stay here with the others. I promise you." Frantic, she grasped the front of his damp cloak. "Please Junno. I beg of you"

Suffering an agony of indecision, he stared down at her pleading expression.

Denied by its master, the mastiff whimpered beside Catherine.

At length, the big man muttered, "You'll stay 'ere."

"I promise," assured Catherine, hastily, "a thousandfold."

When Junno left the cavern in pursuit of his cousin, she found the two older Romany once more standing quietly beside her. She knew that before leaving Junno had spoken to the one who had led the nomadic escort. He gave her a reassuring smile. "Do not doubt, *cara*."

Catherine nodded, plucking at the vibrant jet pendant beneath her riding attire. She did not doubt. She simply did not understand.

★ ★ ★

There was no cavern to offer sanctuary. Fargange had been left behind, hopefully still holding within its prehistoric rock what was precious; and always had been. The only other place to be found in the silent, pristine bleakness was Barney Throup's ale-house.

Junno led his cousin to what was little more than a hovel within a hamlet of likeminded buildings residing under the outlandish name of Boggle Hole. His greatest fear was that the bolt might be shot against hostility. A prudent thumping upon the warped planks of the ale-house's door aroused the landlord's avarice. An insight into Throup's grimy hospitality was revealed by wary degrees. The landlord's thin features, dominated by his hooked nose, radiated surprise upon seeing the big Romany and blanched the colour of the snow on his doorstep upon setting eyes on the Master.

Throup could not turn back time nor could he refuse the coin of the realm. He welcomed the two powerful Romanies as if they were the warlords of King Midas. His scrawny progeny was ear-jerked away from the warmth that was grudgingly flaring in the smoky hearth. He hissed out the corner of his mouth to them in an attempt to stop them from gawping at the Master, who seemed to be in some sort of difficulty. Afraid of the notorious Gypsy, whatever his condition, Throup's skinny wife scuttled with her ragged brood to the rear of their dismal abode.

Throup served ale in two dented mugs. He then slunk away with grovelling politeness to mutely bully his cowering family. It was clear that their wariness of the unexpected customers was partnered by a curiosity even his sly nastiness could not stem entirely.

Trying to show appreciation of their downtrodden trade, Junno took a swig of the ale. His guts welcomed the warming effect of the murky brew. After glancing at his distracted cousin to reassure himself, he stood up and ambled over to the miserable fire. He warmed his hands, smiling across the gloomy interior of the hovel. Upon sitting down again, he straggled the rough bench opposite Shadiz, using his great bulk as a casually placed shield against round-eyed stares.

" 'as it cum back yet?" he asked, quietly, in their language. He was deeply disturbed by Shadiz's condition, the like of which he had not seen for a long time.

He was sitting with his head in his hands, elbows resting on the filthy, ale-stained boards. Eventually he gingerly parted his trembling hands. He blinked several times. The big man tossed one side of his wet cloak over his shoulder and passed a gentle hand over Shadiz's haggard features, close to his bloodshot eyes, and was relieved to see a flinching reaction.

Suddenly, the shadowy door of the ale-house burst open. Immediately, Junno's hand went to the hilt of his sword. His cousin paid dizzy, bleary-eyed attention to the youngsters bursting through the door in a shower of powdery snow.

Their arms full of snowy logs, the girl and the boy breezed into the hovel, bringing with them a mixture of winter's breath and refreshing youth. The door, responding to the boy's deft backward kick, slammed shut behind them as they giddily juggled the kindling in their arms. Intent upon dumping their loads, they were halfway to the fire when the presence of customers, their identity and the atmosphere they had evoked put a dampener on their playfulness and slowed their snow-trailing footsteps.

So amazed was Junno to find such richness in the poorest of places, he found himself looking towards the mother for clues to the origin of the girl's attraction. The doubt he harboured, even in his charitable heart, was quickly dispelled when Mistress Throup moved into the weak light of the candle stubs. Ignoring the grubby fingers that clutched at her ragged skirt, she was obviously afraid for her daughter, and not for the first time, suspected the big man. He realised that apprehension came as second nature to the bones of beauty worn away by hardship.

He had dismissed the youth almost immediately. His nose marked him out as being Throup's son, his eldest judging by the width of his shoulders and lanky height. His sister was a different matter entirely. Her prettiness lit up the dreary place. Her freshness shone like a ray of sunshine in the grime. Her innocence sent a cold shiver down Junno's spine.

Not wishing to look, but forcing himself to do so, it came as no surprise to find Shadiz was digesting with a predator's keen gaze her long fair hair, her sparkling blue eyes set within delicate features and her figure wrapped within layers of drab rags.

The big man was flooded with horror. As an immediate consequence, he wielded the aversion to physical contact like a weapon. Gripping Shadiz's arm, he spoke with uncharacteristic forcefulness in their language. "Let demon lie. D' y' 'ear?"

Black eyes focused with difficulty on Junno. He intensified his grip.

Shadiz tried to pull away.

"D' y' 'ear me?" reiterated the big man, maintaining his hold.

For a moment Shadiz's narrowed gaze radiated menace. Then, he shrugged.

Not entirely convinced, Junno did however relent and withdraw his detested lock upon his cousin's arm. At a loss how best to proceed, he went against the grain of bitter experience and shoved the other, untouched mug across the rough planks of wood masquerading as a table. "Tak a drink," he advised, gruffly.

Shadiz gave a sour laugh. He leaned back against the moist, flaky wall. His slit-eyed glare dwelt upon the mug for several thoughtful seconds. All at once, he lashed out, sending the mug and its contents flying through the smoke-infested air. Both landed with a dull thud and a watery whoosh at the feet of the young girl.

For a long moment, feral black eyes devoured her while she stood frozen with fear.

Junno heard the agonised groan.

Shadiz got to his feet. He swayed, briefly hanging onto the splintery edge of the table, and then made his unsteady way to the door. He went outside, leaving Junno the sole object of the Throups' apprehensive attention. He rose and tossed a few coins across the hovel.

The landlord caught them deftly, wearing an ingratiating smile like a shield. "Nice t' serve y', gentlemen."

Junno's troubled gaze swept over the occupants of the ale-house. "These be dangerous times," he remarked.

"Indeed, they be, sir," agreed Throup.

"I'd guard y'r family well," said the big man, and went on his way to find his cousin.

CHAPTER FOUR

The Way of LIfe

Catherine was plagued by helplessness. The feeling was made worse by the way Junno was trying to disguise his own anxiety.

"I am best avoided. Ill-luck seems to be pursuing me."

Junno was quick to admonish her. "Y' ain't t' talk like that, Rauni." The big, bald-headed Romany instinctively touched the gold earring in his left lobe to ward off any bad *bak* tempted by her miserable observation.

They were in the stables at the rear of the Lodge, and had been since mid-morning, trying to usher into the world a foal that seemed extraordinarily reluctant to be born. Now, as the fall of dusk crept upon occupied and empty stalls alike, lanterns were being lit by a former pick-pocket. Currently a scrawny youth filling out in the employ of the Master, Billy was consumed with worry for one of his precious charges.

The wiry-haired mastiff left behind by the Master, a sure sign that he and his men were engaged in their covert warfare, lay close by, its head resting on its great paws. It had taken to staying close to Catherine when not allowed to accompany its master.

Mary had long since been dispatched to the busy kitchen, her devotion to Catherine having been overtaken by a mildly irritating squeamish streak. As for Keeble, the dwarfish man had grown bored awaiting the difficult birth and had fallen asleep in the accommodating straw of an empty stall.

The pregnant chestnut mare kept moving restively, her sides periodically heaving. As the day had progressed, Junno had become increasingly convinced that the foal had become twisted inside its mother. All his careful attempts to turn it had proved unsuccessful.

He knew his shortcomings, leaving him bemoaning the fact he had no idea of the present whereabouts of Maggii.

Catherine, feeling equally inadequate, knew of whom he spoke. On several occasions, the small, thickset horse master, Maggii, had cured a sick horse at Nafferton Garth when all hope seemed to have faded for the animal, and ensured with his stern expertise a good outcome for her father when one of his mares had experienced a difficult birth.

All at once the hushed, late afternoon atmosphere in the stables was disrupted by the return of men and horses.

Soothing the already agitated mare, Catherine only registered the presence of Shadiz within the sudden activity when first Billy scurried forward and then the big grey dog rose, stretched and moved away, tail wagging.

Talking quietly to his charge, Billy led the stallion away down the wide aisle between the stalls. The black horse cast a mighty shadow over the diminutive stable boy. He was the only other person apart from the Master it would tolerate being handled by.

Showing the full measure of his frustration at not being able to end the mare's suffering, Junno reached his cousin in two wide strides, speaking rapidly in the Romi. As he spoke, Shadiz stood glowering in Catherine's direction. He responded to the big man with a few curt words, stabbing a directional thumb over his shoulder. The gesture propelled Junno out of the stables.

Catherine's heart soared. For she had caught the name of Maggii's son, another wizard with horses. Her heart then began to thump at Shadiz's soundless approach. Showing defiance, for it was glaringly obvious he disapproved of her presence in the stables, especially upon the return of his men, her attention returned with deceptive ease to the pregnant mare.

Saying nothing, he ran a gentle hand down the mare's quivering side, assessing for himself the horse's condition.

Catherine's gaze was drawn to his blood-stained knuckles.

"Ain't mine," he informed her without looking up.

"Oh, good," she answered, briskly. "Lemon and pumice will remove it. But then, you probably knew that already." Feeling the weight of his sharp, black-eyed look, she continued to stroke the mare's velvet neck while speaking soothingly to the pain-wracked animal.

It was the nearest he had approached her since he had vanished into the snowstorm over three weeks ago. She had not discovered what had taken place out upon the treacherous moors. By the time Junno had returned to the large cavern in which she and the Romanies had waited, the snow had stopped falling. He had assured her that Shadiz was in a 'passable' condition. He would not elaborate further, proving his loyalty. Since then, whenever Shadiz encountered her at the Lodge, he made certain a rigorous distance was maintained, and that the duration of any meetings was only fleeting. Indeed, he seemed determined to steer clear of her altogether.

No matter how hard she tried to make light of it, the undeniable consequence of his aloof manner was a dull ache midway betwixt head and heart. Time and again, she found herself wondering what she had done wrong. What boundary had she inadvertently overstepped? Or was it more likely his conduct stemmed from the inevitable outcome of the impulsive promise he had made to her dying father?

" 'ow long she been like this?" asked Shadiz, low-pitched, glancing towards the open doorway of the stables.

"For most of the day, I'm afraid," responded Catherine, marvelling that he had not marched away from her.

To fill the awkward silence which had sprung up between them, she gave a brief outline of how Junno and herself had tried to help the mare give birth. She sensed she was not the only one to view Junno's return with relief, especially as he was accompanied by Maggii's son.

Short and muscular like his father, Conor had also inherited Maggii's curly red hair, an unusual trait in the Romany creed. Catherine could see he was assessing the condition of the mare as he strode towards her. Junno was clearly giving him the same explanation she had just given to Shadiz.

Richard hurried into the stables. He pushed past the two

Romanies. Exhibiting a single-mindedness of purpose, he headed for the stall where his half-brother stood.

"Have you informed her?" he demanded, wheezing slightly. Halting, he ignored the animal's plight. His insistent glare switched from Shadiz to Catherine and then back again to his leader.

Shadiz's barbarous countenance had developed an expression halfway between a scowl and a sneer.

"Informed me about what?" asked Catherine, gladly standing aside to allow Conor to examine the mare.

Richard's exasperated sigh became a short, chesty cough. "You heartless ba." He checked himself. Turning to Catherine, he explained, "We were making our way back to the Lodge, when we chanced upon a skirmish between a company of troopers and a single horseman."

It sounded sickeningly familiar. Richard had her full attention.

"At first we were unaware of the rider's identity. Upon drawing close, I recognised Benjamin Farr. You may recall he has made several visits to the Lodge, carrying dispatches from Prince Rupert. Until recently, I served with him on the prince's staff. Naturally, we sped to Benjamin's assistance. Our superior numbers ensured we routed the troopers, but not before Benjamin was seriously wounded."

Catherine's mind was flooded with painful images, conjured up by the scant details she had been given about her father's ordeal two months earlier.

"You must accompany me and ascertain what can be done for Benjamin," Richard urged. His thin, pale face was ruddy with hectic concern. Ignoring everyone else, including the formidable presence of his half-brother, he took hold of her elbow. It seemed to him that she had worked a miracle upon Shadiz aboard the *Eagle*, which was precisely what his good friend was presently in need of.

"Where's Farr?" The Master's brusque, whispery question arrested Richard's attempt to steer Catherine away.

"In the hall," he tossed over his shoulder.

It was a forgone conclusion what was coming, Catherine realised. But Richard was far too focused upon enlisting her skill as a healer.

From the outset of her taking up residence at the Lodge, two restrictions had been imposed upon her. She must not stray beyond the high, drystone wall encircling the ancient Lodge and the other renovated buildings. She was also required to stay out of the main hall that served as barracks for the Master's men. The first she found restrictive. The second seemed a sensible precaution.

On the whole, she had found her guardian's followers to be a friendly, likeable lot. Mainly lawless outcasts, every one of them had been given a place and a purpose by the Master. All were fiercely loyal to him and respected his commands, even those few men she was glad to avoid. She was convinced that upon her appearance at the Lodge, he had made it clear to them that they were required to adhere to strict guidelines whenever they were anywhere near her. A prime example had been when they had led their weary mounts into the stables upon returning from their latest mission. She had got the impression it had gone well. When they had realised her presence in the stables their euphoric male banter had been swiftly terminated.

"She ain't goin' in 'all."

So great was Richard's outrage, it precipitated a coughing fit. "You would condemn Benjamin to death. You damned heathen," he managed upon ragged breath.

Shadiz smiled with his lips only. *"Begone, dull care! I prithee begone from me! Begone, dull care, you and I shall never agree."*

The men in the stables, though they continued to care for their horses, were surreptitiously viewing the exchange between the Master and Richard Massone.

Clearly there would be no special dispensation for the wounded man. Catherine's mind worked on urgent wings before Richard could make matters worse by becoming embroiled in yet another dispute with his half-brother and leader. After living under the same rickety roof as both of them for several weeks, she had come to understand the full measure of their mutual animosity. Indeed, she would've had to be suffering from chronic myopia not to.

"Junno, do you think you could possibly carry Benjamin Farr into the library?"

"He cannot be moved," put in Richard.

"Better he be moved and examined than left to die where he lays," Catherine pointed out.

"Aye. I reckon I could lift lad," affirmed Junno, from the other side of the pregnant mare.

Catherine felt it would be wrong to take issue with the Master's authority on this occasion. She made certain her gaze was more questioning than challenging. She simply wanted to be allowed to help someone without causing further friction.

Meanwhile, Richard chafed against the delay.

The Master regarded Catherine with fathomless, slant-eyed blackness. He commanded, "Tak Farr into library."

★ ★ ★

" 'ow's 'e doin'?"

In spite of their mutual knowledge of his soundless ways, Tom and even Junno found themselves reacting to Shadiz's whispery inquiry. It was close to midnight, a slumberous atmosphere reigned throughout the Lodge, yet he had entered the fire-crackling peace of the library without either man noticing.

He strolled out of the shadows around the door and made his way across the sparsely furnished chamber to where Benjamin Farr lay oblivious on the pallet that, like himself, had been carried into the library from the main hall. The half-consumed candles flickered upon the gaunt signatures of a life and death struggle in his handsome features. When Shadiz lifted the sheet covering the fair-haired man, the linen bandages wrapped around his upper body were evidence of the sword thrust which had almost taken his life, and could still.

Getting slowly to his feet, Tom said, "Lad's 'oddin' 'is own." While walking stiffly away from the fireside chair, opposite the equally ancient one occupied by Junno, he saw Shadiz glance across the chamber to where Catherine lay curled up on the grubby sheepskin rug, asleep beneath Junno's cloak. The flames in the nearby stone hearth danced upon her fair-white hair, turning the long strands into gold and silver. For a fleeting second an emotion stirred in his scarred face.

Tom halted next to his tall leader, overlooking the wounded man. "Lass's dun 'er best fer lad. Now, 'tis a matter o' waitin'."

Without comment, Shadiz turned his attention to where Richard was sprawled asleep on a stool, his head pillowed on his arms on the rough table. Moving silently with palpable malice, he kicked his half-brother awake.

Richard straightened automatically. His bemused gaze swept around the library, coming to rest briefly on Benjamin Farr, before travelling upwards.

"Shift y'rsen," the Master commanded, harshly. "You're on duty."

Apart from Tom and with the exception of Junno, everyone at the Lodge took their turn at guard duty, either as commander of the watch or part of the constant, tree-bound surveillance. Tom, who compensated for his aged limbs by being in charge of the duty roster, knew very well that it was not Richard Massone's turn to be commander of the watch. Studying Shadiz, he decided against pointing out the fact.

After Richard had left the library, coughing, befuddled by robbed sleep, Shadiz remained standing beside the table, his stern gaze lingering on Catherine's sleeping form. "Is she comfy?" he demanded. "Laid like that?"

"She must be," assured Tom, mildly, "she be 'ard on."

Shadiz said no more. He started to sift through the paperwork stacked on the table.

Tom sat down again and took up his pipe, exchanging a glance with Junno. The big man's manner was carefully noncommittal. Tom had come to expect nothing less from him. He had learned a great deal from Bob Andrew about what had taken place during the *Eagle's* voyages to and from Ijuimden. Being attentive, he had pounced upon the few pieces of information Junno had let slip. And then, of course, there was Shadiz's behaviour. All of which added up to ... well, Tom wasn't quite sure.

Silence resumed its nocturnal tread, only now the tenor of its footfalls within the library had developed a disquieting heaviness.

Since his return to the Lodge, Shadiz had discarded his long, leather coat and broadsword. Before very long, the wad of documents he had been browsing through were flung down dismissively. Thereafter, he prowled the chamber.

"Lass certainly knows 'ow t' 'elp folks," commented Tom into the deep hush.

Shadiz responded, scathingly, in Romi. Perplexed, Tom looked hopefully at Junno for a translation. Disappointing him, the big man simply shrugged, pitching his own loyalty against that of Tom's.

The wounded man moaned.

Responding immediately, Tom called upon his rickety knees to once again hoist him up. He crossed to the pallet. He had been the first person to view Benjamin Farr's condition when he lay in the hall before being moved by Junno into the library. The bloody damage caused him to hold out little hope for the young man's survival. Only when Catherine had examined Prince Rupert's messenger and begun to tackle his deep chest wound had his initial sense of futility started to fade. He knew from what Bob Andrew had told him, that she had saved Shadiz's life, for which he would be eternally grateful to her. And he had seen how she had treated minor ailments and injuries since coming to live at the Lodge. Witnessing her mature skill practised upon Farr had boosted his already high esteem of Sir Roger Verity's extraordinary daughter.

Eventually Farr settled down again beneath Tom's gentle touch.

"She can't be comfy there?" announced Shadiz, suddenly. He had terminated his prowling and now stood glaring at Catherine's sleeping form. "There's too many soddin' draughts in 'ere."

They were, after all, in a near derelict, medieval building. In keeping with the rest of the Lodge, the stony ambience of the library, though filled with cosy firelight, was far from palatial. Moreover, the March nights still possessed an undeniable sting that curled with icy fervour around the edges of the leather curtains, hung with manly carelessness at the unglazed windows.

Tom saw his surroundings with a fresh insight. He had, he

realised, grown accustomed to the ancient crudeness, even welcoming it as home, with Shadiz.

"Aye, you're right, lad," he responded. "Best get dear bairn t' 'er bed, then."

What he had not expected was the fleeting expression of alarm. Without another word, Shadiz turned on his heels and stalked out of the library.

Junno sighed. Smiling sympathetically at Tom's bewilderment, he got to his feet.

A short while afterwards, the big man closed the door to Catherine's chamber quietly behind himself. Despite his prodigious size, he had managed to tuck his charge into the bed she shared with her old nurse-maid, without waking either of them, nor had he disturbed Mary, asleep upon the narrow bed formerly used by her young mistress. He had even managed to build up the fire in the small hearth.

After a great, silent yawn, he prepared his bedroll, consisting of a couple of colourful blankets and a straw-filled pillow, as he did each night, stretching out before the door of Catherine's chamber, in spite of her constant protests. In an effort to appease her, he had pointed out that the narrow landing was warmer and certainly drier than his usual, open-air bedchamber. He had, however, admitted to missing the stars, also his wife, Lucinda and their son, Peter, both of whom Catherine knew well.

"She settled?"

The barely audible inquiry came as no surprise. Junno straightened. "Aye. Rauni'll rest easier now, I reckon," he informed the deep shadows.

As usual, the mastiff was with his cousin. The big dog padded on scratchy toes to the door of the chamber and whimpered. Junno twitched its spiky ears in a persuasive manner, afraid it might disturb at least one of the chamber's occupants. When the tall shadow turned to go, the loyal mastiff went to heel.

"Shadiz."

The tall shadow halted and half-turned.

Junno continued to speak in their language. "Can I say summat?"

"If y' must."

"Y' 'urtin' 'er."

There was a deep pause.

Then. "Better this way than tother."

Junno sucked in his breath. His cousin's unique thoughtfulness towards Catherine made him quick to repudiate the bitter statement. "Y'd never do tother t' Rauni."

There was deep pause. Then. *"Multi quidem facilius se abstinent ut non utantur, quam temperent ut bene utantur."*

Junno sighed heavily. Time and again Shadiz wielded knowledge like a shield. He had no idea that the Latin words of St. Augustine meant, *'To many, total abstinence is easier than perfect moderation.'*

★ ★ ★

Such was his wonder at the newborn, Billy had almost overcome his awe of the Master. Only when his leader's demeanour altered and his interest in the welfare of the foal terminated abruptly did the stable youth's enthusiastic explanation wither on his nibbled bottom lip. The Master moved away, a silent menace in each purposeful stride he took down the wide aisle between the stalls. Billy was bewildered. All seemed peaceful in the stables. Indeed, there seemed merriment within. He could hear male laughter mingling with that of Miss Catherine's.

"What y' gonna call 'im?"

Catherine swung round. Despite her surprise at Shadiz addressing her, she was careful not to alarm the day-old foal and its mother. She was vaguely conscious of Bill Todd and the other men to whom she had been speaking melting away.

Standing in the neighbouring stall, his arms resting on the partition, he raised a quizzical eyebrow. Like the previous evening, when he had returned to the Lodge, he was dressed for battle. It was how she regarded his long black coat, the huge broadsword slung across his back and the wickedly curving sword at his hip.

Taken unawares by his presence let alone his question, she

turned back to the gangling, brown foal to ponder its name. Conor's expertise had prevailed. Less than thirty minutes after she had left the stables to care for Benjamin Farr, the foal had been born. It seemed none the worse for its prolonged birth, nor, fortunately, did its mother.

"May I know the Romi for Lucky?"

"Bakalo," he informed her. He shrugged. "Good as owt."

Nodding, Catherine was pleasantly surprised by his manner. Gone had the remoteness. In its place was a neutrality bordering on politeness.

All at once, he looked downwards. Scowling, he straightened.

Catherine heard playful yaps and groaned inwardly. Stepping closer to her side of the stall's partition, she spoke in conciliatory haste, "That will be Patch's litter." She gave an apologetic grimace. "They're getting very boisterous."

"Ger off me bloody coat," commanded Shadiz.

The campaign had been taken up by canine youthfulness, impervious to the dictates of the Master. He stepped smartly out of range of restive hooves. Whereupon Catherine caught sight of the trio of brindled puppies, tugging in a very determined manner on the hem of his leather coat.

She scurried round to the pups who were by now swinging giddily, growling in unison. The mastiff moved out of her way, apparently disgusted by the spectacle. "Will you keep still," she implored Shadiz, her voice shaking with merriment. She grabbed hold of the back of his coat, careful to avoid the great sword, and, one after another, nipped the pups' noses. Deprived of air to continue the fierce impersonation of their elders, each in turn let go, their small, lithe bodies rolling in the abundance of straw scattered about the flag-stones. They were shooed away by her, and therefore directed their mischief at several kittens prancing by. She turned back to Shadiz, anxious to see what the fiasco had done to his mellowed attitude, only to glimpse behind him a fast approaching herd of youngsters clamouring to see the latest edition to the stables.

Hoping to ward off trouble, she stepped neatly around Shadiz in order to position herself between him and the on-coming children. The group was a mixture of ages. Clearly, the older ones had become aware of the presence of the Master. Coming to a brisk halt, they stopped their excited chatter and attempted to restrain that of the younger ones. All stared up, fearfully round-eyed, at the tall, fearsome Master.

Catherine's reassuring smile included the entire group. When she twisted around to face Shadiz, she felt hands grip her cloak, rather like barnacles attaching themselves to a rock in defence against an incoming tide.

"They've come to say hullo to Bakalo," she told him, brightly. Inwardly, she was preparing for the storm she felt certain would descend upon all their heads, hopefully hers most of all. And, indeed, Shadiz's glowering countenance did nothing to alleviate her disguised unease.

His glare raked through the fear-struck children. "An' what t' bloody 'ell are they doin' 'ere?" he wanted to know in a low-pitched voice chipped out of January ice.

Vigorous in her maintenance of a sunny facade, Catherine told him, "Well, I fear you are not aware, how could you be, but the truth of the matter is, a number of the children, particularly the younger ones, were missing their mothers when they came here to the Lodge each day to labour for your men. With their fathers away working on the land or on fishing boats, some of the older grandparents were finding difficulty in coping with the youngsters." She took a deep breath. "So I, well, I thought it would be nice for them if they were to accompany their mothers to the Lodge. The older ones care for the younger ones, and do not normally stray far from the kitchen. They ... er ... liven up the old place, as it were."

"Liven old place up, eh," growled the Master, hands on hips.

"Well, yes," affirmed Catherine, her rosy, fine-boned face wearing a fixed persuasive smile.

Junno, who had been grooming his huge Clydesdale, walked up and stood behind the immobile children. Like Catherine, the big man, who towered over everyone present including his cousin, was careful to portray a conciliatory manner. Nevertheless, she could sense the tension within her protector.

His arrival brought his cousin's unpredictable attention whipping around him. "Next, you'll be after bringin' Lucinda an' Peter 'ere," rasped Shadiz.

"Well, it certainly would be nice for Junno. Have you given a thought to how much he must miss his wife and son?" Catherine commented, impulsively.

"Lucinda tak's care o' puri daia," put in Junno, defending his cousin.

Several of the Master's men, talking amongst themselves, entered the stables. It was clear they had arrived to collect their respective mounts in preparation to accompany their leader to wherever he was bound that morning. Not immune to the air of tension in the stables, they curtailed their chit-chat and stood in watchful silence, unable to proceed further.

"Y' didn't think t' consult me?" mused Shadiz, switching to French.

"Oh, I did," exclaimed Catherine, conversing in the same language.

"Aye?"

Unsure how to proceed with her mercurial guardian so as not to make the situation worse for the frightened children, she shrugged her shoulders, stirring her long fair-white hair. "For all of a couple of seconds."

Unbelievably, thankfully, mirth was fermenting in those incredible black eyes.

"I realised you would discover the presence of the children at the Lodge sooner or later," She cleared her throat. "I was hoping it would be later."

She watched as Shadiz's manner changed significantly, and thought she had blundered by her flippancy, prudent though it had been, until she realised that Richard had appeared behind her, having made his way through the Master's men and the children, all silent and still. He, too, was dressed for departure, his longbow and quiver of arrows hung about his thin person. Ignoring his half-brother, he appeared eager to speak with her. "Would you attend Benjamin? Tom believes he has succumb to a fever."

Catherine nodded, urging the children to return to the kitchen, promising them they could see the foal later. Behind her, she heard Shadiz address Richard, but failed to catch the gist of his characteristically low-pitched words. Looking in Richard's direction, she saw how he was holding his own counsel with a visible effort. As usual, whatever Shadiz had said was meant to antagonise his half-brother. She conveyed her intention to return forthwith to the library and Benjamin Farr. Smiling his gratitude, trusting her healing skills, Richard walked away to saddle his horse.

The mastiff rose off its haunches, hopeful of accompanying his master. Shadiz accepted the stallion's reins from a wary Billy.

"You're definitely y'r father's daughter," he remarked, softly.

"I shall take that as a compliment."

"Aye. Y' would."

Eager to return to her patient, Catherine gave him a farewell smile, saying with a quick curtsy, "Keep safe. I'm afraid I'll be here still when you return." Hurrying out of the stables, she could feel his black gaze piercing her back until she emerged into the morning sunshine, and even then experienced a lingering sensation.

It was only when she was entering the kitchen on her way to the library that she realised Shadiz had not banished the children from the Lodge.

★ ★ ★

Benjamin Farr drifted over hot plains. His one burning desire was to make the people, toiling below his wingless flight, comprehend the terrible risk. Somehow, God help him, he had to convey to them the danger that threatened all of them. They, in their kindness, had taken him in, now he must find a way to warn them of Neptune's curse.

Even before Catherine reached the library, her heels having picked up Mary and Keeble on the way, it became clear that Benjamin Farr had indeed developed a fever. His delirious outbursts were reminiscent of the *Eagle's* voyage. They made Catherine cringe. She hurried across the darkened chamber to kneel next to Tom beside the pallet. It was easy to discern the unnatural heat as it rose up from where Farr twisted and turned, battling inner demons. The linen bandages around his upper body were still in place despite his restlessness, but were stained with fresh blood.

"Can y' do owt fer lad, luv?" asked Tom. The craggy lines in his brow were deepened further by his anxiety for the young man.

Catherine grimaced. "I've had good practise of late."

Busy with her patient, she missed Tom's quick, sidelong glance.

"I'll go and mix the herbs," she said, rising. Clutching her velvet skirts, she paused. "In the meantime, Keeble draw back the hangings from the windows to allow air in here. Tom, while I am away, would you bathe him with cold water." Farr's feverish ramblings made her feel unaccountably troubled. "Of what does he speak, do you think?"

"Family 'e's lost in war, per'aps?" suggested Tom, grimly.

Catherine continued to stare down at the young man she had met on a couple of occasions, when he had been delivering correspondence from Prince Rupert to the Master. In spite of the good impression he had made upon her, a foreboding chilled her.

"Luv?" Tom's concern now ran deep for her. "Y' be all right, me luv?"

She came back to herself. Taking a shuddering intake of breath, she nodded. And hurried away to prepare the herbs. "Yarrow and woundwort for the bleeding, betony for the fever, perhaps vervain...." she mused in an attempt to escape the vaporous sensation which persisted down the shadowy hallway to her stillroom.

CHAPTER FIVE

Sailing

Catherine entered the broad pasture at the rear of the Lodge. Accompanied by Keeble, Mary and Bessie, her pace was curtailed by the latter's infirmity. Nothing could diminish the elation in her step or the grin of success on her young face.

Making slow but satisfactory progress towards full health, Benjamin Farr was resting next to Tom on the makeshift bench. Junno was sitting nearby on the ground, his back against the grey stone of the well. All three men were viewing Richard's expertise with the longbow.

Not wishing to disturb his next shot at the slice of circular wood he had strung up upon the ivy-smothered wall enclosing the pasture, Catherine and then Mary and Keeble paused. Only Bessie continued forward, muttering about the intolerable condition of her bloated legs. Benjamin rose slowly and motioned for the old woman to take his place on the bench.

Richard took his shot. After his arrow had found the centre of the target with unerring accuracy, he turned, saw Catherine and smiled. He was joined by both her and Benjamin. It was the first real opportunity she had had to examine his longbow without fear of instigating black sarcasm from his half-brother.

Her interest was clearly appreciated by Richard. He explained, "My longbow is just under five feet in length. It is made of yew, though maple or oak can be used. And is quite light." He invited her to hold the weapon to demonstrate his point. "The longbow can be used whilst on foot or mounted. An arrow discharged from either position is effective up to one hundred and five yards. But I have shot further with success, around two hundred and sixty yards. Some consider the weapon to be outdated. I find it to be reliable. More so than a musket, especially in the heat of the moment."

Benjamin, smiling, a hand unconsciously upon his injured chest, gave the impression he had heard the information on more than one occasion.

"What are the markings inscribed upon the weapon?" asked Catherine. She soon returned the longbow to Richard, her heightened sensitivity causing touch to be unpleasant.

"I have been informed the inscription is of Celtic origin."

"By whom?"

Richard did not answer immediately. His handsome features had taken on a taut appearance. "Shadiz," he muttered, grudgingly.

"I see," murmured Catherine, catching Benjamin's reserved eye. "Speaking of Le Grande Master," she continued, lightly. "He has finally given his permission for me to journey to Whitby."

Instead of appearing pleased, Richard informed her, "The stipulation for your excursion being that I must remain under guard at the Lodge."

His despondent words swept away all of her happy anticipation.

Seeing her crestfallen expression, he quickly assured her, "I do not cast blame upon you in any way." He placed a conciliatory hand upon her arm. "Please believe me."

She caught his quick glance in Junno's direction. The big man, she noticed, had stopped whittling on the piece of beech wood and was looking their way, a frown upon his large round face. She smiled at him. Although he returned the gesture, his attention remained mainly upon Richard.

"We will speak about this later," said Richard, squeezing her arm, before stepping away.

But they had not spoken before Catherine set off to Whitby the following morning. Although excited about her hard-won visit, she was unable to forget that Richard was being held against his will at the Lodge.

★ ★ ★

155

"According to one of the books my father gave me, it was upon the banks of the River Esk that Whitby was founded many centuries ago by the marauding Angles led by Ida, the Flame Bearer. Is this thing safe?"

"It be a coracle," answered Megan, primly, as was her nature. Even the way she sat in the trim, little craft made it clear she was a fifteen-year-old turning a stately forty.

"H'm. Is it safe?" repeated Catherine.

Bob Andrew's oldest daughter gave her younger sister a meaningful look. "It'd be if she'd stop muckin' about."

"I ain't," retaliated Tessa, gripping the tiller, her legs thrust out in an unladylike manner beneath her grubby dress. "Just cos I can 'andle *Tilly* better than you."

Boasting a square sail, the coracle was actually being handled quite well by Tessa on the lee side of Tate Pier. She sailed the little craft past differing types of vessels, including her father's ship. Having had her cargo unloaded after her latest voyage, the *Eagle* rocked sedately alongside the weathered stonework of the quay, an elderly aunt viewing a youngster frolicking upon the ruffled, glistening water. The river harbour was the life-blood of Whitby. East of the isolation of the rugged moorland, the North Sea fed the Esk and the fisherfolk who lived beside its shore.

Dubious about her present activity, Catherine watched a flock of wheeling herring gulls. Half-listening to their persistent, discordant chatter, her mind drifted along the pathway of her visit, hitherto viewed with rather more pleasure.

She had received an invitation to celebrate Megan's birthday. It was not often that Megan's father was at home for such an occasion. Catherine felt honoured to be asked by a family she had come to regard with deep affection. Megan, just a year younger than herself, and Tessa, her twelve-year-old tomboy sister, along with their mother, Laura, were allowed to visit her at the Lodge, making a novel change for all three while Bob was away at sea, often on the Master's business. Arriving on the previous afternoon at the captain's cottage overlooking the harbour in Haggerlythe, she had spent an enjoyable evening by the Andrews' welcoming hearth; and a night squeezed cosily between Tessa and Megan in their narrow bed after maidenly chatter.

The following day, while visiting the Friday market with Laura and her daughters, Catherine had tried not to allow the sight of the Master's watchful men positioned around the many stalls within the broad market square leading off Church Lane to diminish her enjoyment. She had rubbed shoulders with country women carrying huge baskets in which to store their purchases when they rode home on pillion saddles with their husbands. There had been many townsfolk there, too, both selling and buying, having emerged from the steep, narrow wynds leading from the communal yards. Her enjoyable inspection of the stalls only came to an end when Bob and Junno had thought it best if the females were not present while the public whipping took place of several determined beggars who had thought to make capital out of the folk of the prosperous port. Catherine knew her huge bodyguard was only too aware of the Master's commands.

Shadiz had very reluctantly allowed her visit to Whitby only after a great deal of persuading from herself, Tom and Junno.

"Look, Mamma and Papa and Keeble are waving."

Brought back to the present aboard the coracle, Catherine looked over her shoulder towards the summit of the slope leading down to Tate Pier where Junno and the little man were standing with Bob and Laura. She received an unpleasant shock.

The next time Tessa spoke, she sounded far less happy. "Ain't that…?"

"Yes," Catherine confirmed, annoyance giving her voice a sharp edge. She had a vision of her guardian frog-marching her back to the Lodge.

" 'e don't look pleased about summat," observed Megan, apprehensively.

As Catherine watched it became clear to her that Shadiz was berating Junno. Her suspicions grew when he flung down his swords and coat and yanked off his boots.

"What's 'e doin'?" asked Tessa, narrowly avoiding a collision with a skiff loaded with lobster pots.

"Will y' watch where y' goin'," snapped Megan.

"*Ye gods and little fishes!*" exploded Catherine. "I don't believe it."

Megan and Tessa glanced at her set features and then quickly turned back to view the Master's purposeful entry into the murky river water. He began to swim towards their small craft.

"What's 'e doin'?" repeated Tessa in a frightened whisper.

"What's it look like," retorted Megan.

Catherine became aware of their mounting terror. She took a deep breath in an effort to calm herself. "I shouldn't worry. He simply wants to join the voyage." Scowling as her guardian swam closer, she called across the intervening distance, "You'll have all of us in the water if you try to get aboard."

In no time at all, Shadiz was upon them. He made no attempt to climb into the coracle. Instead, treading water, he demanded of Tessa, "Can y' get alongside 'em?"

With one accord, the girls looked to where the knot of fishing boats he had indicated were secured alongside the quay aft of the *Eagle*. Struck dumb, Tessa nodded.

"Do it," instructed Shadiz.

Preparing to set sail on the incoming tide, the fishermen quickly realised Tessa's intention. Several leaned over port rails and hauled the girls' craft against their much larger ones. Meanwhile, Shadiz had climbed aboard one of the fishing boats. He eased himself into the coracle; watched with interest by everyone around the harbour, Catherine noticed. Dripping wet, he positioned himself in the waist of *Tilly*, careful not to counterbalance the lighter weight of the girls. Megan and Tessa stared at him. Both girls appeared quite terrified. Feeling sympathy for them, Catherine awaited the explosion with gritted teeth. She received a brilliant grin.

"Y' forgot…." began Shadiz. A few seconds elapsed while he rummaged in his leaking jerkin. "Y' forgot…." he repeated, looking up and glancing from one sister to the other. "Megan?" Responding to her name, Bob Andrew's oldest daughter managed a timid nod. Shadiz turned back to Catherine. "Y' forgot Megan's gift."

"I did?" said Catherine, taken aback. Bemused, she accepted the bundle he held out to her. She stared down at the soggy green velvet, tied up with exquisitely embroidered green ribbon. After which, she looked up and stared at Shadiz.

He continued to grin across the boat at her. "Well, ain't y' gunner give 'er it?"

She would have loved to thoroughly vilify him. She would have loved to hug him. He was the most infuriating man. With a grim effort, she regained her composure. Smiling at Megan, she murmured, "Happy birthday, my dear." And handed over the gift, as interested as the two sisters to see what the bundle contained.

"But y' bought me that lovely shell necklace in market," pointed out Megan.

"'Cos she forgot t' fetch that from Lodge," put in Shadiz, easily.

"How true," muttered Catherine.

Their little craft had bobbed away from the fishing boats of its own volition due to Tessa's preoccupation with Shadiz's arrival. While the attention of the girls dwelt exclusively on the gift he had delivered, he moved with quiet skill to take over the handling of *Tilly*. By the time all three had discovered that Megan had acquired a silver hairbrush, they found themselves sailing out of the River Esk.

"Where's 'e takin' 'em?" asked Laura, anxiously.

"Never fear, luv," Bob reassured her. "'e can do nowt wrong on watter." Concern gathered on his weatherbeaten face. "Land be tother thing."

He surveyed the verdant landscape above the long shoreline where the sky-blue North Sea fell with an unfailing beat upon the desert-yellow beach.

"They be well covered," stated Junno.

Bravado coupled with the desire not to disappoint Tessa, who had spoken often of her wish to take her sailing in her treasured *Tilly*, had resulted in Catherine being afloat. Perversely, her doubts about being on the water with the Andrew sisters were dissolving while making good headway away from the populated confines of the River Esk. Sailing in the tranquil coastal waters, Catherine had to admit that it was not just the change of course. She felt more at ease with Shadiz's presence at the helm.

The southerly breeze not only filled *Tilly's* square sail, but it also blew away the gossamer cobwebs. They had become wound around her spirit without her realising. Eyes closed, she took a deep breath of sea air. In her mind's eye came a vision of Stillingfleet Forest. It was as if the mighty entity approved of her invigorating surroundings. Sentinels of the Lodge, the presence of the ancient trees formed a barrier against a hostile world. Yet, here she was, presently a dot upon the sea, feeling remarkably safe.

Upon opening her eyes with a contented sigh, she found Shadiz had released the helm to Tessa. He proceeded to instruct the tousle-haired, freckled-faced youngster in the handling of *Tilly* in deeper water. Her love of the sea, any stretch of water, and her tutor's patient manner had mitigated her fear of the puissant Master. Complete with tongue protruding concentration, she sought to put into practice what she had just been shown about the nuances of trimming the already stretched canvas to gain the best possible benefit from the obliging breeze.

Glancing at Megan, Catherine saw she was still dazzled by the sunlit brilliance of her birthday present, unexpected by both of them. She had noticed how the attention of the sisters had been drawn, surreptitiously, to the left side of Shadiz's face. Yet again, a pang of guilt assailed her as the wind brushed his long black hair away from the disfigurement. The April sunshine pounced on his gold earring when he turned his head and looked at her. There was no trace of harshness in his dark features. She was never sure how long they remained quite still, their eyes locked. The only thing of which she was certain was the timeless affinity beyond sea and shore. And his smile.

CHAPTER SIX

Visitors

"Your visit to Whitby was enjoyable?" asked Benjamin Farr.

Catherine's prompt smile was full of happy memories. "Oh, to be sure."

The strong smell of herbs betrayed her use of the small storeroom leading off from the large, medieval kitchen. Drying plants, hanging from the ceiling beams above their heads, swayed in the draught coming through the half opened door. Benjamin had benefited greatly from their healing properties. After he had been brought to the Lodge, Catherine had almost exhausted her stocks of yarrow and woundwort in an effort to staunch the flow of blood from the deep chest wound that had threatened his life.

Fortunately, his sliced flesh was knitting together quite well. She was presently applying comfrey to assist the healing process.

Because it was Benjamin who asked how she had gained her herbal knowledge, she felt comfortable explaining how Shadiz's grandmother had taught her about the healing properties of herbs. And went on to admit, in spite of having had such an exceptional teacher, she had been unsure about her ability to heal Shadiz following the fire at Ijuimden. She understood her trust in him was not misplaced. Yet, on occasions, she experienced a vague, uneasy sensation due to Benjamin's presence at the Lodge.

In appearance, he possessed a superficial likeness to Richard, being also tall and fair-haired. But whereas Benjamin's handsome features reflected a robustness, despite his recent injury, Richard's were prone to an unhealthy pallor. Also, Richard was the thinner of the two well-bred young men, the stoop of his shoulders being more pronounced when his chesty complaint was at its worse.

Their temperaments were very different. Richard was highly charged, loathed to suffer slights, imagined or otherwise. A prey to his weakened constitution as well as his half-brother's malicious nature, he seemed to be constantly on the defensive. Benjamin, on the other hand, was content to observe in a good-natured manner in the background of any gathering, and got on well with everyone at the Lodge. During his convalescence, he had taken on the role of secretary. Catherine had noticed how his quiet efficiency seemed to have gained the approval of even the Master.

Possibly due to their surroundings, their conversation turned to Richard and his latest bout of ill-health, now overcome due to Catherine's attendance upon him.

"I'm glad to see Richard has resumed his duties. He was able to accompany the Master when he rode out yesterday," Benjamin commented.

Catherine's worries regarding Richard's frequent bouts of chesty incapacity were plain. "I wonder he has the strength to draw that longbow of his some days."

Fastening his cambric shirt, Benjamin gave a soft, knowing laugh. "Where he finds difficulty in drawing breath, he will always summon the strength needed for the weapon. I have seen it so on more than one occasion."

"How long has he shown a preference for the longbow?" she asked, recalling the unpleasant sensation she had experienced when handling the weapon.

Benjamin shook his head. "I know not." He watched in thoughtful silence as Catherine replaced the pot of comfrey in its place on the crowded bench that stretched the length of one side of the small chamber. Struck by a memory, he added, "The first time I saw him with the weapon he presently owns was when he accompanied the Master to my home close to Richmond to meet Prince Rupert. A place convenient for both, which they have used on more than one occasion."

"And what, pray tell, did your family make of the Master?"

The returning glow of health drained from Benjamin's face. "My father and older brothers are no more," he murmured.

Her amused tone altered immediately. "I am sorry," she responded, touching his arm. She knew all too well the pain of loss.

With a visible effort his manner brightened. He teased Mary about her zealous pounding of the herbs.

Her curiosity piqued, Catherine returned to the subject of Richard's longbow. "I wonder from whom he got such a weapon with those inscriptions?" she mused aloud.

"Me."

Upon hearing the softly spoken word, Catherine and Benjamin both turned in surprise towards the narrow doorway to find the Master lounging there, arms folded, the mastiff at his feet. Behind them, Mary jumped so violently she sent the wooden bowl full of crushed nettles flying across the long bench. Behind the Master, in the normally rowdy kitchen, Catherine realised there was little noise save the whimper of a fretful child, hastily stifled.

"Oh, hullo," she said. "You're back."

"I reckon so," Shadiz murmured with the kind of grin which did little for her shaken composure. She did not care for the glint in his black eyes as they surveyed the small chamber, taking in the various cats and dogs, some bandaged some not. His attention dismissed Catherine's quivering maid and settled upon Benjamin.

"Well, Benjamin Bunny. She mended y' yet?"

"Just about, sir," Benjamin replied, mildly.

Shadiz nodded. He straightened, favouring Catherine with a quick appraisal. "Y' look suitable," he remarked.

"I do?" she responded, glancing down at her plain blue gown, "Oh, good."

"We've visitors," he informed her.

"We do?" She was puzzled. Apart from the constant messengers, visitors to the Master's headquarters were a rarity. She responded warily to his overly polite gesture for her to precede him from the small chamber. His soundless, overbearing presence pursued her to the door of the library, where she was brought up short. Not because the broad chamber was ablaze with candles and she had arrived from the gloom of the hallway. Nor did the sight of Keeble filling to perfection the role of serving page or Richard playing the courteous host make much of an impression upon her.

It was the sight of the visitors to the Lodge that stabbed at Catherine's heart.

The subject of Gianca, the woman's name Shadiz's delirium had ripped from him while aboard the *Eagle*, had not been addressed. Was she now faced with the solution? She tried to observe without spite.

There was a young woman, clearly gently bred, kneeling in rich attire before the fire Tom was presently building up for her. She appeared to be a couple of years older than herself. She was slender to the point of unhealthy thinness, which was vaguely reminiscent of Richard's build. Her long, curling auburn hair, her entire appearance was dishevelled. Within the delicate structure of her face there was exquisite, pale beauty scattered by starry freckles. Catherine tried to ignore the cold, sick feeling in the pit of her stomach.

The grey-haired woman sitting in the nearby chair was the young woman's mother, judging by the strong family resemblance. The years had given her refined loveliness a notable elegance. She, too, looked the worse for wear.

It crossed Catherine's mind that despite the rainy nature of the day, in all probability, they had arrived, *en masse*, to oust her. She swallowed nervously; envisioning a battle royal.

Shadiz brought her doorway hesitation to an end. He took hold of her reluctant hand and escorted her into the library as if they were entering the court of King Charles. As he swept her past Richard and Keeble, they both paused in serving mulled wine to the rain-soaked, mud-splattered ladies, taken aback by their leader's formality.

The two visitors froze upon the Master's arrival. Their obvious apprehension of his powerful strangeness gave Catherine pause for thought.

"M'lady, may I present my ward, Catherine Verity, daughter of the late Sir Roger Verity of Nafferton Garth, Driffield."

Several moments of perfect stillness followed hard on the heels of his courtly introduction. Once the women had managed to tear their mesmerized gazes away from him, Catherine was scrutinized by them. Inwardly cringing, she glanced up at Shadiz as he intertwined his fingers with hers. Without looking at her, he managed to convey with that simple act reassurance to shore up her flagging confidence.

The mother made an effort to mask her speculative thoughts. She rose and stood almost protectively between her fawn-like daughter, hunched fearfully by the fire, and the Master. Her brown-eyed gaze was warm as it rested on Catherine. "My husband and I were acquainted with your father, child. A good man. We lament his untimely passing."

Close up, the woman's shadows of hardship were evident, making Catherine feel ashamed at her initial reaction to her and her daughter's appearance at the Lodge. Whatever had befallen them haunted their genteel faces. Rising from her respectful curtsy, she returned the older woman's smile. "I thank you for your concern, Madam."

The woman's apparent calm regard of the dangerous Master showed her metal when dealing with a difficult situation. "Ward, you say?"

Although he had lowered both their hands he had not released Catherine's. Unsmiling, he softly answered, "Aye. I obey 'er father's dyin' request t' keep 'er safe."

Incredulity flickered in the woman's features. The brief slip was chased away by her inbred sense of courtesy, an incongruity in such coarse surroundings.

Responding to the same inherent spirit, Catherine said, "My security and well being are assured here, in what has become my home since my father's demise."

She almost yelped out in pain such was the sudden grip exerted upon her hand. She turned questioningly in Shadiz's direction. He was staring down at her in a disconcertingly earnest manner. Instead of apprehension, she felt a warm glow down to her toes. A smile, a scowl, she wasn't sure which, threatened to break through the brutal darkness. Almost with relief, she thought, he swung round in Junno's direction as the big man entered the library, carrying a bundle of logs. "An', as y' see, m'lady. She's protection aplenty."

While mother and daughter blanched at Junno's indisputable size, Shadiz turned his attention to Richard. "An', o' course, there's *a verray parfit gentil knight....*"

The sneering inference was plain. Flushed, Richard endeavoured to maintain a dignified silence.

Shadiz switched his unpredictable attention back to the ladies, but addressed Catherine. "Now, I'd best introduce, Lady Anne Fairfax an' 'er daughter, Moll. Misplaced family o' Sir Thomas Fairfax, Parliamentarian Commander in the North o' England."

★ ★ ★

The Lodge never really slept. There was always someone guarding, planning, finding themselves a meal or simply reflecting on the progress of the war during a few snatched minutes of relaxation. This was why, despite the lateness of the hour, Catherine could hear the rumble of male voices coming from the kitchen while occupying the adjacent chamber she used to dry and mix the herbs. Yet, be it day or night, she never felt threatened by any of the occupants of the great, tumbledown edifice. And it was not simply because the protective bulk of Junno was always close at hand. She had quickly come to understand no one at the Lodge challenged the Master's authority. If anyone had an unsettling affect on her, it was the Master.

He did so now. She experienced a strong sense of him moments before he strolled into the small, candlelit chamber, silent as a cat on the prowl. Gritting her teeth against the sudden tremor in her hands, she continued to prepare the herbal potion.

She felt his appraisal of her. It made her acutely aware that she was standing at the long bench in her night robe, an embroidered shawl draped about her shoulders, her fair-white hair falling loose to her waist. She knew no relief when he shifted his gaze downwards to her task, or when, still without a word, he sauntered around the restrictive chamber. The mastiff was with its master. It gave a great yawn and flopped down at her feet, swishing its tail in answer to her quiet greeting.

Her guardian's enigmatic presence seemed to reverberate around the rough stone walls and from the low ceiling beams, he had to avoid, to the stone-flagged floor. She made no comment as he picked up various jars, studied them for a time and then replaced them with care either on the bench or on the long uneven shelf above.

Eventually, Shadiz came to a halt a few feet away from her, watching as she picked up the small pan Junno had just brought her from the ever-present fire in the kitchen and infused the mixture of elder flower and honey with the hot water. Satisfied with the potion, she looked up at him, as usual dwarfed by him despite her slender, straight-backed height.

"Does it ail, again?"

Ignoring the sardonic tone, pitched low, she shook her head. "The potion is for Moll Fairfax." She glanced at Junno, lingering in the doorway. "She has a slight cold and cough and is unable to sleep."

After the Master had left the library, following his courteous introduction of her to the wife and daughter of Sir Thomas Fairfax, Catherine had learned how they had come to be at the Lodge. They had become separated from Sir Thomas following the defeat of the Parliamentary forces at Adwalton Moor. By a miracle, they had proclaimed, they had managed to slip through the lines of the jubilant Royalist enemy. Having made their way to Selby with extreme difficulty, they had heard from a passing carter that the Royalist troops had entered the market town. Unsure how best to proceed, fearing for their safety, mother and daughter had taken refuge in a spinney. Shortly afterwards, they had been discovered by several warlike gypsies, who had taken them to their leader, who had turned out to be the Master, much to their horror. While he had remained adamant about their transportation to the Lodge, Richard had managed to make the journey less fraught by securing several respites for Lady Fairfax and her daughter, who was not in the best of health.

Catherine suspected Shadiz would make capital out of his find, but had been careful to say nothing of her fears to the anxious ladies. She had got the impression Richard was of the same mind. Exchanging a glance with him, both of them had been aware that if he tried to champion the ladies' cause he would undoubtedly seal their fate. It made the situation all the more galling for him.

Now, several hours later, she had the opportunity to try and discover the Master's intentions. But then again, being realistic, she realised she was probably whistling in the wind.

"What are your intentions regarding Moll and her mother?"

Shadiz remained silent.

Tensely willing him to give voice to an acceptable answer, Catherine viewed yet another leisurely turn around the small chamber. He avoided meeting her questioning gaze, which she refused to shift despite an inner compulsion to do so.

At length, he countered softly, "What'd y' 'ave me do wi' 'em?"

"Hand them back to their rightful owner," she answered, promptly.

Dubious humour flashed across his scarred features like lightning splitting the gloom of night. "Just trot through 'alf o' bloody Crop-Ears' army an' knock on their commander's door. By the way, 'ere's y'r family y' went an' lost.

> Give me the avowed, erect and manly foe;
> Firm I can meet, perhaps return the blow;
> But of all the plagues, good Heaven, thy wrath can send,
> Save me, oh save me, from the candid friend."

"Be that as it may," snapped Catherine, her cheeks burning fiercely. "I'm convinced, if you put your mind to it, you could find the means to accomplish their return."

There was a grim silence.

Shadiz watched her, black eyes veiled, as she sighed repressively and picked up the mug containing the herbal potion for Moll Fairfax. His eventual answer lacked heat, and was somewhat guarded. "I've a tendency t' be bloody-minded."

She turned to him. "That is because you consider you have to be." Tears sprang into her eyes, maybe because it was close to midnight and she was tired. "On this occasion," she added, quietly, "I would beg you not to be."

Halfway down the torch lit passageway, being followed by Junno, she heard a pot shatter and hoped it was not one of importance.

★ ★ ★

Benjamin Farr told himself he was repaying a debt. But he knew he was deceiving himself. Each time he had visited the Lodge, carrying documents from Prince Rupert to the Master, against all the odds, the fascination had grown.

That was why, following the present mission, always supposing he survived, he had leave from the Master to seek release from his position on the prince's staff. If successful, he would become one of the Master's men. He would embark upon unorthodox missions such as the present one, which had him strolling through the enemy's town, looking out for an old friend who, if he felt so inclined, could have him strung up within the hour.

Counterbalancing the chilling thought was the familiar compassion of the man he sought. Trying to feel confident in that knowledge, Benjamin continued through the battle scarred streets of Kingston-Upon-Hull.

The inhabitants had chosen to turn away from the monarch who had conferred the grandiose title upon their east coast port during better times for both. By their defiance, their backs were now well and truly wedged against the bank of the murky River Humber. For while they held out for the Parliamentarian Cause, the North East of England had become ruled predominately by Royalists. It had become the domain of the powerful Master.

A grin of relief shot fleetingly over Benjamin's youthful, handsome features when he finally located the object of his deceptively casual hunt. The tavern had certainly seen better days. Situated close to the substantial wall encircling Hull, it had taken a battering in recent times from the various attempts by the Royalists to break the stubbornness of the populace. The wall had stood firm, parts of the tavern had not, giving it a rakish appearance.

It was, he thought, typical of the man he sought to reside in such an abode, homely in spite of its shattered windows and missing chimney pots, rather than requisitioning a grander billet as no doubt the other Parliamentarian commanders had done, safe within the nucleus of the once prosperous town.

Playing the idle observer to a hopefully acceptable degree in the narrow thoroughfare while remaining alert to every movement in his vicinity, he was deciding how best to proceed when he caught a glimpse of the man himself striding across the rubble strewn tavern yard.

Benjamin seized his opportunity.

Leaving the April sunshine outside, he slipped into the interior of the stables with light-footed caution. Fortunately there was no one else present around the occupied stalls to challenge him apart from the man with whom he wished to speak.

Moving quietly through the gloom, he approached the tall, slender man. "Sir Thomas."

Sir Thomas Fairfax broke off from saddling his horse. He turned and peered through the unreliable light within the stables. "Benjamin? Benjamin Farr?"

"Hello, sir."

Following a brief, astounded pause, Sir Thomas swiftly located a lantern and struck tinder. The flickering light fell upon Benjamin's wary smile. Sir Thomas strode forward and caught hold of his shoulder in a hearty grip, his thin, bearded face alight with joy. "What on earth...? How on earth...?" Before the younger man could offer an explanation, the Parliamentary commander grew serious. "Do you now support Parliament?"

"No, sir," replied Benjamin, honestly. "My loyalty remains true to King Charles."

During the present civil strife, many men cut their cloth to suit their needs, changing sides as they saw fit. It was clear that Sir Thomas was relieved Benjamin was not one of those. He noticed the interest his unexpected visitor was taking in his bandaged left hand. "I was unlucky enough to be shot in the wrist during a recent battle," he dismissed. "But, what of you? What folly brings you here if you maintain your loyalty to the crown?"

Benjamin was about to explain the reason for his arrival in Hull, expedited by the Master's Romanies, when footsteps caused both men to twist around to see who was entering the stables. Sir Thomas had the presence of mind to push Benjamin behind his horse, startling them both.

Benjamin had already recognised the approaching voices.

The two men were soon upon them. One was tall and slim, his reserved manner reflected in his solemn face. The other was smaller and muscular, curly-haired and grinning. It was hard to recognise them as brothers, but Benjamin had. Sir Thomas was ordering them away on a bogus errand when he took the deliberate step away from the deep shadow of Sir Thomas's chestnut mare.

Jonathan and Jamie Muir gaped at him in complete amazement.

Sir Thomas murmured his disapproval of the younger man's action. But Benjamin was gambling that his lifelong friends would not betray him, especially when they discovered the nature of his mission. Although Jonathan and Jamie Muir had chosen to serve on the opposing side in the Civil War, having like so many put aside friendship and even family ties, they were still the next best thing to brothers he had since the slaughter of his father and two older brothers. They had grown up in neighbouring manors in the Yorkshire Dales, not many miles away from where Sir Thomas resided at Denton Hall in more peaceful times.

"Dear God!" exclaimed Jamie, running a hand through his thick, curly hair, a habit of his when he was vexed. His incredulity caused him to miss Sir Thomas's admonishing glance. "What the devil are you doing here?"

"My question, exactly," put in Sir Thomas, dryly.

Standing thoughtfully beside his younger brother, Jonathan returned Benjamin's smile, much to the latter's relief.

Without further ado, Benjamin switched his full attention back to Sir Thomas. "Sir, I bring you tidings of your wife and daughter."

The poor man was suddenly not a commander of renown. He was simply an anxious husband and father. "We became separated," he muttered, staring uncertainly at Benjamin. "Since then, try as I may, I have had no news of them." It was plain he feared the worst. Why else would the young man walk into the enemy's den?

Benjamin was quick to reassure him. "Rest easy, sir. Both your wife and daughter are safe."

Fairfax immediately exhibited enormous, heartrending relief, evidence of his deep love for his family. Benjamin recognised the measure of distress he must have suffered in not knowing the fate of his missing wife and daughter.

"Oh, thank the Lord," murmured Sir Thomas. He took a deep, calming breath before continuing. "I see, now. You risked your life to bring me good tidings. But can you not inform me of their whereabouts?"

This was the tricky part about which Benjamin had a few reservations. If he were ambiguous in revealing details, no matter how noble-minded Sir Thomas was, he could very easily jump to the wrong conclusion.

"They are safe," he said into the waiting silence, "within the Master's protection."

"And what ransom does the foul gypsy want?" exclaimed Jamie, sourly. He glowered at his old friend. "I never imagined you to be that bastard's mouthpiece."

Stung by Jamie's comments, dismayed by Jonathan's silent disapproval, Benjamin did not at first realise Sir Thomas was smiling. Indeed, he was beaming with an even greater degree of relief. The Parliamentarian commander put up a hand to silence any further protests.

Taken aback by his reaction just as much as the two brothers, Benjamin explained, "I have come to escort you to where they await you, sir. Perhaps, Jonathan and Jamie could accompany you? For no doubt you will need protection upon the return journey."

"If there is to be one," muttered Jamie.

Benjamin ignored him. "Shadiz has ordered me to make it plain to you, sir. He gives you his word. Your wife and daughter are safe. And will remain so."

"That," answered Sir Thomas Fairfax, "is good enough for me. Let us depart forthwith, gentlemen."

★ ★ ★

Carrying various size vessels destined for replenishment at the well, Catherine headed for the rear pasture. She was accompanied by Keeble and Mary, both similarly laden.

Clanking around a ragged clump of hawthorn bushes, she almost fell over Shadiz, who was sitting cross-legged on the grass. His arm shot out and steadied her before she toppled onto the wicked-looking broadsword he was sharpening.

His irritated expression turned to one of dark amusement as Catherine, muttering a few choice words, struggled to regain her hold on the pots that threatened to descend on him. Only when she had sorted herself out did he release her. There had been strength in his hold and yet enough gentleness not to have left a mark on her arm. He resumed his sharpening of the broadsword.

Keeble and Mary had continued to the well. Catherine was about to follow when Shadiz, asked in his customary whispery tone, "Satisfied?"

She knew immediately he was referring to the Fairfax family being reunited. "Very," she replied, her humour instantly changing.

Acting spontaneously, she planted a kiss on the top of his head. Straightening, she was pleased with herself for yet again not showering him with her difficult load.

His sharpening action arrested, Shadiz's long black hair fell away from his face.

The undisguised anguish in his black eyes promptly wiped the smile from Catherine's face and took her breath away. While she stood frozen, totally nonplussed by his reaction to her impulsive appreciation, he rose soundlessly in one fluid movement and then was gone, leaving her staring after him.

★ ★ ★

Lady Anne Fairfax entered the cosy, candlelit parlour. Weary after the trials of the past week, she was only too pleased to sit at ease in the house her husband had commandeered for his family upon their arrival at Hull. He had characteristically chosen one that had been vacated some time previously by an alderman with self-preservation in mind. With a grateful sigh, she sank down into a high-backed chair beside the warming fire. Laying her grey head against the polished wood, she closed her eyes and relived in thoughts the journey of freedom.

Although it had been without incident, there had been the ever-present threat of an unwanted encounter, even on the isolated byways that Thomas and Jonathan and Jamie Muir had all felt safer taking. They never caught a glimpse of the gypsies who had apparently shadowed their progress until the walls of Hull had appeared in the distance. Then a well-armed nomad had materialised before them, bowed to Thomas and vanished again.

Thoughts of their sinister leader sent a cold shiver down her spine. She still found it hard to believe that her husband was acquainted with the gypsy. Yet it had been quite apparent upon their meeting at the rendezvous north of York that they were no strangers to one another.

The door of the parlour opened. Sir Thomas entered the quiet chamber and immediately crossed to his wife. "Are you not feeling well, my dearest?" he asked, his noble countenance creased with concern.

She opened her eyes and gave him a wane smile.

Crouching down beside her chair, he covered her hand. "How is Moll?"

Lady Anne smiled. "Sleeping peacefully."

"She is well?"

"Thanks to Catherine," she answered, thoughtfully.

"Verity's daughter?"

"Indeed." Her expression changed to one of censure. "Relieved as I am to be reunited with you, husband. I must say, I am displeased with you."

"How so, my dearest?"

"When you arrived to collect Moll and I, the impression I received was that you were familiar with that gypsy. Can this be so?"

Sir Thomas sighed. "Yes, my dearest."

She gripped his uninjured hand with something akin to urgency. "Why on earth would you have dealings with such a savage creature?"

"I realise you must find him … different," he answered, evasively.

She shuddered, saying softly, "One side of his face looks as if he should be in Hell and the other side appears as if its flames have branded him." Taking her cue from her husband's expression, she went on, "You have not seen the disfigurement before?"

Sir Thomas shook his head. "No, I have not," he admitted.

His wife broke into his speculative thoughts. "Thomas, you must extract Catherine from his clutches."

"My dearest, I have no jurisdiction over him," he answered, mildly, "I very much doubt anyone has."

"That is precisely why she must be helped. She is such a dear, sweet child; younger than Moll. Whatever was her father thinking, if he were capable of thinking correctly at the time of his death. Benjamin is also at that derelict place, though I know not why. Perhaps, he can be prevailed upon to assist you in spiriting her away. He has always thought highly of you."

Sir Thomas considered her patiently. "Tell me again how Shadiz spoke of her."

"He tried to claim Catherine was under his protection," she said, doubtful in the extreme. "He said he had promised her dying father, Sir Roger Verity. But who on earth would trust his word?"

"I do," admitted her husband. "Is not your presence here proof of the integrity of his word? Granted, he probably does not give it often. When it is, I can assure you, it can be relied upon, my dearest."

CHAPTER SEVEN

The Seeds Already Sown

" 'ow's Catherine?" asked Tom upon meeting Mary coming out of the kitchen.

"Feelin' a might better, sir."

"What ails 'er?"

Mary took one look at the Master and promptly fled down the narrow passageway leading to the stone staircase.

"Tis monthly curse," explained Tom, turning stiffly towards his young leader.

Shadiz grunted and swung smartly away.

Tom chuckled quietly to himself. It had been a long, long time since he had seen the lad's colour rise.

★ ★ ★

"If I could just show you?" said Catherine to her group of helpers, willing or otherwise. "I've marked out the square to be dug over. It's not that big, really." She pulled a face, a mixture of an ingratiating expression and hope. "If you wouldn't mind first clearing away the grass and the weeds. That way the soil will be less prone to sprouting all manner of unwanted visitors."

There were murmurs and nods of understanding.

"Right, then," she prompted, brightly, "shall we make a start?"

The inspiration had come to her during the night she had laid awake, listening to Bessie's rhythmic snoring. In an effort to stop herself from dwelling upon Shadiz's inexplicable reaction to her show of gratitude for reuniting Lady Anne and her daughter Moll with Sir Thomas Fairfax, she had tried to concentrate her unruly mind on her store of herbs. It was while performing a mental inventory that the inspiration had struck her. Why not create a herb garden in the rear pasture? She would have to find a spot away from where the Master's men practised and the enclosure where the horses grazed. And it would have to be protected from the busy hens. Fortunately, the broad, grassy clearing to the rear of the Lodge, bordered on three sides by the stable block and other outbuildings, was large enough to accommodate the needs of everyone. Close to the kitchen seemed to be her best option.

The next day, while the spring sunshine boded well for her venture, dappling the young leaves of the surrounding forest, she had enlisted the help of Mary and Keeble, Bill Todd and Danny Murphy.

The Master had appointed Todd, the heavyset, jovial brother of the bo's'un of the *Eagle*, and the lean, taciturn Murphy as her temporary protectors after he had given Junno leave to visit his son when tidings had reached the Lodge of Peter's fall from an unbroken horse he should not have been anywhere near.

"I used t' 'elp out in a garden," Keeble said, dreamily, to no one in particular. "She'd lovely roses."

"Who did?" asked Mary, shyly.

The little man's large head came up. Appearing embarrassed, he glanced around at his fellow workers. Confronted by their grins, he shrugged his crooked shoulders. "She was very lovely, like her roses," he admitted with an awkward little laugh.

"Y' full o' surprises," commented Bill Todd, merrily, getting on with his digging.

"May I join in?"

Catherine paused in her battle with a stubborn weed. "Oh, hullo," she said, smiling up at Richard. "If you're feeling up to it, by all means. All help gratefully received."

While he picked up a trowel and, sinking to his knees beside her, set to work, she explained her intention, at the same time assessing his ability to undertake physical labour. He had not been well of late, having caught yet another cold, which had made his chesty cough worse, obliging her to administer coltsfoot.

Nowadays, beg, steal or borrow, she always made sure she had a good supply of the herb that when turned upside down had a striking resemblance to a foal's slender leg and hoof.

"Y' all look busy," observed Tom, coming up behind them. He was leaning heavily upon the stick Junno had fashioned for him out of a length of stout oak. He, too, had not been well of late. Earlier that morning, in an effort to ease the ache in his swollen joints, Catherine had given him an infusion of bogbean and meadowsweet, adhering to the adage, *It made old men young*'. She had also given him a separate infusion of foxglove for the nagging pain in his chest he had finally admitted to. Smiling down at her, he listened while she outlined her plan for a herb garden. "It be warm work," he commented, glancing up at the cloudless blue sky above the broad, forest clearing. "I'll fetch y' all mugs o' summat."

Catherine watched his slower than usual progress to the kitchen's open door. "Richard, how old do you consider Tom to be?" She wiped away a strand of hair from her eyes that had escaped her long braid, leaving a streak of dirt across her cheek.

Richard paused in slicing up tufts of grass. Sitting back on his heels, he gently brushed the soil from her face. "Well, he was one of my father's farm stewards a while before I was born," he said, his direct gaze eloquent.

"Was he really," replied Catherine, her manner carefully noncommittal.

"He lived and worked on Fylingdales for many years, with his wife, Janet."

"I see," she murmured, resuming her self-appointed task. Tom had spoken to her about his late wife and their farm, but never mentioned that it had been part of the Fylingdales Estate. "So, it would be fair to say he's…" She pulled a cautious face. "… getting on a bit?"

"Long in the tooth, he would put it," remarked Richard, grinning. "He does remarkably well."

"I worry about him," she admitted, digging so strenuously she bent her trowel.

"I worry about you," stated Richard.

178

"Oh, I'm fine," Catherine responded, offering a cheerful reassurance in the hope it would stem an awkward outpouring. "My father always maintains … maintained life's too short to worry about what might have been. Get on with the need to be."

Richard stopped working again, his smile wistful. "I would liked to have known your father." When he saw Danny Murphy taking an interest in their conversation, he resumed the attack on the tough grass. "He would surely have failed to condone your presence in this place," he added, grimly.

"Oh, Richard," she said with a patient sigh. "We've had this conversation before. No doubt I will one day return to Nafferton Garth." She experienced a sudden pang of loss.

"And Shadiz remain your guardian?" he queried.

When she did returned home, would Shadiz still consider himself to be her guardian? Would he visit her? She thought not.

"My father wished him to be my guardian. And I have always trusted my father's judgement. Besides, Shadiz has not done a bad job … considering."

"Considering…." Richard broke off. Apart from emitting a chesty cough, he was silent for awhile. Eventually, he asked, "You enjoyed your visit to Whitby?"

"To be sure. I went to the market with Laura and the girls, searched for fossils on the shore with them. Even went sailing. H'm, it was good."

"Would you care to reside there?"

She was jerked out of her brief reverie by Richard's unexpected question. "Can you see the Master allowing that to happen?" she countered, trying to keep the conversation from descending into thorny territory, rather like the one they were presently tackling . "It took an enormous amount of cajolery for a short visit." She was loathed to mention his detention at the Lodge during her time at the port.

"Laura and her daughters would love to have you stay with them on a permanent basis," he continued, undeterred, "Or, there is always the Abbey House. Lady Cholmley would welcome your company, especially with Sir Hugh presently the commander of Scarborough Castle."

"Do you know, I'm sure one of the books brought from home has a chapter upon how the monks set out their herb garden at Easby Abbey."

"Catherine, are you listening to what I'm saying?" he muttered, sharply.

"Richard, I'm going nowhere," she declared. "Besides, I've grown quite fond of the old stones," she added, surveying the rear of the ramshackle Lodge. She did not mention that the old stones seemed curiously hollow when the Master was away as he was at present.

Danny Murphy had started to wield his spade close to where Catherine and Richard were working.

Eventually, Richard broke the uneasy silence that had developed between them. "He doesn't trust me."

She knew immediately to whom he referred. "The running battles make that glaringly obvious," she replied, regretfully. Glancing sideward, she saw his expression harden. He stopped digging and stared into the middle distance. "You must not allow him to goad you," she urged, gently.

With a frustrated sigh, he straightened. His cough erupted and got the better of him.

Catherine rose also. Ignoring Danny Murphy's pointed scowl, she put a sympathetic hand on Richard's arm.

Breathless, he muttered, "He believes me to be contemplating ways of smuggling you away from here. Given half the chance, I would. No matter what you say, I am convinced, were he here, your father would thank me."

"If my father were here, I would not be," retorted Catherine. A thought struck her. For her own sake, she promptly dismissed it. She was flattered by Richard's feelings for her, yet they embarrassed her. Relenting in the face of his transparent emotions, she urged, "Please, Richard, do not do anything untoward."

A shadow of a smile passed over his lean, earnest face. "You are very special," he murmured, looking down at her.

Catherine offered him a comical grimace.

Danny swung his spade in their direction. With one accord, they both resumed work on another grassy yard.

"What of the future?" Richard asked, kneeling, emulating his half-brother's customary low-pitched tone.

"Oh, that will take care of itself," she muttered, extracting long rooted weeds out of the fertile soil.

They both worked on in silence. Then, Richard said, "I'll always be ready to care for you."

"Oh, look," exclaimed Catherine. "Here comes Tom with the promised refreshments. And a troupe of young helpers."

★ ★ ★

"Tom, *please*. Just sit down. Here, by the fire," coaxed Catherine with suppressed urgency. "There's no desperate hurry to change the guard. In fact, I'm certain it can change itself."

"I'll see t' it," said Danny Murphy, striding out of the kitchen, leaving Bill Todd hovering anxiously beside her.

They managed between them to settle Tom on the battered settle, Bessie's habitual perch beside the perpetual fire in the inglenook fireplace. The great, medieval kitchen was filled only by evening's hush, the women and their children having been escorted home to their own hearths.

Prey to an awful foreboding, Catherine watched Tom bend forward, gripping his chest. His craggy features were creased in agony. He had begun to sweat copiously.

Behind her, Mary shuffled, scared out of her wits. Without taking her attention away from Tom, holding onto his clammy hand, Catherine sent the girl to prepare foxglove, as she had taught her, ensuring that it was a larger dose than the one she had administered to him earlier in the day. She dispatched Keeble after Mary, giving the anxious little man something to occupy him.

"What ails 'im?" demanded Shadiz from the doorway.

There was an unfamiliar note in his low-pitched voice. Moving silently forward past Todd, the mastiff at his heels, he sank down onto his haunches close to where Catherine was kneeling beside the settle.

Tom tried and failed to give the attention he was receiving a gesture of dismissal.

Shadiz put a hand on the older man's tense arm. Catherine saw the gleam of keen assessment in his black eyes. "Easy, Father Time," he urged, softly.

Knowing he would want Bill to remain at her side, she asked, "Can you stay with him while I prepare the herbs?"

"Go," commanded Shadiz, motioning needlessly to Todd.

Scrambling to her feet, Catherine dashed out of the kitchen. A feeling akin to panic made her inwardly bemoan Mary's unskilled tardiness. She quickly got a grip of herself, fortified by Shadiz's timely appearance. He had been gone from the Lodge with a sizeable company of his men for some considerable time.

Not Tom.

The words drummed in her head as she took over from Mary's over-cautious attempts to infuse the herbs. He had come to mean so much to her since she had started to live at the Lodge.

She returned to the kitchen, careful not to spill any of the precious mixture in her haste. She found Shadiz had not moved. He was speaking quietly of mundane matters. Although rough-looking from his warring activities, the great broadsword upon his back and the scimitar at his hip, once again she sent up a silent prayer of thanks for his presence.

Upon bending down to him and gently calling his name, Tom looked at her with pain-blurred eyes. She assumed a tone of brisk confidence. "Now, if you can manage to drink this, it will help to relieve the pain. Tom?"

He nodded slowly, breathing with difficulty. Yet, however much he was willing to oblige her, it soon became apparent that he found it impossible to move, trapped in the grip of chest pains.

Shadiz shifted his position in order to lend support. Catherine held up the mug to Tom's blue-tinged lips. Between them, over the next few minutes, they made certain he drank the herbal potion. Afterwards, with great care, Shadiz lowered him back down in the fireside seat.

"Now what?" he asked, straightening, grim-faced; staying beside the settle.

"We wait," she murmured, watching Tom's agonising discomfort and praying the herbal potion would soon take affect.

Bill Todd left the kitchen as Keeble returned with the cover that Catherine had asked him to bring. While she wrapped the blanket from her bed around Tom, the little man sat down cross-legged close to the settle, staring up at his old friend, gently rocking to and fro.

Eventually, after a gruelling wait, Tom's breathing became easier. His aged hand gradually relaxed upon his chest. He gave a deep sigh. And slept.

"Go," the Master commanded Keeble, "make it known he is not to be disturbed."

Catherine exhaled ragged breath which seemed to have been pent up for hours.

Shadiz bent his dark gaze on her.

She nodded shakily in response to his unspoken question. She was trembling so much she was in danger of dropping the empty mug Tom had drank from. Saying nothing, Shadiz took it from her. She could not speak. It was the tears sparkling in her blue eyes that spoke volumes.

Catherine sensed Shadiz's hesitation. A second later, he placed an arm around her slumped shoulders. Desperate for his solace, she leant into him, breathing in his wild masculine scent mixed with the smell of smoke. "Not Tom...." she whispered, brokenly, "I could not bear...."

"Nowt'll 'appen so long as 'e's got you around," he said, giving her a reassuring squeeze. She stood quietly beneath his arm thankful for their nearness. It proved to be all too brief.

Voices coming from the rear pasture gave warning that the tidings of Tom's indisposition had not reached all of his men. His arm slipped away from her just before the companionable group entered the warmth of the huge kitchen. He stepped protectively in front of Catherine; all at once as hard as nails.

Seeing the Master's expression, quickly followed by the sight of Tom asleep beneath the blanket on the settle, brought the men up short. They were told in no uncertain terms, "Get what y' need, then get out." When Catherine made a move to assist them, Shadiz detained her by circling her wrist in a discreet grip.

After his men had left, nodding respectfully to her, she remembered that Shadiz had also just returned to the Lodge. "I'll prepare you a meal."

"Y' don't need t'," he objected, finally releasing her wrist.

She shrugged, yet again glancing at Tom's sleeping form. "I'm not going anywhere."

Moving away from him before he could protest further, she filled a trencher with chicken stew from the great black cauldron hung over the fire and sliced thick wedges of bread. After taking off his long leather coat and putting aside the broadsword, Shadiz poured himself a drink of water. He had ignored the stone ale jug on the large, well-scrubbed table. She had never seen him touch anything other than water all the time she had been at the Lodge.

Serving his meal after he had sat down on the bench beside the table in the middle of the kitchen, she gave him a quick warning, "Careful how you sit on that or else you'll go arse over tip."

He looked at her sharply. "Less o' that," he chided. His tone was at odds with the shadow of humour on his dark features.

"I was trying to be descriptive," pointed out Catherine. "To see you do such a thing would be a feat in itself."

Shadiz stood up .

Laughing, for she knew there was no threat in his manner, she backed away from him a couple of paces, holding up a defensive hand. Puzzled, she watched as he took sideward steps into isolation. He performed a forward somersault with fluid ease in spite of his powerful height. She was still staring at him in total wonder after he had resumed his seat and began to eat.

"Thought y'd like a bit o' entertainment," he commented, amusement in his black eyes.

"By showing me how light you are on your feet," responded Catherine, dryly.

"What else've y' picked up since comin' 'ere?"

"I brought a pocketful of dubious observation along with me," she admitted, ruefully. "My father used to berate me. I teach you all manner of text, he would say, and you spout kitchen vulgarity. *Les enfants terribles.*"

His genuine laughter startled her. "Just like Roger. 'e wanted everybody t' be scholars. *An' let a scholar all Earth's volume carry.*"

While he continued his meal, she wandered about the cat and dog strewn kitchen, giving a caress here and a tender word there. She knew that like Junno, he thought nothing of having dogs around but considered cats, matchkos, nothing short of vermin.

Shadiz washed down the last mouthful of stew with a drink of water. "'e dunt seem bad, now."

"True," she answered, following the direction of his gaze to Tom's sleeping form. "Foxglove is excellent for the relief of pain." After a moment's hesitation, she added, "And ... weak hearts." She felt the weight of his suddenly intense gaze upon her.

"What's up?" he asked, softly. "Kore?"

She wanted to ask him one question but, taking herself by surprise, instead she petitioned an answer for the question that had plagued her from the outset of their acquaintance. "Why do you use my middle name?"

★ ★ ★

He entered the library before retiring in search of an appropriate book, and discovered he had a visitor.

There was the usual searing thrill, akin to finding a wild creature in one's home. Yet, he was pleased to once again welcome the tall, dark man. And relieved. It had been a substantial length of time since the extraordinary fellow's last nocturnal visit to Nafferton Garth. He had begun to fear the worst.

It was his habit to never approach too close. But he knew his books, old friends every one, and, by dint of a little pert straining, could discern his visitor's choice.

"Ah, Hades," he murmured, "Lord of the Underworld."

His visitor looked up and grinned, whether in greeting or in confirmation, it was difficult to ascertain.

He went away in search of nourishment, and returned before long with fruit and water, knowing the man's preference.

"What has always intrigued me," he said, setting down the silver tray close to where the other man was standing, book in hand. "Whether or not Persephone's conduct was due to her eventual regard for Hades, or the welfare of the Earth, or her mother, Demeter's well being?"

The other man regarded him in enigmatic silence.

"I have often wondered if her other name, Kore, was not offered as a clue. Was it a derivative of her being? Was she, in fact, Hades's soul?" He smiled, shrugging his shoulders, feeling a might self-conscious. The fellow must think him addled-brained with such late night musing. "Just a thought," he added. "In any event, I consider Kore to be a pretty name. That is why, much to my late wife's dismay, I chose Kore as Catherine's middle name."

The goblet shattered in his visitor's hand.

★ ★ ★

Catherine awaited Shadiz's answer, aware that she would most likely not receive a truthful one. Or, indeed, one at all. He was looking her way but it was plain his thoughts were elsewhere. At length, he focused fully upon her young, hopeful face once again. "Roger considered Kore t' be a pretty name," he muttered, dismissively.

She had been right. Trying to get anywhere with him was like getting blood out of a stone. But she did have a far more pressing question. The one she had meant to voice in the first place. She continued to wander around the kitchen.

"What's this, a Barbary Roast?"

"What's that?"

"Y' don't want t' know." He sighed repressively, pushing his empty plate away. "What else y' got on that mind o' yours?"

"How old is Tom? Do you have any idea?"

186

"'ow old be me?"

"Y'r near enough four, lad."

" 'ow old be y'?"

"As old as me tongue an' a bit older than me teeth."

The black-eyed child frowned, bewildered.

The man laughed, swinging him up onto his shoulders and striding homewards. "I be the grand age o' thirty-four, m'lad. By 'eck, y'r gettin' a 'eavy lump."

★ ★ ★

"Father Time'll be about fifty-nine," Shadiz informed her, eventually. "Why?"

The draught prone candlelight shone on his motionless earring and her indecision. For Tom's sake she had to voice her doubts; her hopes. She stopped before Shadiz. Meeting his jet-black regard, she said, "I can only do so much for Tom, I'm afraid. And … I am afraid. I was wondering. He is in no condition to travel, as you no doubt have gathered. So … I was wondering if perhaps Mamma Petra could be persuaded to come here to see him." When he held his own counsel, being his usual fathomless self, she went on briskly, "She will no doubt have left the winter quarters at Nafferton Garth by now?" He nodded. "Well, could you prevail upon her to visit the Lodge."

Probably goaded by her pleading expression, he answered in a half-whisper, "She does 'er own biddin'. I ain't sure…."

"You could try," exclaimed Catherine, her primary concern being for Tom. "Her knowledge is far greater than mine." Rashly, she added, "You know this to be true."

"Do I?"

"Yes," she retorted, meeting his mesmerizing eyes unflinchingly.

After a brittle pause, he asked, "Y' reckon she'd cure what ails 'im?"

"He would stand a far better chance of recovery with her care."

187

"Two o' 'em don't exactly see eye t' eye?"

"I did not realise they were acquainted."

"Oh, aye. 'e believes 'er t' be a meddlin' old choviar, witch. An' 'e might've summat there. She believes 'e's a turpid. Translate that any way y' like." He shrugged. "If it'll 'elp Old Father Time," he said in final agreement.

"Less o' the old," muttered Tom, opening his eyes upon them.

"Tom!" Catherine exclaimed. Hurrying to him, she dropped lightly to her knees, the grass-stained skirt of her plain brown gown billowing out around her. Placing both hands upon his knees, she scrutinised him. "How are you feeling?"

His haggard face creased into a wane smile. "Better, luv," he reassured her. "Whatever y' give me, it did the trick."

"I'm so glad the potion helped," she said, happy to see him awake and, better still, not in pain.

His attention switched to Shadiz. "Lass can tak' care o' me well enough," he said, with unexpected forcefulness, "I don't want that old 'ag anywhere near me."

Curious about Shadiz's reaction, Catherine half-turned in his direction. His raised eyebrow underscored his recent warning. But, surely, she thought, looking from one to the other of the men, he could prevail upon Tom if it was in his best interest to have the White Witch attend him. Or was it a case of Shadiz not wanting to prevail upon his grandmother? Whatever the obstacle, she was worried. Although she was flattered by Tom's confidence in her, she was convinced he was in need of the White Witch's stronger medicine. It far exceeded her paltry knowledge.

"But, Tom."

"But nowt, luv," retorted Tom, emphatically. Seeing her downcast expression, he softened his manner. "Y'all I need t' keep me goin'."

Shadiz got to his feet and stretched. The mastiff followed his example. "Told 'er y' wouldn't entertain anyone else." He prepared to leave the kitchen, picking up his coat and broadsword from the stone-flagged floor.

"Benjamin's gone off t' see Prince," Tom told him, sitting

forward on the ancient settle. The effort left him somewhat breathless, but he continued, "'e's left y' out dispatches that've come while y' been gone."

"Will Prince Rupert allow Benjamin to join you here in Yorkshire, do you think?" asked Catherine. She continued to harbour a niggling doubt about Benjamin Farr. Not understanding why, she found the misgiving irksome whenever it raised its ugly head, for she quite liked the quiet, calm young man.

Shadiz gave her a quick, calculating look. "'e'll find Rupert's been victorious against Meldrum. So…."

"Meldrum?" broke in Tom, hastily. He took a breath. "D'y mean Newark's been relieved, lad?"

"Aye," replied Shadiz, leaning against the rough stone wall close to the large cooking hearth. "Rupert was at Chester, preparin' for Irish comin' t' England, an' recruitin' troops, mostly in Wales, when 'e got deluged by Charles's messages, orderin' 'im t' do summat about siege o' Newark. So, bein' the ever loyal nephew, right off, 'e marched for Newark wi' musketeers from Shrewsbury an' reinforcements from Midlands. An', o' course, wi' 'is cavalry."

"An' was successful," put in Tom, grinning, accepting a drink of mulled ale from Catherine.

"Meldrum didn't expect Rupert t' shift so bloody fast," observed Shadiz.

Catherine wondered if the Master's recent absence meant he and his men had played a part in the relief of Newark. During her time at the Lodge, she had learned, among other things, that on occasions Shadiz and Prince Rupert combined their exceptional, militaristic talents. Thinking out loud, she said, "The Parliamentarians consider Sir John Meldrum to be one of their finest commanders. Wasn't his intention to take Newark in order to sever King Charles's line of communications with the North?"

Shadiz's attention dropped like a polished stone upon her. She rearranged her woollen shawl beneath his jet scrutiny. Glancing at him through her lashes, rather than annoyance, his expression contained approval. And sparks of pride, she foolishly deceived herself.

Having noted the indulgence which characterised his leader's attitude towards Catherine, Tom felt safe in admitting, "She listens."

Shadiz's hard mouth twitched. "Summat else y' brought wi' y'."

Satisfied with the folds of her shawl, she looked up at him. "Twigging, I call it."

"Y' would," he commented, softly. "Well, whatever Meldrum's intentions. They come t' nowt. 'e lost a few thousand odd muskets, about as many pistols, most o' 'is ammunition, along wi' about thirty odd cannons. An' was sent packin' Hull way. Owt else you've been twiggin' o' late?"

"H'm," Catherine murmured, hoping to creep out of the corner in which she had inadvertently strayed. "There is always the threat posed by the Scots signing the Solemn League and Covenant with the English Parliament. That never did bode well for King Charles. Although, it has to be said, since they put their names to the document, and as a consequence gleefully crossed the Border into England, the weather has been their greatest enemy." She was warming to her subject. And seemed to be getting a fair hearing. "When they laid siege to Newcastle, they expected to encounter little resistance from either the place or its Lord, but that proved not to be the case, they discovered to their cost. They thus got themselves bogged down before the city walls and are having to rely heavily on supplies being shipped to them from Scotland via the North Sea. There is, after all, little or no help forthcoming from their vicinity. Newcastle has made quite certain of that by devastating the area. Unfortunately with the progression of the season and therefore an improvement in the weather are they likely to up-sticks and head our way?"

"Not if I've owt t' do wi' it," answered Shadiz, ominously.

"In a similar way to Newark, Yorkshire, where you hold sway, stands between the North and the South. Surely, therefore, you would be a prime target?" Catherine pointed out.

"I've allus been that ever since joinin' this damned farce," he commented, flatly. "Me aside, York's temptin' t' Scots, Crop-Ears. Bloody lot o' 'em."

From his seat by the fire, Tom looked up at his young leader. After a couple of irregular heartbeats, he averted his gaze for fear of being detected. Shadiz's unguarded expression brought about a heartrending pain not unlike the alarming one he had experienced in his chest a short time ago. It could not be dissolved by Catherine's herbal medicine. He looked at her. Did she realise the lad was becoming more and more at ease with her, far more than Tom had seen him with anyone, himself included? Did she have any idea as to the reason for the rapport? Despite her intelligence, her caring nature, her easy, affectionate manner, all of which had captivated everyone at the Lodge, she was still very young; innocent.

"Would the Scots attack York?" Catherine asked, apprehensively.

"Right now, they ain't likely t' entertain notion o' aimin' for York wi' Newcastle left undefeated at their backs," Shadiz reassured. "Besides, their quarters at Corbridge were raided an' prisoners an' weapons delivered t' Marmaduke Langdale, a fine upstandin' gentleman."

Matching his ironic tone, she exclaimed, "Oh, you have been busy!"

Softly laughing, the Master pushed himself away from the kitchen wall and started to stroll away.

Catherine called to him when she realised Tom was finding it a struggle to rise.

"Don't fret, luv," muttered Tom, frustrated by his weak condition.

Shadiz was already back beside them. "Come on, Father Time," he said in a jocular manner. "Let's get y' t' y'r bed."

Tom was hauled to his feet. Knowing the younger man's aversion to physical contact, once he was upright, albeit on shaky legs, Tom let go of Shadiz's arm. He was surprised when support continued to be given.

"My turn t' put y' t' bed," remarked Shadiz, grinning.

The barely audible words caught Tom off-guard at a vulnerable time. His smile was constructed out of memories, misted by the dust of years. Wistfully, he commented, "D' y' recall 'ow Janet've devil's own job wi' y'? Aye, especially on summer nights."

Stood by the settle, Catherine's interest was greatly spiked. Tom had spoken to her on many occasions about his late wife. She had never before heard him speak of Janet and Shadiz in the same breath.

Shadiz lifted his head and met her curious blue gaze. "Tom an' Janet reared me for first five years."

"After that," stated Tom bitterly, compounding the moment of revelation, "'e were left t' drag 'issen up."

Shadiz dispassionately quoted,

"An' so, from 'our t' 'our, we ripe an' ripe,
An' then from 'our t' 'our, we rot an' rot:
An' thereby 'angs a tale."

He would not leave her alone in the kitchen. From its worn threshold, he gave a piercing whistle, summoning Todd and Murphy.

Catherine stood with Tom, conscious of his need for support and his effort not to encumber her. While Shadiz was momentarily distracted, she tried again to persuade Tom to allow Mamma Petra to visit the Lodge on his behalf. Puzzled by his firm refusal, she asked, "I don't understand. Why do you harbour such bad feelings towards her? I realise she is a little odd. Well, incredibly odd. But, when all is said and done, she is Shadiz's grandmother."

"That's just it," retorted Tom in a fierce whisper. "Lad'd be better off wi'out 'er." He took a deep breath, a hand going to his chest. "Old 'ag's got some kind o' grip on 'im. I'm certain o' it."

Shadiz returned with his two dutiful men. He looked at Tom and Catherine in turn. "What's up?" he demanded.

Catherine felt Tom's pressure on her arm. "Nothing," she replied, brightly. "I was just telling him to take care." She pulled a longsuffering face. "And he wasn't well-suited."

As Tom and Shadiz started to make their way from the kitchen, of necessity at a slow pace, Keeble crept into view. The little rag-tag man gave a whoop of joy at seeing the improvement in Tom's health.

192

"Anybody'd reckon I'd been at death's door," grumbled Tom.

Catherine bit her lip. Keeble laughed, not at all put out by his friend's dour reaction. He hobbled after the two men, tossing a happy grin in her direction.

He was not the only one to look back at Catherine. Shadiz paused beside the flaring torch set in a sconce on the wall by the lop-sided door. Its flickering light illuminated in vivid detail his disfigured cheek. "What y' doin' now?"

"I'm going to tidy up here and in the herb chamber."

"Leave it t' tothers," he commanded.

She took exception to his arrogant tone. "I'm quite capable."

"It's late. Y' look worn out. Go t' y' chamber." When Catherine began to object a second time, he added, "Then y'll be close if Tom needs y'."

"I'm not bad now, lad," put in Tom.

Shadiz ignored him. He met Catherine's irritated look with an impervious black stare.

"Y' do look tired, luv," Tom told her.

"So be it," she declared, not immune to his silent plea.

Shortly after entering her chamber, there came a polite knock on the door. Mary opened it. Seeing the girl's expression, Catherine approached the door aware of who was standing there. Head down, Mary scurried back into the chamber, leaving her mistress to face the Master.

Catherine glimpsed Bill and Danny lounging at the head of the gloomy stairs. Her stiff attention returned to Shadiz. She kept silent, still fuming over his high-handed attitude.

"Forgive me." He shrugged. "I just want y' t' rest." His quiet honesty took her by surprise

"As you pointed out, I am close to Tom in my chamber."

He nodded. And seemed curiously reluctant to walk away. He stirred restlessly, glancing at his two men. Their attention seemed to be directed elsewhere.

Catherine looked expectantly at him. "Was there anything else? Is Tom settled for the night?" she asked, awkwardly.

"Aye. 'e seems all right," he assured her, his distinct voice pitched low. He stood without speaking for a couple of moments, scowling into the middle distance. Then he turned to her. "Y' not t' fret."

"I'll try not to," she answered, her heart pounding. She was held fast by the odd, searching expression in his direct gaze.

Bessie's querulous voice calling from within the chamber ended the curious pause. Released, Catherine smiled. "Well, er … I bid you goodnight." She was loathed to do so.

He nodded, and made to go and then turned back to her. "You're well guarded."

"I know. Thank you," she answered with a smile.

As he nodded again and made to go a second time, Catherine hesitated before, murmuring in a detaining manner, "Er…" Upon him responding, she said, "You look tired yourself." While in the kitchen she had noticed the telltale signs of lack of sleep. Uncomfortable with his guarded silence, she went on, "I could prepare a sleeping draught, if you wish?"

"Not poppy, nor mandragora
Nor all the drowsy syrup of the world,
Shall ever medicine thee to that sweet sleep."

After quoting Shakespeare, he gave her an enigmatic smile. "No thank you."

PART THREE

EARLY SUMMER

"Follow thy fair sun, unhappy shadow,
Though thou be black as night,
And she made all of light."

CHAPTER ONE

No Man is an Island

'Fine knacks for ladies, cheap, choice, brave and new.
Good pennyworth, but money cannot move.
I keep a fair but for the Fair to view;
A beggar may be liberal of love.
Though all my wares be trash, the heart is true.'

"Missy? Be y' alright. Missy? You've gone reet pale!" exclaimed Mary, distressed.

"Though all my wares be trash...."

Catherine had been wrenched back to when she had been concealed, with Shadiz, in the *Eagle's* secret hold earlier in the year, when he had quoted the line of poetry he had failed to finish. Her quick recovery was due to Mary's nervous disposition. She did not want the girl dashing off in panic and disturbing Tom in the neighbouring chamber. "H'm. I'm just a little weary," she assured with calm duplicity, closing the book of poetry with a shaky hand.

Outside, Stillingfleet Forest was alive with wind and rain. Branches could be heard creaking ominously. Fresh spring leaves were giving a fair imitation of a storm tossed sea as the vibrant air raked through them. The strong wind moaned with eerie shrillness around the Lodge while the heavy rain beat down upon the renovated fossil. Stony cracks were overflowing leaks, grassy hollows were becoming deep pools and soaked men on guard duty among the dripping forest canopy were growing increasingly depressed as the inclement day crawled by.

Better off by far, while Bessie enjoyed her afternoon nap, Catherine and Mary sat before the small, glowing hearth in

Catherine's chamber, made cosy by the possessions her guardian had transported for her from Nafferton Garth.

They had just concluded another of Mary's reading lessons. Making good progress, she was fascinated by Catherine's collection of books. Picking up one of them from the sheepskin rug, frowning in concentration, she deciphered the title with her newfound knowledge. "A ... d ... es."

"Hades," prompted Catherine, kindly.

Upon opening the leather bound book, Mary stared at the drawing to which a random flick of the pages had brought her. Her eyes widened in apprehension. "'e looks mighty fierce."

Catherine laughed. "Hades is the god all mortals encounter upon death according to Greek mythology. They pay Charon the ferryman one obol to row them across the River Styx to the Underworld."

A shudder passed through Mary's thin frame. She snapped the book shut as if attempting to trap the myth within. More closer to home, she came from a community in which dark tales of the moors abounded.

Catherine took the book from her and began to leaf through the well-turned pages. "Hades is a much maligned god. Contrary to popular belief, his realm is a just one. Only those who behave with great impropriety during their lives have reason in death to fear the wrath of his judgement. They are mainly the souls who are consigned to Tartarus." She came to a page showing a drawing of a young woman.

"Who be that?" asked Mary, twisting around to get a better look.

"She is Persephone," explained Catherine, "Hades snatched her from her mother, Demeter, the goddess of the fruitful earth. He carried her off to his kingdom and wed her."

"Were she in love wi' 'im?" Mary wanted to know in a shy manner.

"Not to begin with," replied Catherine, reflectively. "She hated him for what he had forced upon her. In time, her love for him blossomed."

"An' did they live 'appily ever after? Fanny Rice says a good tale allus 'as 'appy endin'."

Smiling, Catherine went on, "When Demeter could not be persuaded to end her mourning for her daughter, which had plunged the earth into barrenness and famine, Zeus, Hades's brother, intervened. When it was discovered that Persephone had eaten the seeds of a pomegranate, the food of the dead, tying her irrevocably to the Lord of the Underworld, Zeus forced a compromise. Persephone would spend eight months of the year with her mother, Demeter, and in that time the earth would prosper. The rest of the year she would live with Hades in his domain."

"When it be winter!" put in Mary, enthusiastically.

"Exactly."

"When did Per ... see."

"Persephone," supplied Catherine.

" She'd a queer name," commented Mary.

"She is also known as Kore. The Maiden."

Mary's narrow, pasty face was elongated by a startled expression. "But ... that be what I've 'eard Master call y'," she whispered, fearfully, glancing to where the door stood closed in shadow.

"I can only presume my father must have mentioned my middle name to him at some point," Catherine remarked, glancing at the portrait of her dead father, hung upon the ancient stone wall. She came across the page Mary had seen moments before. Staring down at the artist's impression of the god, Hades, she continued, "My father wished to name me Kore. However, my mother, would not hear of it being my first Christian name. Like Hades and Demeter, they came to a compromise. I was called Catherine after my maternal grandmother and given Kore as my middle name. Only my father ... and my guardian ... have used it."

Mary switched from Catherine to the drawing. "Y' know, 'e looks like Master," she whispered, in fascinated horror.

"H'm," responded Catherine.

'I am what I am.'

Once again Shadiz's words echoed. Catherine closed the book. "Enough of myths for one day." She stood upright, trying to ignore the quiver within. "I'll just go and see how Tom is doing," she announced, gesturing for Mary to stay where she was.

"Tom be alright, ain't 'e, missy?"

"Yes, of course he is," answered Catherine, emphatically. "He just needs a little rest. I think he must have been overdoing things of late."

Stepping out onto the narrow landing, she found Bill Todd and Danny Murphy still on guard. Leaning against the wall close to the wildly flickering torch jammed into an old sconce, they were surrounded by weird shadows that briefly reminded her of myths from forgotten places.

She liked Bill Todd. His humorous view of life was highly entertaining. She wasn't so sure about Danny Murphy. There was no doubting his efficiency. The trouble with him was that she could sense nothing beyond his hard-shelled reserve.

Catherine smiled at the two men, who had broken off from talking quietly together at sight of her coming out of her chamber. "Just going to look in on Tom," she told them, pulling her shawl tightly about herself to ward off the cold air prevalent on the landing.

Shortly after entering Tom's chamber, where he had remained on her advice since the previous evening when Shadiz had escorted him to his bed, they both heard Richard's voice raised in anger. After exchanging dismayed looks, while Tom sat forward in the bed, Catherine quickly retraced her footsteps.

Upon opening the door, it became immediately apparent to her that the atmosphere on the landing was charged with tension. Danny Murphy had Richard pinned against the shadowy wall, a restraining arm across the other man's thin shoulders. Bill Todd was beside the two men, trying to go about his duty in a more conciliatory manner.

Catherine prevailed upon Richard to desist in his furious resistance. Danny Murphy remained muzzled by a grim determination to detain Richard.

At the head of the stairs, Keeble stood arrested by the confrontation, the plate and mug destined for Tom forgotten in his small hands. His large face reflected his surprise, and a trace of smugness. Suddenly, his expression altered.

"Tom!"

The startled exclamation penetrated the commotion. Everyone cast quizzical looks in the little man's direction, and then followed his anxious gaze to Tom's blanketed appearance in the doorway of his chamber.

Catherine went to him, disconcerted by his presence. Exerting reassuring pressure on her hand upon his arm, he sought the reason for the disturbance.

"I simply wished to visit your chamber in order to inquire about your health," Richard explained, angrily. He again tried to escape Danny Murphy's grasp. Murphy responded with a corresponding measure of aggression. Whereupon, Bill Todd attempted to use his bulk to muscle-in between the two slimmer men.

"Enough, you lot."

An uneasy lull followed Tom's exasperate command. He looked questioningly at Bill Todd. But Richard didn't need Bill's awkward explanation, having recognised the Master's malicious influence.

"Well, y'd best come in, anyways," muttered Tom, looking tired and drawn, "I ain't standin' 'ere any longer. This place is full o' flamin' draughts."

Catherine saw Richard stiffen, furious resentment clearly uppermost in his mind when Bill looked uncertain how best to proceed. Warned by her reluctance to follow him back into his chamber, Tom returned his weary attention to the three men. "If it be like that, one o' y' come in wi' 'im, for god's sake."

Danny Murphy retreated from Richard with an antagonistic look. "Y' go," he told Bill, curtly.

Richard finally entered Tom's bedchamber, followed by Bill Todd, who henceforth remained against the closed door, barely visible at the borderline of the candlelight.

Catherine poured Richard a drink of water from a flagon she had previously brought for Tom and took the full mug to where he was standing beside the lively hearth, trying to control a fit of coughing. "Are you...."

"Well enough," snapped Richard, hoarsely, accepting the old mug. He drank while she made a point of watching Keeble serve Tom his meagre meal.

"I'm sorry," he said, handing back the empty vessel, "That fiasco was none of your doing. Why on earth should I inflict my rancour upon you?"

"Lads're just doin' what they've been told t'," put in Tom from the bed.

"By that black-hearted." Richard broke off. He took a calming breath. "Again, I apologise," he added, looking towards Catherine.

"No need," she dismissed, moving away. She supported Keeble in his efforts to persuade Tom to eat a little of the fresh baked biscuits and cheese.

Richard walked up and stood beside the bed. "May I *now* inquire after your health?"

"Not so bad, lad. Thanks t' dear lass, 'ere," Tom responded, taking hold of Catherine's hand.

Her thoughts were elsewhere.

"Luv?" questioned Tom.

"I have often wondered," she began, self-consciously. "This is your chamber. Richard has another. And I occupy the one in between. The other two are used to accommodate supplies, ammunition and goodness knows what else."

"Plunder," put in Richard.

Ignoring his sour interruption, Catherine continued, "Where does Shadiz go at night? Into the hall?"

"He visits his latest wh ... mistress," suggested Richard.

" 'e ain't got one," Tom was quick to point out, glancing at Catherine, " 'e gave up 'is chamber for you, luv. Not that he used it much. 'e's allus been one fer not much sleep."

"No doubt he kept you and your wife on your toes when he was young," she commented, with a wise grin.

Immediately, Richard's attention snapped around to her. Frowning, he then scrutinised Tom.

The older man answered the unspoken demand in a defiant tone of voice. "Lad told 'er 'issen. 'ow me an' Janet brought 'im up fer first few years." After the briefest of hesitations, he went on, "An', I intend to tell 'er more."

"You cannot," objected Richard with all his might. "She does not need to know anything about him," he continued, almost choking on the bitter words.

"Yes, I do," Catherine put in, emphatically.

"He is nothing but a murderer. And a ravisher of innocence."

"No one is entirely black, Richard. Nor is anyone scrupulously white. There are only different measures of grey," she replied, quietly. The memory of a carnage strewn harbour blighted her words that had captured the attention of the men.

"Whatever y' may think, lad," commented Tom, ending the thoughtful pause. "I don't see owt wrong in tellin' dear lass."

"I don't, as well," piped up Keeble. He glared at Richard from where he sat cross-legged on the bed at the opposite side of Tom to Catherine.

"So," said Tom, laying back on the stacked pillows, "leave if y' don't want t' 'ear what I've got t' say. Either that, or 'od y'r row."

Richard shook his head in dismay. Frustration quickened his footsteps as he turned away from the bed. Yet, instead of leaving the bedchamber, he strode back to the small, stone hearth. Thereafter, he stood in critical silence, his back turned upon the other occupants, staring at the sunset flames dancing on the sacrificial logs taken from the forest.

"Now we've got that sorted," muttered Tom.

He was interrupted by Bill Todd. "Tom, I ain't able t' leave alone," he pointed out, stepping into the candlelight. "An' if y' don't want me t' 'ear what you've got t' say?" He glanced at Richard's stiff back with discernible unease.

"Aye, well. I reckon y'll know a good lot o' tale. Them bits y' ain't 'eard afore, I'd ask y' t' keep 'em fer Miss Catherine's ears alone," Tom replied, knowing the other man to be trustworthy.

Looking relieved, Bill nodded and disappeared back into the shadows.

"What about me?" asked Keeble.

Tom looked at the little man in surprise. "You've earned y' place 'ere, old friend." He sighed. "Now, where do I begin?" he murmured.

"Ab incunabilis," suggested Catherine, tucking her legs beneath her on the bed.

Tom frowned.

"From the cradle," Richard translated, unexpectedly, from his place by the fire. He turned to face them, but said no more.

Tom shook his grey head. "Nay. Afore that. Crib were left empty." His eyes grew misty as he allowed himself to be guided by the hand of time. "Twenty odd year ago. Oh, it'll be well over that. 'ow old be y', lad?"

"Twenty-three," answered Richard, sitting down in the tapestry-backed chair that Catherine had insisted Tom have in his chamber.

"About twenty-eight years, then," stated Tom, mildly surprised. "Tis true what they say. Time flies, alright. Anyways. In them days, I lived an' worked on Fylingdales Estate. Me wife, Janet, 'elped out at 'all. Lord Richard liked t' run what Bob'd call a tight ship. Don't get me wrong. 'e were a fair man. A good, strong man. 'e did 'ave one weakness, though. She lived wi' 'im at the 'all. Aye, Gianca were a beauty, right enough, wi' eyes t' bewitch any man."

"*Gianca?*" exclaimed Catherine, stunned.

"Yes, Gianca," muttered Richard.

"Y've 'eard name afore?" asked Tom, sharply. "Aye, o' course. Bob told me."

She glanced at Richard's set features. "When Shadiz was feverish on board the *Eagle*."

"So lad did say 'er name, then," mused Tom, "I thought Bob'd mis'eard."

"He heard correctly," answered Richard, tersely.

"Aye, well," resumed Tom, "'is Lordship would've given that Romany lass the moon if it'd been 'is t' give. 'e wanted t' wed 'er, no matter what anybody said. An' there be much said about it, on quiet, like. But, accordin' t' my Janet, Gianca kept refusin' 'is offer. Summat made lass say no, even when 'is Lordship found out she were carryin' 'is bairn. It weren't fer lack o' love fer 'im. She returned 'is feelin' tenfold. But when lass's time come…" Tom sadly shook his head. "Well, as they often do, things didn't go well. Not well, at all. Poor Gianca lived only long enough t' give 'er son a name."

"Shadiz," murmured Catherine, softly.

"Nay, luv." Tom hesitated. Then he added, "Sebastian."

"Sebastian," she repeated, savouring the name.

"Aye. Shadiz's lad's Romany name. It were given t' 'im by 'is grandmother, accordin' t' Junno."

"I see. I think," she murmured.

"Y' might when y' 'ear rest o' what I've got t' say." Tom became stern. "Y' not t' use it on 'im, lass. Ever." He turned his attention to Richard. "Y' knew it?"

The younger man shook his head.

Tom appeared momentarily to regret his decision to divulge the precious secret. "Y' use it an' 'e'll kill y'," he warned, bluntly. "Y' 'ear?"

Richard slowly nodded.

Hopeful that the younger man might heed him, Tom continued. "It were biggest shame. Lass'd been so full o' life. An' now she were gone." He sighed reflectively. "'is Lordship were beside 'issen wi' grief. Nobody could make 'im understand danger t' 'is son. All 'e really knew was that 'e'd lost Gianca. In finish, Janet carried bairn t' our farmhouse.

"When 'e did finally get 'od o' 'issen, 'is Lordship wouldn't set foot in our 'ome t' see 'is son. 'e told us we could bring up bairn so long as 'e were kept out o' 'is way. Y' see, Janet an' me, we'd no family. So, despite circumstances, we were over moon. As bairn grew, we told 'im not to fret cos we weren't 'is true family. That we loved 'im all same. We were goin' t' tell 'im about 'is Lordship an' Gianca when he were older. We weren't given chance.

"Y' see in time, I suppose 'is Lordship came t' realise 'e needed an 'eir. A legitimate one. So, about two years after Gianca's death, 'e wed a French woman, 'ellena somethin' or other. 'e'd met 'er when 'e escorted Queen 'enrietta Maria on a visit t' 'er family over there.

"T' give Lady 'ellena 'er due, she must've found a big difference when she come t' Fylingdales after the fancy places she'd been at previously. Not that 'all weren't, ain't, grand. It were clear from start she thought world o' 'is Lordship. I ain't so sure about 'im. An' it weren't mine or anybody else's place t' know.

"Anyways. Life went on as usual. That's until Lady 'ellena were wi' bairn. That's when trouble started. She found out about lad bein' wi' us. Even though 'is Lordship never bothered about 'is son, she demanded 'e get rid o' 'im. French woman's obsession grew each month she were carryin' bairn until physician warned 'is Lordship she were in danger o' losin' it, accordin' t' Janet.

"In end, 'e gave in t' 'er demands. 'e made arrangements fer lad t' go live wi' 'is sister at York. Twas an 'eartbreakin' time fer me an' Janet. We begged 'is Lordship t' be allowed t' take bairn away from Fylingdales. We promised t' leave area altogether. As a family. 'is Lordship wouldn't 'ear o' it. I still ain't sure why.

"'ow d' y' tell a five year old 'e 'as t' leave all 'e's ever known? Moors, sea, beasts in fields an' what 'e took t' be 'is family." Tom shook his head. The bright ache of tears was in his brown eyes. He looked at Catherine and gave her a thin smile as she took his hand in hers. Her own blue gaze shone with unshed tears. "We never stopped tryin' t' change 'is Lordship's mind right up t' time bairn were taken from us. I'll not forget that day as long as I live." He fell silent, gazing into the middle distance, haunted by the tinder-dry past. Catherine increased the physical pressure of her commiseration. In truth, she could not speak for the lump in her throat.

"Janet were never same. She'd been given a little soul t' tend an' then 'ad it torn from 'er. She never stopped frettin' fer 'im. We both knew lad weren't meant fer a place like York. 'e were a wild spirit even in those days. We weren't far wrong. Just two months after 'e'd gone from Fylingdales tidin' came o' 'is disappearance from 'is Lordship's sister's 'ouse. The searches found nowt. Mine didn't, either. I scoured York. It were no good. We clung t' 'ope bairn'd find a way back to us. Only, months turned into years, an' still there were no word o' 'im.

"Janet never did set eyes on lad again. Bless 'er. But I did. One night, about a month after I'd laid 'er t' rest, I were sittin' by fire, broodin', when I slowly got feelin' I weren't by mesen anymore. I turned an' there 'e be, after all them years o' wonderin', just standin' there near t' door, watchin' me. 'e'd got into place wi'out a sound.

Lad were ... a stranger, I suppose. Then 'e grinned at me. An' 'e looked so like 'is ma. 'er wild, dark colourin'. 'er eyes. Just ... so much.

"Anyways, that night were summat like today, wet an' windy. Me an' lad'd been talkin' fer a while when next thing I knew, 'is Lordship were stridin' into me cottage tellin' me about collapsed fences an' stock roamin'. When 'e caught sight o' lad, 'e looked like 'e'd seen a ghost. If lad were as shocked as 'is da, 'e didn't show it.

"O' course, 'is Lordship recognised lad, wi'out a doubt. There were no mistaking them black eyes. Summat seemed to snap inside o' 'im. 'e started rantin' on about 'ow lad was foulin' Fylingdales by 'is presence. 'e accused me o' 'arbourin' gypsy vermin. Lad never said one word in 'is own defence. I'll never forget way 'e just stood there while 'is da called 'im all filthy names 'e could lay tongue t'. 'e even went s' far as sayin' lad murdered Gianca. Oh, God. Then 'e marched for'ads an', afore I knew it, 'e 'it lad wi' such force 'e knocked 'im flyin'. An' 'e wouldn't give over."

Tom sighed, a lifetime's worth of regret. "If lad ain't been pushed t' defendin' 'issen, I swear t' y', 'e wouldn't've got out me cottage alive. An' then, all 'e did were shove 'is da away afore 'e could use 'is sword on 'im. 'is Lordship lost 'is balance an' fell back on hearthstone. 'e passed away right there in front o' us. I swear t' y', an' God Almighty, it were accident. If owt, twas 'is Lordship's own fault."

"Oh, no!" cried Catherine, dismayed.

"Aye, luv. Lad were ... I ain't sure. Sort o' odd. I begged 'im t' go, get away. 'e wouldn't listen. Instead 'e took 'is da up t' 'all. I ain't a clue what took Lady 'ellena's breath away most. The sight o' lad or 'er dead 'usband in 'is arms.

"I tried tellin' 'er what'd 'appened'd been accident. I ain't got far afore French woman flew, screamin', at lad. That scar across 'is cheek, it were 'er doin' that night. 'e tossed 'er away an' were leavin' 'all when Richard come downstairs. 'ow old would y' be, lad?"

"Ten." Came the curt reply.

"Aye, y' would be," agreed Tom, continuing, "Richard'd no notion o' 'is 'alf-brother. Lad soon put that t' rights, tellin' 'im

207

everythin'. Poor Richard just stared at 'im, 'is 'alf-brother, an' then at 'is dead da. After that, Lady 'ellena screamed at menfolk who'd gathered in 'all to keep lad from goin'. When they tried, lad took down 'alf a dozen in no time. Rest thought better o' it.

"After lad'd gone, Lady 'ellena accused me o' 'elpin' 'im t' murder Lord Richard. She was nigh hysterical. I tried defendin' mesen. Tried t' make 'er understand 'er 'usband's death'd been a terrible accident. It were no use. I fled afore she made me a scapegoat."

Tom shrugged forlornly. "The next few years weren't much. I wondered about a bit, mostly in these parts. I was always careful t' keep me distance from Fylingdales 'all. In that time, I didn't come across lad. But that ain't t' say I didn't 'ear o' 'im. 'e weren't often in England. Whenever 'e was there were allus tales t' tell.

"Anyways, as time went on summat queer 'appened. Tales got stale. So, I reckoned 'e ain't been around for a bit. Afore long, when I was in Scarborough, I 'eard tell o' a gypsy bein' 'eld up at castle, awaiting trial. Them folk I talked t' told a tale o' a drunken rampage.

"Summat made me go t' castle. I couldn't get a toe-'old inside dungeons. So, I made mesen a plan 'cos a queer notion'd got stuck in me 'ead. You'll understand gap 'ere when I tells y' I got well pickled. I must've done some damage, fer when I come back t' me senses, I were in a cell wi' three others. Rats in a rat-'ole.

"Well, there be me, gatherin' me wits an' me bearin's, when such a bellowin' started up. So, I takes a squint at sort o' cage affair suspended between full cells. There were this ... wretch ... inside. Dear Lord, 'e looked so young an' yet so old. Wild-eyed. A wild thing ... caged. I soon realised....." Tom's tremulous voice faded away.

He bowed his head, shaking it slightly as if he still could not comprehend what he had witnessed. The memory of that time had wreathed him in a haunted air. Swallowing convulsively, Catherine gently stroked his arm. He looked up, his craggy features filled with sorrow. Catching sight of her stricken look, he muttered, "Ah, luv." He gathered her to him and henceforth she listened to what he had to say leaning against his shoulder.

"Guard brought lad a flagon. Boasted about 'ow it be full o' cheap, raw liquor an' 'ow they kept lad quiet wi' it. Aye, an' lad took it like 'e were a man dyin' o' thirst. After 'e'd finished it off, 'e were quiet again. An' then afore cage were raised again, 'e got a good beltin' t' make sure 'e stayed quiet. Helpless, I watched same performance day in, day out afore me release.

"When I were freed, I 'ung around castle gates wonderin' 'ow t' get lad out o' that 'ell 'ole. I'd t' do summat. That was when I come across Keeble. Or 'e come across me. One o' two. Anyways, we got t' talkin', an' after we'd both been round 'ouses a few time, so t' speak, we found out about our mutual interest. Accordin' t' 'im…." Tom looked encouragingly at the dwarfish man.

"Master be me captain," Keeble revealed. But then his proud grin faded and the expression on his long, ugly face grew melancholy. "Just afore time Tom talks o', I come t' England. I've kin 'ereabouts. Master give me leave t' visit 'em while 'e went about 'is business. I was t' meet 'im at Whitby three days 'ence, where 'is ship was berthed. But 'e didn't come, not after three weeks. Like Tom, me an' 'is crew 'eard tales an' went t' Scarborough. When I did meet up wi' Tom, I explained t' 'im I'd found out Master'd been captured after gettin' drunk an' causin' 'avoc an' destruction. I been told it took most o' garrison t' subdue 'im. I bribed one o' soldiers an' 'e told me they were keepin' 'im quiet wi' ale until French Dowager o' Fylingdales an' 'er brother, Francois Lynette, got back from France for Master's trial."

"So," said Tom, taking up the story once more, "Keeble told me about lad's cousin, Junno. So we tracked 'im down. I ain't sure why, but, at first, 'e were reluctant t' 'elp us. By all accounts, 'is grandma, Mamma Petra, ordered 'im t'. Some o' the Romany folk 'elped, as well as Keeble's crewmates. Anyways, let's just say between us we got lad away. Lord, I never want t' go through owt like that again. But little did I know worse was t' come. We got Bob t' delay *Eagle's* sailin' until we could get lad aboard. The lad's ship sailed wi' us. Guardin' us. Everybody remembers that voyage. I put a stop t' damned 'og-wash they'd been givin' lad in castle. An' then it started. Just imagine, luv, if y'd a body y'd given 'erbs t' day in day out, an' then stopped 'em even though that body felt they needed 'em, demanded them. That's what it were like. We all fought on that voyage. Lad most o' all. 'e fought against us an' 'issen. It were just a good job Junno'd come along. It'd taken 'alf a dozen o' us t' 'andle lad in same way 'e did." Tom sighed. "Anyways, after a bit, lad won battle. Be time we sailed into Med, he'd beaten most o' the cravin'. I don't think 'e's won war, though, cos y' never see 'im take ale or owt else like it.

"Down years, 'e were away most o' time, mostly in Mediterranean, I reckon." Tom looked at Keeble for confirmation.

"We'd our adventures," replied the little man, with a mischievous grin.

"Aye, well," muttered Tom, stroking Catherine's long fair-white hair, "I stayed at Whitby. Queer thing. Lad always come back, even if it were just fer a few days."

After Tom had finished speaking, a deep, reflective hush settled on the occupants of the bedchamber, which had become darkened by the hour and the continuing force of the storm lashing the Lodge. Tom was lost in the labyrinth of time. Keeble appeared to be, too, wearing an unfamiliar expression. Accept for the occasional cough, Richard had neither moved nor spoken for a long time.

Catherine digested all that she had heard, none of which rested easily in her thoughts. She had questions. "You say Mamma Petra gave him his Romany name?"

"Aye, luv," replied Tom. "Though 'ow she come across 'im, Junno ain't said much about that. Just that 'e were taken in by tribe."

She sat upright. "How did he become involved with Prince Rupert?"

Tom shrugged his shoulders on the pillows. "I ain't a clue, luv." He glanced at Keeble. He, too, shrugged, indicating his own lack of knowledge.

"First we knew o' 'im 'avin' owt t' do wi' present troubles," Tom told her, "was when 'e come t' Whitby about a year ago. 'e recruited Bob an' *Eagle*. This place was found an' men started appearin'. It's gone on since then."

"I wonder if my father had anything to do with him joining the Royalist Cause?" Catherine mused aloud.

"Tis possible," remarked Tom, "One things fer sure it's benefited cos o' lad."

Keeble slipped off the bed and prodded the fire back into life. The upsurge of flames burnished her long hair as she turned towards the place where Richard was sitting in the tapestry-backed chair. The increase in firelight revealed the consequence of an afternoon engaged in retrospective pursuit. Her heart went out to him, but she dare not show it. For he was proud and defiant in the face of life at the Lodge with his half-brother. She felt sure that he too had learned a great deal in the revealing of Shadiz's life. He saw her interest in him. "No doubt you are wondering how on earth I come to be in residence at this godforsaken place?" he said, lifting an ironic eyebrow in a manner that was faintly reminiscent of his half-brother.

"The thought has crossed my mind on more than one occasion," she admitted.

He sat forward in the chair. Resting his elbows on his knees, he gazed at his outspread hands. "I ask myself that question every day." He looked up at her. "Or, at least, I used to." His eyes betrayed his feelings. Catherine tread gently upon them. He had become a close and trusted friend. She knew he wished for more from her. Having to accept the smile she offered, he launched into the details of his own life path.

"After my father's murder … death … call it what you will, my mother's younger brother, Francois Lynette, was installed at Fylingdales Hall. This was due to me not being of an age to take on my birthright. And, at the time, my mother was so distraught at my father's passing.

"I welcomed my uncle and looked upon him as a mentor. He assured me, and I saw no reason to doubt him, that he would assist my mother to run the estate until I had completed my studies. Whenever I inquired about the day-to-day business of Fylingdales, he made light of my interest. He would stress that I had years ahead of me to become immersed in the management of the estate. When I had completed my studies, he insisted I travel around Europe and enjoy the sights before I took on such a weighty responsibility. If I tried to object, my mother would invariably lecture me about how fortunate we were to have Francois assisting us.

"Eighteen months ago, I returned to Fylingdales intent upon claiming my inheritance and taking over the reins of authority. Due to Francois's attitude in the past, I realised it would take time for me to fully get to grips with all that that entailed. As you may have gathered it was not to be. I became heartily sick of Francois's interminable, silk-tongued obstacles and my mother's intractable manner. In frustration, I turned my back on Fylingdales. I even thought of reclaiming my inheritance by force. But that would have proved futile. Over the years, Francois has built up a small army of experienced retainers. And, of course, at the outbreak of the strife in England, he had an excellent motive for increasing his force, with my wealth. And my mother's blessing.

"The war made a difference. It gave me the breathing space I needed. Unlike Francois and my mother, I did not support Parliament. Not because I wished to be contrary to them. My loyalty remains with the monarchy. Therefore, Benjamin and I decided to postpone our investigation into the violent passing of his father and brothers and instead we joined the staff of the King's nephew, Prince Rupert.

"It wasn't until Benjamin and I accompanied Rupert to Yorkshire that I discovered Shadiz was involved in the war. We rendezvoused with him at Benjamin's home close to Richmond. I had, of course, heard about the Master and his exploits. Even that he was a gypsy. Yet, I had not made the connection. My uncle has always maintained he is the scourge of the Mediterranean, along with his accomplice, Nick Condor. He and my mother were and, no doubt still are, kept informed of his movements. Her hatred of Shadiz seems to have grown into an obsession. She would go to any lengths to exact revenge."

"Did Shadiz realise who you were?" Catherine asked.

"Oh, yes," replied Richard, getting to his feet all of a sudden. He took a brisk step towards the hearth and rested a fist upon the irregular stones. "At sight of me ... he fell about laughing. When I revealed our ... relationship ... to Prince Rupert, he was quite taken aback." He shot her a sidelong glance. "It has become an inevitable reaction."

"I can imagine," remarked Catherine, recalling her own astonishment. After a short pause, she added, "Forgive me, but I still don't understand how you come to be at the Lodge with your half-brother?"

"To be honest, neither do I," replied Richard, candidly. He was about to say more when he heard a distinct, sickeningly familiar voice, pitched whisperingly low.

"Surely, *little brother,* ain't y' sittin' tight for me t' bite off more than I can chew. *The Spider taketh 'old wi' 'er 'ands, an' is in kings' palaces.*"

The atmosphere in the bedchamber altered irrevocably. No one was immune to the menace of Shadiz's unexpected presence.

Keeble darted about lighting more tallow candles to replace those that had been extinguished by the passage of time. In the process the subject of the stormy afternoon was revealed. Shadiz was leaning against the closed door, his arms loosely folded over his long, wet coat. His gold earring sparkled between strands of his soaked hair. The mastiff lay quietly at his feet in a puddle of its own making. Revealed also, Bill Todd was standing ramrod straight a self-preserving distance away from his leader.

" *'as fer 'im who voluntarily performeth a good work, verily Allah is grateful an' knowin',*" quoted Shadiz. He salaamed, glittering jet aimed at Tom.

Pale and drawn, the older man felt no regret. For he was sure in his rapidly beating heart he had done what was right. He had spent the last few months observing words and actions, and the significant lack of both on occasions. By doing so, he had done away with mystery and gained an ache he wanted desperately to ease, not for himself.

"The tale served as a distraction on a dull afternoon," commented Richard, stiffly. How long had Shadiz been standing there, listening?

"O, little brother," murmured Shadiz, "y' sellin' y'rsen short."

After a hefty pause, in which equal degrees of animosity and contempt flashed between the half-brothers, Shadiz pushed himself away from the door. "I suggest y' tear y'rsens away from fireside tales," he said, brusquely. "*Eagle's* in trouble in Mercy Cove." The clamour of alarm was checked, and ridiculed, by his dark expression. "Aesop, the teller o' tall tales an' the 'older o' life's small mysteries, I'll leave thee the usual guard. I'll tak y' along, little brother. An' wi' luck, the fishes might rejoice this night."

Bill Todd opened the chamber door and swiftly vanished. Keeble hobbled after him, grinning. Moving more slowly, Richard paused at the door. Unable to withstand his half-brother's arrogance any longer, he muttered, "One of these days I shall end your days and nights."

"You're welcome t' try," responded Shadiz, dismissively.

Despite the need for prompt action in response to the *Eagle's* plight in Mercy Cove, he did not seem inclined to follow his men from the chamber. Lingering at the door, he made the open invitation plain, which Catherine declined. She made her point by leaning against the edge of the bed, arms folded. Without acknowledging her, Shadiz slammed the door shut with the heel of his boot. Henceforth, he roamed the bedchamber; a soft-footed brimstone threat.

Troubled by the blue-lipped strain on Tom's face, Catherine watched Shadiz warily. "You must not seek your justice when there is no one around to defend."

"Aesop," he snapped, still pacing. "Only cowards insult dyin' majesty." Glancing fiercely apologetic at Tom, he added, "Dammit, I ain't meant it that way." In the next breath, he rounded upon Catherine. "Since when've you given orders around 'ere?"

"I live here," exclaimed Catherine, straightening. "Remember!"

" 'ow in the bleedin' name o' all that's damned 'oly am I ever likely t' forget?" he growled. "Y've 'alf animals in neighbourhood 'obblin' around in bloody splints. By each day that dawns there's more o' 'em. Bleedin' matchoes. A man can't move wi'out 'im brekin' 'is neck over a 'erd o' twitterin' brats. There was nowt mentioned about women fetchin' their bloody bairns till you come along. D'y realise, you've got me men pickin' a petal 'ere an' a petal there. Like a bunch o' cavortin' nancies. *We must get these 'erbs t' the lady.'* An', o' course, they're fallin' over each other t' 'elp y' in that bloody plot o' y'rs. The one I never sanctioned."

"Harken to him," invited Catherine turning briefly to Tom, who by now was sitting bolt upright in bed. "He lives as if civilization is unfashionable, and requires the same of all of us." She did not wait for Tom's anxious response before turning back to her scowling guardian, her fair-white hair swinging about her waist. "Well, maybe you can survive at such barren heights. *I* cannot."

"So y' turn this place into."

"A home," she retorted. "What other have I? You won't condone my return to Nafferton Garth." They faced each other, the fumes of their respective emotions rippling between them. "Is there no part of you that wishes for somewhere? Someone?"

Plainly, he was not conscious of the backward step.

"No one even lays a hand upon you. They dare not," observed Catherine, bluntly.

Tom got out of bed, regretting his rheumatic knees, ignoring the sharp twinge in his chest. "Luv," he murmured, warningly.

Shadiz had become perfectly still. He stared down at Catherine. At last. "Woman, what hast thou to offer me?"

His barely audible tone of voice brought Catherine up short. Her colour high, she met his gaze. His expression was as clear as mud. "If you would only seek, there is..." She cast about impatiently for the correct words. "... kindnesss and...."

The travesty of mirth was tossed at the draped window as Shadiz twisted away from her.

"You will not even allow anyone to know your birth name!" she exclaimed.

Shadiz rounded on her. Tom's arm came up protectively.

"Kore! For the love of God. *Let me breathe!*"

There was a shocked pause, in which he took the time to acquaint himself with his own desperate words. Then, he went. And, rigid, Catherine could do nothing to prevent his rapid departure.

★ ★ ★

"Mary, do you know the way to Mercy Cove?"

"Nay, missy."

"Never mind. It is of no consequence, Mary."

"Billy, in stables, does, missy. It's where 'e 'ails from."

★ ★ ★

Men were gathering in the courtyard. Their idle, dry hours in the main hall had been washed away by their leader's summons. They had become accustomed to being called upon to work in the foulest of weathers.

Falling in crystal sheets, the cheerless deluge bounced upon the hillocks of cobbles, causing the hooves of the ill-suited horses to skim over the reflective slickness. Above dripping manes and plastered hair, lost in the evening's premature darkness, the wind-inspired rustling of the forest sounded like conspiratorial whispers in a lofty cathedral. The ancient, renovated Lodge stood firm, bleeding weak light upon soaked cloaks, wet jowls and the timeworn, detaining hand upon the stallion's bridle.

For the briefest of moments, Shadiz looked as if he might thrust Tom aside.

"Damn me any way y' like, lad," declared Tom, looking upwards, quickly becoming soaked to the skin, "but, I ain't sorry one bit I got me say in afore Richard."

Catching his name on the capricious wind, full of curiosity, Richard drew rein alongside his half-brother.

"Y' forgotten where Mercy Cove is?" rasped Shadiz, dismounting.

The mounted men followed Richard out of the courtyard as their leader seized Tom by the arm and marched him back into the Lodge. "What's point o' Kore lookin' after y' when y' go do a bloody stupid trick like that?" In the hallway, after berating the older man for venturing out into the stormy evening, Shadiz didn't wait for an answer.

"Lad," said Tom, "I knows way o' things."

Cold, wet, shivering, he braced himself for what might break upon him for encroaching on forbidden territory. He watched in resolute silence as his young leader halted and slowly turned back to him. Tom found himself staring through a crack in the door.

"Father Time, y' can't begin t' comprehend. So, please, do me no more favours."

"No man is an island, son," observed Tom, standing alone in the empty hallway.

★ ★ ★

"Billy, Mary informs me you know the way to Mercy Cove?"

"Should do, Miss Catherine. Born an' raised there. Y' know, there be trouble in Cove tonight. Master's gone t' see."

"Yes, so I understand. I was wondering, Billy, could you guide me there?"

"Ee, Miss Catherine, as much as I'd like t', it's more'n me life's worth t' tek y' away from Lodge. Master's made it plain. None o' us is t' even allow y' through Stillingfleet."

"I see. Well, I understand you must obey him."

"D'y wish t' see 'ow fares *Eagle*, me luv?"

"Oh, Keeble! It's alright, Mary, don't take on so. Yes, that's it. I'm so afraid for Bob and his crew. They showed me such kindness on the voyages to and from Ijuimden."

"Well, I tell y' what, me an' Billy could tell sentries we've been ordered t' carry rope t' Master. If y' an' Mary leave Lodge wi' Glaisdale women, quiet like, me an' Billy'll meet y' near village track out o' Stillingfleet. Mary knows where I mean. But what about Bill and Danny?"

CHAPTER TWO

Kindness Would, The Waves Will

"Oh, Lord! What've y' done t' Bill an' Danny, missy?"

"They are sleeping, Mary. Don't worry. Come on. Your mother and the rest of the women will be leaving soon."

"I ain't altogether sure about this, missy. What if Master finds out?"

"H'm."

★ ★ ★

The half-brothers stood side by side on the edge of the tall, ragged cliff, bracing themselves against the ferocity of the storm. For once they were in agreement.

The *Eagle* was in dire straits.

Both men were aware that Bob Andrew was accustomed to the North Sea's propensity for tempestuous weather, and therefore must have set his ship on a heading for Mercy Cove. Unfortunately, on this occasion, the large sweeping bay seemed not inclined to honour its compassionate name.

Aided by the full moon, a celestial orb riding high in the riotous heavens, Shadiz and Richard, the men from the Lodge and a cliff top full of locals watched the *Eagle's* desperate passage through a turbulent sea. Her tattered sails flapping madly, her helm seemingly ineffectual in the prevailing conditions, she was being driven by the gale force wind towards a rocky outcrop that marked the farthest reaches of the shore.

A horrified gasp whipped through the onlookers when the merchantman surged upwards on the foaming crest of a maelstrom

218

of towering waves. Adhering to their age-old cycle in a riotous mood, the waves then pounded upon the half-submerged outcrop, dashing the hapless ship upon the rocks amidst wild, flying surf. Within a heartbeat, the subsequent, powerful drag of the remorseless sea caused an ominous retreat. The *Eagle* slithered over jagged stone teeth protruding out of chaotic water.

To the onlookers on the cliffs, it seemed as if the merchantman's fate was sealed.

A fragile hope of salvation came from the gradual realisation that the North Sea was being prevented from devouring the merchantman entirely. Its own raging strength had grounded her at a perilous obtuse angle in a stony vice. Thwarted by the rocks, the maddened sea crashed over her submerged stern and far up her vulnerable decks. The moonlight revealed how the exhausted men trapped aboard the imprisoned merchantman were struggling to survive.

Shadiz turned away from the cliff edge. *"Their hands outstretched in yearning for the farther shore."*

Richard caught the words above the strong wind. Before moving away, Shadiz gave him a hearty slap on the back that rattled his lungs. Richard stared after him in amazement. After months, it remained extraordinary to hear his uncouth half-brother quote such luminaries as Virgil, and do so in Latin.

By the time Richard rejoined him, Shadiz was issuing orders to the men from Mercy Cove and Boggle Hole, two miles down the coast.

Ropes had been carried on broad shoulders to the vantage point of the cliff top, an instinctive action on the part of the fishermen. All of them had, at one time or another, lost a companion or a family member to the North Sea. Their respect was paramount. Their knowledge beyond compare. And, like the crew of the Eagle, they had come to recognise Shadiz as being a fellow creature of the waves. A Sea Gypsy. Richard knew he was involved in their secondary occupation of smuggling. His suspicions were well-founded. His participation blocked at every turn. This galled him. He considered himself to be far more intimate with the coastal communities he had known since childhood than his worldly half-brother.

Belatedly, he realised that Shadiz had ordered him to produce the coils of rope brought from the Lodge. Because his response was tardy, two of the Master's men deposited the thick hemp at their leader's feet. Shadiz seized Richard's arm and spoke in his ear. "Gather 'orses together. Secure 'em two abreast behind each pair."

Richard hurried through the sodden, windswept crowd, pondering the reason for the task. He left the stallion where it was tethered for fear it would revolt without its master's authority and panic the other horses. Like him, the Master's men were curious about the procedure that took them some time to accomplish. Answering their leader's moonlit gesture, the men started to coerce the column of horses towards the cliff edge. The women and children peered through the rain while husbands, brothers and fathers helped to position the reluctant animals. By which time several of the old-timers had knotted together all the other ropes, creating one lengthy strand.

Returning to his leader, and seeing his long, leather coat, boots and weapons discarded on the muddy ground, Richard understood what Shadiz was proposing to do. Getting a ripe impression from the tight-lipped fishermen, he, too, considered the undertaking in such atrocious weather little short of madness. Unlike them, he made sure his opinion was heard. "Have you lost your wits? You'll never make it across *there*." He thrust out a soaked arm, indicating the narrow strip of hostile shore bordering the storm-tossed sea.

Impervious to all opposition, Shadiz started to wind the elongated rope around his upper body, from right shoulder to left hip. When he had finished, he held out the loose end to Richard.

But Richard had more to shout about. "So be it. I'm coming with you."

"T' 'od me 'and," retorted Shadiz, loudly. The moonlight revealed his nasty sneer.

John Cox, one of the older fishermen of vast experience, had the courage to intervene. "Master, 'is Lordship's reet. If rocks don't get y', watter will."

Having adjusted the hemp waistcoat to his satisfaction, Shadiz looked up and grinned. Cox took a step backwards, finding the weird, silvery mirth intimidating.

Once again Shadiz thrust the end of the rope at Richard.

"What about Francois?" Richard bellowed through the wind and rain. "Should he discover what is going on, which is highly likely, he will sprout wings and arrive just in time to see you break your damn fool neck."

It was clear from the Master's authoritative demeanour that he would not tolerate any further attempts to persuade him to give up his bid to cross the seashore. "Fasten this end o' rope t' lead 'orses."

Recognising with fury the futility of any further objections, Richard snatched the irritably proffered rope. He was marching away when he was struck by an inspiration. Turning back, he yelled, "Listen to me."

Shadiz shoved him roughly away in the direction of the stamping horses. In his determination to be heard, Richard grabbed his leader's wet shirt sleeve, and was promptly repulsed in a vicious manner. He tried again, shouting from a prudent distance. "Let me fire an arrow, with the rope attached, over the shore."

"Bloody crackpot notion," retaliated Shadiz. "Rope's too damned heavy. Besides, y' bow string'll get soaked."

Indicting over the cliff edge, Richard made himself heard. "Not if I work fast enough. And if I shoot from down there with four arrows tied together."

The windblown words appeared to give his leader pause for thought. He seemed to gauge the feasibility of Richard's suggestion. The sudden withdrawal of moonlight behind scudding clouds gave the indistinct shore an almost palpable menace; as if Nature was daring man to step into its wild blackness.

Approval came with a stern warning. "Y' not t' follow me. Y' come back up 'ere an' supervise 'orses. Understand?"

Nurturing his endeavour, Richard nodded.

Shadiz continued to wear the rope wound around his rain-dripping jerkin as first he and then Richard were lowered over the cliff edge by several of his own men.

He unwound the rope from around himself while Richard, his back turned upon the raging elements, extracted four arrows from the canvas bag attached to his sword belt beneath his cloak. He was careful to keep the goose feathers within the protection of his cloak until he and Shadiz could work together. Kneeling in the shelter of the cliffs, they secured the rope to the shafts. Time was of the essence. For once the bowstring became wet there would be no chance of firing the bundle of arrows across the shore. Shadiz found a handy crevice in which to keep the arrows viable. Richard swung the leather bag holding his longbow off his back and deftly strung it, again using his cloak and what little sheltered the overhanging cliff gave to shield his actions.

As soon as he straightened to take the ambitious shot, Shadiz stepped clear of him.

The force of the wind was less severe in the lee of the sandy cliffs. Yet the arc of variation was still a real possibility. Richard, standing braced in the deep sand, quickly perfected his aim and fired.

Both men watched through the driving rain the flight of the connected arrows across the rocky shore; a dark-winged gull trailing a ponderous serpent in its wake. Above them, from their vantage point on the cliffs, the many onlookers held their breaths as the fickle wind carried the shafts through the obliging moonlight. Then the feathered venture began to fall swift and graceful. When it appeared not to land in an inauspicious spot, a spontaneous cheer was swept away by the vibrant air.

"Clever. Bloody clever."

The words swept past Richard. He grinned at his success, and, though he was loathed to admit it, the rare praise. The hope he still harboured to accompany Shadiz to the stricken merchantman was dashed when his leader signalled those above to hoist him upwards.

Shadiz was left alone. The pendant he wore had escaped from beneath his sodden shirt. He briefly gripped the white stone set in engraved silver before thrusting it safely against his wet skin. He embarked upon the perilous trek across the hazardous seashore.

"*Kindness!*"

"Can we not go faster, Billy?"

"Not in this weather, Miss Catherine. Is Keeble an' Mary still following' on 'is mare?"

"Yes. Please, Billy, let us make all possible haste."

★ ★ ★

From the outset, Shadiz found the going taxing. The wind tore at his long, soaked hair and clothes and roared in his ears. The driving, needle-sharp rain stung his face. It seemed the foul mood of Nature had become embodied in a powerful brute ready to hinder every stride he endeavoured to take. The mad spark which made him forever push against the impossible stood him in good stead. All too soon thought became primeval; survival optional.

Destined to help those men trapped aboard the *Eagle*, the rope Richard had fired over the shore became his own lifeline. It lay across stretches of glutinous sand and between clusters of treacherous rocks. Each foot-sucking or skidding step drained his tremendous strength but not his implacable resolve. He felt as if he had stepped out of time and was struggling in a landscape reminiscent of Tartarus.

Before long he encountered sprawling patches of kelp. Their pungent slime carpeted most of the rugged stony mazes through which he was obliged to go. On several occasions he was forced to make arduous detours, hoping to once again locate the rope in the swirling darkness by touch or pure instinct. Only when the full moon escaped her prison of storm clouds did her mystical rays make the searches less tedious.

Lethal rocks that readily tore open a misplaced hand were metamorphosing into a mountainous range of boulders. Set like jewels in Celtic granite that had been honed since time immemorial by the North Sea, cold-water pools existed at the heart of each looming cluster. Their width heralded his hard-fought approach to the wild dark sea laced by ghostly white breakers.

It was within one such rippling, enclosed pool that he came upon the end of the rope. However, his efforts to drag both it and the still attached arrows clear of a half-detected, stubborn vice were met with little success. Resigned to investigate the problem before proceeding, he clambered over a couple of slick boulders. In doing so, he slipped on a random patch of kelp that blended insidiously with the night and as a consequence lost his footing. Unable to get a grip on the smooth stone, he plummeted into the rock pool which quickly threatened to be bottomless.

By perverse instinct, he still held the rope. Because of a pernicious twist, the sodden hemp became locked around his wrist, ensuring a pendulum effect that caused him to hit one wickedly serrated side of the pool and then the other.

Yet the result of his hapless plunge into the ice-water chamber was dross when compared to the elation. Trapped within the declining air bubbles, the emotion signalled a release. The struggle had been an illusion. All that would remain would be driftwood on the shore.

It was unfortunate that at that precise moment the voices erupted in his smug mind.

'Hold the Moon.'
'No one is infallible.'
'In Stygian cave forlorn.'

★ ★ ★

"Missy! Oh, missy. What be wrong? Billy, why's Miss Catherine dismounted? Missy, please! Y' must get up. Y' can't stay down 'ere in mud. What ails y'?"

"No! *Mithral Bel cay lay. Canast fay nay par.*"

★ ★ ★

It was to the accompaniment of exclamations of dismay that the people on the cliff top had witnessed the Master's moonlit disappearance between the collection of large boulders. Fearing the worst yet praising the indomitable authority they respected, they waited in anxious silence for him to reappear.

Richard, for reasons of his own, had decided not to watch Shadiz's progress across the dangerous shore. Yet the cries of alarm had propelled him to the grassy cliff edge overlooking the sandy stretch from where he had discharged his longbow.

"Come on, you bastard."

★ ★ ★

'Kore, let me breathe.'

★ ★ ★

It was the horses, tethered in pairs, that brought the crowd's hushed stillness to an end. Putting great store in skittishness, men sprang to do Richard's throat-punishing bidding. Urgent hope on their rain washed faces, they persuaded the equine column backwards.

Close by an old salt was struggling to squint through a dented spyglass with his good eye. It was snatched away from him. Richard, seeing this, in turn seized it from Ned Locke's son. Through the spyglass's scratched lens, grateful for faithful moonlight, he discerned feeble movement. Immediately, he bellowed to the men pulling on the horses.

Having been hoisted up by cliff top horsepower, Shadiz lay half in, half out of the rock pool, immune to its bitter chill. He refilled aching lungs in a concaved chest with painful gasps of ragged air, interspersed with bouts of retching. Blood from the cut in his forehead he had sustained when he had been thrust against the brutal sides of the deep pool trickled into his eyes, diluted by rain water.

When he had recovered sufficiently, he hauled himself back onto his feet. He swayed and leant against one of the boulders that formed the Ring of Nemesis. Still breathing rapidly, he wiped the sleeve of his wet shirt across his forehead. Against his cold skin, the moonstone still retained some of its previous warmth. His trembling hand closed about the pendant. He raised it to his lips, acknowledging its power to salvage and defeat the goddess of vengeance.

The weariness deep in his narrowed gaze was not entirely due to the tremendous physical demands of the violent night. He sought the dynamic entity he revered after the Maiden. Eventually, after taking deep breaths of replenishing sea air, he resumed the struggle to the stranded ship.

Gripping the arrows which constituted the end of the rope, having managed to extract them from a deep crevice, he toiled around the castellated boulders and waded through the plentiful, sea-fed marriage of rock pools.

His reward was not reassuring. Buffeted by rough, waist-high sea and blasted by the persistent wind and rain, he paused and regarded the *Eagle*, aground on tenacious rocks and listing heavily.

One last mighty effort saw the end of his self-imposed task. The vindictive wind snatched away his deep sigh. He leant his bleeding forehead against the merchantman's rearing timbers.

'Beware that you do not lose the substance by grasping at the shadows.'

The thought floated away when he became conscious of Bob Andrew and his crew straining over the low slung starboard rail. He stepped out of the shadow of the bowsprit, sailing uniquely above his head. A rope was tossed down, enabling him to scale the *Eagle's* uncovered hull.

Seamen who had thought themselves to be doomed stepped back on the tilting, sea-infested main deck, nervous of giving effusive praise to the sinister Master. Yet gratitude for what he had achieved shone in the kind of night all seafarers dread. For even though they had spotted movement on the cliff top, rescue had seemed a cruel illusion. To them, the only certainty as the *Eagle* had run aground was death in a cove that should have shown mercy. The first inkling they had gleaned of possible rescue was when the rope had been launched over the shore. Then, like those folk safe on land, they had strained through the silver split darkness in an effort to watch the progress of the extraordinary Gypsy, for they were convinced it could be no other, hopeful that the Devil would take care of his own.

He remained as inscrutable as ever.

Trying to keep a foothold on the *Eagle's* decks, those that were not completely under water, was hard enough without having to probe the oblique merchantman for a secure place to fasten the precious rope Shadiz had carried on board. The mizzen mast with its splintered yardarms was impossible to access while the aft sections remained submerged. Due to its shaky condition, the foremast was ignored. In the end, the mainmast seemed to be the most likely option. It remained intact despite its torn, flapping canvas and rakish angle.

What the captain and the crew of the Eagle would have given for a warm fire, a mug of ale and the arms of their loved ones around them, they contemplated sacrificing in exchange for a slice of the Master's impressive vigour. A matchless rogue he certainly was. A deadly one at that. He was also a man of unfailing charisma. And, knowing this, their own spirits jaded, their upturned, rain-washed faces drawn and grey with exhaustion, they watched his shadowy figure scale the mainmast with something akin to awe.

In truth, Shadiz trusted no man to finish the task he had started by duplicity. Having secured the end of the rope to the head of the lopsided mainmast, he signalled to Richard on the cliff top.

While he waited for a taut result from the coercion that was surely taking place on trampled land, he gazed over the widow-making sea; reflecting on a fire in a Dutch port cheated and a rock pool denied. By kindness? That bleak abyss to which he had grown accustomed was being encroached upon by a soulful power he had never envisaged during all the long, empty years.

A definite tension on the rope brought him back to the night's hazardous endeavour. It now stretched high above the forbidding seascape. Letting his speculative thoughts swirl away in the vibrant air, he tested the feasibility of the lifeline with a cool-headed flair that caused many of those watching to grit their teeth.

Thereafter, aided by the Master, perched upon untrustworthy wood, the apprehensive seamen traded the remains of the yardarm for the rough, wet rope that had become their means of escape from a watery demise. One after another, they embarked upon the awkward, windblown, rain-pelted monkey climb which had to endure until outstretched hands grasped them from the cliffs. Those who faltered were encouraged by their concerned audience, bellowing above the ruthless elements.

Eventually, only Bob Andrew remained braced at the base of the mainmast. It seemed the captain of the *Eagle* was happy to keep it that way. The Master had other ideas. His impatient curses circulated in a disjointed manner around Bob.

Lithe as a cat, Shadiz followed.

Bob got the gist of the younger man's opinion. Bravely he bellowed, "I ain't leavin' 'er. Mebbe there's a chance on mornin' tide?"

He missed the respect of one seaman for another. Also the opportunity to object further before he was bundled up the tilting mainmast by strength he could not overcome. Once upon the shaky yardarm, bent against the lofty fury of the wind, he listened in resentful silence as Shadiz poured words into his ear.

"In morning, so long as this lot abates return afore high tide. Bring a skeleton crew. Tell 'em from Cove an' Boggle 'ole t' be on 'and wi' their vessels. Wi' a bit o' luck they should be able t' tow old cow off those bloody rocks."

"You're stayin'?"

"Aye."

Bob relented, feeling guilty after the risks already taken. "I'm sorry, lad. Tis 'ard t' leave 'er when she's this way."

"No doubt Laura an' y'r bairns'd agree," retorted Shadiz.

Realisation dawned on the Captain. Too late. Shadiz had set him in motion along the lifeline with a no-nonsense push.

Alone on the merchantman, aware of the build up of tension in his temples, Shadiz began a thorough tour of inspection. He was establishing how much damage the hatch covers had sustained, mainly by touch, when he noticed vague movement on the lifeline.

"Allah deliver me from bloody 'eroes," he muttered, moving off to another part of the crippled ship.

Minutes later, Richard slithered down the mainmast faster than he would have liked and plummeted into the seawater upon the *Eagle's* uneven main deck. Rising up and balancing himself against the unpleasant tilt and churning water, it took him a while to get his breath back while fighting the coughing spasm. Irritated by his relief at there being no sign of Shadiz, he picked his way over the ship's ruined fittings.

"Don't tell me. Y'r speciality be pipin' mournful laments."

Richard turned to find a tall shadow solidified into black menace. "Perhaps you have an ulterior motive for remaining on board alone?" He attempted to mask his wariness by casually wading away.

Moving fast, Shadiz barred his way. "Suppose y' tell me what's on y'r mind."

"Was the courageous trip a disappointment?" challenged Richard, loudly. "What happened? Did fate take a hand? Or did you simply lose your nerve? What a pretty sight she would make up there on the cliff. Her kindness is boundless, even for the lowest of creatures."

His unfortunate choice of words drew a violent response that relegated him to the waterlogged deck. Face down in icy seawater, he spluttered and coughed. His own rage triggered a swift recovery in order to go after his loathsome half-brother. It was his misfortune that life had pitted him against a half-blood Romany and a full-blooded mercenary.

Shadiz side-stepped his attack with fluid ease. The next moment, Richard found himself once again stretched out full length spluttering in seawater.

Bending, Shadiz rasped into his ear. "Employ procedure by all means. Just make sure when y' do y' ain't soundin' off like 'erd o' irate bulls."

Richard attempted to raise himself from swamped humiliation. He was promptly slammed back down by a vicious foot in the middle of his back.

" 'eed me. *Don't* let 'er stray into our argument."

Richard managed to twist awkwardly around. "She should be nowhere near you."

This time, he was already avoiding Shadiz's nasty rejoinder. Having rolled away from the kick aimed at his ribs, he sprang to his feet, making sure to balance himself against the perilously steep angle of the ship.

"Dammit, Massone. Grow up." If Richard had not been in a mood to contemplate his half-brother merely in an hostile light, he might have realised that Shadiz's intolerance was due to him becoming preoccupied with something other than aggression. "This ain't place for an adolescent brawl."

"You think not?"

But Richard was not given the opportunity to object further. He was suddenly spun round, and then found himself in a powerful grip. While his arms were pinioned at his sides, from over his left shoulder, he was called upon to use an unfettered sense.

"Listen, y' bloody 'ot-'ead. Listen, dammit."

Richard was not attuned to the different characteristics of the sea in the same way his half-brother was. He suspected Shadiz of foul play, knowing the other man's malicious ways. Only when he felt the sloping deck shudder beneath him did he curtail his infuriated struggle and begin to take note of the strident creaking being emitted by the merchantman. Looking across the low starboard rail, he realised the sea was not running as strongly as before. The buoyant power which hitherto had maintained the *Eagle's* precarious balance in the grip of the rocks was becoming prey to tidal retreat. As a result the ship was listing inch by deadly inch further to starboard.

"Find me light," commanded Shadiz, thrusting Richard away.

In an instant, Richard was once more the obedient lieutenant. His hasty search in the pitch-blackness below decks was regularly punctuated by wrong turns and blows from unseen obstacles. He had no idea where he was when his questing fingers alighted upon a lantern and then tinder. Snatching up both, his prayer was that they had not become infected by the seawater like most things aboard the merchantman, himself included. It took precious minutes for him to find his way back topside and then locate his leader in the cargo hold. After a couple of fumbling attempts, he managed to light the lantern. A murderous shift to starboard of the *Eagle's* cargo was revealed. If the big barrels were left across heavy crates and the fat sacks were not rescued from beneath both, the ship would tear herself asunder on the merciless rocks.

The two men set to work in an attempt to avert disaster. Separately and together, they transported load after load up the arduous slope, wedging barrel against crate and sack against barrel in whatever way they could, conscious throughout their laborious, uphill struggle of the crippled ship's woeful, shuddering moans. Although they were often beaten back down the infuriating tilt by sodden merchandise they had just put in place, they persisted, wading in several feet of seawater, until at last they had accomplished by sheer determination and brute force a bizarre mosaic of cargo at the port side of the hold in an attempt to counterbalance the shift to starboard. Still complaining about her plight, the *Eagle* settled at a steep angle to await the morning's tide.

Richard was worn out. Coughing, he collapsed in the water swilling about in the hold. When he had got his breath back, he saw reflected in the weak light of the lantern the terrible toll the night's endeavour had taken on Shadiz.

"Get out o' 'ere."

Richard got to his feet, staring down questioningly at his half-brother.

Keeping his head bowed, crouching in the water, Shadiz ploughed both hands into his long, soaked hair. "Tek that wi' y'."

"What's amiss?"

"Get out," Shadiz rasped with sudden savagery.

Too tired to argue, Richard picked up the lantern and left the hold.

"Kindness." muttered Shadiz to the sea-whispering darkness.

★ ★ ★

"Missy, we can't stay 'ere. We'll get blown off the rotten cliff. Please, do as Billy asks, an' let's tak shelter wi' 'is folk."

231

"You three do so. I cannot leave."

"I'll seek shelter 'ereabouts," volunteered Keeble.

★ ★ ★

After a great deal of awkward coaxing, far more than Richard had anticipated when he had entered the lop-sided cargo hold, Shadiz stirred. A second or two of disorientation then he was in full command of himself. By which time, Richard had straightened and moved away. He watched in thoughtful silence while Shadiz sat up with a half-stifled grimace on the soaked crates that had served as his bed.

"What's 'our?"

"Almost dawn," answered Richard. He made his way topside. It had been a long, cold night, leaving him in no mood to fence verbally with his half-brother.

Getting to his feet, stirring the murky water in the hold, Shadiz scrutinised the cargo he and Richard had stacked at the portside as a counterbalance to the merchantman's dangerous, tidal listing. The flickering glow from the lantern left by Richard showed that little within the constructive jumble of barrels, sacks and crates seemed to have moved significantly. Meanwhile, he tried unsuccessfully to grasp a hazy part of the night.

There was something else he couldn't quite grasp. It manifested itself in an incongruous uneasy feeling.

The chilly pre-dawn greyness enfolded a peaceful world. A gossamer mist shrouded the rugged shoreline. The outcrop of rocks upon which the *Eagle* had run aground was gradually being covered by the placid surf-ridged off-springs of the previous night's heavy sea.

Balancing close to the ship's rearing bows, Richard failed to notice his leader's bare-foot approach.

"There 'e be, the fair guard on the lonely decks."

Richard swung round, eager suddenly to rub salt in the wound of Shadiz's absence. "And where were you?"

" '*ell*," muttered Shadiz, looking to the east where the first

232

tentative blush of dawn was creeping over the horizon, *"is a circle around the unbeliever."*

Defeated by Arabic, not wanting anything further from the waspish tongue of his half-brother, Richard silently followed Shadiz's lead on a tour of inspection. The two men found the *Eagle* remained vulnerable but that she was managing to hold her own in relatively calm waters.

Daylight was growing stronger, the mist dissipating. It was becoming clearer that there was activity worthy of note on the distant cliff top. As the swelling North Sea glistened in the rosy dawn, men began to cross the rocky shore by lofty means.

Bob Andrew boarded his ship by the unconventional route of the mainmast. Richard was perched on the uneven yardarm to greet him. After taking in the younger man's ripening bruises, the captain descended to the deck to find Matt Pearson explaining to the Master why the majority of the skeleton crew were his own men. The renegade son of a fisherman, Pearson was expressing the thoughts of his peers, in the process hoping to pacify their hard-faced leader. "If owt's t' go wrong, sir, we reckon we stand a better chance than tothers who've women an' bairns waitin' on 'em. Sir."

Their voluntary presence was an affirmation of his charismatic leadership. For in making warriors out of aimless rogues, he had given them back self-esteem and the dignity of considering their fellow men.

Enigmatic as ever, the Master simply gave a curt nod.

Bob Andrew's relief at being back on board his beloved ship was clear. But when he was taken by Richard to view the mosaic of ruined cargo keeping the merchantman's precarious balance in check, his worries received an unpleasant boost.

Meanwhile, the Master was sending men into the mounting swell upon the sunken aft section to collect the tough ropes from the fishing boats from Mercy Cove and Boggle Hole. Their captains had answered his call to attempt to re-float the merchantman for tow.

The sunlight pounced upon the strong rhythmic movements of the swimmers. Rocked by the increasing momentum of the incoming tide, Shadiz kept his balance far down the steep tilt of the ship. He pulled out each of his men in turn from the sea and directed the distribution of the tow lines they had acquired.

At length all was in readiness. Men were apprehensive yet welcomed the growing strength of the morning tide, hoping it would bring salvation to the grounded ship. They were aboard the merchantman to avert disaster. Yet the thought of doom was an ugly consequence at the back of their minds. Their collective gazes swept the cliff top, once again thronged with anxious spectators. When the Master signalled to the fantail of fishing boats a prudent cable's length away to get underway, they braced themselves at their given stations. He urged them to be vigilant so as to ensure the dripping lines were not hampered by the debris strewn about the ship. He did so in such a way that at a critical time those aboard the Eagle came under his confident spell.

The endless, cascading breakers were rapidly deepening to a critical degree the measure of seawater already swamping the half-submerged stern of the ship. With its daily timing, the rushing tide was also adding to the creamy chaos around her high, beached hull. The rocky outcrop holding her fast would soon be submerged. Its disappearance would herald a buoyancy that just might float her free or result in her remaining a prisoner and facing a death sentence.

Men waited. Some prayed. Others cursed. Stranded midway between both, Bob Andrew was mutely desperate.

Marine timbers shrieked. The shaky mizzen mast wobbled. When it became clear there was a possibility of it being felled by the increasingly violent shudders passing through the assailed ship, those closest to the danger readily answered the Master's sharp command and moved out of danger.

By now thoroughly drenched, all of the men hung onto anything of substance, fearing the Eagle might break up around them; looking to the straining fleet of fishing boats to aid them.

The crews of the tough smacks had crowded on sail, hoping to make capital out of the favourable wind and so increase their combined pulling power. The lines were taut across the dazzling blue sea. But nothing, it seemed, could persuade the citadel of rocks to relinquish their catch of the previous night.

Shadiz's fist hit the splintery port rail, his exasperation plain for all to see. He started up the imprisoned ship. Defying the crazy angle with nautical prowess, he made his way to the trapped bows. Richard was about to follow when ominous scraping noises brought him up sharply. With dread not exultation, he realised the ship was on the move.

Thereafter, all was sunlit, watery confusion.

Men were flung from their stations by the hectic intensity of the sea. While they battled the turbulent water, the meagre consolation that the ship was suddenly free of all stony restrictions was not uppermost in their minds. For now she was adrift in a sea made perilously agitated by her own floundering presence. And since her aft section had erupted out of the aquamarine depths, the increased measure of seawater flowing over her decks was an added risk to her and everyone aboard.

Despite their doubts, the crews of the fishing boats valiantly persisted in their efforts to tow the *Eagle* away from the cheated rocks. They could do nothing about the hazardous pitch and roll. If it continued, there was a real danger of the much larger merchantman becoming their anchor.

For the second time Richard came up spluttering, gasping for breath. He caught sight of Bob Andrew likewise struggling nearby, and motioned towards the ship's bows. Upon their eventual release, the bows had plunged into the sea only to surface minutes later full of teeming, hissing water. The two men staggered to their feet, were almost bowled over by the next powerful wave to swamp the Eagle's already inundated decks and travelled on its foaming crest to the bottom rung of the fo'c'sle ladder. They both caught sight of Shadiz at the same time. He lay above them in the thunderous surf.

Coughing, Richard fell to his knees in the waist-high water beside his half-brother. "Shadiz?" He could not credit the weird mirth.

"Lad?" questioned Bob, confused.

235

If Shadiz had not been aware of their presence before, he was now and got to his feet within a waterfall of sea.

Men were slowly recovering. They became even more cheerful as the *Eagle* gradually stopped emulating a tipsy doxy leaving one tavern for another. Placing a fishermen's faith in the Almighty, the captains of the loyal fishing boats had widened the width of the tow lines, keeping them taut. Their expertise had produced the desired effect while the merchantman was towed away from the shore.

When she had been re-floated, a large measure of seawater had gushed into her already watery hold, disturbing the cargo Shadiz and Richard had wedged at the portside. Men were sent into the inconvenient well to bale out the unwanted ballast and to straighten the troublesome, floating cargo in a further effort to restore the ship's equilibrium.

Shadiz and Bob paid attention to the damage. It was plain most of her canvas and rigging would need replacing. Other parts of the storm-battered ship were in need of repair. Most notably, two of her three masts. An expensive business.

To Bob's immense relief, the Master indicated he would fund the refit.

There remained only one section to be inspected before the flotilla of fishing boats towed her the short distance up the coast to her home port of Whitby. Shadiz hailed the skiff that had hove-to between the merchantman and the fishing boats after delivering the tow ropes in case matters did not go well for the few men aboard her.

Bob wasn't sure how to detain the Master. Yet he felt impelled to do so. "What y' done 'ere. It won't be forgotten in 'urry."

Shadiz stared at the tranquil sea, reflecting the blue of the cloudless sky. "*We're as near t' 'eaven by sea as by land,*" he quoted, low-pitched. He turned inboard, grinning at Richard. "Since y' was so keen t' get aboard, y' can stay 'til they get 'er t' Whitby."

Already feeling nauseous, Richard's first inclination was to become querulous. The eyes of the two men locked. A moment later, Richard swung away from his smirking half-brother.

There was only one way to discover whether or not the *Eagle* had sustained any major damage to her hull. Instead of taking his place in the waiting skiff, while the burly rowers trailed their oars through the waves to prevent a tidal drift to the rocky shore, Shadiz dived off the *Eagle's* port rail. Several times, in different places, he came up for air before resuming the underwater inspection. Surfacing for the last time, he shouted up to Bob, "She's sound enough for tow."

Having reassured himself, Bob and the attentive men both on the merchantman and the fishing boats, Shadiz hauled himself into the skiff. Minutes later, before it grounded on the small pebbly beach below the cliff-hugging hamlet of Mercy Cove, he jumped out and waded through the shallow breakers. Gulls perched on cobles drawn up on the stone slope leading up from the shore squawked and took flight as he walked barefoot through the driftwood and kelp tossed up by the previous night's rough sea.

Awaiting their leader, mounted men crowded the narrow, steep lane flanked by fishermen's cottages, festooned with drying nets, and lobster pots piled up on their doorsteps.

Unusually sombre, Bill Todd stood holding Shadiz's leather coat, boots and weapons. He was grateful for the notable presence of the dark-skinned member of the Master's nomadic force. Behind them, Danny Murphy sat his horse stony-faced, his grey eyes filled with suppressed fury.

Approaching them, Shadiz gave each man a piercing, quizzical look. He came to a halt beside the restive stallion, the ecstatic mastiff at his heels. "Summat tells me y' ain't bearer o' glad tidin'," he grimly remarked to the dark-skinned messenger.

The Romany's native words brought about a momentary lapse before Shadiz's barbarous, scarred face took on a chilling aspect. Wath went on nervously, "Tomas was trackin' out o' Stillingfleet wi' Junno when they sent me after y', sir."

The Master shot Todd and Murphy an encompassing jet-black glare that was akin to a physical blow. Todd's heart quailed while his guts turn over. Murphy cursed under his breath.

Shadiz mounted the stallion. He now understood the source of the troublesome uneasy feeling. "Friggin' *kindness*."

CHAPTER THREE

Consequences

A conspiratorial knot riding double on the longsuffering horses, Catherine and Billy, Keeble and Mary ambled through a sunny meadow where bluebells bloomed in hazy profusion. Joy at the salvage of the *Eagle* had evaporated, just like the early morning mist upon the cliffs where they had spent the night, leaving them jaded by their own audacity. The stark reality was inescapable. There was no possibility of an unobtrusive return to the Lodge.

Catherine was ready to face the admittedly disquieting consequences of her actions. Indeed, given the alternative, she welcomed such an outcome.

While they gave collective thought to their predicament, they were mostly blind to their surroundings. That was why it came as a shock when they were impeded by a large party of horsemen, bristling with weapons. They were forced to halt within the iron ring that had surrounded them with lightning efficiency.

Catherine fleetingly hoped the riders hailed from the Lodge. But then her heart sank into her muddy shoes when she saw no familiar faces. Men-at-arms wearing an insignia of a bold keep surmounted by sprigs of ling upon their breasts were interspersed by buff-coated troopers.

There was a short pause, filled with the creaking of leather and the snorting of horses. A black bird sang sweetly while sparrows twittered in chorus in the soughing trees bordering the meadow. Normality seemed a cruel illusion.

Whether they had encountered the Master's men or the frighteningly smug warriors, in either case, Catherine would have feared for those she had led into disobedience far more than herself.

She felt herself to be relatively safe. For some bizarre reason, she was a prize catch. Yet, the enormity of what she had done, albeit for what she considered a very good reason, hit her hard.

"He's going to kill me," she muttered under her breath.

Keeping the nervous horse in check, Billy felt her words brush the stiff hairs on the back of his neck. He believed she had been referring to the most comely man he had ever set eyes on. His guts clenched even more, but did not betray him. Instead, he straightened his thin shoulders in a determined manner.

In wary silence, the small group from the Lodge watched the undoubted leader of the detaining company walk his high-stepping white mount into the unremitting circle. He halted the splendid Arabian stallion a few paces from them. It tossed its elegant head, long mane flowing, while he encompassed them with a pleasant smile none of them trusted. Thereafter, his sapphire attention dwelt on Catherine. His scrutiny held facets of a successful hunter. She returned the inspection, her head held high, trying not to betray her dismay at the wicked turn of events.

He wore dark blue velvet breeches and doublet of the highest quality, with a tasteful flair at collar and cuffs of intricate lace. A diamond brooch in the shape of an eight pointed cross held his scarlet cloak in place at a stylish angle upon his slim shoulders. Fair hair fell in immaculate waves from beneath a wide-brimmed hat, boasting an array of peacock feathers. Monogrammed soft kid gloves were worn on the shapely hands that held the stallion's reins in a light grip. Despite the finery, it was evident that he was no beautiful popinjay. The sword at his hip was no stylish accessory. His unmistakable air of sophisticated leadership dominated the assembled company, confirming her worst fears. If ever anyone was the counterbalance of her guardian it had to be Francois Lynette. A cobra against a panther.

He had been followed into the circle of warriors by two men, one fair and foppish and the other middle-aged and solid. Both watchful, they remained motionless, slightly behind and to either side of their leader, while he bowed to her in the saddle with a courtly flourish of his feathered hat. Straightening, he followed the gallant gesture by saying in lightly accented English, "Mon cheri, what an unexpected pleasure."

"And you are, sir?"

He seemed entertained by Catherine's procrastination. "I am Richard's uncle," he informed her, as if they had simply encountered each other upon the fashionable streets of York. "I hope he is well?"

"A slight head cold, but otherwise in good spirits," she replied, maintaining her brittle formality.

"Is this what all the fuss is about?" remarked the foppish young man.

The sneer on his effeminate face made Catherine conscious of her dishevelled appearance. Her long, damp hair had long since escaped any means of restraint. Her cloak was also damp, the hem encrusted with mud. The skirt of her plain brown dress was likewise matted. She needed no looking glass to realise her flushed features were dirty. But she was more than willing to be defiant in the face of adversity.

"How would you be aware of the fuss, sir? Having come fresh from the boys' bath house."

By being moved to smile at her spirited response, Lynette deepened the younger man's discomfort, causing the latter to glare at her.

"How fares your guardian?"

Catherine was at pains to keep her tone of voice neutral. "I would imagine he will be disconcerted by the manner in which you have waylaid my companions and I."

Lynette's laconic gaze swept over the others with her.

She felt Billy stiffen, making the horse they shared move restively. Upon catching sight of the knife he was surreptitiously gripping, she placed a restraining hand upon his tense arm. Glancing sideward, she realised Mary was on the verge of fainting through sheer terror. Only Keeble, mounted with the girl on the other horse, seemed reasonably composed. "Master be not far away!" exclaimed the little man.

"I am quite convinced he is mindful of his responsibility,"

Francois Lynette observed, switching back to Catherine. He expertly manoeuvred the high-spirited white stallion alongside Billy's mount, courteously adding, "What say you enjoy the hospitality of Fylingdales Hall. A more fitting environment for your youthful beauty than a forest hovel."

Gerald Carey gave a disparaging snort.

While keeping her features impassive, Catherine grimaced inwardly at Lynette's oblique reference to her age. At present, she probably looked like a twelve-year-old who had been playing in the mud.

Carey and Potter fell in line behind their leader while around them the circle broke and in no time at all the mounted men who had formed it became an impressive escort.

They left behind the wistful meadows around the fishing hamlet of Mercy Cove. Throughout their journey along a series of muddy causey which wound their way over the springtime moors within sight of the North Sea, Lynette maintained an amiable conversation with Catherine. All too soon for her liking Fylingdales Hall appeared in the distance. A magnificent sight, the ancestral manor, built around an imposing medieval keep, was set within parkland cultivated from the moor from which it took its name. She feared what lay within Richard's inheritance and Shadiz's, Sebastian's, birthplace.

Upon what she considered the enemy's stronghold coming into view, Catherine's natural sensitivity caught Lynette's imperceptible relief. The realisation that his chivalrous manner had masked a prudent alertness gave her a measure of satisfaction. He was not alone in believing the danger was over. Upon approaching their destination, the wariness of the strong escort was being replaced by a triumphant air.

And she had made it so ridiculously easy.

The inexplicable dread she had experienced the previous night had made it impossible to ignore the compulsion to journey to Mercy Cove. While doing so, her jet pendant had started to burn her beneath her drenched clothes. In desperation, she had sought to implement the remarkable conduit in order to cast a life line into troubled waters. Yet, despite the absence of remorse for her actions, she could not help feeling guilty about her present situation. Caught on the spike of trepidation, she wondered what Shadiz's reaction would be when he discovered she had strayed into Lynette's clutches. Would it simply be a matter of pride to reclaim what had been stolen from him?

The elegant Frenchman's accented voice broke into her morbid thoughts. "You must be fatigued after your sojourn during such a frightful night. Once we reach the Hall, you shall rest in comfort."

"I thank you for your consideration, sir," responded Catherine, in the same polite manner, "I hope the same applies to my companions?"

"I can envisage no less."

She was not convinced by his smooth assurance. She glanced in Mary's direction. Clinging onto Keeble, the poor girl continued to appear terrified.

In an effort to keep her own anxiety in check, she surveyed her surroundings. She had managed to slip away from the Lodge. If the opportunity arose, it might be possible to escape from Fylingdales Hall. Therefore it would be beneficial to have at least a vague idea of the lie of the land.

She lost sight of the Hall as the route of the large company took them down into a deep hollow. To their left thistles and nettles grew in profusion around the base of dense hedgerows. A black bird sang in the coppice on the opposite side of their path. How could the world seem so right and be so horribly wrong?

A volley of muskets shattered the moorland peace.

Catherine held onto Billy as he struggled to prevent the startled horse from bolting. Turning fearfully, she saw several members of the Fylingdales escort were now sprawled lifeless on the muddy ground. She averted her horrified gaze as they, their faces frozen in alarm, were trampled by the hooves of their own panic-stricken mounts.

In the next rapid heartbeat, she understood who was descending upon them. What she did not recognise was the hostile mood of the Master's men. Two formidable packs, they charged at breakneck speed down both sides of the steep-sided hollow. At the same time more riders cleared the hedgerow to the left and landed with ground shuddering momentum. The three-pronged ambush effectively trapped Fylingdales's men-at-arms and the Crop-Ears troopers. Struggling to combat the advantage gained by the ferocious impetus, they were driven back against the dark stand of trees to their right.

The attack had been formulated with a dexterity that cut the head of the column from the main body. The third prong of the onslaught, those horsemen who had cleared the tall hedgerow with expert ease, were Romanies, led by Junno.

Several immediately engaged Lynette, Carey and Potter, cutting them off from the terrified horses from the Lodge. While the three men were forced to give ground, hard-pressed by superior, aggressive numbers, Junno and the rest of his warlike brethren surrounded Catherine and her small party. Grim-faced, the big man snatched her from behind Billy and set her down before him on his Clydesdale. During the neat transfer, she beseeched him to aid Mary and the others. Bad enough the deaths and injuries her folly would cause this day without those she had persuaded into disobedience being added to the final reckoning. But, already, the surrounding Romanies were seizing the reins of the wild-eyed horses. One of the dark-skinned warriors swung Mary onto his fine-boned mare, averting a petrified collapse beneath flying hooves. Billy and Keeble hung on for dear life as their mounts were turned at speed.

Junno bellowed a command. He was flanked, protectively mane to mane, by all of his brethren, including those who had driven Lynette's command group away and into the serrated ranks of the fierce battle taking place around the coppice, so that while they fought for their lives they posed no threat to Catherine.

The big man's normally placid Clydesdale had turned into a warhorse. The great brute ripped into those inferior horses whose riders sought to flee the bloody turmoil and stamped upon wounded men unfortunate enough to be unsaddled. While the less experienced among Lynette's force had quickly fallen victim to sword thrusts, their surprise having curtailed an effective defence, the majority of his men-at-arms and a knot of troopers, veterans of many such skirmishes, had transformed their alarm into professional resistance.

Although it seemed to Catherine that minutes had been transformed into hours, in truth it had taken Junno and his fellow Romanies a remarkably short time to whisk her and the others away from the determined clash of steel, the harrowing cries of wounded men and the screams of horses.

She had received an unforgettable insight into the activities of the Master and his men. The violence had turned her blood cold. She had caught sight of him in the thick of the fighting. For the briefest of moments his gaze had found hers. In less than a blink of an eye, she had glimpsed what lay beneath the few shreds of civility. She had witnessed the same unmasking of feral malevolence earlier in the year when he had tortured and killed the renegade seaman, Walt Smithson. A tremor passed through her. Junno's arm tightened comfortingly around her.

Even when they had left the churning brutality far behind, the big man did not slacken their fast pace. Encountering only startled sheep, the Romanies sped across the wild, undulating moorland. They were past masters at traversing cryptic ways, even so, transporting their precious load, they remained on the alert. Only when they had reached the outskirts of Stillingfleet Forest did Junno signal a halt.

Catherine lost no time in calling upon him to intervene on behalf of Mary, Keeble and Billy. "Shadiz must understand, they came after me when they realised I was missing from the Lodge. They hoped to find me and guide me back before he learned of my absence."

The big man readily agreed, but the expression on his round, big-boned face, shiny with sweat, showed he was not entirely convinced by her explanation. He hoped his cousin's dangerous fury had been appeased by the attack on Lynette's force. On this occasion, it was not only Keeble, Billy and the little maid for whom he feared.

The wait to see what frame of mind the Master was in following Catherine's rescue was relatively short yet anxious. Before too long, he and his men galloped into view. They reined in their lathered, excitable horses around the large group of Romanies. In an attempt to evade Shadiz's chilling black glare, Catherine established what casualties there were amongst his men. Despite a profusion of sweat, blood and mud, to her immense relief, fortunately none of the wounds appeared to be of a serious nature.

In the fast breathing pause, the restive stallion pawed the ground.

Junno realised he had underestimated his cousin's one, abiding emotion. While everyone else saw only an extremely lethal and unpredictable exterior, the big man was convinced that Shadiz was torn between the inner, conflicting needs to catch hold of Catherine and hug her or to give her a desperate shake for what she had put him through; the like of which no-one else ever could. In the event, he did neither. Junno's compassionate heart ached for him.

The Master gestured for his men to continue through the forest to the Lodge. In passing, Bill Todd gave Catherine a hurt, reproving look. Danny Murphy gave every indication of wanting to throttle her. The Master dismissed the Romanies, too. They went in silence, taking Mary, Keeble and Billy with them. The trio shot Catherine worried backward glances.

When men and horses had disappeared and no other noises disturbed the forest, birdsong once again flourished. A squirrel ran halfway down the trunk of a beech tree, only to scamper back up again when the stallion once more pawed the muddy ground, impatient with its master's stillness on its back.

"Develesko Mush," rasped Shadiz, eventually, low-pitched, "Y're the most bloody infuriatin' chai. Will y' not stay where y' put?"

Catherine decided in defence of herself to be brutally frank. Meeting his withering look, she retorted, "I sensed you were about to do something wildly inappropriate." She clutched her jet pendent. "This was burning me. I could not ignore the warning."

Neither Shadiz nor Catherine noticed Junno's wide-eyed astonishment.

Uttering a string of swift oaths in several languages, Shadiz dismounted. Hands on hips, his tall, broad-shouldered stance rigid, he stood with his back to her. Junno was convinced for the first time in his cousin's adult life he was at a loss to know what course of action to take.

The big man failed to stop Catherine sliding down from his patient Clydesdale. "I left the Lodge by myself. Keeble, Billy and Mary sought to find me before you returned. Please, you must not blame them."

Shadiz slewed round to face her. "Oh, believe me, I ain't layin' blame on 'em. You've got knack o' twistin' folk round y'r little finger off t' perfection."

"Except you, of course!" exclaimed Catherine. "You care about nothing and nobody. Oh, I am forgetting, you thought enough of my father to saddle yourself with me. Well, pardon me, I felt the need to try and keep you alive. Is that so very terrible!"

" 'ow in God's name do I make y' understand?" Shadiz demanded, very, very softly.

Neither Shadiz nor Catherine took any notice of Junno, hovering apprehensively between them.

For the next few moments, though he continued to glare down at her, Shadiz seemed preoccupied. Then, abruptly decisive, he reached for her.

She shied away from him, the glimpse of the predatory beast fresh in her mind.

His expression darkened still further as he shackled her wrist but caused her no pain in spite of his enormous strength. "*You* have no reason t' fear me," he snapped, starting to march her through the forest.

Left behind, Junno swiftly hobbled both the stallion and his Clydesdale. Leaving the two horses to crop the wet grass on the forest floor, he followed in his cousin's decisive wake.

Catherine tried in vain to free herself from Shadiz's grip. He ignored her vehement protests and defiant clutching at foliage.

When she lost her footing, instead of yanking her up by her imprisoned wrist, he briefly released her and then quickly wrapped an arm around her waist to keep her upright. Her feet barely touching the ground, he took her around close-knit trees, through undergrowth that tugged at her dirty garments and down narrow animal tracks. Forbiddingly silent, he ensured she came to no harm. His consideration gave Junno a measure of relief as he kept in hot pursuit, lumbering apprehensively to a mysterious destination.

When Shadiz finally brought their trek through the forest to a halt, Catherine glanced at the big man questioningly. All he could do was shrug his huge shoulders to indicate his own bewilderment.

Both of them surveyed the rough shelter nestling between the trees a few feet away. It had been crafted out of thick, knobbly branches and covered by several layers of leaves and twigs. The doorway consisted of interwoven branches. There was a smoky fire to one side of the shelter. A rather clever contraption made up of different size iron rods held a small, bubbling cauldron in place over the meagre flames. Several crude cooking utensils were scattered about the trampled grass.

The small camp appeared more hermit-like than a sentry post, Catherine decided. She jumped when Shadiz called out.

"Garan," he repeated, loudly. He paced up and down impatiently in front of the shelter, taking Catherine with him. Yet again, she tried to break free, but he stubbornly refused to relinquish his hold on her. Having swapped back to imprisoning her wrist, she wondered if he had any idea he was constantly stroking his thumb over the palm of her hand. "Dammit, Garan, where the devil are y'? None o' y'r bloody games."

"Games be they! Is that what you reckon? A catch me quick around bushes. A hide an' seek betwixt trees."

Both Catherine and Junno stared in astonishment at the person who had spoken in an outraged gravel voice. He was as long as a barge-pole and willow thin. His outlandish garb appeared to have been fashioned out of the same natural materials covering the shelter. His feet were bare. His ancient face was barely discernable through his long, wild hair and his rampant beard, which tumbled in bird nest disorder onto his narrow chest.

"*Games!*"

"Forgive me." Shadiz spoke with a certain amount of restraint. " 'elp me wi' summat."

The man skipped past him and started to stir the murky contents of the cooking pot hung over the fire. "I know what you're 'ere for. Well, there be no long-ears in this pot. Go catch a beastie an' listen to its screams. Poor beastie. Poor, poor beastie."

"I ain't after y'r food," snapped Shadiz. He drew a long, repressive breath. "I want y' t' tak 'er into Sacred Grove an' let 'er see Crystal Pool." He inched Catherine forward while still keeping her within his looming, protective shadow.

Continuing to bend over the fire, despite the abundance of smoke drifting up into his contorted face, the scarecrow-man kept on stirring the bubbling contents of the pot, muttering to himself.

"D' y' 'ear me?"

"Well, there's a thing," said Garan, straightening. He gestured with the wooden spoon, splashing hot liquid into the fire, causing it to hiss like an angry snake. "Do I 'ear y'? Or do I want t' 'ear y'? Interesting. Very interesting."

"What the 'ell?"

Shadiz raised a hand to silence Junno, his attention remaining on Garan. "Will y' let 'er see Crystal Pool?" he asked, tersely.

Garan gave an exaggerated sigh. He walked around the fire, coming to a halt a couple of paces away from Shadiz and Catherine. "Be she pure?" he asked, sniffing suspiciously.

"Aye. She's pure," replied Shadiz. His posture became reassuring as she shrank into him, away from the wild man's blunt attention. "Pure grauni."

"Pure in heart?" persisted Garan, eyeing her intently.

Regarding her, Shadiz cocked his head to one side.

"When you have quite finished." Blushing, she directed her objection at Shadiz, disturbed more than anything by his closeness she had inadvertently encouraged.

"Aye. She be pure in heart," he confirmed, softly, his mesmerizing gaze locked with hers.

Garan rubbed his thin, dirty hands together. "Well, then. Why d' we wait?"

Shadiz started forward with Catherine.

"No! No! No!" cried Garan, waving his hands above his head. "She, alone."

At first, Shadiz seemed reluctant to comply. Only after further prompting from the weird old man did he eventually release her. He gave her a fierce, meaningful look meant to deter any thoughts she might have of bolting. When he spoke it was with a hard edge of authority. "Go wi' 'im."

Seething with impotent rage, Catherine responded with a sarcastic curtsy. Garan giggled and, catching hold of her hand, swept her away from the two tall Romanies.

Junno watched with grave misgivings as she disappeared into the forest with the wild man. Turning to his cousin standing beside him, who was also watching their departure, he said, "I don't understand. First y' move 'eaven an' earth t' get Rauni back, an' then y' let 'er go off wi' that crazy, old man."

Shadiz continued to stare after Catherine. "That crazy old man is more capable o' lookin' after Kore than me an' you put together." He glanced sideward at Junno. "Besides, simensa. If y' recall I'm the one whose crazy. An' she's about t' find out 'ow bloody crazy."

"No," objected Junno, plaintively.

★ ★ ★

Huge oak trees, centuries old, formed a protective circle around the broad forest clearing. Stepping into the Sacred Grove, its spirituality resonated strongly with Catherine. It was a setting of pure enchantment, where the ageless reverence for Nature was encapsulated in every blade of grass and in every leaf and branch. She recalled her father speaking with deep respect of such ancient places. How they had been open-air temples long before the

Roman Emperor Constantine had sanctioned magnificent stones and hallowed mortar.

A huge brown boar stood before the mightiest oak that dominated the rest. Its long, wicked-looking tusks were aimed at Catherine, as if she were a thief come to steal the amazing array of corn shapes, locks of hair twisted in ribbons, fresh spring flowers and strips of different coloured cloths decorating the broad tree trunk, graceful branches and thick, protruding roots.

She slowed despite the tug on her arm by Garan. He twisted around to her. "Oh, you're not to mind Myr. Come, I'll introduce you." She responded to his urging with reluctance, eyeing the brown beast warily. For as long as she could remember she had possessed an affinity with animals, but this was no ordinary creature, she was certain.

It was the impression that man and beast were conversing mutely that made her apprehension waver. Fascinated, she looked from one to the other. And, after a moment, was treated to a wide smile from Garan. "She likes you. Thinks you're a bit dirty, mind. She told me to tell you that you're not to fear her, me or the Crystal Pool. You don't fear me, do you?" He looked pointedly at her.

Meeting his clear grey eyes, Catherine felt as if she was being drawn into a secure domain. His smile was no longer the foolish beam it had been before but a reasoned approach, possessing a gentle compulsion "No," she responded, "I don't fear you."

He held out his hands to her. "Please." Seeing her hesitation, which really had nothing to do with the deplorable state of them, he added, "Oh, I'm sorry." He rubbed them together. Curious, thin gloves, complete with dirty fingernails drifted down to the ground. "There that's better, isn't it."

Blinking, Catherine took hold of the immaculately clean hands. Immediately, she felt a tingling sensation. It started in her hands and crept up her arms.

"Tis quite alright," Garan reassured her, kindly. The warmth in his gaze drove away her alarm. After a moment, he added, "You are worthy of the view."

"I am?"

"Oh, indeed," he answered, tucking her arm in his. Oddly, the smell of decay that had hung about him seemed to have receded. Or she had become accustomed to it. He walked with her into the middle of the grove. She could not understand how she had missed noticing the pool surrounded by perfectly round white stones.

"It's beautiful," remarked Catherine, glancing sideward. To her surprise, the tall thin man now wore a long green robe. Like the odd gloves, the wild garb of a forest hermit lay discarded on the ground. His long hair and beard seemed to have unravelled into snowy neatness. He was now holding a staff almost as tall as himself. It was a mystery to her where it had come from. The top of the staff was an enigmatic face sculptured naturally by the contours of the smooth wood.

"Come, Luna May," Garan invited.

Catherine swallowed convulsively as he led her forwards onto one of the flat stones bordering the Crystal Pool. Each stone had a different rune carved into its vivid whiteness. Looking down at the slightly larger one upon which she was standing, she saw that it had a particularly complicated symbol etched into its smoothness. Looking up at the pool, she thought it aptly named. Shafts of sunlight seemed as if they were being absorbed by the water. The calm surface glistened a mystical, silvery crystal.

"This be the Crystal Pool. The well of past, present and future." Thus saying, Garan bowed low. Speaking quiet words completely foreign to Catherine, he touched its strangely dense surface with the face upon his staff.

She was trembling. The huge boar had paced beside them. It brushed against her, by its nearness seeming to offer support.

"Why has he brought me to you?" she asked, unable to halt the quiver in her voice.

"You are hope. You are peace. You are light in the bleakness. All thoughts. All actions. All are butterflies upon the web to behold. Gather your store."

She was seized by a sudden dread before becoming curiously enthralled by the enchantment of the Crystal Pool.

Junno was the first to catch sight of Catherine stumbling through the trees. He called out to her in an attempt to stop her from veering wildly away from where he and his restless cousin had waited.

Moving in the present moment, what she had glimpsed, past and future, in the Crystal Pool reflected in her wide, staring eyes. Tears had made thin, clean trails down her grubby face. Trembling violently, Catherine made her erratic way to the big man. "Please, take me home," she pleaded, brokenly.

"Kore?"

She flung up her arm and struck Shadiz hard across his scarred cheek.

No one ever struck first, such was his lightning reactions. And no one even attempted to strike with impunity. Yet he had allowed Catherine to do so. Probably realising her intention before she had. It made Junno want to drop to his knees and beg his cousin to give in to the emotion that was swirling in the tormented black eyes and eroding the brutal exterior.

"Don't you come near me!" she cried. "How could you do such a thing?" Angrily tearful, she continued, "I hope you're satisfied. But, you maybe less so when I inform you, I can't remember half of what I saw. Only seeing my father's murder remains perfectly clear." She dashed away from her speechless guardian.

Junno registered the tremor within Shadiz's curt gesture. He hurried after Catherine, knowing that he could give little comfort.

Neither of them spoke as they walked through the forest. Catherine tried to regain her composure while Junno led the placid Clydesdale towards the Lodge. Occasionally he would glance back at her atop of his large horse and she would return his look of concern with a weak smile. But her blue eyes remained haunted.

Upon reaching the Lodge, they were met in the courtyard by a distraught Keeble.

"Tom's been teken bad."

CHAPTER FOUR

Farewell

An icy dread had replaced all other emotions. Catherine raced up the stone steps. Despite his size, Junno was close behind her. Together they burst into Tom's chamber. Brought up short in the doorway, they were confronted by the inexorable dimming of life within the purview of candlelight.

"Tom!"

Catherine's desperate call went unanswered. A frail old man, his face deathly pale, he lay quite still. Rushing to his bedside, she fell to her knees and grasped his hand.

"Oh, Tom."

His eyelids flickered in weak response.

She was unaware of Junno and a tearful Keeble pressing around her or Mary's mother, Alice, standing at the foot of the bed, a sad expression on her ruddy face.

"Tom? Can you hear me?" called Catherine, softly.

His eyes gradually opened. He focused with difficulty upon the lovely, very special bairn who had been thrust into the domain of warriors, whom he had come to love like a daughter. But his words, stored like precious gems, were not for her.

"Sebastian?" came his weak entreaty.

Junno immediately left the bedchamber in determined haste, haunted by the knowledge Tom would not have used that particular name in any other circumstance.

Catherine forced herself to smile. "Fear not, he will be with you ere long," she said. And hoped that her soothing words would prove true.

Guilt-ridden, she realised the time for administrating herbs had vanished in the night she had been driven to follow her heart. The price was proving exorbitant. Not only had she been made to view her father's slaughter, reflected in the crystal mirror of time, now she must kneel, strangled by grief, at the bedside of the man who had become the benevolent replacement in her drastically altered lifestyle.

Cradling his limp, timeworn hand, she tried to keep the silent tears that washed her grubby cheeks out of her voice as she spoke quietly of the *Eagle's* rescue in Mercy Cove; all the while watching the sculptor of death whittle away on Tom's beloved, rustic features. She treasured each moment of capricious life while marking their passage without Shadiz's presence, aware the anticipation of his coming was the single thread keeping Tom connected to life.

Shadiz arrived with his inherent stealth. When the people in the bedchamber realised his presence, Keeble and Alice immediately gave him access to the bed. Catherine cast an anguished look in his direction. She could sense the subtle change in him. Going down on one knee at the opposite side of the bed, he gave her a wary, consoling glance. Thereafter, his attention focused on Tom. "Father Time," he murmured. He had seen too many deaths not to recognise the last moments of life.

The older man's eyes opened. His trembling hand gripped Shadiz's sleeve. Desperate to make best use of the remnants of his span, he tried to speak but words did not come readily.

"Easy," soothed Shadiz.

But Tom's agitation to be heard increased, fed by the dregs of the well.

Shadiz drew closer, a dark, vital force bending over dying wisdom. Listening to Tom's low-pitched words, he shot Catherine an incredulous look.

Indeed, such was his apparent incredulity, it seemed to her that he had momentarily forgotten Tom's imminent demise. Confounded, her speculative gaze held his for several heartbeats. With a visible effort, he tore himself away from her, and looked back down at Tom. She watched as he spoke words that she was unable to catch.

An attempt to shake his head failed. Therefore Tom groped for the hand that he had not held since the time the man had been a child in his care. Then he cast around for Catherine's hand. Seeing his weak effort, she took hold of his right hand. Struggling to accomplish his last act, Tom joined their hands. His fragile smile was directed first at Catherine, and then, gaining persuasive conviction, was turned upon Shadiz.

In the last moments, Shadiz found himself renewing his pledge to keep Catherine safe. Yet again, the quiet oath was given to an older man who would take his secret to the grave; who with his dying breath had deepened, incredibly, exquisite torment.

Holding hands across Tom's shrunken body, together Shadiz and Catherine watched along with the others in the bedchamber as the light of life faded away into another time, another place, unknown to the living.

For a while the silent mourning was broken only by Keeble's heartbroken sobs.

"In the turning of the hourglass, I have been witness to two deaths," mumbled Catherine, continuing to stare at Tom's peaceful countenance.

Shadiz was also gazing upon Tom's lifeless form. "Per'aps, if y'd been 'ere t' see t' 'im...."

"Perhaps, if you had done as I asked and gone to Mamma Petra," retorted Catherine, her voice breaking.

"I was on me way when I got message about *Eagle*," he snapped, snatching his hand away from hers. He stood up in one fluid move. "I ain't able t' be in two bloody places at once."

"Enough. *Please!*" Junno's deep bass voice was mournful, firm and pleading all at once.

After a lingering glance at Tom, Shadiz began to walk away from the bed. As he drew abreast of Junno, the big man gave him a stark, pointed look. Shadiz halted. A muscle flexed in his scarred cheek. Tears on his cheeks, Junno would not be browbeaten by the sinister black eyes. After a moment's hesitation, Shadiz turned back to Catherine. She continued to stare down at Tom, paralysed by grief.

"Go an' see t' men's 'urts," he commanded. After a moment, he added, "D' 'y 'ear me?"

"I'm not allowed in the hall," she responded in a voice bleak with despair. She turned her head and looked at him. Her blue eyes sparkled with a well of tears. They seemed to dominate her hauntingly forlorn, grubby face.

Junno saw his cousin recoil. Shadiz seemed pinned to the moment by his painful indecision. It made the big man put aside his own misery, as he knew Tom would have wanted him to do. For it was obvious, the man who had raised a hated, unwanted bastard for the first five years of life had come to realise his adopted son's untainted passion. More. He had clearly become convinced, in the same way Junno had, that over the time Catherine had lived at the Lodge, her feelings for her improbable guardian was not some girlish infatuation for a powerful leader, an extraordinary man. Even if she in her innocence was uncertain about the emotion, disguising it in the kindly consideration she gave to all.

"Come, Rauni," Junno coaxed, quietly. Stepping forward, he helped Catherine to rise and escorted her out of the bedchamber, followed by a tearful Alice. Keeble stumbled after them, giving Tom one last, distraught look before closing the door.

Left alone in the chamber, Shadiz slowly retraced his footsteps. He stood by the bed gazing down at Tom.

"You must wear your rue with a difference. There's a daisy; I would give you some violets, but they withered all when my father died."

He sighed regretfully. Bending, he brushed a kiss over Tom's forehead.

"Sleep well, Father Time," he murmured. Straightening, he gently pulled the sheet over Tom.

Shadiz took a backward step away from the bed. One arm raised across his chest from waist to shoulder, he bowed.

CHAPTER FIVE

Drowning in Tears

Catherine felt it necessary to apologise to each of the Master's men in turn as she attended to their various wounds, sustained when they had confronted the might of Fylingdales in order to prevent her abduction. Fortunately, their injuries were nothing like the damage they had inflicted upon Lynette's force during the successful ambush. Although it was evident none bore her ill-will, nevertheless Junno stood in attendance.

The last man to enter the small chamber adjoining the kitchen where she kept her herbal paraphernalia was Bill Todd. She didn't know if Danny Murphy was carrying a memento of the fight. Even if he was, she thought it highly unlikely he would seek her help, and for that she was grateful. The last thing she needed at the moment was Murphy's hard-faced condemnation. Bill, on the other hand, was not a man to hold a grudge. Even so, Catherine felt a special apology was required for her actions, which Bill accepted with jolly grace. "Best sleep I've 'ad in ages," was his only remark about the way she had drugged him and Murphy in order to make good her escape from the Lodge. A shadow passed over his wryly smiling countenance when she asked him if they had received a reprimand from the Master.

A deep, distinct voice, barely above a whisper, answered for Bill. "Y' see, bloody daft me. I ain't reckoned t' give a warnin' t' watch out fer one they were guardin'."

Bill developed an embarrassed expression. Uneasy, he shuffled around. And was told to keep still while Catherine finished attending to the shallow sword cut in his left forearm. She ignored Shadiz's presence in the doorway. As soon as she had finished bandaging Bill's arm, he beat a hasty retreat, nodding respectfully to the Master in passing.

Normally efficient in her work, Catherine uncharacteristically sent flying a dish of bloody water and a pot of unpleasant smelling woundwort. They collided in mid-air and, having mixed together, tumbled down onto the stone-flagged floor, just missing the mastiff that had appeared with its master. The large, grey dog gave her a hurt look. Reaching for a handy cloth, she knocked over a pot of comfrey on the long bench, which immediately added to the mess. Resigned to the extra work, she was grateful for Mary's and Junno's help.

"Y've 'ad enough. Go t' bed. Get some sleep," commanded Shadiz.

"I'm allowed to, am I? Now that I've served my punishment," she retorted, dabbing briskly at the discoloured floor. "Besides," she continued, tersely, "I am perfectly well."

"Like 'ell y' are," observed Shadiz, catching hold of her arm and pulling her upright.

"I'm not going up there!" she exclaimed, wrenching her arm free. She swallowed hard, trying to hold back the tears. Watching Junno and Mary as they continued to clean up the spillage, she muttered, "Alice and Keeble are up there ... with Tom."

"Then," began Shadiz, sharply. Taking a repressive breath, he continued in a more moderate tone, "Go rest in library."

"I need some fresh air," Catherine admitted, rubbing her pounding temples. But when he took her by the arm again, she resisted. "You are not taking me back to that place. That Crystal Pool."

"O' course not, dammit."

He anchored her to his side by circling her waist and took her through the busy kitchen. His inescapable presence at least ensured she did not have to stumble through the mire of sympathy turned her way. Though he was obviously taking care with her, the apprehensive women were relieved to see Junno appear soon afterwards. He lingered in the doorway of the kitchen while behind him, quietly marvelling at the Master's conduct, the women resumed their preparation of the evening meal. It promised to be a subdued affair.

The sunny day did not alleviate Catherine's mourning for Tom, and the underlying feeling she had abandoned him. Nonetheless she did find the mild spring air in the broad pasture refreshed her burdened spirit. Several cats and dogs followed her aimless footsteps to her freshly dug plot. She bent down and absent-mindedly stroked wiry-haired canines and feline smoothness. Had it been only two days ago since Richard, Keeble, Mary, Bill Todd and Danny Murphy had helped her to prepare the ground for the herbs she intended to plant? When Tom had brought them mugs of elderflower wine to slake their thirst?

Still fully armed and rough-looking from the attack on Lynette's force, Shadiz stood, hands on hips, watching her. His tribal dark features were set in stone.

Eventually, bone weary, soul weary, Catherine subsided onto the bench close to the well. The assortment of dogs remained with her, showing respect to the mastiff, which rested its spiky chin on her lap as if sensing her sadness and wanting to comfort her. Aware of his dislike of them, the cats slunk away when Shadiz walked over to her. He put a boot on the splintery wood of the bench and leant his arm on his knee.

"What did you say?" she asked, belatedly realising he had brought their mutual silence to an end.

"I said, forgive me. It were uncalled for, accusin' y' o' failin' Tom."

Catherine looked up at him. She felt compelled to reciprocate. "Even if you had not been diverted from going to see Mamma Petra," she said, wretchedness filling her subdued voice, "I doubt even she would have been able to save him."

He slowly nodded. "So," he urged in a half-whisper, sitting down next to her, "y' ain't t' blame y'rsen for Father Times's passin'."

Catherine began to speak, but the words died on her lips. "What?"

"I … I had a choice. I could have remained with Tom. Only."

Her unsteady hand rose to her jet pendant. "The stone grew warm."

She felt in no condition to withstand his soul-piercing attention. Her averted gaze drifted over the trees, soughing gently in the light breeze beyond the half-ruined, ivied wall encircling the pasture at the rear of the Lodge. Like a thousand tiny jewels, yesterday's raindrops sparkled upon the spring-green leaves in the bright morning sunlight. Sparrows, blackbirds, thrushes and squabbling starlings flew to and fro from their newly built nests in the branches of the ancient trees and the many nooks and crannies in the renovated Lodge. From the kitchen came the indistinct buzz of cooks and pot washers and their offspring. From the stables came the murmur of male voices.

"I cannot remember all I saw," said Catherine without altering the line of her glassy stare. "Just the manner of … my father's death." Twisting around to her motionless guardian, trying to shut out the haunting scene she had witnessed in the mystical water, she demanded, "Why did you take me to that place?"

Shadiz did not answer immediately. For a second or two he hung his head. When he moved, his long black hair fell away from his regretful expression. Sinking down onto one knee before her, he took hold of both her arms. "Forgive me, Kore. I simply wanted t' make y' understand." There was no harshness in his barely audible voice. "Y' can't change what's written in the pauni."

"Yet I have," she reminded him, emphatically, meeting his stark gaze, "twice now."

His smile was wistful. "Mebbe y' shouldn't 'ave."

Catherine raised a trembling hand to the cut in his forehead. Saltwater had cleansed the wound inflicted by jagged rocks in the deep rock pool he had inadvertently strayed. She stroked the rough stubble about his jaw and then the discoloured ridges of his scarred cheek. "I am so glad you are safe."

He captured her hand and removed it from his cheek. His tender expression made it plain he knew her thoughts. He was taking her breath away with his deliberate openness. When she saw his moonstone pendant had escaped from beneath his shirt, she touched its silver edge. Its strange markings were so like her own. "You have felt the link, haven't you?"

She was unprepared for the sudden upsurge of wild fury. Startled, her heart began to pound.

"Aye," he growled, the blackness of his eyes deepening. "When y' were taken by Page." He took a shuddering intake of breath, struggling to regain control. A moment later, he gave her a rueful grin. "An', aye. Just afore I were informed y'd took t' y' 'eels. *Again*."

"H'm." Looking again at his moonstone pendant, Catherine caught sight of the blood she had failed to notice before on his shirt where his jerkin had come undone beneath his long, leather coat. "You're hurt."

"I'll live, I reckon."

"You should have told me when I was attending to everyone."

"Y' kept me safe."

There was a deep, locked silence between them for a couple of moments.

"Do you not fear mortality?" she asked, quietly.

"I seek mortality o' those who'd 'arm y'. Y're under my protection."

There it was again. The cold, hard reason. He had given a promise to her father. And, a short while ago, to Tom.

It hurt. Everything hurt. Catherine's face slowly crumbled. "Why did Tom have to go?" she cried, wretchedly. Tears began to cascade down her grubby face. "Why did he have to follow my father?" She gulped, staring up at Shadiz helplessly. "I could not bear it if you....."

"*Sh*. Enough, mandi kom." He sat down beside her again on the bench and gathered her to him. Reaching for the solace he gave unstintingly, goaded by fatigue, the full force of her unhappiness spilt forth.

In time there was silence save for the occasional shuddering sob.

Junno straightened in the kitchen doorway. Soft-footed in spite of his tremendous size, he approached the bench where Shadiz held Catherine's sleeping form possessively close to his chest. He felt like an intruder. Yet with resignation he knew his designated role. Experiencing immeasurable sadness, he halted before Shadiz.

"D' 'y want me t' carry 'er up t' 'er chamber?" he asked in their language.

Shadiz sat immobile, staring down at Catherine. A combination of despair and exhaustion had created deep hollows below her high cheekbones and dark shadows beneath her closed eyes where her long, damp lashes lay. Her pale face was a patchwork of grubby patches and tearstained streaks. The homemade attire she had worn the previous evening, so as not to draw attention to herself when Mary and her had unobtrusively joined the Glaisdale women as they were escorted out of Stillingfleet Forest, was filthy. Only her hands were clean, where she had washed away the grime before attending to those of the men in need of attention. Her long fair-white hair was limp and tangled. Lost in much-needed sleep, she looked very young.

Half-hidden by his own wild long hair, the gut-wrenching purity of emotion on Shadiz's normally forbidding face brought tears to Junno's eyes.

"Bring me water an' cloth," muttered Shadiz, without looking up.

Upon the big man's swift return with a bowl of warm water and two soft cloths, Shadiz carefully washed and dried Catherine's face, relaxed in oblivious sleep. He gently brushed his fingers through her dishevelled hair.

"What the 'ell am I doin' t' 'er?"

Junno being Junno found a poppy in a field of weeds. "Safeguardin' 'er. Just like y' promised the Rai an', just a bit ago, Tom. Y've no choice. Somehow, Lynette, damn him, knows 'e can get t' y' through Rauni. 'ave y' stopped t' wonder 'ow cum bastard were out 'untin' 'er, not y'?"

Shadiz looked up swiftly, his expression sharpening, hardening.

Not altogether surprised, Junno had realised his cousin had been too taken up with getting Catherine back to consider, as he would otherwise have done, the threat posed by Lynette's dangerous knowledge of her movements.

The spectre of a traitor rose its ugly head once more. Had not the seaman, Walt Smithson, given a malicious warning.

"Wouldn't y' like t' know about maggot reet under y'r nose."

"Develesko Mush," rasped Shadiz.

In the lengthy pause that followed, each man tried hard to fathom who could be the rotten apple in a full barrel. Richard was the obvious choice. Too obvious. Like Bob Andrew and the recently departed Tom Wright, Junno did not trust Richard Massone, coming from where he did. The big Romany knew his cousin was not misled by his half-brother's declaration for the king, which was why he was kept under surveillance and at arm's length when it came to the war politics at the Lodge.

The force raised by the Master included men from various, dubious backgrounds. Yet all were fiercely loyal to their strange, charismatic leader. Also, the folk of the district, be they of the sea or land, had prospered greatly since he had established his headquarters at the Lodge. However, it was not overlooked by either Shadiz or Junno that Walt Smithson also had been a part of the close knit community in a rugged, isolated area.

Junno, who had not been at the Lodge the previous night, asked, "Who could've known 'er whereabouts? When she left 'ere?"

"God knows," rasped Shadiz. His next few words, pitched low, held a ruthless threat. "But I intend t' find out."

Catherine gave a ragged sigh in her sleep, interrupting the troubled thoughts of the two men.

Shadiz's dark attention returned to her immediately. "She must be guarded." It was an indisputable statement. He brushed a strand of hair away from her face. His thumb caressed her pale cheek. "Even against 'ersen."

To Junno's surprise, he rose with Catherine cradled in his arms, and carried her into the Lodge. Junno followed, his kind brown eyes filled with consternation when not possessing a warning to those people who viewed their passing.

After quashing with a fierce scowl Bessie's lamentations about her young mistress's deplorable state, Shadiz closed the door of Catherine's bedchamber. Junno settled down to guard her sleeping presence within.

Shadiz lingered in the shadows on the landing. "Resolve's crumblin'. Y' must guard against *Want*, simensa."

CHAPTER SIX

The Nightmare Watcher

Rather than stay in the dingy interior of Barney Throup's ale-house on the outskirts of Boggle Hole, upon receiving a mug brimming with weak ale from the nervous landlord, Shadiz ducked under the low lintel and strode out into the afternoon sunshine.

The mastiff settled at his feet while he leant against the pitted stonework of the hovel and watched Throup's ragged brood playing tig-o-ring on the beach below.

In their midst was Throup's eldest daughter. She dashed about trying to catch first one then another of her giggling, agile siblings, her fair hair flying in the breeze coming off the North Sea and burnished by the sun. Her lovely young face was alight with merriment, the movements of her slender body unconsciously graceful.

When the game finished, Throup's notorious customer drank the ale in one, long pull, trying to get rid of the bitter taste from a different murky brew. After tossing the empty mug to the landlord hovering in the doorway, he mounted the black stallion and rode away in the direction of Scarborough. But not before he had given the fair-haired girl one last glance.

★ ★ ★

Catherine came awake abruptly.

Crying out against elusive dreams, she grasped Bessie's thick, comforting arm. She was desperate to leave behind on her pillow whatever had stalked her dreams. Whatever it was, she was unable to describe to Bessie or to herself.

The blind old Romany woman put away the misshapen roots and tossed away the bitter dregs out of the drinking vessel. Satisfied she had once again reinforced her authority, she would await the outcome.

CHAPTER SEVEN

Keeping the War in the Family

For centuries the inhabitants of Scarborough had lived beneath a fortress of one sort or another situated upon the great bluff of rock over three hundred feet high. Dominating both land and sea, the Romans had considered the lofty plinth to be an excellent place to establish a signal station. But it was the Normans, the great castle builders, who really took advantage of the ideal location. Concurring with history, both Royalists and Parliamentarians had seen the potential in securing the castle at the outbreak of the Civil War. Sir Hugh Cholmley had declared for Parliament.

His change of heart had been forced upon him a year later in 1643.

The castle had been besieged by a substantial Royalist force for several weeks when Prince Rupert's emissary had entered under a flag of truce. Instead of respecting Cholmley's position as Governor, the Master had addressed the Yorkshire men who made up the beleaguered garrison, appealing to them with down-to-earth eloquence. As a result, the gates of the castle had been thrown open to the Royalists. As for Cholmley, having wisely changed his coat to suit the overwhelming demands of those under his command, he had hung onto his position by his fingertips. By doing so, he had delivered a frustrating blow not only to the Crop-Ears' Cause but also to Francois Lynette at Fylingdales Hall. Meanwhile, the Royalists had acquired not only a mighty fortress but a harbour of strategic importance through which supplies of munitions could be imported, mainly from the Master's associates in Mediterranean countries.

Cholmley was reminded of the demeaning events when he was

obliged to get to his feet in courteous response to his unexpected guest's hasty entry into the wide, sunlit chamber. Throughout his greeting of the young Lord of Fylingdales, he paid surreptitious interest in the array of colourful bruises sported upon sickly paleness. He was moved to offer a reviving glass of claret. Tossed back with little thought for its smooth texture, the welcoming drink brought a faint glimmer of colour to the younger man's hollow cheeks.

Richard had arrived post-haste from Whitby, trying hard to ignore the lingering nausea swilling about in his guts during the wild ride over the moors. He had dutifully witnessed the arrival of the crippled *Eagle* in her home port after the difficult tow up the coast by the fishing boats from Mercy Cove and Boggle Hole. Once thankfully ashore, he and the Master's men who had made up most of the skeleton crew rode away from Whitby on borrowed horses. But whereas his half-brother's loyal followers returned to the Lodge, he had headed down the coast to Scarborough.

Having gained entry to the castle, Richard made it plain to the portly Governor that he had not arrived on the Master's business, rather to seek his aid regarding a personal matter. His request was delivered without preamble.

It caused Cholmley to retake the elaborately carved seat at his large desk. He averted his gaze from the younger man's expectant features, his expression making plain his answer.

Sour bile hit the back of Richard's throat. His steps were brisk as he strode away. Thereafter, he stood rigidly by the breezy narrow window, failing to appreciate the familiar panorama from the commanding height.

Beneath the isolating escarpment of the castle, the imposing houses of captains and merchants were ranged upon a haughty level above the neighbourly jumble of cottages in steep, narrow lanes. Their disjointed roofs clustered around the harbour, red-tiled stages for the raucous songs of sharp beaked herring gulls. Shrunk by distance in the mellow light of late afternoon, fishing boats, their crews busy with their nets, bobbed alongside merchantmen being either loaded from the stone quays or unloaded onto them.

Eventually, feeling the strain of the difficult silence that had developed, Cholmley began, "My dear fellow."

The door was thrust open, startling the two men in the stone chamber.

Cholmley rose to his feet, looking from one to the other of his visitors in an apprehensive manner. "Well met, sir," he said to the Master. "May I offer you a glass of claret to slake your thirst?" Even as he uttered the nervous words, he felt like biting his tongue.

The gypsy shot him a piercing, ironic glance.

He did not seem surprised by Richard's presence. His derisive grin did nothing to soften his barbarous countenance. "I'm interruptin' summat, I 'ope," he murmured.

Having turned back into the chamber, Richard remained tight-lipped and defiant.

"We were just having a discussion," began Cholmley.

"I want Dobson's troop." The Master walked with soft-footed menace further into the chamber and perched on the Governor's imposing desk, arms folded, long legs stretched out in a casual manner that was intimidatingly deceptive. "Now."

Even though the sharp command had been barely above a whisper, Cholmley's tense nerves visibly quivered. "Of course," he responded, automatically.

The atmosphere in the quiet chamber was fermenting with inflamed spleen. Glancing from one to the other of his visitors, he did not relish becoming a buffer between the gypsy and Richard Massone, no matter how much he sympathised with the latter, whom he had known since childhood. It remained a source of amazement that the young Lord had defied his mother and uncle and joined the gypsy's gang of rogues, given respectability under the guise of war and the foreign prince's patronage.

Upon closing the door quietly behind himself, sickened by his own pathetic deference, he did have the satisfaction of recalling how several years earlier he had ordered the detention of the notorious gypsy in the castle's dungeon, and what form that detention had taken.

After Cholmley's departure, Richard found it impossible to

withstand the dangerous, feral patience. "I presume you are about to inform me that by coming to Scarborough, I have flouted your authority. That I should have returned forthwith to the Lodge after landing at Whitby, like the rest of your faithful lapdogs." He took an angry step forward, eyes narrowed. "Who are you but a misbegotten brat with gutter-scum inclinations who has found the perfect carriage for your vile talents."

His half-brother switched from studying his boots to Richard's flushed features. He waited until the other man had finished coughing, then softly asked, "An' the reason for y'r visit?"

"To obtain sanctuary for Catherine," Richard admitted, forcefully.

Shadiz regarded him, black eyes fathomless. "An' Cholmley's response?"

Richard wavered for a moment before retorting, "He is of the opinion that the castle is not the appropriate setting for her. I must agree there."

"So?"

"He suggested she lodge with his wife at the Abbey House at Whitby."

Shadiz nodded slowly. "I see." Still resting against Cholmley's desk, he glanced in a leisurely manner at the paperwork strewn there. "I'm surprised y' ain't considered Fylingdales," he remarked.

Richard stood mid-chamber, holding himself tensely. "The thought has crossed my mind." He was not about to admit to his half-brother that he had dismissed that course of action. He would not give his uncle the chance to make capital out of Catherine's presence at the Hall. It still remained a mystery to him why she was of importance to both Francois and Shadiz. "Catherine is an extraordinary young lady, who has my highest admiration. I will not stand idly by while you ruin her reputation," he declared. Lifting his chin in a challenging manner, he added, "I will not allow you to harm her ... as you did Elizabeth."

When Shadiz, his expression impassive, pushed himself off the desk and started to walk forwards, Richard watched him warily, his hand going instinctively to the hilt of his sword. Shadiz said nothing, despite his half-brother's emotive condemnation. He merely gestured for Richard to proceed him to the door of the chamber.

Richard's hesitation was eroded by the gypsy-dark restraint. He headed for the door of the chamber, wondering if Shadiz's remote silence could possibly mean he was finally experiencing guilt over what he had inflicted upon Elizabeth.

Such a suspicion was ruthlessly quashed when, upon reaching the door just ahead of Shadiz, he was slammed into its carved panels. Henceforth, he was pinned against sharp chiselled ridges. Both of his arms were piniored together and pushed far up his back. The bones in the left side of his face felt as if they would shatter at any moment. He could barely breathe while his chest was being crushed by Shadiz's malevolent weight. Even the inclination to cough was being squeezed out of him. He could smell ale on his half-brother's breath.

"Y' even think about yappin' t' any other sod about Kore's presence at the Lodge an' I'll do away wi' y'," rasped Shadiz into Richard's ear.

"She would condemn your murder of me," managed Richard.

"Who said owt about murder? I'd 'ave y' shipped off t' Algerias. An if y' mention owt about Elizabeth t' 'er, I'll 'ave y' castrated an' sold t' Malik, Bey o' Tunis, as a eunuch for 'is 'aram."

Richard swallowed hard, in so far as he was able. He had no doubt his half-brother would carry out his threats. He felt helpless. Cast down spiritually, he felt lost in the maze that life seemed to have fashioned around him. Only his growing love for Catherine gave him any hope of salvation.

The cruel pressure intensified. "D' y' 'ear me, Massone?"

The defiant stiffness gradually left Richard's hard-pressed body like a despondent sigh. He nodded, awkwardly.

Shadiz released Richard's right arm. Keeping hold of his left one, he pulled his half-brother backwards and then opened the door. He thrust Richard out into the passageway. Coughing, trying to get his breath back, Richard cannoned into Cholmley.

Caught off guard, the solid, thickset Governor careered

backwards. Unable to regain his balance, he tumbled down in the middle of the passageway.

A sentry sniggered in the gloom.

"No time fer sittin' on y'r arse. There's a war on, y' know," commented the Master, propelling Richard before him down the passageway.

CHAPTER EIGHT

A Surprise Hello

A respectful silence fell upon the entire courtyard. The Master's men and the Romanies, an arm across their chests in an age-old salute of their creed, formed a spontaneous guard of honour as Tom's coffin was carried out of the old Lodge.

Having lifted her onto the bench seat of the open wagon in which Tom's coffin had been placed, Shadiz swung up beside her and took up the reins of the team of horses.

Earlier that morning, he had given her the opportunity to say the kind of private farewell to Tom she had been unable to give her father. Once inside the darkened bedchamber, a supportive arm about her shoulders, he had led her to where Tom lay in the oak coffin. And he had held her close while she had regretfully sighed and quietly wept. Thereafter, he had kept her at his side.

It came as no surprise to Junno that his cousin was going to drive Tom on his last journey. With a heavy heart, the big man climbed into the back of the wagon and sat down at the opposite side of the coffin to Keeble and Bill Todd.

As a further mark of respect to one whom all of them had held in high regard, the majority of the Master's men had asked if they could form an escort to the cliff top church at Mercy Cove where Tom was going to be buried next to his wife. Wanting the best possible protection on the day, their leader had given his permission. But taking no risks, he had split his Romany force so that the Lodge would not be stripped of an effective guard. Half were supporting those few Gorgio who had elected to remain behind on guard. The rest were to be the nomadic eyes and ears of the cortege.

The tidings of Tom Wright's death had spread like wildfire across the moors and up and down the coast. Once clear of Stillingfleet Forest, the folk from Glaisdale, Beck Hole and Egton Bridge, riding double on horseback or crowded in wagons, joined the procession to Mercy Cove. Also a full troop of cavalry, which at first sight alarmed Catherine.

"I've borrowed 'em from Scarborough," Shadiz told her, soothingly. Clearly, he was not taking any chances of being waylaid on a day when the entire district knew his movements; and those of his ward.

"The more the merrier," she murmured, flatly.

Following a nod of acknowledgement from the seasoned commander of the troop to the Master, the well-armed cavalry remained in place until the rear of the cortege came abreast of their position by the side of the rutted causey and then they fell in behind the sombre procession.

The north wind defied the sunny nature of the morning. Its chilly presence stirred the lacy leaves of bracken and the spring-yellow gorse. Catherine had been dreading this day. Constantly aware of the manner in which Tom was accompanying them on the ride to Mercy Cove, she watched the faithful mastiff loping alongside the wagon. She was glad of Shadiz's presence beside her instead of leading the long column, as Richard was doing. The sadness of Tom's demise had touched them all, causing Richard to stay silent when he had been positioned far away from Catherine by his half-brother. He was in the moderate company of Benjamin Farr. He had returned to the Lodge the day after Tom's death, his inclusion in the Master's force having been countenanced by Prince Rupert.

"It's a Standing Stone," explained Shadiz, having apparently noticed Catherine's interest in the tall monolith several feet to the right of the winding causey they were presently following. "They're scattered about the moors, in places where the Olas worshipped their Spirits."

"Olas?"

"The Ancient Ones. Celts who roamed this land, markin' the

passage o' the seasons. Their days were measured by their needs. T' 'unt animals livin' on moors an' in forests. T' catch fish in streams. T' forage for berries an' roots. The Stones they erected were t' 'onour the Spirits o' Nature. Theirs was a cycle o' moon, stars an' sun, given t' 'em by the Creator. Trees were their guardians. Forest glades their churches. Crystal Pools were the windows their wise ones looked through t' catch glimpses o' the world o' Spirits. They considered theirsens part o' the great tapestry o' life. Threads woven around land an' above it; wind, clouds, sea and sky."

"How do you come to know of them?" Catherine asked, in wonder.

"Garan," answered Shadiz, giving her a cautious sidelong glance.

She was struck by a startling realisation. "Garan is a Druid?"

"Aye."

"What my father learned about Druids came from you," she mused, thoughtfully. "Little wonder, I was unable to find a book about them in the library at home."

"Roger was intrigued."

"I can imagine."

"I was goin' t' arrange for 'im t' meet Garan. But never got round t' it."

"I did in his stead," commented Catherine, pointedly. Curiosity got the better of her. She ended the ponderous lapse in their conversation. "How did you come to meet the Druid?"

"I sought 'im out?" admitted Shadiz, urging the team of horses up a steep slope.

"You did?" she remarked, holding onto the bench seat as the wagon dipped backwards. She glanced over her shoulder. Between them, Junno, Keeble and Bill were steadying Tom's coffin. "Why?" she asked, turning back to Shadiz.

"T' ask permission t' set up camp in Stillingfleet. It were Garan who suggested Lodge."

"Really." She was astonished that he had sought approval for his intention. "The people around here, they know of Garan, I presume?"

Shadiz shrugged. "Most are descendants o' Olas."

"So what does that make them?"

"Whatever they want t' be, I reckon."

They were silent for a short while. Catherine surveyed the passing moorland. She heard the call of an unseen bird stalking through the bracken. It should be raining on such a grievous day, she decided. Tears from heaven. The vast, undulating panorama, beneath a sweep of sky she felt she could reach up and touch, lent a haunting dignity to their journey, as if the land knew they were journeying to bury one who had once tended its bounty. Tears misted her eyes. She had to think of something else. "What faith do the Romanies follow?" she asked, abruptly. Digesting her own question, a little self-conscious, she added, "I've never thought before."

"Whichever one keeps 'em safe from persecution," Shadiz told her, a harsh note in his quiet voice.

"Why are they so reviled?" she wondered aloud.

He gave her a calculating glance. "Y' ain't 'eard o' tale? 'ow Roms were the ones who made nails fer Cross?"

"No, I haven't," she admitted, taken aback.

He shrugged. "If it weren't that, it'd been summat else." He steered the team around the sharp bend in a causey thick with the muddy aftermath of the heavy rain a few days before. "Gorgio bein' kennicks, house dwellers, ain't keen on nomads."

"That is so wrong. My father considered them no different from anyone else."

"An' never pressed them t' attend 'is church," remarked Shadiz, approvingly. After a moment, he continued, "Roms bend the knee t' Devel, the Creator. In the open air. T' do owt else would constrict 'em."

"Like the Druids?"

"Aye."

He must have divined her ill-repressed curiosity. "What?" he asked, softly, giving her a patient, sideward look.

Catherine met his black regard with care. "Do you possess beliefs?"

He turned his attention back to the uneven causey they were traversing. "In Arabia, I'm 'eathen. In other parts o' the Med, I'm 'eathen. I've fought against Christians. An' I've fought against Moslems. They all bleed same."

"And in truth?"

"Every child is born into the religion of nature; its parents make it a Jew, a Christian or a Moslem," he quoted.

"A child is born; and the sparks fly upwards."

She was a victim of gooseflesh upon hearing his rare, genuine laughter.

"That was what my father maintained," she told him, ruefully.

" 'e were a good man, wi' integrity. Garan's got same quality. 'e can be a bit crazy. The years done that t' 'im. But 'e talks sense about nature o' earth an' sea. An' 'ow we're all a part o' it, not apart from it."

"You are a Pagan, then?" suggested Catherine, totally absorbed by his candour.

"Again, most'd say 'eathen," he responded, with a quick grin. He shrugged, growing serious. "A Pagan ain't what the Church'd 'ave y' believe. They ain't consumed by the sinful evils thrust on folk by Cantin' Preachers. Early Christians faced wi' the power o' the Druids took the Pagan festivals an' turned 'em into Christian ones. T' be 'onest, I reckon religion's bane o' mankind. Because o' it, for centuries men've been at each other's throats in an effort t' impose their different beliefs as being the one truth. Ain't that part o' what's up wi' England right now. Them in Parliament can't abide Charles's zeal for all things elaborate in worship. Some'd say popish. They maintain simplicity is close to He o' Fire an' Brimstone. I reckon Beng, the Devil, created religion, an' been laughin' up 'is sleeve ever since."

"Yet you are taking Tom to Mercy Cove for a Christian burial?" she observed, softly.

"'onour thy father," he said, barely above a whisper, staring straight ahead.

The funeral cavalcade arrived at Mercy Cove mid-morning. A great number of people had gathered around the fishermen's

Church of St. Peter, within sight of the blue, sparkling North Sea. Swelling the ranks of land based mourners, they had come from every seafaring community from Staithes to Scarborough.

Catherine joined Laura and her daughters while Bob joined those men who had volunteered to shoulder Tom's coffin. The bluff captain appeared very close to tears. Laura shed them for him. Many a night, she had sat by the fire in Tom's reassuring company while the girls had slept and Bob had been away aboard the *Eagle*.

Fortifying her weakened control by her intention, Catherine called upon Laura and her daughters to proceed her into the church. She hung back in order to speak to the Master when he had finished giving orders to his own men and those from the garrison at Scarborough Castle to secure the surrounding area.

Before Richard could join her, she walked up to her tall guardian. "You are coming in?"

He looked past her at the squat, weathered church, rapidly filling up with mourners.

"For Tom," she urged.

His critical black gaze scanned the cliff top graveyard. The iron ring he had set up was in place. Almost reluctantly, he looked down at her, saying nothing. She met his hooded regard with a persuasive expression. Though her attention remained on him, she was conscious of Junno blocking Richard's path to her.

Shadiz sighed repressively. Then turned towards the church.

Remaining where she was, Catherine cleared her throat and gazed pointedly at his weapons.

He thrust an irritable scowl her way. Yet, without further prompting, he swung the broadsword off his back and then removed the scimitar at his hip. He thrust the weapons towards Benjamin, who hurried forward to receive them. "Keep watch," snapped the Master.

He and Catherine, with Richard and Junno following, were about to enter the church when a commotion erupted some distance behind them. They all paused and looked to where a coach and its sizeable escort had been halted by the Master's men beside the low drystone wall surrounding the breezy churchyard.

Though the quality of the coach confounded her, Catherine thought at first the late-comers were being discouraged from attending Tom's funeral due to the large number of mourners already present. However, upon hearing Shadiz's short, malicious laugh and seeing Richard's disbelieving reaction, her curiosity was aroused.

From where she was standing in the protective company of the men, she watched a group of women alight from the coach which bore an elaborate coat of arms on its highly polished door. Due to their finery, even with a view restricted by horsemen, her first impression was of ladies-in-waiting. While they stood in an apprehensive knot, a small, stately lady was handed down from the coach by a liveried footman.

At sight of her, Richard swore shockingly.

Startled, Catherine glanced at him.

Barely seen in the opposing groups of well-armed men, the small woman's demeanour made it plain she was not unduly perturbed by her hostile reception.

The Master gave a sharp whistle, turning Benjamin as he hurried to take charge of the situation. He then motioned to his latest recruit. Benjamin obediently escorted the women towards him along the grassy path between the graves while his men kept the new arrival's resentful escort at bay.

Seeing her at close quarters, Catherine was impressed by how regal and dainty the unknown lady appeared. She was not young. The silver of her immaculate hair, glimpsed beneath her flimsy veil, revealed the passing of the years. Otherwise, her aristocratic beauty seemed barely touched by age. Her black velvet cloak was beautifully embroidered with fine gold thread. Beneath, she wore a gown of black silk. Her kid gloves were monogrammed with presumably her initials. The manner in which she conducted herself amply made up for her lack of stature, no more than five foot. Here was nobility looking down, from a heightened mind, on inferior mortals.

"Mother, what on earth are you doing here?" Richard asked in curt bewilderment.

Catherine shot him a sideward glance. She looked back in amazement at Richard's mother.

Lady Hellena gave her son a cold appraisal. "Have you lost your manners living in that hovel? Are you not going to introduce me to your young companion?" She turned her severe attention upon Catherine.

Richard flushed at the sharp, accented rebuke. Unclenching gritted teeth, he said, "Mother, may I present, Catherine, the daughter of the late Sir Roger Verity of Nafferton Garth, Driffield."

Sensing the unpredictability in Shadiz's watchful amusement, Catherine executed a perfect, deep curtsey. The austere inspection continued, much to her discomfort. For Tom, she had worn her dark blue velvet cloak and, in the absence of a black gown, had chosen one of sombre grey.

"Catherine," continued Richard, formally, "You are in the presence of Lady Hellena. The Dowager of Fylingdales. My mother."

"I am honoured to meet you, my lady," said Catherine with due courtesy.

The brief pause was filled with tense anticipation of the Master's reaction.

"Now we've got that ov'r wi'," he remarked, laconically.

Lady Hellena was obliged to strain, without appearing to do so, to grasp the gist of the gypsy's words. She had forgotten how ridiculously quietly he spoke. An event of more lasting import had taken place on that fateful night twelve years ago. An event she had recalled throughout the long years with festering hatred.

Her initial appraisal whilst approaching him had revealed to no one her involuntary reaction to the towering, deeply disturbing youth who had become a notorious man and a formidable leader. As a wife and mother, she would forever hold him in abomination. She continued the inner struggle to disguise her virulent rage, to not award him any satisfaction. Yet the demand was raw. Why should he be standing virile and arrogant when her husband had lain those many, empty years in his premature tomb? And Elizabeth … Oh, Dear Lord, sweet, innocent Elizabeth!

She could not bare to acknowledge him, even when, stepping to one side, he bowed to her, indicating with sardonic gallantry that she should proceed into the church. Instead, she moved forwards, saying to no one in particular, "I come to honour a faithful worker."

"The same worker y' 'ad driven off Fylingdales."

Lady Hellena studiously ignored the whispery remark, salted with biting mockery.

Keeble appeared at the door of the church, in search of Catherine. When he caught sight of the Dowager of Fylingdales, he stopped abruptly. His jaw dropping, shock was stamped upon his over-large face.

A hush, more of inquisitiveness than of mourning, descended on the large congregation upon their entry into the overflowing church. Catherine found herself walking beside Lady Hellena. The Dowager addressed her in a stern tone. "You are nothing like I imagined. The sort Richard always harkens to. The Hall stands ready for you, if at any time you find yourself free to choose your abode."

Having ended up beside his half-brother, a pace behind the women, Richard heard his mother's words with mixed feelings.

"She's fine where she is. I'll deal wi' any bastard who tries to make out otherwise," Shadiz rasped, "an' bloody well 'ave done".

Lady Hellena half-turned, her manner condemning. "Remember where you are, *gypsy*."

She swept down the narrow aisle, pursued by her women. Their royal progress rustled past the crowded pews. Those who worked and lived within Fylingdales's domain acknowledged the Dowager dutifully.

Richard glanced at his half-brother. He had suffered the haughty rebuke in glowering silence. It was becoming increasingly noticeable how Shadiz kept himself well in hand whenever he was in Catherine's company. Indeed, Richard was in no doubt that had she not been present upon his mother's appearance at Tom's funeral, the outcome might have been quite different.

The large congregation peered with cautious, sideward fascination as Catherine moved in the lofty shadow of the Master.

The entire district knew of her presence at the Lodge. Although the women from Glaisdale who worked there seemed curiously reticent to gossip about her, she continued to be a subject that spiced the locals' everyday, hardworking lives.

Being the object of interest proved difficult for Catherine, particularly under the present circumstances. She felt obliged to put on a brave face, even when her gaze rested on Tom's coffin. Expertly made by two of the Master's men, former carpenters turned thieves to feed their families, it rested on two large, upright stones before the simple altar. Both the wildflowers, Shadiz had watched her picked earlier that morning, and the polished oak upon which they lay were lit by a shaft of sunlight streaming through the tiny stained-glass window funded by plentiful catches.

Taking their places in the front pew across the aisle from Lady Hellena and her retinue, Shadiz and Richard flanked Catherine. When Parson Ellerby, a small, balding man made visibly nervous by the presence of the imposing Master and the august Dowager of Fylingdales, began to honour Tom's passing, the two men closed about her, united in their concern for her, both aware that the funeral rites for Tom included the farewell she had been unable to give her father. Catherine was grateful for Richard's support. But it was Shadiz's subtle shift which brought his arm in contact with hers that gave her the greatest comfort.

After the poignant ritual had been completed, and Tom laid to rest beside his late wife, the many mourners prepared to disperse. It was then that Shadiz spoke to Richard, "Why don't y' escort y' ma 'ome. Seens as 'er brother ain't 'ere t' do 'onors. I must o' pressed 'im too 'ard."

Richard was mightily tempted to denounce the over-innocent suggestion.

His mother intervened before he could voice an objection. "Indeed, Francois's indisposition is due entirely to your rabid concern." She gave a contemptuous snigger. "I am informed of her continued ignorance."

Stood a little apart, talking to Laura and Bob Andrew, Catherine glimpsed the dangerous change of expression on Shadiz's barbarous, scarred face. His gold earring flashed in the sun as he rounded upon Lady Hellena. In an effort to avoid trouble, Catherine stepped smartly to her guardian's inflexible side. At the same time, resigned to his fate, Richard took firm possession of his mother's arm and led her away. Although he spoke in the Romi, Catherine had a fair idea of what Shadiz would like to do to the Dowager of Fylingdales. She persuaded him in the opposite direction, and was unaware of how a large number of people viewed with wisely-muted wonder his compliance, albeit murderously glaring.

Riding back to the Lodge upon a sadly empty wagon, Catherine turned to Shadiz, putting a tentative hand on his arm. "Thank you. I don't know what I would have done without you."

A muscle flexed in his scarred cheek. "Y'd o' coped."

"Not as well, I fear."

Gathering the reins in one hand, he gently squeezed her hand resting on his arm with the other. There was admiration, pride and another, involuntary emotion in his black eyes as they rested upon her. "Y' did well, Kore. Tom an' y' father would've been proud."

CHAPTER NINE

Dancing in the Dark

"Looks like we're gettin' 'em all t'day."

Upon their return to the Lodge, they discovered a well-armed contingent of Romanies awaiting them, apart from those Shadiz had left on guard at the Lodge. Following his ironic comment, he swung off the wagon and then lifted Catherine down onto the sunlit cobbles.

Despite Mamma Petra's blindness, both Shadiz and Junno bowed their heads in respectful salutation to their grandmother.

The Romany matriarch was sitting on the ground close to the leafy entrance to the rear pasture. She had obviously spurned the offer of the stool a Gorgio had carried out for her from the kitchen. It stood unbidden at the edge of the colourful blanket spread upon the grass.

Junno's wife, Lucinda, and his son, Peter, had accompanied her to the Lodge.

Catherine knew Romany custom dictated that before she welcomed them, like Shadiz and Junno, she must first pay her respects to the Puro Daia. She did so by curtseying in the same formal manner she had when being introduced to Richard's mother.

"Thy haste be in vain, Posh-Rat," remarked Mamma Petra, surprisingly in the Gorgio's language.

"Aye," replied Shadiz. To Catherine, he explained, "When I were called t' Mercy Cove, I sent a messenger."

"Thy call didst not inspire my presence for the pur givengro."

"It was my fault," said Catherine, "I was not here to help Tom."

"Thee cast thy spirit for succour."

Catherine was scrutinised by the strange, hollow eyes, set in a small, deeply-lined face. She knew better than to repudiate her motive for leaving the Lodge that fateful stormy night. Mamma Petra's inner vision missed nothing. "I was unable to withstand the call." She looked down, embarrassed by the admission. It was one thing to admit the motive to herself, and Shadiz, it was another to have the world know.

The old Romany nodded her head, stirring her long, grey plaits. "Thee followed thy onna."

Catherine, her cheeks flushed, half-turned to find Shadiz watching her with considering eyes. "Heart," he translated, low-pitched.

"Instead of my head," murmured Catherine, meeting his gaze through her downcast lashes.

"Be not muladi."

"Y' ain't t' be 'aunted by Tom's passin'," Shadiz again translated, adding his own silent reassurance.

"Thou hast blossomed, chavnay," remarked Mamma Petra, shrugging off her black, woollen shawl. "Spoken is thy use of the pattriensis."

Thankful to leave aside the reason for her disappearance from the Lodge, Catherine curtsied once again. Compliments were few and far between from the White Witch. "I am honoured to have been taught by you. I use the herbs to heal whenever I can."

Mamma Petra spoke sharply, in their language, to the fidgeting child. He immediately burst out from his mother's loosened restraint. Laughing, Junno scooped up the tall, robust boy and spun him around. Peter giggled in delight, holding onto his grinning father.

In danger of being knocked over by their playful antics, Catherine was moved out of the way by Shadiz while she was greeting Lucinda.

Dressed in colours that contrasted brightly with Mamma Petra's sombre attire, the young Romany woman looked briefly towards Shadiz and inclined her head tentatively. Catherine sensed her wariness of him. She noticed Lucinda glance at his hand lingering upon her arm, presumably in case the whirling dervishes grew close again. She was fond of the attractive, considerate young woman, three years her senior. Over the years, since her father had offered winter shelter at Nafferton Garth to Mamma Petra's tribe, the two of them had grown quite close.

The tousled-haired youngster, his chubby dark face filled with merriment, hailed Catherine as Junno halted their twirling and placed him back on his feet. He dashed somewhat dizzily over to her.

"Hullo, my love. And how are you?" she greeted, bending down. She was glad to see the youngster looked fully recovered from his fall off an unbroken horse. The accident had caused his father to rush to his side. "I see you have overcome your bump."

Peter's reply was in the Romi.

"Give tongue to the Gorgio," Mamma Petra ordered him, sternly.

For a brief second, the child scowled. The fleeting expression startled Catherine. Kindly she explained to him, "I cannot understand you otherwise, my love."

Peter's small fist opened. "I you flower bring," he said, revealing a botanical specimen beyond identification.

"Well, thank you. I will treasure it always," she promised, straightening.

Peter's bright grin faltered as he looked up at Shadiz. He had taken a backward step closer to the heavy skirt of her grey, mourning gown. There seemed to be awkwardness on both the part of the child and the man.

While Mamma Petra was being settled in the rear pasture having refused point blank to enter the Lodge, Catherine asked, "You are unused to children?"

"Like a lot o' things afore you arrived," came the low-pitched reply.

★ ★ ★

Following the biggest meal they had been called upon to prepare,

285

the women from Glaisdale regrouped to take a well-deserved rest in the large, medieval kitchen, still warm from their busy hours of cooking. Also present were those women who had accompanied their husbands to the Lodge, including Laura Andrew and her daughters. All had made a contribution to the preparation and the serving of what had been an appetising and companionable send-off for a good friend. The younger children were presently asleep, either on their mothers' laps or curled up at their feet. The older ones were gathered around the kitchen door, talking, playing the occasional game and daring each other to spy on the weird, old Romany woman in the rear pasture. In the courtyard, the Master's men mixed easily with the captains and crews of a number of ships, including the *Eagle*, the fishermen from up and down the coast and the men of widespread moorland hamlets. Even a goodly number of the Master's Mulesko Dud, his Romany will-o-the-wisp force, had joined the Gorgios.

That such a great many people had been allowed to gravitate to the ancient Lodge was testament to the Master's high regard of Tom Wright. By their presence, the night had developed into a celebration of his life. Catherine had become certain that Tom, in spirit manifested by genial, wistful thoughts, was with everyone during the fire-bright, convivial evening. Having overheard numerous anecdotes while helping to serve the open air meal had made her believe he would live on in cherished memories.

Ignoring Shadiz's glaring displeasure at her menial tasks, Catherine had watched unobtrusively while his dark, charismatic influence had drifted through the large gathering. His leadership qualities had already evoked respect and a fierce loyalty. Because of his present casual manner, the men believed they were getting a rare glimpse of what lay beneath his austere bearing. It had occurred to her that he just might be taking the opportunity to further bind men to him. Probably doing so with Tom's blessing!

Having stayed awhile in the rear pasture talking to Lucinda, Catherine had become chilled. Upon entering the welcomed warmth of the kitchen, she searched for her shawl. Not finding it in any of the likely places she looked, speaking to a number of the women in passing including Laura Andrew, she decided to seek the shawl elsewhere.

The sable gloom of the lofty, stone hallway made her shiver. When she heard a sudden burst of masculine laughter in the courtyard, despite the cold atmosphere, she paused at the bottom of the indistinct stairs.

It had become no longer possible to deny the truth. The rich emotion had beaten against the walls of commonsense until they had collapsed despite her best efforts. How ridiculous would he consider her if he ever found out. Perhaps, he would be flattered. She grimaced. More likely, he would look upon the development as another reason to view her as a burden. Giving herself a mental shake, she started up the worn stone steps. But then finally recalled where she had left her shawl.

The fire in the library's great stone hearth had been allowed to dwindle down to glowing ashes. Unlike the well-attended blaze in the courtyard. The brightness of its well-fuelled flames lit the area around the glassless windows while the rest of the chamber remained in darkness.

Catherine's footsteps slowed. She became aware of a sense of peace in harmony with the surrounding forest. Happily baying humanity receded for several precious moments. For despite the night's merriment, deep within her, she had sensed the underlying loss that had overlaid her own sadness, and her own heartfelt longing.

At odds with herself, she began to blindly cast about for her shawl, the light coming from the courtyard being of little help.

"Y' lookin' for summat in particular. Or just 'avin' a good rant?"

"*Ye gods and little fishes!*" exclaimed Catherine, drawing in a startled breath. "I believed you to be out there."

She was not even sure from which direction Shadiz's seemingly disembodied voice had come. Fleetingly, she wondered if the whispery challenge had sprang from her own thoughts. Thoroughly shaken, she snapped, "What are you doing skulking around in here?"

"Skulkin'?" he repeated, his soft tone amused, "I asked y' first."

"I am certainly not skulking," she retorted, indignantly, "I found it chilly in the pasture and decided to find my shawl. Mary said she would help and Junno volunteered but I said…."

"Y' gabblin'."

"So would you be if you had been damn well pounced upon."

"Y' ain't t' blaspheme."

"H'm." Catherine took a moment to try and calm the pounding of her heart and reduce her rapid breathing. "I'm sure you went through the wrong door."

"What?"

"You should have been a great wild cat." The rash statement struck a cord. With less irritable force and more consideration, she added, "Prowling the moors."

There was no response for a few moments. When next he spoke it was from close behind her. "Nay. Give me form upon the deriav. Within the waves."

She turned to find his tall shadow looming over her. Relieved he was not a figment of her imagination, she peered upwards, trying to define features. It was the unexpectedness of his presence that was causing her to feel shaky, she decided. "You possess an aversion to being land locked?"

"Y' never enjoy the world aright, till the sea itself floweth in y'r veins."

A warm, strong body brushed against her legs. As always, the mastiff was with his master and had also come to greet her, in a more tactile manner. "And Tom would wait," she murmured, stroking the dog's shaggy coat. "Hoping for your return."

" 'e who waits, Allah praises for 'is patience."

Catherine became aware of the strange sounding music that had begun in the courtyard. Turning towards the bright windows, she listened to the rise and fall of masculine voices. Out in the night, the enthralled silence of the listeners accompanied the haunting, tribal requiem.

"They sing for a Gorgio thought well o'. A poorano pral."

Tears sprang into her eyes as a result of the honour the Romanies were paying Tom. The rhythmic sound of boots beating upon cobbles attested to the physical accompaniment to the ancient, foreign chant.

"They dance for 'im, t' 'elp 'im t' 'is Duvvel. 'is God."

"Are women allowed to dance?" she asked, quietly.

Her elusive shawl was placed around her shoulders. "Aye."

Catherine grasped each tasselled end of the woollen shawl and, with arms outstretched, held it out behind her. She began to sway in time to the lilt of Romany voices, finding their ritual offering hypnotic.

A couple of moments passed before she heard what sounded like a mug being placed on the black bulk of the table close by. After which, she felt the nearness of Shadiz's arms, stretching out, matching hers, surpassing them. She became acutely conscious of his powerful body shadowing her movements. Their steps of lamentation took them first to their right and then to their left, then backwards and forwards. Together, without touching, they traversed the covering darkness in expressive silence.

Inch by inch, moment by moment, grief became absorbed by another potent emotion. It brought togetherness that vital step closer.

Catherine's back came to rest against the rise and fall of Shadiz's hard chest. She tilted her head back so that it lay in the shelter of his broad shoulder. His hands drifted with infinite gentleness upon her outstretched arms, up and over her shoulders, skimming lightly down the soft mould of her breasts. He wrapped his arms around her waist, leaning over her, breathing into her hair. His wild mane brushed against her sensitive face. She was surrounded by his warm, masculine scent. Giving herself up into his tender keeping, she slid her hands down the strong muscles of his thighs. She kept her hands spread upon him while they moved as one. This time swaying to the harmony of their irresistible courtship.

Overcome by their heightened sense of one another, by the silent passion of their unique melody, they found it impossible to deny the need for each other. Suddenly halting their faltering steps, Shadiz lifted Catherine off her feet and turned her towards him as if she was of no consequence and held her close as if she was the most precious treasure in the world he had roamed endlessly.

They sought each other with matching desire. Their kiss quickly blossomed into the exquisite honesty of lovers. The one true emotion toppled barriers, swept away resolve. Beyond bone and muscle, beyond mind and thought, essence recognised essence and merged for a joyous heartbeat in eternity.

The long journey deep within their twin souls had become intolerably starved of air. Shaken beyond all expectation, they reluctantly drew apart, but were loathed to separate more than a hair's-breadth. Continuing to hold her possessively against him, he barely possessed enough breath to whisper her name, achingly, into the silk of her hair. Clinging to him, afraid to let go, she smelt the ale upon his rapid breath, experienced the lingering roughness of the stubble about his jaw and cherished beyond measure his unbridled accessibility.

She was innocent, but not naive. Trembling, she understood the pressing hardness their wondrous embrace had aroused. And knew the swell of her breasts, crushed against his chest, and the heat in places she hadn't known existed was her own body's response. Indeed, her entire being yearned to defy convention and be truly one with him. He had only to lay her down on the old sheepskin rug before the glowing embers of the hearth and she would offer up her innocence to him. Instinctively, she knew he was the only one. Where he led she would gladly follow.

The door of the library opened. Men's voices were heard.

Benjamin Farr glimpsed a flash of hair, shades lighter than his own, in the light of the lantern he carried. A reflex action, he banged the door shut behind himself, in the faces of those men out in the passageway. Ignoring the grumbles beyond, he put his back against the ancient, pitted wood. A little more presence of mind and he would have extinguished the revealing light of the lantern and save himself further embarrassment. It was not only the Master's jet glare that was making him feel exceedingly awkward. He had seen enough to realise who was being concealed behind his leader's back, for the reaction to his entry into the library had been uncharacteristically tardy. As unwanted confirmation, Catherine's shawl lay on the floor.

Being tactful to the point of blindness, Benjamin said, "Sir, I apologise for disturbing you. There is a group of fishermen from Boggle Hole wishing to speak with you."

"What for?" Shadiz demanded, harshly.

"They would not divulge the reason. They did assure me the matter is of importance and that you would be interested in what they have to say."

Benjamin watched as the Master seemed to ease himself forward slightly. He had one hand behind his back.

"Aye, all right."

Benjamin hesitated.

"Wait. Out yonder."

Tersely dismissed, Benjamin escaped through the smallest crack of the door.

The moment they were alone again in the darkness, Shadiz swung round, exclaiming, "Develesko Mush. D'y understand what y' do, mandi kom?"

Catherine's hands remained beneath his loose shirt. They had slid lightly from his deeply scarred back as he turned to face her. She buried her long fingers in the thick mat of hair upon his chest. "I wanted to make sure you were not injured after what happened with the *Eagle* in Mercy Cove. You would not let me look the other day."

"Believe me, y' done plenty o' damage," he reprimanded, wryly.

He had kept an arm around her, tightly masking her with his big body, when Benjamin had been present. Both of his arms now drew her back to him, making it plain he was loathed to let go of her. Loving the sensation of him, her arms slipped around his muscular body and up his back again beneath his shirt. The temptation was too great. There was a compulsion within both of them to recreate the spark that had kindled such a potent response between them. Their embrace was, if anything, even longer, deeper than before. Their bodies melted into one another. Incredible sensations ravaged them while they teetered on the threshold of ecstasy.

"They are waiting," she reminded him, eventually, breathlessly. His gentle kisses down her neck were making her tremble afresh.

"So've I," he murmured against her stretched throat.

"I suspect there would be much eye rolling were I to walk out of here, now," Catherine observed, striving to think straight, to think at all, "I could always climb out of the window, I suppose."

His soft laughter brushed against her ear and sent shivers down her spine.

"Allus thought that was fella's doin'."

His repressive sigh made it clear he was aware of the implication if she left the library while the hallway was occupied. If he had thought to order Benjamin to have the fishermen return later, Catherine would have been able to make her escape without anyone being any the wiser. As it was, they were left with no option but to have the fishermen from Boggle Hole enter the library while she was still present. In order for them to do so without being aware of her, keeping her close, he led her to the tall-backed chair beside the large hearth and sat her down facing away from the door. Yet he seemed as unwilling as her to break the precious, gossamer spell they had spun between them no matter who was waiting for him.

Shadiz crouched down before the old chair. He was appalled at how close he had come to giving into the long-standing, tormented ache for her. A tremor went through him. She, in loving response, stroked his arms at either side of her on the chair arms. In the darkness, lost to her, there was a flare up of self-loathing. She was so very vulnerable. And *Want* was so very, very dangerous.

"I do not fear you," Catherine informed him.

Her quiet words shook him, almost as much as her pliant, virginal ardour. Had she, with her incredible empathy, read his mind?

She felt the muscles in his arms grow tense beneath her caressing fingers and was aware of his animal-like stillness. "I know you would not hurt me."

Her words brought forth a growl of anguish deep in his constricted throat. "Kore. Nowts more important than y'r safety."

292

When he laid his head in her lap, responding to his amazing vulnerability, she bent lovingly to him. Her fair-white hair fell over him like a protective cloak.

At last, with some irony, she murmured, "You are needed."

He stirred reluctantly. With great tenderness, he placed a hand on the nape of her neck and drew her to him over the short distance that separated them. He kissed her receptive lips, lingeringly. Afterwards, he rested his forehead against hers and, barely above a whisper, he quoted,

"There is a lady sweet and fair,
Was never a face so pleased my mind,
I did but see her passing by…"

Gaining his full, towering height, he obviously could not resist bending one last time to brush the top of her head with a fleeting kiss.

While he strode across the library, Catherine barely noticed the mastiff sitting down beside her and leaning against her legs, as if answering a command. She stared into the darkness. Stunned, she recited the last line of the poem to herself.

Galvanised into action by the Master's curt summons, the six fishermen shuffled into the library and congealed into a nervous knot around the half-closed door.

Catherine watched Shadiz's overbearing shadow retrieve what she believed to be a mug from the black shape of the table. He then strolled past her with an imperceptible glance. She was aware of him leaning casually against the high back of the chair in which she was concealed. "Well?" he demanded.

Revealed in the light of the lantern Benjamin had left with them, the fishermen were intimidated by his manner. It was in icy contrast to the easy-going influence that had drifted around the courtyard. They were simple men, carrying the broad toughness to cast a net to its width, earned through indifferent seas and inclement weather. At present, they were of a mind that loyalty was a demanding task.

Jim Precious displayed the commendable resilience needed to captain a fishing smack out of Mercy Cove, and to address the

Master. "Sir, we ain't sure we're stickin' our nabs in like, but lot o' us reckon, while we're 'ere, y'd like to 'ear about summat that 'appened tother neet, when *Eagle* were in trouble." Half-turning, he tugged on the sleeve of a short, burly young man who was absorbed in looking around the shadowy library. He spoke in a quiet, coaxing manner, "Sammy, I want y' t' tell Master what y' told us."

Sammy Tate gazed at Precious vacantly. Taut patience showed on the older man's weatherbeaten face. "Y' remember. What 'appened t' y' neet *Eagle* were nearly lost."

"Tell...?"

"Aye. Tell, Master."

Sammy glanced at Shadiz and then swiftly looked down at his dirty boots, clutching his woollen cap in his big hands. " 'e did ask me t' tak a message," he mumbled.

"Who?" asked the Master, sharply.

Sammy looked up, an expression of childlike apprehension on his large, chubby face. He shook his head. "I not know." He darted a nervous glance at Precious. The burly fisherman nodded encouragingly. Sammy went on, " 'e were behind me. I were wi' little 'uns. Jim told us not t' go near cliff edge. It be dangerous."

"Tell Master what 'e asked y' t' do," prompted the older man.

" 'e sent me up t' big 'all."

"An' y' went?" queried the Master.

"Oh, aye," Sammy was pleased to confirm.

The voices of Shadiz and Precious clashed. Both men were getting exasperate, for different reasons.

Secreted in the chair, Catherine was silently fuming at their handling of a restricted spirit. While the mastiff persisted in leaning against her legs, she twisted awkwardly around and managed to place a hand on Shadiz's back, hoping to instigate restraint.

"Tell Master what message 'e told y' t' deliver, lad," urged Precious, quickly.

"Er," answered Sammy. He thought hard for a couple of moments, his ruddy features contorted. Then, with painstaking care, he said," 'e told me t' tell 'em up at big 'all that gypsy's whore were on Fylingdales Moor." Sammy grinned in triumph.

"Y' mean Miss Catherine?" rasped Shadiz.

" 'e does, sir," Precious put in, with placating haste. " 'e means no 'arm, sir. 'e be but a simple soul."

"But y' call 'er…."

"Catherine Verity is *not my mistress*," insisted Shadiz, his voice low and ominous.

The men standing around the door of the library fidgeted beneath his all-encompassing glare.

"Did y' recognise 'is voice?" demanded the Master.

Like a sensitive child, Sammy was troubled by something he did not understand. They had told him the Master would be pleased to hear what he had to say. They had forgotten, like a child playing on the floor when adults gossip, he had been present during their speculative conversations. Confused, he looked to Precious for guidance.

"Master wants t' know if y'd 'eard voice afore?"

"Whose?" asked Sammy.

Precious gritted his teeth, well aware of Shadiz renowned wrath. " 'im that told y' t' go t' Fylingdales 'all."

Sammy lifted his big shoulders in a childish shrug. "I not know."

That seemed to be as far as anyone could get with Sammy Tate. After a nod from the Master that was both acknowledgement of their effort and aloof dismissal, the man-boy was shepherded away by the fishermen.

Passing them with some urgency as they jostled each other in their relief to escape the Master, Junno entered the library. Like Benjamin and the fishermen before him, he carried a flickering lantern. It shed light upon where his cousin stood close to a chair. He spoke in their language.

Recognising her name, Catherine waited. When she was certain the big man was not about to get a response to mitigate his obvious agitation, she called out, "I'm here." The faithful mastiff remained stubbornly against her legs. To Shadiz, she said, "Your guard dog won't allow me to move."

Shadiz spoke a Romi word. The big dog rose and shook itself.

At the same time, Shadiz walked around the chair and offered Catherine his hand. Accepting the gesture, she got to her feet. Whereupon, Junno's relief shattered into heart-stopping fragments.

He scrutinised the couple he was confronted by. Alarmed by such an unmistakable impression, reinforced by the way his cousin had kept possession of Catherine's hand and entwined his fingers with hers, he was desperate to know what had transpired to bring the elusive bond into sharp focus so that now it was a palpable entity living between them.

Shadiz spoke to Junno in their language. Catherine did not care for his tone. Whatever he had said seemed to satisfy his watchful cousin to a cautious degree.

Catherine and Shadiz regarded each other clearly for the first time since she had entered the library. What they had shared was acknowledged by both of them. She smiled up at him. He answered her in the same sincere manner, taking her captured knuckles to his lips.

Suddenly, he gave frowning thought to something that bothered him alone. He hesitated for a further moment before asking, "Will y' come wi' me t' see Garan?"

Recognising the plea in his black scrutiny of her, Catherine recoiled nevertheless.

"I ain't meanin' for y' t' go t' the Crystal Pool again," he reassured her.

"Then, why?" she asked, bewildered and not a little afraid. She sensed his struggle to find the right words.

"I want 'im t' perform the rite o' 'andfast."

" 'andfast?" exclaimed Junno.

Shadiz's face grew hard. Switching from Catherine to the big man, he spoke harshly. "Out o' mouths o' babes, an' bloody simpletons. The damned lot o' 'em reckon she's my mistress. I need t' prove t' all an' sundry that she ain't a ratvalo looverni. An' all o' 'em understand 'andfast. 'alf o' 'em round 'ere practise it afore goin' t' church."

Junno continued to appear incredulous, and once more thoroughly alarmed.

"I hate to sound like the poor relation of an ignoramus, but what exactly is handfast?" asked Catherine, warily.

After a notable hesitation, Shadiz informed her, "It be Druidic ritual."

"And that is?" urged Catherine. She had not recovered from the last Druidic ritual. It had given her dreams of terrifying proportions.

His deep, distinct voice had elements of nervousness. " 'andfast is when two become 'onourably one."

CHAPTER TEN

Family Truths

Frustrated. Agitated. Richard could do little but pace the confines of his chamber.

That he should occupy the one he had called his own since leaving the nursery at Fylingdales Hall had been taken for granted. It bore little resemblance to the one he occupied at the ramshackle Lodge. He wished with all his heart to be within Stillingfleet Forest rather than trapped in pernicious splendour. For trapped, he most certainly was. Worst still. There had been no courtesy involved in Shadiz's suggestion that he should escort his mother back to Fylingdales Hall; simply ill-will.

He was haunted by the sight of Catherine riding away from the churchyard, where they had buried Tom Wright, in the company of Shadiz. He flung himself into another bout of teeth-grinding pacing. At the same time, fighting the urge to cough.

At long last the tension he had woven around the chamber was relieved by a perfunctory rap on the door. He moved swiftly, wrenching it open, to find Henry Potter conversing with two guards in the broad, candlelit corridor.

Squat and dour, Potter stepped deliberately into the chamber before Richard could escape its confines. His grey, beetle-browed gaze scanned the rich furnishings and the four-poster bed with its damask hangings. There were only a few personal items scattered around the chamber. They had been unused for some considerable time.

"I have not spirited up an army while I have been incarcerated," snapped Richard.

Potter gave an ill-humoured grunt.

Making brief eye contact with the older man, Richard realised Potter was hard pressed to forgive him for the way he had deceived him on board the *Eagle*. His protection of Catherine had meant he had also been forced to keep Shadiz safe. Richard could well imagine the sardonic tongue-lashing Potter had received from Francois. In respect of failure, his uncle and his half-brother were very much alike.

The two guards, not much older than Richard, stood smirking at either side of the door of the chamber when he was allowed to pass through it. They remained close on Richard's and Potter's heels. Behind them, a perfumed breeze rustled down the long corridor, lined with family portraits. Upon reaching the head of the horseshoe staircase they were joined by Lady Hellena and her women.

For the evening, her habitual black attire was softened by Flemish lace and the allure of gemstones. Although her matronly women did not adhere to mourning hues, their gowns were of sombre taste. They halted in a dignified, watchful knot while Lady Hellena's critical gaze scanned her son's attire; neat for Tom's funeral but far from presentable in her undisguised opinion. "Your hair is far too long," she observed. A moment passed. She sighed impatiently and then snapped, "Well?"

Richard managed to hold onto his temper. The fact that she had inspected him as if he were a recalcitrant child rankled enormously. Adopting stiff courtesy, he proffered his arm to her. The rest fell in behind as they led the way down the grand staircase. For the first few steps, he was conscious only of his resentment.

"You are entranced by the girl?"

Richard glanced sideward at his mother, knowing to whom she was referring. "I have sought to be a friend to Catherine in the difficult situation she has found herself," he replied, tightly. "Nothing more." Henceforth, as they made their stately descent, he kept his attention centred on the servants bustling into the main hall carrying silver trays loaded with steaming dishes.

"That is not what I have heard."

Reaching the bottom step, he stopped and turned to her. "From whom?"

She ignored his blunt thrust. Intolerant of his tardiness, she pressed him to continue.

There were a great many people gathered in the glittering sea of candlelight. A goodly half of the convivial throng seated at the long, oaken tables were known to Richard. The local gentry, attired in York bought finery, were always flattered to be invited to dine at Fylingdales Hall. Those unknown to him were present, he presumed, due to a common interest in the Parliamentarian Cause judging by their plainness of dress. Stern-faced warriors, devoid of female companions, they kept their attention steadfastly on their trenches. His uncle's senior commanders were seated on a nearby table, conspicuous by the insignia upon their more stylish doublets and their jovial manner.

Word of his presence must have flown around the turrets, for there were broken conversations and speculative glances cast his way as he escorted his mother the considerable length of the splendid, vaulted hall.

Upon reaching the imposing dais, Richard's smouldering gaze switched from the familiar tapestries hung above the oak panelling to his uncle. Immaculate as ever, Francois was wearing sea green sprinkled with diamonds. While Richard led his mother to her seat, he noticed his uncle seemed to be experiencing difficulty showing off his courtly manners. He tried to make light of the way he was steadying himself with one jewelled hand upon the high table, covered in Irish linen and resplendent with ancestral silverware. Upon closer inspection, it became plain to Richard why his mother had gone alone to Tom Wright's funeral. Francois's handsome face was bruised just below his left eye and around his jaw. His bottom lip was slightly swollen. There was a jagged cut across his neck, half-hidden by the fall of his fair hair. Blood from the wound had stained the froth of lace erupting from his doublet. When he resumed his seat, he did so with care, and then sat with his left leg thrust out at a cautious angle.

After taking the tall-back chair with notable enmity between his mother and his uncle, Richard's attention was drawn to where Fylingdales's younger officers occupied a couple of tables further down the hall. He scanned with vindictive pleasure their bloodstained mementoes of the Master's whirlwind ambush in Longdrop Hollow, where he had ruthlessly thwarted Fylingdales's abduction of Catherine. Richard wished he had been present instead of earlier being ordered by his malicious half-brother to remain aboard the *Eagle* while the crippled merchantman was towed to her home port of Whitby.

A manifestation of his thoughts, the tang of lemon civilized the haddock. His appetite would not pay homage to the culinary expertise of his mother's French cook. The slice of white fish swam around his plate, propelled by his abstractedly tuned cutlery. He felt like a fish dragged out of the murky waters of his half-brother's domain and hoisted onto a place of prominence in the magnificent fountain of his stolen heritage. In bondage to his hate, he realised with something of a shock how he had grown accustomed to moving in the black shadow cast by Shadiz.

Assuming a detachment not unlike the suits of armour stood to attention around the hall, worn by ancestors during the various struggles of different centuries, he surveyed the regimented banqueting tables. Fate had nailed him to a board betwixt two worlds. He watched the servants, resplendent in the blue and green livery of Fylingdales, move with practiced ease around the polished boards, serving the gregarious people pleased to be included in the Hall's sumptuous hospitality. Meanwhile his mind's eye traversed the community sharing a common goal with homespun pride at the Lodge. Shadiz's sphere of influence, he could only ever fathom from the ragged fringe.

Self-absorbed, he failed to catch the gist of Lynette's question.

His mother uttered a stinging reproach. "If you were not scowling at all and sundry, you would have heard what your uncle asked of you?"

Locked between them, Richard was of a mind to get up and walk away. How far he would get was reflected in the presence of the two guards standing in the shadows behind his chair. With bad grace, he asked, "I beg your pardon, sir. What did you say?"

Lynette's sapphire gaze continued to rest upon his nephew

while his dulcet words were meant for his sister. "Do not be too hard on him, mon cherie. After all, he is but keeping up appearances."

Lady Hellena scoffed at such a notion. "You give him far too much credit. By now, the gypsy will have discerned the ruse."

A hot flush gushed into Richard's pale face.

Francois Lynette shrugged eloquently. "He still serves as a conduit."

Vibrating with fury, Richard shot to his feet. His furious objection was interrupted by the clatter of dishes. In his haste to vacate his seat, he had overlooked the deftly floating servants. Steaming slices of beef were now strewn about the dais, resembling autumn leaves in the thick mud of herb gravy.

"Now see what you have achieved by your tantrum."

"Mother!"

"Sit down!" Lady Hellena commanded, impatiently waving away one of her officious women. "You are making a spectacle of yourself. Just as you appear to be doing over the Verity girl."

Lynette sighed with gracious regret. "Mon ami," he persuaded, suavely indicating the chair from which Richard had risen so precipitately.

Following the clatter of flying dishes, the conversation buzzing around the main hall had lapsed noticeably and then resumed with a monotonous tone. Faces, politely expressionless, with hooded eyes glinting with curiosity, were directed towards the high table. Gerald Carey, sprawled decorously in a chair at the head of the table closest to the dais, was wearing an expression of sneering mirth.

Richard slowly resumed his seat. No one spoke as the mess he had created by his impulsive action was cleared away and replacement dishes arrived. He pushed his away, knowing one mouthful would choke him. Without looking to either right or left of him, he rasped, "I am my own man. I will no longer have you determine my future. Either of you."

"Your hope for the future is transparent," said his mother. After eating a dainty mouthful of vegetables from the Hall's extensive kitchen garden, she added, "As always you deceive yourself. The gypsy is far too possessive of Catherine Verity to countenance your involvement with her."

Richard turned his fair head and looked at her. "It was you." He glanced at Lynette. "And you." He looked back at his mother. "Who deceived me." The turmoil within threatened to erupt into a coughing fit. "As for Catherine, she has no part in any of this sorry affair."

Lady Hellena was mordant. "You are too absurd for words. Have you not realised yet? The gypsy is in love with her."

"Now it is you who is being absurd, mother," Richard flung back.

"I think not," Lady Hellena snapped. "He is obsessed with her. He worships her. And has done for a very long time."

CHAPTER ELEVEN

Handfast

It did not take long for the rosy glow and merry sounds abounding around the old Lodge to fade into the distance. The trees appeared to blend together, shrouded in the velvet night. Catherine's sixth sense flared outwards, discerning beyond sight and sound the benevolent protectiveness of branch and leaf. Up ahead, the invading light of the lantern seemed to float of its own accord through the ancient forest.

She was riding in front of Lucinda on the broad back of Junno's Clydesdale. Following the decisive lantern, the big man's indistinct bulk was leading them along a forest track created by foraging animals. Apart from the horse and the dog, Catherine was the only person to not perceive with unease the sensation of watchfulness pursuing their wordless passage through the nocturnal world.

Junno's dismay at Shadiz's determination to seek out Garan and have him perform the Ritual of Handfast had not stopped him from obediently escorting Catherine to the stables, collecting Lucinda on the way. He had thrown a blanket over his resting steed for the two young women, and then led the great, patient beast to where his cousin had awaited them beyond the convivial gathering in the courtyard.

It was thoughts of their destination and the man prompting their journey through the forest Catherine found intimidating. It was hard to equate the amazing tenderness he had shown her with the anger he had displayed since talking to the fishermen. He had not spoken to her when they had joined him. Or even glanced in her direction. So to imagine, with girlish glee, that the ritual would mean anything to him other than the reinforcement of his authority was a misconception she would not allow herself to make no matter what their ardent encounter had meant to her. He could simply have been missing a favourite mistress. No doubt there was a veritable bevy of beauties on the Mediterranean island Keeble had told her about, where the Master and his fellow corsair, Nick Condor, had their base. He exerted an extraordinary hold over less formidable souls. Therefore his present course of action must be the result of his furious indignation at his rare, noble intention of safeguarding her for her late father's sake being apparently misconstrued.

"Garan."

Despite its night-time existence, Catherine instinctively knew they had reached the place Shadiz had marched her to a few days before. More disturbing, she sensed with trepidation the nearby presence of the mysterious Crystal Pool. The mighty oaks she had encountered, unlike the rest of Stillingfleet, were its ominous sentinels. She felt their gnarled bark bristle. And heard their leaves rustle an eerie warning. A cold shiver ran the length of her stiff spine. Lucinda's hold on her waist intensified.

"Garan."

Shadiz swung the lantern around in a circle. Wary eyes shone fleetingly within successive areas around the untidy hermit camp in the wildly protesting light.

"Garan."

"What be this cackling? No slumber will I gather."

The disembodied voice wafted to them on a gentle breath of air, more like a sigh of relief. Seeking its origin, they were defeated by a conspiracy of dark design until a ragged shadow materialised behind them.

"Sleepin' was I."

Shadiz swung around. "I come t' ask a boon."

"It could wait not 'til a body gets its true reward?" The barely discernible figure shunned the light of the lantern.

"I want y' t' perform 'andfast," said Shadiz, without preamble.

"Indeed!" cried the wild man. "An' why should that be? Are you so afraid the maid'll wait not?"

In spite of her misgivings, Catherine smiled. Such candour was rarely practised upon the Master.

"An' which is it to be? Or can it be greed means both?" the wild man mused aloud, shuffling in the Clydesdale's direction. The big, brown horse half-turned in his direction, but not with the apprehension present in its master's response.

"Lucinda's Junno's woman," stated Shadiz, tersely.

"So tis the one y' brought afore y' would lay wi'?"

"No," emphasised Shadiz, sharply.

"Then why do y' disturb the night?"

There was a brief pause. Then, his exasperation mixed with superstition, Junno spoke to his cousin. "We're gettin' nowhere 'ere."

The quiet laughter was melodious, the rippling of a brook over water-worn stones. "What is Time wonders the Great Oaks as they pass into another Age."

The alliance of darkness had shrouded the change. Although their blinded eyes had been defeated, their cautious instincts attempted to fathom the transformation. The tall man by whom they were now confronted wore a long robe. He needed no light to reveal his flowing white hair and beard. The mastiff sat on its spiky haunches, staring at the gleaming white tusks of the boar.

Garan allowed them time to become accustomed to his priestly aspect, and then spoke to Shadiz, who he knew was not adverse to it. "What you ask is the impossible."

Shadiz's tense aura made it plain he was very rarely thwarted, especially by someone armed only with a seemingly innocuous staff. The ethereal beauty of moonlight entered the clearing, making it abundantly clear to all how his fierce gaze was spearing the compassionate one of the Druid.

"Handfast does not adhere to convenience. There is no place in its rites for selfish advancement. The hand is given freely to hold another's heart. If that is what you wish ... so be it. Otherwise, turn about and go forth to exalted stones, devoid of free air. Trap yourself and the girl in cynical demands."

"And the demons?" retorted Shadiz, much to Catherine's bewilderment. "What would you've me do wi' 'em?"

Junno's rumbling protest was ignored.

Garan smiled. "They are witless monsters whose defeat is surrender."

Shadiz had become perfectly still, contemplating the moonlit ground at his feet. His long black hair concealed his expression from the silver rays. Catherine was at a loss to know what to say to bring the odd pause to an end. It was Junno who spoke, pleadingly. "Let's leave this place."

Looking up, his cousin shot him a cold glance everyone present could discern. Shadiz then switched to Garan. "An' if I submit t' y'r wishes?"

"The Fates decree," stated the Druid, smiling faintly.

Shadiz stared into the forest.

Catherine sensed his inner turmoil, without understanding its true nature. When at length he gradually turned in her direction, it crossed her mind that he was more likely to bolt rather than endure any kind of ritual. When he started to make his way across the clearing to where she was sitting atop of Junno's horse, she envisaged a leave taking with remote and chilling courtesy. She was proved wrong.

He halted beside the Clydesdale. Catherine felt Lucinda stiffen behind her. Uncertain herself about his intention, higher than him for once, but not by much, her heart had begun to beat wildly. Scrutinising her beautiful young face, framed by her long fair-white hair, fine as any gossamer bridal veil, his black eyes softened. Catherine responded to his smile. She heard Lucinda's sharp intake of breath.

His actions considerate, Shadiz lifted her down from the horse's back.

"Does the maid understand what you ask of her?" asked Garan.

"Why don't y' enlighten 'er," Shadiz responded, quietly, reluctantly withdrawing the possessive arm he had wrapped around her waist.

Catherine felt suddenly unsettled. Was she expected to endure another ritual similar to the one when the Druid had taken her to the Crystal Pool? Throughout she had been aware of it awaiting hearts and minds to seek answers in its mystic clarity. Since her previous visit, it had given her baffling dreams of frightening regularity.

Garan inclined his white head. Smiling, he held out his hand. "Walk with me, Luna May. Be not afraid."

With one last glance at her motionless guardian, feeling the warmth of his protective presence, Catherine went with Garan to the other side of the forest clearing, her hand tucked within his. He said nothing, the boar by his side like a faithful mastiff.

"He simply wishes to honour the oath he gave to my father," she found herself saying, "And, he was annoyed when it was implied that I am his mistress. So, I presume, by offering to Handfast with me, he is trying to protect my reputation. Even if I am not a stainless character."

Garan halted, turning to her. "Does he know you?" he asked, regarding her with wise grey eyes.

"Better than I know myself, sometimes," replied Catherine. Comprehension dawned. "Oh, no. I didn't mean in that way," she explained, blushing. "Well, that is to say, he has ... well, we have embraced on a couple of occasions." She shrugged, embarrassed, dismissing her own words. "And tonight, I don't know ... maybe he was in need? He has been drinking. He doesn't normally."

"I see," murmured Garan. "What do you consider the future holds in store for you?"

She felt suddenly sad, lost. "I have no idea."

"Try."

An owl flew from one nearby branch to another. "I would spend my life in this place," said Catherine, softly, her attention caught by the soundless flight. "At the Lodge." Helplessness swept over her. Turning towards the forest, hoping the strange old man or her keen-eyed guardian would not see her threatening tears through the moonlight, she went on, "Being realistic, when he considers the risk to me, whatever that might be, has passed. Well, then, I'd imagine, he will frogmarch me back to Nafferton Garth. And, afterwards, heave a great sigh of relief."

"Within the depths of the forest, there are many hidden pathways," he responded.

"I don't understand."

"That, Luna May," he answered, squeezing her arm, "Is yours, and his, downfall."

Catherine sighed, wishing there were clear signposts upon the highway of life. She looked across the clearing. And knew instinctively Shadiz's black gaze had never left her. If it had been any other man, she would have considered his faint smile to possess an element of nervousness. In the next moment, she saw him stiffen and half-turn. Curious, she followed the direction in which he was glowering, but could see nothing of what he had obviously glimpsed in the forest.

"Oh, dear," muttered Garan, "I suppose it was to be expected."

A company of Romanies entered the clearing. They were on foot. Mamma Petra was mounted on her sturdy pony.

The arrival of their grandmother had an impact on both Shadiz and Junno. The big man stepped smartly between the old, blind Romany woman and his cousin. Encountering the menace of Shadiz's towering rage, Mamma Petra's escort closed around her. She remained composed on her disgruntled pony.

Catherine was eventually allowed to break free of Garan's restraining grip. He stood and watched as she ran across the clearing. "Fly to him, Luna May. Know your fate."

Junno raised his thick, muscular arm to ward off Shadiz at the same time as Catherine dashed up to them. Shadiz sidestepped the protective action that inadvertently swept her off her feet. In an instant, the world vanished into a void darker than night.

CHAPTER TWELVE

Heartache

Catherine regained consciousness slowly. When she tried to move, her head hurt abominably, making her feel sick and dizzy, making her groan.

"Easy, Kore. Stay put fer once."

Disorientated, it took a tremendous effort, but, by degrees, she established that she was cradled in Shadiz's arms. All she could do was rely upon his gentle strength.

A pewter mug was held against her lips. The contents smelt familiar, but in her confused state she was unable to identify the herbal brew. "Drink, Kore."

She complied with the imperative command as best she could. Then once again slumped against him, her eyes forced shut by the brilliant vortex.

After a while the White Witch's herbs began to take affect. Looking up at Shadiz, Catherine was unable to differentiate between an exasperated scowl and fierce anxiety. "It wasn't my fault?" she murmured, dizzily.

"I'm sorry, Rauni. It were mine," confessed Junno.

Movement increased the bell-pounding throbbing in her temples. It was with difficulty that her blurry gaze found the big man. He was down on one knee beside his cousin. His expression of regret jogged her foggy memory. She had a vague recollection of a muscular arm swinging towards her.

"No," rasped Shadiz. "It were me. If I ain't been turnin' me 'og out."

Touched by his self-condemning honesty, her hand rose shakily to his scarred cheek. She failed to register Junno's retreat over the flattened grass.

Mamma Petra spoke in the Romi, making her presence felt.

Seeing hostile clouds gather above her, Catherine slid her fingers to Shadiz's hard mouth in a feeble attempt to prevent a retort to whatever his grandmother had said. Intense and haunted, his black eyes returned to her swollen face. He gently removed her persuasive fingers from himself and brushed her palm with a light kiss.

Mamma Petra spoke again, commandingly.

Despite Shadiz's gaze remaining on Catherine, the clash of wills between the old Romany woman and her youngest grandson stretched mutely between them. The undeniable prod of apprehension made Catherine struggle into a sitting position. Although Shadiz supported her effort, he kept her in the shelter of his shoulder. She saw they were in the rear pasture beside the fire. Its continued warmth dispelled the chill of the night air. That the night was late enough to have become quiet around the Lodge went unnoticed by her while the atmosphere around the fire was charged with tension.

At last, in impatient words Catherine could understand, Mamma Petra said, "Thou wouldst seek a forest path to nowhere. Thou be Posh-Rat. Thou be half. Command that half do I. Turn thy hand and complete the cycle. Give of your heart's messenger."

A foreigner entering a strange land, an expression of crippling uncertainty seeped into Shadiz's face.

Catherine recalled how Tom had believed that Mamma Petra possessed some kind of hold over her grandson. She had been sceptical of his belief. Now she wasn't so sure.

"No!"

The heartfelt cry emanated from Lucinda. The usually calm young woman pleaded with Mamma Petra to desist. Her uncharacteristic agitation disturbed Peter's slumber. He lay close to his mother upon a bright, patchwork blanket. Bewildered by her objection, Catherine watched as she hastily soothed her son. When Lucinda looked up, their eyes met in a frank exchange. The natural progression was to look to the boy's father.

He flinched.

Catherine showed no condemnation, simply acceptance of Peter's existence. For during the evening, as the meal had been served, it had become plain to her from whom he had inherited the dark scowl that had kept children twice his age from usurping his place by her side. And those eyes. Although both Lucinda and Junno possessed Romany coals, Peter's were the image of slanting jet.

Her husband's comforting arm around her slender shoulders, Lucinda struggled to follow the doctrine of her creed and henceforth obey the stern-faced Puro Daia. Yet, she was not alone in wanting to speak out. Junno supported the courage his wife had shown. "Wi' respect. Let 'im do it in 'is own time. It's comin'."

Mamma Petra was scornful of the temperance they urged. "The past liveth in the present. The future wilst know of its shadow."

"If you are referring to Peter?" put in Catherine.

"Nay," dismissed the old Romany woman, with an irate wave of her small, wizened hand.

Catherine's questioning gaze took in the people around her. The fire highlighted the wedded dismay of Junno and Lucinda, and flickered upon Mamma Petra's stony, blank-eyed resolve. She turned to Shadiz. "I don't understand."

He would not look at her. Instead, he seemed hypnotised by the blaze.

"Give up what thee made for her."

Aware of the build up of tension within Shadiz because of their nearness, Catherine fully expected a foul dismissal of Mamma Petra's uncompromising command. Bracing herself, she marked the agonising pause with surprise that melted into disbelief that pitched headlong into distress.

She watched his lids descend upon the mesmerising flames. His long lashes tightened. At last came an exhale of ragged breath, heralding submission. His hand moved upwards and gripped his moonstone pendant. Galvanised into further action by his grandmother's brusque prompting, he wrenched the silver chain from around his neck. Long moments went by. He did not stir, the moonstone locked in his fist.

"Shadiz?" murmured Catherine, desperate to know why he had done such a thing.

He opened his compelling black eyes. The gaunt ruins of his austere composure took her breath away. In the next thunderous heartbeat, she received the moonstone. Her two hands were folded with infinite care over the pendant. Saying nothing, keeping his tormented gaze bent upon her, he raised her locked hands to his forehead and then placed them over his heart in what appeared to be a symbolic gesture.

"Thou wilst give forth the utterance."

Shadiz baulked at her command. Still holding Catherine's locked hands against his heart, he moved restively, caught in Mamma Petra's weird snare.

Catherine felt his agony as if it was her own. He shouldn't be struggling. Why was he struggling?

"Thou wilst do as I say. If thee be such a coward, complete thy offering in the rightful tongue."

When Shadiz eventually spoke, Catherine could barely hear his words. She could not understand them.

"Be gone. I wilst be there when thou hast need of me," dismissed Mamma Petra.

His relief palpable, Shadiz released Catherine and stood upright in one fluid movement. Tearing his remorseful gaze away from her, he disappeared into the night. Only the mastiff followed.

Tears of frustration burnt Catherine's eyes. "Will someone please tell me what is going on?" she protested, standing up unsteadily, her head pounding. She looked to where Shadiz had been swallowed up by the concealing darkness around the Lodge. Junno moved to her side and supported her. Lucinda hurried to the other side of her, as if she feared Catherine would dash after Shadiz. Mamma Petra commanded all three of them to sit back down.

Junno and Lucinda lingered around Catherine.

"Thou wilst learn nought but chaos if thee were to go forth. Sit ye down, and gain knowledge thou seeks."

Catherine stood her ground, ignoring the pain in her head and the hot throbbing in her bruised face, but not the terrible ache in her heart.

She could feel her jet pendant warm against her throat, and the moonstone cold as ice in the palm of her hand. She opened her trembling fingers and stared down at the pendant Shadiz had given to her in such a ritualistic manner. Around both jet and moonstone were broad, silver borders inscribed with identical, rune-like markings she had thought she knew so well, until now.

"Kammoben Bister is what thee beholds. Made they be for friends parted, family members following paths separated. And lovers. It be the ritual of Poorano Pattrimishi. The stone shalt alight the silver text to cry a warning. When giveth by hand, there be a declaration."

"A declaration?" repeated Catherine, bewildered. "The words? What did they mean?"

Mamma Petra tutted.

Her large grandson told her quietly, "Rauni ain't ... aware."

That he had chosen their language, as had Shadiz when obeying his grandmother, piqued Catherine. *"Ye gods and little fishes!"* she exclaimed.

"Besh!"

The blind eyes bore into Catherine with sinister power. She was accustomed to the instruction. It had been delivered many times before when the White Witch had been teaching her how to administer the medicinal herbs. She sighed, her shoulders sagging. "Forgive me," she mumbled, sitting back down on the woven blanket. Lucinda knelt beside her. Junno sank down onto his haunches and started to prod the fire with the head of a large axe.

Mamma Petra said. "Thy existence became known to me when the Posh-Rat cometh to seek my aid. Insistent was he that I accompanied him to the dwelling of a Gorgio close to Driffield. Thy malady defied the Gorgio's remedies. Thy steps were treading homewards. The fools consider the flow of juices can wash away a body's poison. Thy state overcometh doubt, forged with the Posh-Rat's declaration of my skill."

"You are referring to the illness when I was twelve," recalled

Catherine. "My father told me how you cured me. And, I remember you being at Nafferton Garth that winter while I was recovering. And, of course, winters after that." She frowned. "But, I don't ever recall seeing Shadiz."

"Objections," continued Mamma Petra, "They issued not from the Gorgio. He be fair of deram. Nay, the tatcho was concealed by the Posh-Rat."

"Tatcho?"

"Truth," Junno told her, turning away from the fire.

"Why would he do such a thing?" asked Catherine. "What possible difference would it have made if he and I had met?" It seemed to her the more she was told, the more baffling circumstances became. The only thing which did make sense to her was that her father had not been responsible for stopping her from meeting Shadiz.

"Maketh myself clear, didst I not?" responded Mamma Petra, sharply. "When the Posh-Rat didst bring me to thee, his fear was rampant. When time passed well for thee, he asked thy father grant two goodly deeds. That he remain concealed from thy knowledge. And that he be allowed to give thee through the pathway of thy da the Kammoben Bister. He wished to keep thee safe within the Rom tradition."

After a moment or two of difficult contemplation made worse by her persistent headache, Catherine gave voice to the only conclusion she could find. "For my father's sake."

"For thy sake."

"Me?"

Mamma Petra's lined features showed her irritation. She shook her grey head in grim disbelief. "Thou is being thicker than a mailo."

" 'ave a care, I pray y'. Wi' all respect," urged Junno.

Although she could not comprehend the big man's quiet words, Catherine saw that they did have a slight mellowing affect on his grandmother. The old woman went on, "We believe it hath origins before thy sickness. By then the Posh-Rat's feeling for thee had already set down deep roots. Beneath the moon, they are too well grown to be escaped. Though he would rip them up, for thy sake. Deceit hast altered the pathway of fate. He didst not seek guardianship, though he craved glimpses. He considered himself beyond contact. Now, he sees nought but the need for loss. He sees nought but dishonour in his obsession for thee. And yet knowst not how to go forth on any highway. Lost is he in his consideration for thee."

A precious moment of tremulous exultation was overcome by sensible disbelief. Catherine said, "Forgive me, I believe you to be mistaken. Whatever consideration he has shown me has been due entirely to his respect for my father."

"Besh, tupid," retorted Mamma Petra. "More blunt, shall I be. Souls bent on destruction fell upon the discovery of the Posh-Rat's *love for thee*. That knowledge was wielded to put fear into thy father. He became the sacrifice. Thou became the bait in the trap. And thusly remain."

It was more or less what Shadiz had told her while they had been locked together in the secret hold on board the *Eagle* when Lynette's men had boarded the merchantman in the middle of the North Sea. He had, however, allowed her to believe that his friendship with her father was the reason for him becoming her guardian. In reality....

'Yet will I love her till I die'

She swallowed hard, remembering the last line of the poem Shadiz had failed to finish when they had been in the library earlier in the evening. The tremulous exultation had returned, and was spreading. To be pursued by mortified guilt. She made a painful journey through the months since her first encounter with Shadiz in Colonel Page's campaign tent.

"Is that the reason why he went alone to the Crop-Ears camp and led them away?"

Mamma Petra inclined her grey head. "When that didst not see him ousted, he chose foreign flames. But they didst nought but lick him. Desperate, he took to the water."

Catherine went rigid. Lucinda gasped. Aghast, Junno demanded. "Are y' sayin' he tried those times to seek death?"

Unmoved by their reaction, Mamma Petra said, "An wilst again."

Catherine was choking on her despair. "We must go after him!"

"Aye," agreed Junno, forcefully. "We can't leave 'im."

"Are thy ears blocked? Didst thou not hear me say I wilst be there when he hath need?"

When Lucinda put a comforting arm around her trembling shoulders, Catherine barely noticed. "All because of me," she muttered, devastated. An horrendous thought struck her. "What happened at Scarborough, when Shadiz was imprisoned in the castle's dungeon? Was that after my illness? Was I responsible for that, too?" Consumed with guilt, her desperate gaze ranged over the three Romanies.

Mamma Petra's customary stern expression had not altered, unlike those of Lucinda and Junno. Lucinda appeared oddly shamefaced. Junno's massive body had stiffened to a significant degree. He paced around the fire until his grandmother called him sharply to order. Thereafter, he stood gazing at the Lodge, his usual good-humoured features roundly condemning.

Catherine was taken aback and made apprehensive by the reaction to her question.

Mamma Petra told her, "The Posh-Rat knew closeness to thee. He didst not know how to respond. Beng was within him. He caused Lucinda hurt."

"Puri Daia!" cried Junno, swinging back to face them.

"And giveth her his seed," continued Mamma Petra, undeterred by the big man's urgent interruption. "Me, he didst blind."

"Oh, my god!" exclaimed Catherine, stunned.

"I didst tell him to stop drowning in his cups."

Junno forestalled his grandmother. "So 'e 'it 'er an' robbed 'er o' sight."

"This is what thee hast feelings for," stated Mamma Petra.

"Yes," answered Catherine, emphatically. "Whatever the man is."

PART FOUR

LATE SUMMER

"Yet follow thy sun, unhappy shadow."

CHAPTER ONE

Flight to Nowhere

There was blood in the fountain. Not his.

He perched precariously on its inconvenient ornate rim, legs braced, watching his back as best he could, ready for another onslaught. All around him men glistened with sweat and were breathing heavily, just like him. Many, to their obvious chagrin, bore the signs of the confrontation he had instigated by his resolve to flee.

Domestic matters had come to a standstill. From all quarters in the broad, sunny Quadrangle servants stood agog, watching the spectacle of the young Lord of Fylingdales defying his uncle. All were aware of the family rift. None had expected to see it be so blatantly demonstrated.

Now that the dye had been impulsively cast, a single-mindedness of purpose drove Richard on. He twirled the blood-stained sword he had snatched from one of his smug guards, rashly inviting the men gathered around him to try and take revenge for their bruised egos. Although his chances of escape were remote, he took grim satisfaction in his slender advantage. For he suspected, or rather hoped, that they had been warned not to do him mortal harm while awaiting the arrival of their leader. Whereas, if the opportunity arouse to accomplish escape, he would not hesitate to inflict the killer blow.

"The gypsy is in love with her."

Ever since he had heard his mother's derisive words, he had been even more desperate to slip out of the silk manacles detaining him at the Hall. He had readily supplanted one emotion for another. His savage half-brother knew nothing of love, but everything about murderous lust.

He had failed Elizabeth. He was determined not to fail Catherine.

The upsurge of resolve brought about more fierce bravado, and an even keener eye for that elusive opening in the equally determined ranks of Fylingdales's men-at-arms.

It was the younger, more fanciful ones who posed the greatest threat. Those who given the chance would gleefully inflict a far more humiliating defeat upon him than their comrades wishing only to exercise a prudent measure of brute force.

All were destined to be disappointed.

Francois Lynette appeared in the Quadrangle. He sent the servants scurrying back to their duties with an impatient flick of a graceful hand. His handsome face still bore the marks of his brutal encounter with the Master. The slight limp was barely noticeable as he made his way down one of the neatly paved paths bordered by well-tended greens and fragrant borders, intricate knot squares and wreathed arches. Taking in the situation around the splashing fountain, he took his time passing the stone benches and haughtily crumbling statues that had once graced the imperial soil of Rome.

At length, cool and calculating, he halted a few paces from the three-tier fountain and, looking up, considered his nephew balanced on its rim. His men closed about him, not least because he was unarmed.

"What do you think you are doing?" His mellow, accented voice was infinitely patient, his smile indulgent.

While the fountain persisted in sending cool water down the back of his doublet and breeches and into his boots, Richard's defiant expression deepened into a stormy grin. He fought the need to cough. "Go to the devil," he retorted somewhat hoarsely.

Lynette gave a delicate sigh. "Could it be we are trying to save you from that Dark Devil, mon sweet?" He surveyed the damage Richard had accomplished on his men. "He has brutalised your skill."

"Bastard has done many things," rasped Richard, staying alert. He was aware the Fylingdales men were wanting to prove themselves to their leader after the violent fiasco.

"Therefore, you are truly ready to thwart him?" mused Lynette.

Stung by the gossamer accusation, Richard raised his sword a fraction higher.

In response, his uncle's men moved protectively closer to their leader. A challenge rippled through their bloodied ranks.

"Oh, come now, mon sweet. Your fear for Catherine Verity is what goads you into action."

Richard's furious objection was cut short.

He was tackled from behind by Gerald Carey and two of Fylingdales stalwarts. The struggle in the sunlit water of the fountain was shortlived. Although he knew himself to be overwhelmed after having allowed his attention to stray, Richard maintained an obstinate struggle while being disarmed, fished out of the fountain and pinioned in a vindictive grip by half a dozen men.

It was while he was being force marched back to his chamber in order to dry out and cool down that the door of the Dowager's Solar opened. He had not regained sufficient composure to respond with much civility when informed his mother wanted to speak to him.

"I have nothing to say to her."

He would have continued to the imposing staircase, the central feature of the entrance hall, but his guards responded to Lynette's command. They pulled him to a halt and jerked him around to face the mordant presence of his mother.

Towering resentment and sour defiance uppermost in his mind, Richard stood between his equally wet guards, his long hair plastered to his skull, water dripping from every part of him onto the parquet floor.

It seemed his thin-lipped mother had little to say to him. For without speaking, she walked up to Richard, and without appearing to overreach herself, she struck hard across his face.

Her women gathered in the oval doorway of the solar stifled their unanimous gasp. Francois Lynette raised a regal eyebrow at his sister's stinging reprimand.

As for Richard, he was angered and shaken by it. After ruthlessly driving down a coughing fit into the caustic pit of his guts, he demanded, "How long have you wanted to do that, mother? Since Elizabeth was raped and murdered?" For a moment, he looked past her, saying to his uncle, "It is a long held suspicion of mine, she has never forgiven me for not being there that day to defend my sister. Though, god knows what I could possibly have done against that bastard and his foul hoard." His bleak gaze returned to his mother. "Over the years since we lost Elizabeth, it has become increasingly plain to me that you would readily swap one offspring for another."

"Enough," commanded Lynette, stepping closer to the embittered tableau of mother and son.

Lady Hellena broke her condemning silence. Her accented voice was chilling. "For once he speaks the truth. This maudlin son of mine, to whom inheritance must be countenanced."

With one last icy thrust at him, she turned and walked away.

CHAPTER TWO

Breaking Point

"He loves me? He loves me not?"

Catherine posed the questions, picking at the petals of a daisy. And then felt guilty for torturing the flower.

She was supposed to be tending her newly created herb garden in the rear pasture. Instead, she knelt beside it and stared at the blackened grass marking the spot where the fire had been several nights ago. She sighed. Bless them, they must have got it wrong.

No matter how strong Mamma Petra's mystical powers were, she was human, after all, with human failings, granted not many, but just enough to leave a margin of error regarding her enigmatic grandson's emotions.

Yet, try as she may while half-heartedly stabbing the loosened soil with a bent trowel, Catherine could not stop herself from sifting through the tantalising evidence presented by the adamant old Romany. Such irresistible reverie carried in its wake an abundance of mixed feelings. Was her existence to blame for Shadiz's abuse of his grandmother and Lucinda? And for his capture at Scarborough when he had been riotously drunk?

No. They had to be wrong. He was twelve years her senior, and about a hundred years in worldliness. A charismatic leader, who could snap his fingers and have any woman he wanted. To believe for a moment that he was not only in love with her but had been for years was to court disaster.

Yet why had he given her the jet pendant by way of her father? And why, to apparently complete a Romany ritual, did he wear a moonstone pendant with runes inscribed on the silver border exactly the same as hers? Why had he shown her such remarkable tenderness in the library? And afterwards ritualistically given her his own pendant at his grandmother's prompting?

What was she supposed to believe?

"Ye gods and little fishes!"

The see-saw emotions plagued each day without sight of Shadiz. And made her nights unbearable. They had gradually coalesced into an unremitting sensation. A defining knowledge of love and empathy. Reassurance was in the air. But no one could tell her otherwise. Instead, she had told them to let go of false hope and give in to the temptation to seek out answers.

After five long days and nights, Junno had finally heeded her.

With the notable loss of Tom and Richard's prolonged absence, the big man had taken charge at the Lodge. No coercion had been required to dispatch search parties. The men willingly scoured the land for their leader. To no avail. Even the Romanies returned to the Lodge cast down by their lack of success. Speculation was rife. Catherine caught the whispers around her.

One thought sustained her. If she was Kore, salvation was possible. If it were timely.

Eight days after Tom's funeral word reached the Lodge that the Master was presently in Whitby. The tidings came from Bob Andrew and was conveyed along with a sense of urgency by Sam Todd. Bill's older brother, the bo's'un of the *Eagle*, clattered into the courtyard on a borrowed nag and quickly made it plain that someone's attendance was needed at the port. All eyes shifted to Junno.

Standing head and shoulders above the men gathered around him and Catherine, the big Romany writhed in a vice of conflicting loyalties.

Catherine had been drawn from the rear pasture by stark fear. Her advice was simple and prompt. "Go."

"Ain't that easy, Rauni," he bemoaned, scratching his bald head.

"Then, I'll go with you."

"Y' can't," he cried with increased agitation. "I can't leave y' 'ere. I can't tak y' wi' me."

"Then you condemn both of us," she protested in a voice bleak with despair.

Staring down at the tall, slender, well-bred girl, Junno knew she was not referring to herself or him. Consumed by his anxiety, which had grown with each day Shadiz had remained absent from the Lodge, he had missed the new maturity sparking within her distinct, ethereal beauty. She met his anguished look in silence, yet her entire trembling demeanour pleaded with him. Dark imagery sprang up between them. He was moved to gently touch her arm. But how could he reassure her? If she only knew the true extent of the damage done already.

Unbeknown to Junno, the day after Shadiz had disappeared into the accommodating night, before leaving the Lodge with her son and Mamma Petra, his wife had sought out Catherine and issued a warning.

The two young women had met on the threshold of the kitchen, and at Lucinda's bidding found privacy of sorts in a leafy corner of the rear pasture. Usually placid and discreet, never forceful, Lucinda had probed Catherine's feelings for Shadiz. Taken aback, Catherine had found it hard to conceal the truth. As a result, Lucinda had seemed appalled and, in no uncertain terms, warned her against becoming involved with her husband's dangerous cousin. She had left Catherine in no doubt about her worries for her safety. Shaken, Catherine had realised that it was not just a case of a jealous thrust from a scorned mother. She knew how much Junno meant to Lucinda, even though he was not the father of her son, and she had seen for herself how the Romany woman appeared ill at ease whenever Shadiz was close by.

But, standing in the courtyard awaiting Junno's decision, Catherine accepted that Lucinda's warning had been in vain. Her feelings for Shadiz had been forged in blood and tears. They had gone beyond the point of denial.

"Tis only what you've expected these many days," Junno admitted, regretfully.

Catherine nodded, biting her bottom lip, trying to hold within the torment that was not hers alone.

His large hand on her arm grew tight, an indication of his

reluctant conviction. "I want most o' y' t' escort us t' Whitby," he told the men.

★ ★ ★

The large group of riders clattered over Spittal Bridge and swept past the industrious cacophony coming from the boatyard. They hastened down the dusty highway running parallel with the shrunken River Esk. Various vessels rested idly in the mud uncovered by the low tide. Off to their right, the weathered, stone-built cottages tumbled down the steep cliff , interwoven with uneven steps, canting wynds and yards. In no time at all, the riders were entering the sunlit confines of Church Street. Their curtailed progress was met by startled gazes from Whitby folk who retreated from their lathered mounts.

Self-contained in cold dread, Catherine was dismayed when Junno insisted on her remaining with Laura Andrew in Haggerlythe, the narrow lane overlooking the wide mouth of the estuary where the captain's cottage was situated. The big man left Danny Murphy in command of the substantial escort which had accompanied Catherine and himself to Whitby. Then, he went in search of his cousin.

Upon entering the common room of the Lobster Pot with his older brother, the big man and Benjamin, Bill Todd gave a long, low whistle. Stunned, the three men halted.

"Told y'," muttered Sam Todd, continuing forward to his captain.

Bob Andrew was sitting in the midst of shattered tables and upturned benches, his head in his hands. Looking up gingerly, he nodded with care in answer to his bo's'un's concerned inquiry. With Sam's help, he got to his feet. Meanwhile the astounded newcomers scanned the vandalised common room. They were discovering for themselves what little remained of the rough furnishings, ale-jugs and prized nautical decorations. Strewn amongst the debris, battered men were coming to terms with their injuries in an atmosphere permeated with spilt ale and shock.

328

Junno needed no telling who was responsible for the damage. "Where's 'e now? D'y know?" he asked, wading through the splintery wood, fit only for kindling. He halted beside Bob and took in the other man's dishevelled appearance. "Y' be all right?"

"Aye," answered the captain, succinctly, wiping away blood from a nasty gash in his cheek. "What the devil's up wi' lad?"

Lifting his huge shoulders in a noncommittal shrug, Junno reiterated, "Where's 'e?"

"I'll show y'," said Keeble from the door of the wrecked tavern.

Junno gave the axe wedged in the thick boards of the door a passing glance as he returned into the sunshine. Bob was slower. On the way out of the tavern, he offered up a silent prayer. For it had become painfully obvious that nobody but the big Romany was capable of dealing with Shadiz in his present, self-induced condition.

Hooked by perverse interest, Burt Brewer's customers, exhibiting various degrees of stiffness, left him to contemplate his ruined business. Keeble led the men to the head of a flight of stone steps at the rear of the Lobster Pot. What Junno saw on the foreshore below, between Tate Pier and Fish Landing, caused his heart to sink into his boots. At that moment, he would have given anything for Tom's fatherly support. Bracing himself, he started down the slimy steps. The men took heed of his gesture to stay where they were.

Benjamin longed to accompany the big man across the muddy ridges of the foreshore. Having returned to the Lodge after succeeding in being released from Prince Rupert's service in order to serve the Master, he had found his leader missing and his men at a loss to know his whereabouts. Bound into the expectant silence against his will, he watched with the rest as Junno made his way past fishing cobles sunk in the mud awaiting high tide, and the various bits of flotsam and jetsam successive tides had delivered to the riverbed below the harbourside cottages.

The men were not the only ones to view the unusual activity on the foreshore. Many small-paned windows were filled with curious faces. The narrow heads of wynds had become crammed with interested bystanders. On Fish Landing, fishermen stood amidst lobster pots, nets and wicker baskets. Opposite them on Tate Quay, seamen had also ceased work and congregated around stacked crates, barrel and sacks.

Concentrating on the lone figure, Junno trudged over a pile of crisp mussel shells. Despite all his good intentions, his mud-sucking footsteps faltered. A few feet away from him, his cousin groped for an ale-jug sunk in the watery mire. Judging by the way Shadiz cursed, the earthenware pot had obviously lost its remaining contents. In a rage, he flung the fat vessel towards the burgeoning measure of river water. Missing his mark, he succeeded only in frightening nearby gulls and unbalancing himself. He fell heavily onto his knees.

While twisting around, his bloodshot eyes focused on the big man through lank strands of his long, black hair. A nasty sneer tightened his slack-jawed drunkenness. "Well, well. Bastards sent fer bleedin' Colossus." All at once, the sun burst from behind the clouds starting to gather over the port, making him close his eyes and bend his head. "Y' can sod off." He groped blindly for the ale-jug, apparently having forgotten he had tossed it away. "Where th' bloody 'ell...."

Junno stood in silence, hurting to the core of his large, compassionate being.

"I ain't goin' any bleedin' place." Shadiz's defiant words were slurred. He gave a chilling grin. "I'm waitin' fer the bitch. This time ... I'll be ready for 'er."

"Y' sacrificed another t' 'er," Junno murmured, regretfully. "Didn't y'."

When the sun once more disappeared behind grey clouds, Shadiz's black, feral eyes opened but remained heavy-lidded. "Y' should o' guarded 'er, simensa," he hissed.

"I tried," answered Junno, quietly. "The Puro Daia saw what'd befall."

"Outwitted by a blind seer. Ain't we all." Shadiz thrust out a grimy hand, stabbing a black-nailed finger at the big man, adding, "Not this time."

"Y' can't go on like this."

"'Tis at an end," spat out Shadiz.

He suddenly took a sharp intake of breath and gripped his temples. Bending forward, he hammered his head upon his knees. Blood stained his filthy breeches as a result of the demented savagery.

It was too much for Junno. He drew closer to Shadiz, only to have his attempt at a solicitous approach violently rejected.

He tried reaching out with a heartfelt plea, "Think o' Catherine."

Shadiz grew unnaturally still. When he did eventually straighten, the big man saw his cousin's eyes were dense and glazed. The tears were cleaning away the grime from his unshaven jowls. In a strangled voice, he muttered, "I am." He gasped in pain. Gloved in the mire of their dank surroundings, his hands released their vicious grip upon his temples and descended to pluck with the same ferocity at his stomach.

Junno frowned. He was sadly accustomed to the agony of blind, irrational violence. On this occasion there was a different element to his cousin's manic behaviour. He was bent double. Both his arms were now wrapped tightly around his middle.

When Shadiz began to retch with gut punishing force there was little Junno could do but stare at the oozing blood. There was a strong temptation to put the blame on the known intolerance of ale. But commonsense told him the notion was wishful thinking. This was certainly something he had not encountered before. He bent over his cousin. Before his worries could manifest themselves into constructive action, Shadiz reacted with venom to his benevolent shadow. Although his breathing was laboured after the bout of sickness, he managed to twist away from the big man. Engrossed in his concern, the sudden movement took Junno unawares. He failed to combat the blow from the ale-jug his cousin had randomly laid hands upon in an upsurge of blind fury.

Cast down into the muddy ridges, it took the big man a few moments to recover from the stunning blow. He sat up, shaking his muzzy head, expecting Shadiz to still be close by. When he discovered he was not, he scanned the foreshore. Cursing, he scrambled to his feet and was quickly in pursuit of the stumbling figure.

Adhering to its twice daily ritual, the influx of the North Sea into the Esk Estuary was broadening and deepening the river, causing the fishing boats and merchantmen to rock at their berths in the harbour; and allowing a sufficient measure for a berserk intention.

A potent mixture of dismay and panic drove Junno into the water after Shadiz.

The sun had made another spectacular appearance from behind the ominous clouds. Its rays struck the disturbed surface of the Esk, transforming mundane greyness into burnished silver. Dazzled by the inconvenient light, it took Junno a couple of moments to realise the unsteady figure had stopped struggling against the drag of the water and disappeared beneath its surface. Hesitating only to take a swift deep breath, he too sank down into an airless, silt-drifting environment.

From stacked yards and threadlike wynds, from neighbourly cottages and tavern windows, from ships and fishing boats, from the unnaturally quiet quaysides, a goodly part of Whitby's inhabitants waited with bated breath. Only the herring gulls, wheeling above all manner of curiosity, continued to give squawking life to the port. Doubts about the big man's ability to stem the Master's astonishing behaviour hung on a wind that threatened rain.

Benjamin Farr had no memory of descending the stone steps. He vaguely registered he was standing on the foreshore and that Bob, Keeble, Bill and Sam Todd had followed his example. Their collective attention was riveted on the river. When the gilded surface of the Esk exploded into a thousand grubby, sunlit gems, not in the least relieved, they watched the trial of strength between the two powerful men, oblivious of their hypnotic footsteps towards them.

A dispassionate observer, the sunlight glinted on a stiletto blade. It flashed with deadly purpose between the Romany cousins while they remained locked together amidst a glittering nimbus of discoloured spray.

" Almighty!" exclaimed Bob Andrew.

With one accord the five men broke free from the restraint of disbelief. Stung by their own inaptitude, forcing Junno to fight alone, they dashed across the remaining porous terrain.

After Benjamin and Bill had tossed their sword belts to Bob, they left him and Keeble to fret in the shallows and waded out from the foreshore, followed by Sam. In doing so, they kept grimly focused on the spot where Shadiz and Junno had once again vanished beneath the river's agitated surface. Silt infested waves born out of the underwater struggle were lapping against Benjamin's chest when an eruption took place a few feet away.

"Watch out fer that damned dagger!" bellowed Bob, pacing the Esk's rippling edge.

Junno needed no warning. The big man had realised the moment he had entered the water in an effort to extract his cousin from the riverbed that he would be fighting for his life. For both their lives. Shadiz's crazed fury had turned in on itself, but having been thwarted was now being directed at his cousin. As a consequence, Junno was having to wield his great strength simply to hold his own.

The younger men were eager to help him. Bob wasn't so sure. He called out a warning, this time to Benjamin and the Todd brothers. They ignored him. Instead, closing in on the combatants, hampered by tall waves coming from the trial of strength, they attempted to get behind Shadiz. Unfortunately, in an attempt to avoid Shadiz's savage thrust with the dagger, Junno inadvertently frustrated their joint endeavour with a reaction that was borne out of self preservation.

This time when Shadiz tried to escape with grotesque purpose, all four of the men dived after him.

Bob stood cursing all and sundry in his frustration while Keeble crept steadily further into the rapidly broadening Esk. The captain was in the process of calling the little man back onto the muddy ridges of the shrinking foreshore when a Romany appeared suddenly at his elbow. His nerves already stretched like frayed ratlines, the swarthy man's soundless manifestation startled him. He was about Bob's age and similar to him in robust build. He was not alone, Bob soon realised.

"They need all 'elp they can get," he said, watching as several Romanies waded past Keeble, heading for deep water.

"They go to look out for yours," the Romany told him, without taking his dark eyes from where his brethren had quickly and quietly sank beneath the disturbed surface.

In a matter of seconds they reappeared, dragging Benjamin, Bill and Sam up to the surface with them. Although a great deal of furious thrashing went on, the Romanies prevented the outnumbered Gorgios from intervening further.

His attention momentarily deflected from the conflict between Junno and Shadiz, Bob envisaged another battle royal and attempted to quell the growing argument between the young warriors of two cultures. "Lads. We've enough goin' on," he bellowed across the intervening distance.

The older Romany beside him shouted in the same sharp manner in the Romi.

An uneasy truce lasted until Junno and Shadiz once more reared up locked together, shattering completely the agitated surface of the river. Thereafter separate, water-borne struggles were renewed. Bob cursed and looked to the Romany beside him for support. Before either of the two men could intervene a second time, a slender object came winging their way. Both of them ducked to avoid it. And both looked behind them at the dagger that had stabbed the churned up mud.

"Thank God," muttered Bob.

It was Junno who roared at Romanies and Gorgios alike, with breath he could ill-afford to spare. Both sets of young men halted their wrangling. Treading the muddy river, they became united in their scrutiny of Shadiz and Junno. With their attention now centred on the two cousins, they realised that the struggle between them had diminished considerably.

Despite being fastened in Junno's powerful arms, Shadiz

persisted in his bellicose attitude. There was a remarkable forbearance in the way the big man dealt with the flailing remnants of his cousin's bizarre wrath.

All at once Shadiz's whole body seemed to contract. Junno could do little other than transform restraint into much needed support during the bout of violent, bloody vomiting. Totally spent, Shadiz offered no further resistance when Junno dragged him out of the river. Burdened with his cousin, the big man fell heavily onto his knees on the dismal foreshore.

He had won the horrendous duel, at a cost he would not easily forget. But, for now, he had a more pressing struggle to contend with. A crushing foreboding caused him to handle his cousin roughly.

While Benjamin, Bob, Keeble and the apparent leader of the Romanies closed about Shadiz and Junno, the other men remained a few paces away, watching. Of them all, only Bob and the older Romany were not thoroughly soaked.

"What be up wi' lad?" demanded Bob.

Junno did not respond. All else he was familiar with. But not this. Not the obvious pain or the terrible sickness.

It began again. This time going on for even longer. When the sickness came to a ragged end, Shadiz writhed in agony, far more than he had done before.

" 'e'll spew 'is damned guts up afore long," exclaimed Bob, thoroughly perturbed.

"This cannot be just the ale, surely?" observed Benjamin, crouching down.

Junno had come to the only possible conclusion. In his desperation, he shook Shadiz. "What've y' teken?"

His frantic question was of little use. Shadiz was beyond answering.

The Romany beside Bob met Junno's distressed look. Comprehension flashed between the two men. In their language, Imre Panin said, "What was it that went missing from the Puro Daia's great bag at the Lodge?"

Junno shook his head. "I ain't sure," he muttered, striving to hold onto Shadiz. "Rauni might know."

In a place where life was mostly humdrum, or downright hard at times, the unusual was highly entertaining. So while the rest of Whitby digested what had already taken place, the folk living in Haggerlythe were spilling out of cottage doors and windows in an effort to watch the continuing spectacle. Their view was being hampered by the throng of Master's men and Romanies within the narrow lane.

Catherine froze on the doorstep of Bob's cottage. Her worst fears, fuelled by her jet pendant, were realised when she saw the crowd of sodden, dirty men making their way down the lane, with burdened urgency. Having eyes only for Shadiz, slumped in Junno's arms, she dashed towards them. Overcoming his surprise at the sight of this leader's dire condition, Danny Murphy was immediately on her heels. Behind him, slower to overcome their shock, Laura and a protective pack of the Master's men followed.

For Junno, Catherine's fair-white hair was like a beacon of hope. " 'e's teken summat," he cried, breathlessly. He laid Shadiz on the cobbles. "Summat out o' Mamma's great bag. I ain't a clue what. D' y?"

Falling to her knees, Catherine recalled Lucinda's parting words when she had been leaving the Lodge. *Belladonna is missing from Mamma Petra's herb bag.*

Shadiz's clothes were soaked and covered in mud. There were flecks of blood on his blue lips. His eyes were tightly shut. Framed by plastered strands of his long wet hair, his dark, scarred face was a mask of torment. Though he was clearly oblivious to his surroundings, his big body convulsing in horrendous pain, he suddenly clawed at Catherine.

"Oh, dear God! This is beyond me," she admitted in wild-eyed despair.

Tears of frustration sprang into Junno's eyes. "Y' must do summat?" he pleaded.

"My view be summer bright," said Mamma Petra, from behind them. "Didst I not say, I would be ready when the Posh-Rat hath need of me?"

CHAPTER THREE

Impasse By Design

"*Mithral Bel cay lay. Canast fay nay par.*"

The glow from melting candles thrust motionless shadows on the white-washed walls at the top of the steep ladder-staircase in Bob Andrew's cottage. Benjamin Farr was leaning against the shadowy wall on the narrow landing, staring down at his boots. Laura Andrew was sitting on the top step. Her arms were around Catherine's shoulders. She was balanced on the narrow tread below, every fibre of her being twisted in tense knots. Her jet pendant hung around her neck and Shadiz's moonstone were both in her tight, unfailing grip.

"*Mithral Bel cay lay. Canast fay nay par.*"

She chanted the Romany words continually without understanding their meaning, simply clinging to the memory of their power to resurrect on the *Eagle*. Only the whispered mantra against death stirred the profound silence laying upon the landing and ladder-staircase and below in the semi-darkness of the parlour where Bob and Keeble sat.

Their helplessness a bane, those present had suffered in muted, downcast spirits the agonised groans and the tormented moans coming from the other side of the closed door. Now only the quiet movements of the two people in the bedchamber with Shadiz could be heard.

Catherine had wanted so very desperately to be with him. But neither Mamma Petra nor Junno would allow her to remain with them while the vile stuff he had swallowed was swilled away. She had argued, vehemently, against being dismissed by her former teacher, reminding the old Romany and her grandson of what she had already accomplished. To no avail. The White Witch had been adamant. And adding his voice to hers, Junno had sought only to spare her from witnessing the horrendous procedure he had seen his grandmother perform a couple of times before.

"Mithral Bel cay lay. Canast fay nay par."

Catherine continued to chant, the faith in her ability to sense direction shaken, leaving an excruciating uncertainty.

Eventually, the door to Laura's and Bob's bedchamber opened. The first reaction of those waiting nearby was a moment of paralysing trepidation.

Then Catherine slowly got to her feet. Laura rose, keeping a supportive arm around the younger woman's trembling shoulders. If need be, it would be there to comfort. Glancing at Catherine as she stepped onto the landing beside her, Laura's heart went out to her. She looked so young, pale and vulnerable. Laura knew what it was like to fear for a man. Feeling slightly guilty, she just wished it wasn't Shadiz for whom Catherine was so desperately worried.

Benjamin had straightened. He joined Catherine and Laura in regarding Junno in expectant, braced silence.

The emotional and physical exhaustion etched into the big man's round face was under-lit by the wavering candlelight. He began to speak, stopped and cleared his throat. "Come, Rauni," he murmured, holding out a hand to her.

Catherine gripped the two pendants, jet and moonstone, even tighter. The chant persisted in her cringing mind as Junno's unusually cold hand led her into the bedchamber. Just before entering, he put Benjamin's and Laura's minds at rest with a slight, grim nod of his bald head.

Approaching the bed in which Shadiz lay, her heart pounding, her breathing suspended, Catherine sought signs of life. And to her boundless, heady relief found them in the rise and fall of his chest beneath the patchwork blanket. She felt the warmth of her jet and his moonstone pulsating in her fist.

Trembling uncontrollably, she sank down onto her knees beside the bed, and scrutinised the ghastly hollows and ravished flesh of his remarkable face, stripped bare of harshness, of that charismatic vitality she associated so closely with him. His long, midnight eyelashes lay upon the dark smudges beneath his closed lids.

"All hast been done within my power. The pull of the pattriensis wouldst have been ignored if thee had not call unto him," said Mamma Petra, demonstrating her weird knowledge.

She was sitting in a rocking chair beside the small casement window. It had been opened, allowing the tang of the sea, borne on the mild wind, to cleanse the stale air in the candlelit chamber. Having been forged in leaden clouds during the previous day, raindrops had been set free sometime during the night. Threads of dawn were creeping over the North Sea beyond the harbour.

Before returning her attention to Shadiz, Catherine looked at the White Witch's familiar leather bag, open on the polished floorboards. It was surrounded by an assortment of herbal mixtures and various lengths of hollow willow sticks. Perturbed by their discarded presence, and the cauldron beside them, her attention returned to Shadiz. To find his fragile gaze upon her as if she was an amazingly beautiful angel come to his bedside.

A vibrant thrill shot through Catherine. Her eyes gazed brilliantly into his, half-closed by exhaustion. Taking his hand, moving closer to where he lay, she bit her trembling lip, smiling and frowning at the same time; not really sure of what she was doing.

Shadiz attempted to speak, but could manage only a rough, hoarse sound that obviously caused him pain.

Junno was quick to appear beside the bed. Leaning over, he supported his weak cousin while Catherine held up the mug he had handed her to Shadiz's sore lips. She was careful how she gave him the drink, but even so, he began to choke on the water. Junno raised him up further until the retching brought about by the rawness of his throat had come to an end.

After laying Shadiz back down with a gentleness that was so much a part of his compassionate nature, the big man gave Catherine a reassuring smile before returning to the other side of the chamber and joining his grandmother near the open window.

Shadiz lay with his eyes closed, struggling to get his ragged breathing under control. At length, he sought Catherine's hand. Upon her responding, he gave a feeble tug so that she would sit upon the bed.

"Forgive me," he managed with difficulty.

"You cannot go on like this. Pursuing self-destruction," she protested, shakily. "You are tearing yourself apart. And me."

Shadiz opened his eyes and gazed up at her. His black eyes revealed agony of the spirit.

Distressed, Catherine would have said more had she not been interrupted by Mamma Petra.

"Thou be a boon and a burden to the Posh-Rat."

"Puri daia. Please, no more," objected Junno.

Consumed by a sudden impulse, Catherine twisted around to confront the blind old Romany. "For all your foresight, you saw me only as a boon to cure whatever ailed him. You made quite certain of that. You implanted the words within me. Yet it was he who gave me the twin of his moonstone pendant. Their connection has made those words more potent than you ever foresaw."

Whatever Mamma Petra retorted in a condemning tone caused Junno to scowl at her, and Shadiz to very nearly come off the bed.

Unnerved by both of their reactions, Catherine understood she had been verbally flayed for speaking in such a manner to Mamma Petra.

While trying to settle Shadiz down, made easy by his fragile condition, Catherine could sense waves of virulent emotion wafting across the bedchamber to her from the old Romany woman. And was certain he could, too, by the way he gripped her hand protectively with the small amount of strength within him.

Even when she had been a pupil of the White Witch, learning the properties of the different herbs and how to administer them, there had been no warmth in the old Romany's manner. Catherine had accepted the trait as being part of her difficult, austere character, and had mentioned nothing to her father about how uncomfortable it made her feel at times.

If she were to believe what had been imparted to her at the Lodge, with irritation by Mamma Petra, the enmity had begun to manifest itself at that early time. Now, in Bob's bedchamber, she realised her ability to sense the emotions of others had not played her false.

Shadiz was holding her hand that possessed his pendant. He slipped it out of her hand. It was clear what he wished her to do. But she could not accomplish it alone.

Junno quickly answered her pleading look. Reaching the bed, he once again supported his cousin, this time so that Catherine could slip the mended silver chain around Shadiz's neck. While she bent towards him, her own jet pendant swung forward. Shadiz raised a trembling hand and catching hold of the stone drew it to his lips. The gesture brought tears to Catherine's eyes.

After Junno had laid Shadiz down again, and Catherine had made him comfortable, both her and the big man saw how he fought the sleep his ravished body demanded. A feeble shadow of his usual commanding manner, he nevertheless made it plain he wanted Catherine to remain at his bedside and Junno to watch over her, glancing pointedly to where his ominously silent grandmother was sitting. Shortly afterwards, he had no option but to submit to restful slumber.

Junno reinforced his ailing cousin's wish. " 'e'll only fret if y' go, Rauni." With a gentle squeeze of her shoulder, he added, "Y' need t' rest easy. I'll not be far away."

Catherine answered with a grateful smile.

She knew it must have been Junno who had stripped off his cousin's filthy clothes and washed away the mud. Yet the reek of the foreshore still clung to Shadiz. All that Catherine cared about as she lay down beside him on the bed was his slumberous breathing and the warmth returning to his big body next to her.

CHAPTER FOUR

Wench Who Serves

"Great Spirit hear my cry. Beloved of mine in safety keep."
Junno had lifted the veil. Responding to Catherine's plea, he had supplied the translation with a solemnity that gave the words undeniable credence. Their meaning remained potent while spoken in either the Romi or in her own language. Their influence was beyond her comprehension. She was simply grateful to whichever benevolent angel had reinforced the silver thread betwixt jet and moonstone on those occasions she had uttered the sacred words in desperation.

Believing the words also to be a declaration of joyful life, they made the fresh air smell even sweeter. Each intake of breath was taken for both of them. For Catherine was aware of how fretful Shadiz was growing at being trapped indoors by the slow pace of his recovery. Though she had been persuaded outdoors by him, she still felt guilty about leaving him. She had not done so in two days and nights.

Catherine was not alone in enjoying the fresh air. Having remained with her in the captain's bedchamber throughout, Junno had been called upon to escort her out into the sunny morning by Shadiz. Benjamin had accompanied them from the cottage in Haggerlythe to the wooden rail at the top of the slope leading down to Tate Pier. He had guarded the bedchamber, looking through the half-opened door now and then to see how the Master was faring. Standing between the two thoughtful men, Catherine was glad of their company. Their quiet devotion had been a welcomed contrast to Mamma Petra's austere presence.

The last few days had taken its toll. Both men wore the same expression of indelible aftermath. As no doubt she did.

Junno was nothing like Mamma Petra's other grandson. Catherine's encounters with the gentle, bald-headed big man at Nafferton Garth, where his grandmother's tribe had passed the winters since she was twelve years old, had sparked a friendship which, since he had become her protector at the Lodge, had developed into a fond closeness. She had grown accustomed to being in his mighty shadow. His great height possessed a slight, self-conscious stoop that was typical of the unassuming Romany. Benjamin, on the other hand, was straight and slender as a ship's mast. Catherine glanced at his handsome, boyish features. His shoulder-length fair hair was being stirred by the same brisk wind brushing her much longer fair-white locks. Despite the obvious differences in the two men's appearances, their temperaments were remarkably similar. Quiet, caring souls with great strength of purpose, they gave of themselves with no selfish intent. She trusted both of them. And was mystified whenever she experienced those occasional, inexplicable qualms about Benjamin.

Through daylight that seemed unusually bright, she watched the fishermen preparing to sail from the harbour on the incoming tide. They braced themselves against the increasing buoyancy of their hardy crafts as they checked their nets. A rough swell heralded the approach of high tide at the mouth of the River Esk. Its gathering strength was creating a surf-white threshold to the North Sea. Armed with experience, grit and a measure of luck, the fishermen of Whitby would return with their sea-washed decks laden with cod and haddock, the silver of the port.

Catherine was glad Junno's huge frame was blocking her view of the muddy ridges between Tate Pier and Fish Landing. She did wonder if his back was deliberately turned upon the dank foreshore because he, too, could not bear to look upon the place where he had been forced to fish his cousin out of the Esk.

"Weren't me!"

When Shadiz had been in a condition to do so, he had made the hoarse declaration.

It had become known that someone had raided the White Witch's bag when she had visited the Lodge. Despite Mamma Petra making it plain to her and Junno that her flawed grandson had courted death on more than one occasion over the past few months, Catherine was not convinced that this time he was the culprit. Shadiz had previously indicated there was a bad apple in his orchard. Why else would he have charged his cousin with the task of being her bodyguard?

"You are a burden to him."

Mamma Petra's accusing candour echoed.

According to her, Shadiz's knowledge of her had been withheld, even by her father. A startling fact she found hard to believe. Yet the vagaries of fate had seen her stumble unwittingly into his turbulent life and, if Mamma Petra was to be believed, made it a living hell.

And, Lord help her, she was beginning to believe, with a vulnerable hope that could be so easily shattered, the stunning revelations tossed her way with something akin to icy resentment by the old Romany woman.

During her vigil either at Shadiz's bedside or curled up beside him, their conversations had been far ranging. Apart from discussing the satisfactory condition of Nafferton Garth, during which she discovered he was a regular visitor, she also benefited a great deal from the remarkable breadth and depth of his self-seeking knowledge. She learned about the world in general, and a little of his in particular.

Though she had longed to, Catherine had refrained from asking him about events closer to home. Not least because of Mamma Petra's continued, dour presence in the bedchamber.

Shunning the unpleasant shadow Shadiz's grandmother cast upon her thoughts and turning away from the activities in the harbour, Catherine gazed instead upon the array of cottages tumbling down the steep cliff below Abbey Top.

"What do you suppose has become of Richard?" she wondered aloud.

No one had seen him since he had left the cliff top graveyard where Tom had been buried to escort his mother home to Fylingdales Hall. Of late, everyone had been too preoccupied with his half-brother to pay much attention to his continued absence.

"Dunno that y' need fret," Junno remarked.

Benjamin and Catherine regarded the big man. Shrugging, he added, " 'e's more'n likely bein' 'eld against 'is will. Aye. But I doubt 'e'll cum t' much 'arm."

"I hope you are correct," commented Catherine.

When Junno suggested they return to Bob's cottage, Catherine immediately agreed. Retracing their footsteps back to Haggerlythe, in spite of Junno's confident words, she could not help feeling uneasy about Richard's conspicuous absence.

Surely, his mother would ensure no harm came to her son? On the other hand, from what she had seen of him, and been told about him, Francois Lynette was quite a different matter. If Richard were to be disposed of, Lynette would undoubtedly benefit. By all accounts a younger son sent out in the world to seek a good position, the Frenchman must have become accustomed to ruling Fylingdales over the years he'd kept his nephew at arm's length from his rightful inheritance.

Upon stepping into Laura Andrew's neat parlour, Catherine, Junno and Benjamin were treated to the appetising aroma of a simmering stew. Catherine saw the frowning glance Junno gave Mamma Petra. She was sitting on a stool by the open window, her wizened hands clasped in her lap. Her long, grey plaits lay against her black attire. Oddly, her dislike of being in a Gorgio's house had not stopped her from remaining at Bob's cottage. Catherine had thought that once Shadiz had shown reliable signs of recovery, she would have mounted Gabriel, her irascible pony, and gone on her way. She found the old Romany woman's continued presence disturbing. Junno evidently found it perplexing.

Megan sat at her mother's feet, trying to veil her interest in Lucinda, who was sitting beside Laura on the settle. Her younger sister, Tessa, was sprawled over the colourful, woven mats on the stone floor, playing a lively game of sticks and stones with Peter. The sturdy, black-eyed boy merrily hailed his father. Junno's smile waned as Mamma Petra called sharply to Peter to speak in the Gorgio's tongue. After a momentary lapse, the five-year-old's enthusiasm for the game resumed when his father got down on his knees beside him. He continued to be fascinated by the novelty of being in the home of a Gorgio. The daughters of the house had repeatedly shown him around, as if they lived in a splendid manor, and each time they had been entertained by his bright-eyed wonder.

After spending a few minutes joining in the youngsters' fun, the big man looked up at his wife and asked, "'e still quiet?"

Lucinda nodded. She had been accepted by the Andrew family far more readily than Mamma Petra. Her affable nature and willingness to help in any task had soon bridged the gulf of culture. Yet, even when Shadiz's health had shown signs of improvement, Catherine sensed something was troubling her.

All at once, Junno raised his bald head and looked towards the open window close to where his silent grandmother was sitting. Seconds later, the other people in the parlour became aware of voices out in the lane, their tenor not the jocular banter that had been heard occasionally during Shadiz's recovery.

The Master's men had kept up their vigilance in Whitby, especially in Haggerlythe, since he had been taken to Bob's cottage in terrible agony. No one was taking any chances, least of all the big man, who remained in command of his cousin's force. Even when he had gone for a walk with Catherine and Benjamin, Junno had insisted upon a well-armed escort. Apart from the Master's Gorgio force, Catherine suspected Junno had deployed members of his will-o-wisp Romanies in nooks and crannies.

Lounging next to the door of the cottage, Benjamin reacted immediately when a loud rapping came upon it. He pulled it open, allowing Bill Todd to stride into the parlour. At sight of Bill's troubled expression, Junno got to his feet. He was about to seek the reason for the other man's arrival, for it was obvious Bill had not come merely to give a routine report, when he was interrupted by his son's exclamation.

"Konko!"

The attention of everyone in the parlour promptly swung away from Bill Todd to the startled boy and then in the direction he was staring, wide-eyed. They were just in time to see Shadiz slide down the wall at the bottom of the ladder-staircase and subside onto the floor.

Junno scooped up his son and swung him towards his wife. At the same time, because Shadiz was thoughtlessly naked, Laura shepherded her daughters into the tiny kitchen at the rear of the cottage. She was followed by Lucinda, with Peter squirming in her arms.

The men started forward to their leader. Catherine was ahead of them. She dropped to her knees beside Shadiz, deftly tossing the skirt of her gown over his nakedness, her concern for him serving to spare her blushes.

"What on earth do you think you are doing?" she demanded.

He gave her a weak smile. *"Praise be to Allah for small mercies."*

"Allah is not here, dammit," retorted Catherine. "Nor should you be."

"Y' ain't t' blaspheme."

Clutching the hand he had raised somewhat shakily to her cheek, she pointed out, "You would make a saint curse." The expression on her young face was at odds with her remonstration. He responded by drawing her close and murmuring his special name for her into her long hair.

Catherine revelled in his living warmth. Leaning against him, she was aware of the coming together of their jet and moonstone pendants. Shadiz pulled back slightly from her, his gaze locking with hers. "The angel weren't back when I woke up." He took possession of her hand and kissed her knuckles. "Y' alright?"

She nodded, giving him a tremulous smile.

Guilt-edged concern haunted his black eyes, those deep, dark-ringed pools dominating the bones of his roughly bearded face. The gaunt manifestations of his lethal excesses had given his scarred cheek stark prominence.

Bob Andrew strode through the door, which, following their surprise at Shadiz's appearance in the parlour, no one had thought to close. He displayed the same urgency Bill had done upon his arrival, but when he caught sight of Shadiz slumped on the floor, he came to an abrupt standstill. The disquieting tidings he had

347

learned on Tate Pier while checking the *Eagle's* seaworthiness following her repairs after she had run aground in Mercy Cove completely slipped his mind. He found himself following the example of the other men. Comments had been made when the Master had kept Catherine at the Lodge earlier in the year. Cautious gossip stamped on by Tom. Yet no one had truly believed that the gypsy's cold, vicious heart could ever be melted. Until now.

A breath of wind closed the cottage door.

Junno roused himself from his troubled musings. Realising belatedly he was not alone in studying Shadiz and Catherine, he tried to divert attention from them. "What's amiss?" he demanded.

At which point it seemed to dawn on Shadiz that he and Catherine were being watched with undisguised interest. His black gaze lost its warmth as he looked away from her.

Feeling the chill of the Master's attention, the broad, muscular brother of the *Eagle's* bo's'un opened his mouth to speak but was forestalled by the captain. "Lynette be at Saltersgate!"

"Aye," put in Bill, in possession of more information, " 'e's got Richard wi' 'im."

Everyone in the parlour heard a faint curse.

Whatever feeble condition he was presently experiencing, nevertheless the men looked to the Master for direction.

Catherine had felt him tense at the tidings of Lynette's and his half-brother's presence at the moorland tavern several miles east of Whitby. She saw the rapid rise and fall of the moonstone pendent on his chest. He straightened, insofar as his lingering weakness would allow. His attention remained on Catherine. Fearing for him, she had no time to dwell on the bond that was already strong enough for her to realise what he was contemplating. She shook her head. He squeezed her hand and gave her a crooked, apologetic smile.

"Give me summat, puri daia."

Catherine voiced her objection, "No! You must not risk the need in your condition."

Young though she was, she possessed considerable experience with herbs, including those which could very easily bring about dependency whilst giving support. In her teachings, the White Witch had warned her against administering the poppy. Indeed, her father had forbidden her to use the flower's potent essence.

"Y' ain't fit t' go any place," Junno told his cousin forcefully.

Shadiz scowled and snapped. "I'd be wi' some o' 'er stuff in me."

Catherine had heard the big man's sharp intake of breath upon hearing his cousin's demand. She had seen the apprehensive glance he had given their grandmother. She no longer felt sure Mamma Petra would rebuff her youngest grandson. Was this development what had kept her in a Gorgio's home?

"Not the poppy," she protested, looking at the old Romany woman, who continued to sit impassively in the chair beside the window.

"I'll go," announced Junno.

" 'e's well backed," Bill warned him, a hand on the hilt of his sword.

"So'll I be," retorted Junno.

" 'ell's teeth," muttered Shadiz. "I'll do once I've got some o' 'er stuff down me," he repeated, a hoarse note in his angry voice.

"That's allus if y' can keep stuff down," Junno pointed out, tersely. "Nay. I tell y', I'm off. Be told fer once. Benjamin'll stay wi' Rauni. I'll leave lad a good lot t' be on guard." Fielding an uncharacteristic challenge, he met his cousin's haggard animosity.

Although Shadiz was in no condition to argue, he still persisted in doing so. Catherine, Benjamin, Bob and Bill could not understand the words that raked the tense air between the two Romanies. At length, she could stand it no longer. "This is getting us nowhere."

The two men broke off, each with bad grace. Shadiz sagged against the wall. Weakened further by his stubbornness, his brow glistened with sweat. Worried, Catherine laid a hand on his chest, her fingers soothing within the mat of black hair that rose and fell at an alarming rate. He covered her hand comfortingly, but his narrowed gaze remained on the big man. She knew he was accustomed to Junno's placid nature soaking up, without offence, the sharp barbs of his volatile nature. She knew he was accustomed to men obeying him. Her intuition told her he was seeking a reason beyond the obvious why Junno was ready to defy him.

And it seemed as if Junno was determined to have the last word. "If y' ain't o' been out y'r 'ead y' wouldn't 'ave teken 'er brew."

"Develesko Mush! 'ow many more times. It weren't me," retorted Shadiz, his breathless agitation increasing. But then his chest stilled beneath Catherine's solicitous, restraining hand. He looked at Junno with a scowling, calculating jet gaze. Low-pitched, he demanded, "What y' on about ...'er?"

Furious colour drained from Junno's round face. He appeared mortified.

"It be me."

Everyone in the parlour turned to where Lucinda had spoken from the low doorway leading into the kitchen. She was nervously twisting the edge of her colourful shawl.

During the stunned silence, Laura could be heard urging her daughters to take Peter to hunt for mussels. There was a scrabbling in the kitchen, presumably for a suitable basket, and then the sound of the back door closing. Soon afterwards, Laura came to stand beside Lucinda. Unsure of what had happened to cause everyone to focus on the young Romany woman, she stepped aside upon Junno reaching his wife.

He spoke to her in a low, urgent voice. Lucinda looked up at her tall husband and gave a slight, resigned shrug. She brushed away the tears on her dusky cheeks, only to have more course down her sorrowful face.

She glanced in Mamma Petra's direction and then, with a visible effort, looked towards Catherine and Shadiz. Biting her lower lip, she lurched away from Catherine's shocked gaze and Shadiz's piercing regard.

When she spoke in a shaky whisper the entire parlour listened in disbelief.

"Twas me who snatched nightshade from Mamma's bag. I thought by doin' it at the Lodge, it'd be 'ard t' know who'd took it." Keeping her eyes downcast, she added, "An'... I used it in ale."

350

"Why'd y' do such a rotten thing, lass?" exclaimed Bob, looking perplexed. His mouth twitched with his own guilty spasm beneath his wife's glaring rebuke.

"I ... I did it ... t' get me man back," Lucinda admitted, so quietly everyone had to strain to catch her hesitant words. Junno had placed a comforting arm around her drooping shoulders. She went on, "Twas easy t' make out I were a serving wench at Bagdale's tavern. An' just as easy t'... t' drop stuff in the ale." Tears were streaming down her distressed face. "I ... I just wanted 'im back fer a little while, now and then. For Peter's sake."

Her resolve deserted her. After another apprehensive glance at Mamma Petra, she buried her tear-stained face in Junno's broad chest. Her shoulders were shaking as he enfolded her in his large arms. At the same time, he glared at Shadiz, ready to quell any vicious retaliation.

Yet anger did not emanate from Shadiz.

It was Catherine who was ready to spit blood despite her previous high opinion of Lucinda.

It took several moments before she realised Shadiz was watching her. He seemed to fortify himself with a deep shuddering breath, clearly waiting for her to condemn him for his wretched indulgence that had left him vulnerable to ill-will; unbelievably from Lucinda.

"You are not infallible," she murmured, softly.

She had told him so once before, while they had been in the secret niche on board the *Eagle*. Their world had spun inexorably since then.

His tense shoulders slowly relaxed. He answered her as he had done before. "That's a relief."

Due to their involvement with each other, both Shadiz and Catherine at first missed the presence of Mamma Petra beside them.

"Believeth mine presence in this Gorgio's dwelling be for nought?"

When Catherine looked up, she was confronted by a blind, malicious smirk.

CHAPTER FIVE

A Pawn's Movement

When the moorland tavern several miles to the east of Whitby had been invaded, not by the smugglers that reputedly arrived with their illicit liquor, but by a well-armed company from Fylingdales Hall, those customers enjoying a mug of ale and a reflective pipe in the common-room of Saltersgate had beaten a hasty retreat. Outside, they had encountered more men-at-arms standing around their tethered mounts, on guard despite the mugs they were being served by a flirty wench.

Richard Massone abruptly halted his infuriated pacing of the long, narrow common-room, narrowly missing hitting his head on one of the crooked beams spanning the low ceiling. "I keep telling you!" he exclaimed, swinging around. "He will not come."

"We shall wait, mon sweet," responded Francois Lynette, unruffled by his nephew's aggravation.

He was sitting on one of the crude benches before the meagre fire as if he was reclining beside one of the Hall's grand blazes. Having on arrival an hour ago made clear his aversion to ale, he seemed content with the wine of dubious origin served by the cautious landlord. The half-empty mug stood by his elbow on the rickety table, little more than a plank of sea-worn wood between two barrels. "Would you not like to discover if his regard for you is greater than that he possessed for Elizabeth?"

Richard promptly interrupted his pacing a second time to once again whirl around in his uncle's direction. "Do not mention her in the same breath as that bastard. Damn you, leave her to her rest."

Lynette inclined his golden head by way of acquiescent. "Indeed, your sister deserves her peace." He ignored Richard's glare. Arranging his velvet cloak about his slender legs, he added, "I wish only to demonstrate your worth."

Sitting on the bench opposite his leader, Gerald Carey sniggered. "Your worth could be measured by the yardstick of how fares the gypsy."

Richard had been relieved to put Fylingdales Hall behind him. His so-called home had been nothing more than a glorified prison for almost two weeks. When he had questioned the reason for the journey across the moors and their destination, he was hard-pressed to believe half of what his uncle had told him. He was left wondering what had really taken place at Whitby and, more importantly, where was Catherine? All of which added salt to his boiling resentment at not being able to escape Francois's clutches.

"He will not come," he insisted, curtly. He loathed being dangled as bait, and resented the futility of such a ridiculous measure.

Francois Lynette simply gave an eloquent shrug. "We shall see, mon sweet."

Richard spoke through gritted teeth, fists balled at his sides. "The ruse is up. If it was ever viable. You and my mother have badly underestimated the gypsy. The fact that he is a villain blinded both of you to the way he has lived and prospered by his wits. He will not come because he tires of the game." He was about to say that his half-brother wished to keep him away from Catherine, but refrained from doing so, having startled himself with the unexpected thought.

"The Master has been thwarted," murmured Lynette. "He will come."

CHAPTER SIX

Love Her Till I Die

Laura Andrew had managed to wash away the grime of drunken excesses. Her thoughtfulness meant that Shadiz was able to stand up in his own clothes. Having drank deeply from the mug given to him by his grandmother, in spite of Catherine's pleas, he was becoming steadier on his feet. She had sniffed the White Witch's brew as it had passed her, bubbling and hissing, and knew to her chagrin that the herbal brew was laced with the false-giving stamina of the potent poppy. It had caused him to shudder involuntarily and give her an apologetic glance.

Three days ago, Catherine had been overwhelmingly grateful for the White Witch's ability to rid Shadiz's body of the poison that would have surely killed him. For she had no idea how to deal with such a deadly substance; and didn't care to know how the old Romany woman had accomplished the arduous task, though she had her suspicions. Now she was just as shocked and appalled at his grandmother's action as she was at Lucinda's when Shadiz had been too drunk to realise her deadly purpose. As far as Lucinda was concerned, despite her burning outrage, there was a part of Catherine that couldn't quite believe Lucinda capable of such a nasty deed. An inner feeling made her wonder if there wasn't more behind Lucinda's action other than wanting Junno to spend more time with her and Peter. As for Mamma Petra, she couldn't help wondering whether her own remarkable ability to call Shadiz back from the brink was resented by her. Supporting the suspicion, by intuition alone, she got the impression by giving him the strengthening brew, the strange, old Romany woman had been demonstrating her authority over her extraordinary grandson.

Never at ease in her presence, during the past few days, Catherine had become decidedly uncomfortable.

Tom's words echoed once again. *"She's some kind o' 'old over 'im."*

She watched in thoughtful silence as Shadiz gave the empty mug to Laura. Her heart contracted as he spoke to Bob's wife.

"It can't o' been easy takin' in a piece of soakin' flotsam."

His unexpected low-pitched words caused Laura's attractive features to blossom a deep crimson in the shadow of his towering darkness. She bobbed a quick curtsy. " Twas easiest thing in world, sir." Flustered, she added, "Anyways. If it ain't been fer y'r efforts at Mercy Cove," She glanced at Bob. "I'd like as not be a widow, an' bairns'd be wi'out a da."

Shadiz inclined his head, his haggard face unreadable.

The silence following Laura's hasty departure from the parlour was thick with anticipation of the Master's commands.

When he turned towards Lucinda, pierced by his direct gaze, the young Romany woman shrank into Junno's protective embrace. The big man was clearly ready to defend his wife. Yet Shadiz's bleak expression belied his barely audible words. Catherine had been around Romanies long enough to realise he had just thanked Lucinda. Greatly vexed as to why he should do such a thing, she witnessed the look he exchanged with his cousin. An open book, Junno was relieved that his wife had been exonerated for her uncharacteristic deed. Yet, despite the tension leaving him, he continued to appear troubled. Having lost the battle to lead a force to extract Richard Massone from Lynette's challenge at Saltersgate following their grandmother's surprising intervention, he now made it plain he was adamant about accompanying Shadiz to the moorland tavern. Only to be thwarted once more by Shadiz's demand that he remain with Catherine.

She was about to speak up in support of Junno when Benjamin Farr suggested, "Sir, if you will permit me. I will escort Miss Catherine back to the Lodge?"

Junno looked hopeful. Although he had been at the Lodge for a relatively short time, the Master seemed to favour Farr.

"What if Catherine were t' sail t' Mercy Cove in the *Eagle*?" put in Bob. He saw Shadiz's brittle scepticism, and rushed on, "Lads from Spittal've just told me she's ready t' get under sail again."

"An' what about *Endeavour*?" snapped Shadiz.

Bob's weatherbeaten face brightened. "Aye, well. Phil Tate o' *Swan* were tellin' me 'ow Lynette's gunship be laid up at Scarborough. Summat wrong wi' her rudder."

Catherine knew that before he went anywhere Shadiz wanted her safe from any possible attack, overruling whatever she might desire. Her biggest desire was to remain at his side. Knowing this to be impossible, she wanted the next best thing.

"Junno," she said, placing a restraining hand on Shadiz's arm, "accompany him."

The men in the parlour switched from the Master to her, noting her accepted touch. They were beginning to understand why Shadiz was determined to keep Catherine safe. They were beginning to comprehend the unbelievable.

Gripping a convenient piece of furniture, Shadiz growled his displeasure. "Develesko Mush. I've bleedin' vanished."

Looking up at him, Catherine made her feelings abundantly plain about 'vanishing', giving him an insight into the anguish she had recently suffered. "Allow Junno's presence. If I must depart."

"Y' must," he stated, meeting her gaze.

"Perhaps Laura and the girls could accompany me on the *Eagle*?"

"Would it not be wisest for their own sakes, sir?" Benjamin pointed out, with his usual quiet deference. "Considering how matters stand at the present."

Eventually the assembled company received an irritable sigh.

"Y' agree?" asked Junno, his deep rumble the thunder of hope.

Shadiz gave a curt nod. It was obvious he had reservations, but was equally obvious he could not withstand Catherine's wordless persuasion. "Aye. 'ave it y'r way."

Bob hurried away to gather up his family and prepare his newly repaired ship, ostensible for a sea trial along the coast. The other men went away to divide the Master's men, Gorgios and Romanies, between themselves for their respective requirements.

When Mamma Petra found her own way out of the harbourside cottage, Lucinda reluctantly followed, with an equally reluctant Peter.

It was the first time Catherine and Shadiz had been truly alone since the night of Tom's 'wake' at the Lodge. She became aware of his jet study of her. Suddenly, she felt awkward. "I pray you take care." Her words sounded stilted to her own ears.

A merry twinkle entered his black eyes. He bowed to her with a flourish he could ill-afford. "T' be sure, m'lady."

The gallant gesture caused him to stagger into Catherine. Despite his effort to avoid both of them being thrown off balance, his superior weight cause a giddy decent. Both of them landed heavily on the settle.

Initially, she was concerned for him, but then relaxed upon seeing his shoulders were shaking with silent laughter. "Ah, no gentleman me," he commented, ruefully. He righted himself, and before she had a chance to get to her feet, he pulled her onto his knees.

"Try it again when nothing ails you," was her amused advice.

Her mirth soon melted away. Troubled by the consequences of his indisposition, she felt impelled to try one last time to change his mind about seeking out Lynette, even though she knew she was probably doomed to fail. "Is it egotism that prompts your stubborn resolve?" She watched his expression change. "*Pride cometh before a fall*," she added, quietly.

"Y' want 'im extracted?" he bit out, scrutinising her.

"To be sure," admitted Catherine. "I distrust Lynette where Richard is concerned. With Richard out of the way, how easy it would be for Lynette to marry and provide an heir to the Fylingdales Estate, that is if he is not wed already."

Shadiz's response was a crude smirk. He quoted, "*It's not only fine feathers that make fine birds.*" Seeing her bewilderment, he explained, "Lynette'd be 'ardpressed t' make an 'eir." He shrugged, adding, "Although, I suppose it's been done, grudgingly."

"I don't …oh, I see." Her cheeks flushed an embarrassed pink.

"Well, if that is the case, Richard's return to the fold is pressing," she said, primly, and then moved on quickly. "I return to my original point, your half-brother is your least favourite person, so why…."

" 'e's y'r favourite?" he demanded. His arms around her had become tense.

Catherine met his slit-eyed consideration with a steady look. "I have become fond of him."

"Aye," Shadiz retorted on a sour note.

Throughout their conversations while he had been bedridden there had been an unspoken boundary both of them had strayed across only occasionally with a glance or a smile. Whereas, at present, his nearness and responsiveness possessed elements that caused her commonsense to fly out the window, someone had thoughtfully left open. She began to tremble and her heart to pound in her breathless chest at the enormity of what she was about to do. For it had became overwhelmingly vital to her that he understood her feelings for him went far beyond anything she felt for anyone else.

"I love *you*."

Shadiz swallowed convulsively. He made as if to answer, but then remained silent. He stared at her, all dark harshness drained from him, vulnerable upon her delivered truth.

It was at that point her nerve shattered. She looked down, plucking at her gown. "Sorry. I wear my heart on my sleeve." She would have risen, but he stopped her. He lifted her chin with tender loving care.

"Tom told me," he said, softly, "I didn't … I couldn't believe. I reckoned it t' be but the outpourin' o' a dyin' wish."

"He came to realise," Catherine replied, shakily, "though I said nothing."

He smiled. "I ain't, either. Yet the Watcher in the Tower saw all."

He cupped her cheek in his hand, his thumb caressing her lower lip. His breathing had altered and his unsteadiness had nothing to do with the state of his health.

"There is a lady sweet and kind,
was never face so pleased my mind;
I did but see her passing by,
And yet...."

The remainder of the line hung between them as their faces drew close and his lips met hers.

After the dizzying kiss, she urged, "Come back to me." Concern reasserted itself. "With your own strength. Promise me, you will not take again what your grandmother might offer."

He regarded her for a long moment before answering. "I promise."

CHAPTER SEVEN

Brother's Keeper

The afternoon downpour had swept in from the east in collusion with the incoming tide, depriving Whitby and the surrounding moorland heights of capricious sunshine.

With an elegant gesture, Francois Lynette had given leave for his men-at-arms on guard outside Saltersgate, situated at the foot of the steep slope from which the low-slung tavern had taken its name, to make use of the landlord's leaky barn. Their more fortunate comrades in the common room occupied shallow puddles of light.

Alf Wisly, a stockily built fellow, shrewd enough at a critical moment to disguise his association with the Master, and the fact that his ramshackle establishment on the rough track between Whitby and Pickering was a staging post for smuggled goods destined for York and beyond, had pleaded a scarcity of candles for the lack of illumination. Conscious of the dark patches between the rude benches they presently occupied, the men of Fylingdales had grown increasingly conscious of time progressing on the back of a snail, fermenting dubious ale and nerves. Only Lynette continued to appear at ease, waiting with machiavellian patience.

Richard had retired to a bench some distance away from the lowly fire and the grand presence of his uncle. His agitation had brought about an unfortunate bout of coughing. In his stead, Gerald Carey had taken to pacing in and out of the patches of candlelight, proving his nerves were not as robust as those of his leader.

When the distinct, barely audible voice drifted through the subdued atmosphere of the common room, speaking words few if any of those present understood, it fell to Lynette to translate the Arabic text of Omar Khayyam,

"Tis all a Chequer-board of Nights and Days
Where Destiny with Men for Pieces plays;
Hither and thither moves, and mates, and slays
And one by one back in the Closet lays."

With one accord, his men had come to their feet in alarm. Yet, resentful in the extreme, they were obliged to keep their weapons sheathed, such was the decisive manner in which the Master's men manifested their supremacy. Junno stayed Carey's rash impulse. A sullen expression on his beautiful face, Carey's hand fell away from his sword hilt and balled into a fretful fist. Thereafter, he scrutinised the thick shadows along with the rest of the tense men.

Francois Lynette rose with leisurely grace, the injuries he had sustained during the skirmish in Longdrop Hollow having healed sufficiently to be disguised. His attention focused on the darkest corner, he murmured, "Ah, the doom of fate. If we could but be ransomed from La Dame's grasp."

A silent phantom, the Master emerged from the concealing darkness. He strolled halfway down the common room's narrow length and then leant against the short, ale-stained counter.

Having been convinced that Shadiz would not arrive for his sake throughout the long wait his uncle had made him endure, Richard's subsequent astonishment was rapidly overtaken by shock. So distracted was he by his half-brother's gaunt, hollow-eyed appearance, he missed Lynette's wholly involuntary reaction which had nothing to do with Shadiz's eventual arrival. By the time Richard had recovered from the twin lightning bolts, the two leaders were taking stock of each other, black and blue eyes locked.

Their first meeting had been a fleeting, violent affair, which Richard had missed due to his enforced presence aboard the crippled *Eagle* while she had been towed to Whitby. Witnessing a more deceptively peaceful encounter, he perceived the affinity between the two men. Although from very different moulds, they both possessed the same defining traits of powerful, intelligent leadership. Lesser and not so dangerous men looked on with cautious interest.

Francois Lynette ended the deep silence. "Pardon, mon ami, my challenge to your vigour. I do hope it has not proved too problematic?"

Before Shadiz had a chance to reply, Gerald Carey was anxious to inform him, "We have men beyond who await you, gypsy. You are surrounded by Fylingdales's might."

"Y' mean that lot penned up in Alf's barn?" put in Junno, grimly.

Shadiz dismissed the eager intrusion with a bleak glance. Returning fathomless jet to azure speculation, low-pitched he asked, "Were the wait taxin'?"

"I used the time to reflect," Lynette answered, smiling.

"On 'ow t' bell the cat?" Shadiz murmured, raising his eyebrows in sardonic query.

Richard paid little attention to the double-edged pleasantries, being far more disconcerted by Junno's presence with Shadiz. Having been charged with Catherine's safety by his half-brother, it was highly unusual for the big man to have left her side. He chafed against inquiring about her whereabouts in front of his uncle, but was unable to resist the overwhelming urge. "What of Catherine?"

Shadiz ignored him. Though anger did briefly flicker across his unhealthy features.

A giant shadow engulfed Richard. He was informed Catherine was safe without Junno's attention straying from Shadiz.

Richard realised the big man was greatly troubled. His half-brother certainly looked the worse for wear. His casual stance against the rough counter made Richard suspect it was an attempt to keep himself braced upright.

"Would I be correct in thinking sweet young things drive you to distraction? Well, one at least," Lynette mused, lightly.

Richard swore under his breath.

Shadiz deflected the goad. "Don't y'?"

"I am insulted," responded Lynette, giving every appearance of the opposite. He continue to meet the vaguely slanting, piercing eyes. "At the end of days, you are alive, Darkness. No mean feat, I gather."

Shadiz shrugged. "The net's been known t' pull in rubbish. *Se non e vero, e moltoben trovao."*

"If it is not true it is a happy invention," Lynette translated. "For whom, I wonder?"

"For any poor sod who's a likin' fer myths," suggested Shadiz. "What is mythology but fantastic tales."

Lynette put forward a theory of his own. "I am of the opinion that within each myth there exists a kernel of truth." He studied the other man's barbarous, scarred features, as if he were trying to gauge what lay beneath the rough beard, the dark-ringed, sunken eyes and the haggard flesh. "You are the subject of fantastic tales. And thus being so, are younger in the flesh than I credited you."

"I make y' feel old?"

Mirth came readily to the suave Frenchman ten years Shadiz's senior. "You are a whore, Darkness."

Richard gave his uncle a sharp look.

"We two patrol separate landscapes," observed Lynette, assuming a tone of businesslike interest. "Your sphere fares well, methinks."

"I'm just the mercenary who follows orders," responded Shadiz in a whispery tone. Beads of sweat on his brow were glistening in the weak candlelight.

"Oh, come now. You are too modest," said Lynette in mild remonstration. "From what I gather, you were recruited by Rupert directly. By all accounts, the prince was eager to capitalise upon the acquaintance that began prior to this unfortunate business betwixt Charles and his rebellious Parliament."

" 'e pays well."

"I am informed your title is Master?"

The black eyes glittered. "Y're reliably informed."

Intensely human, Junno shifted his weight at the cold irony in Shadiz's voice. He gripped Richard's thin shoulder as he fought the racking cough he could not stem, but continued to remain fixated on Shadiz.

"Think you, there will come a time when the land shall be yours?" Lynette challenged, with curiosity that was apparently idle.

"You'll never lay claim to any part of Fylingdales, gypsy," observed Carey, smugly.

Shadiz sighed irritably. "Y' put up wi' bloody chirpin' popinjays?" he snapped.

"They make for a pleasant diversion," pointed out Lynette, waving a jewelled hand in Carey's general direction. "However, the popinjay does have a point."

"This land needs no master. Mortals who inhabit its slopes're governed by time. They've but mere moments in scale o' things t' lay down furrows. Ultimately, land remains master."

Richard wondered if he had imagined Francois's brief, unguarded response.

Questionable humour stole into Shadiz's gaunt face. "Ain't y' forgettin' legitimate claim? Allus supposin' 'e could shift y' from the usurped throne."

"I have often pondered why *you* have failed to eject him," Lynette countered, switching from Shadiz's mockery to his flushed nephew. "I can only conclude, you are not adverse to the qualities of brotherhood."

"*Chevalier sans peur et sans reproche*," Shadiz quoted, also turning towards Richard, a nasty grin playing within his rough beard.

"I am heartily glad I am not remotely similar to either of you!" Richard informed both leaders, emphatically. "You remain at either end of a despicable spectrum, and will surely one day pay for your deeds."

"Well, that has told us," murmured Lynette, smiling indulgently.

Shadiz did not respond. A sudden, dire spasm had overtaken him, that much was clear. It aroused various degrees of dismay and grim satisfaction throughout the common room.

His rancour pushed aside, Richard shot Junno a hasty sidelong glance. After another second of agonising indecision, the big man took the necessary stride. Shadiz had bowed his head, making it impossible to see his face through the barrier of his long black hair.

He managed to turn his back on the men. Yet, judging by the way in which he was bending over the counter, it was evident to all he was having difficulty regaining his composure.

The expression on his handsome face portraying only polite interest, Francois Lynette stood and watched as Junno bent towards Shadiz and spoke in their language. Shadiz shook his head. The impatient movement threw him off balance. Junno steadied him, and then was thrust away. Thereafter, he remained close, looking on with the rest of the men as Shadiz pulled himself together with an obvious effort. He slowly lifted his head. Moist where it had come into contact with his sweat-bathed face, his wild hair fell back to reveal how weakness and ill-humours had gouged out even deeper shadows. His black glare found Lynette.

A consummate diplomat, the Frenchman responded with cool dignity under smouldering pressure. "Well, Darkness," he said, pleasantly, "I know not what has sustained you thus far. I do confess to feeling somewhat guilty at having dragged you away…."

"From the bed your child-whore keeps warm for you," put in Gerald Carey.

No one in the common room expected the vicious reprisal, least of all Carey.

It came out of nowhere, flying unerringly to its unsuspecting target. The dagger sank with deadly force into Carey's chest. His green doublet was quickly dyed a morbid red by his life-blood. For a horrified moment, he stared down at the tool of death protruding from himself. Then he screamed, and fumbled desperately in an attempt to extract the dagger, only to be overtaken by the inevitable. Before startled gazes, he pitched forward, landing at the feet of his leader, his final expression petrified in disbelief.

There was stunned silence. Not least, because Shadiz appeared unarmed.

Several breathless seconds later, Lynette wrenched his gaze upwards. His unfettered shock had given way to the purity of outrage. "You murdering scum," he flung at Shadiz. The pearls sewn upon his scarlet doublet quivered in the scarce candlelight. "That was crude, even for you."

Shadiz propelled himself off the counter so fast he had driven Lynette backwards to the hearth before anyone realised his intention. In spite of the other, shorter man's aggressive efforts to break the strangle hold, he rammed Lynette against the rough stone of the chimney breast with brutal momentum. The flames of the meagre fire licked dangerously close to Lynette's braced legs. His handsome face was contorted in defiant rage. "In the end, your defence of her will bring you down."

Despite Lynette's jewelled fingers clawing at his flesh, Shadiz was not persuaded to alleviate the savage pressure on his slender throat. "From the gods comes the sayin' *know thyself*," he rasped, "*Mon sweet*."

"From the portal of comfort there appears little succour in the wilderness," grated Lynette, with difficulty.

Perhaps the upsurge of anger that had flared so savagely bright had harvested the blood-red field. Whatever the reason, contempt, a much easier emotion to sustain, replaced the seams of sinister fury within Shadiz's moist face. He slowly released his hold upon the other man, and then lowered his arm. "*Securus iydicatobis terrarum*," he said in a low, controlled voice.

"The verdict of the world is indeed conclusive," replied Lynette, huskily, sliding away from the hearth. He massaged his throat where the deep imprint of Shadiz's cruel fingers could be seen.

The body of Gerald Carey lay between the two leaders. Staring down at his dead follower, Lynette said, "He gave me consolation." He looked up to meet Shadiz's feral glare. "What she would give to you, for I hear she is willing, you forbid yourself." He gave a tight, vindictive smile. "Is she aware of what lies within your reticence? Not her youth or the oath with which you dispatched her father?"

Junno growled.

Shadiz remained unpredictably silent.

Prompted by Francois's words, Richard recalled the verse his half-brother had quoted when he had first arrived in the common room. Had he been right all along in thinking Catherine was a pawn, to be protected? Had her father been a trapped piece? How

366

had his uncle known of Catherine's existence before anyone at the Lodge, with the notable exception of Shadiz?

"Go back an' tell that bleedin' old witch I won't be destroyed. Not by 'er."

His half-brother's icy promise brought Richard back to the present. He watched along with the assembled company of opposing forces as his uncle bent and extracted the dagger from Carey's lifeless chest. He made no attempt to cleanse the weapon. Blood pooled in his palm as he straightened and extended his hand towards Shadiz.

Junno strode forward, raising his sword. Shadiz put up a hand to halt him without looking away from Lynette.

"On your own dagger," challenged Lynette, "which has dispatched a hideous number, I promise to bring you down."

Glittering blue and weird jet, the eyes of the two men remained locked.

Shadiz's right hand covered the blood-stained weapon and the shapely hand in which it lay. Lynette's mouth became a taut, repressive line. Shadiz bent extremely close, and into the other man's ear murmured softly in French, "The Ferryman's already been paid. 'e waits. Get me across the Styx, mon sweet, an' I'll be eternally grateful."

CHAPTER EIGHT

The Missive of the Heart

He sat on the ground, his arms locked around his drawn up knees, staring into the dancing flames of his puri daia's open-air hearth.

She broke the silence, which had lasted for most of the night. "Thy decision, Posh-Rat?"

He stirred then, a ripple of muscle that could have been a resigned shrug, but remained focused on the fire. "Ain't much choice."

Her head came up slightly, marking the bitterness in his barely audible tone. Her sightless eyes bore into his powerful body; a cleansed and guarded receptacle. "She be preserved without thee."

He slowly nodded.

★ ★ ★

"Why do you think he did it?"

"Did what?"

"Came to Saltersgate?" Richard had not waited for Catherine's answer. Instead, he had furnished one of his own. "He came to prove his invincibility to Francois."

"Or retrieve his half-brother because he doesn't trust your uncle. Or your mother, for that matter."

Richard had looked at her as if she had gone completely mad.

She was presently in danger of doing just that.

It had been an interminable week. Each long day had passed endowed with expectation, only to fade by nightfall into painful disappointment that had lasted until yet another dawn. The feeling was worse than before, when Shadiz had left the Lodge intent on

368

seeking oblivion in the ale. This time, his prolonged absence had instigated an ominous sense of conclusion.

In his stead had come a missive.

And now Catherine sat alone on the ragged windowseat in the library, staring down at his surprisingly scholarly handwriting. Loathed to break the seal, she procrastinated, reliving the events of the past few days, including the question no one could answer to Richard's satisfaction.

Upon being rowed ashore from the *Eagle*, having bid farewell to Bob and Laura Andrew and their two daughters, Catherine had prevailed upon Benjamin to allow a visit to the cliff top graveyard overlooking Mercy Cove. As it was clear the might of Fylingdales was currently occupied elsewhere, Benjamin had agreed to her request with only moderate reservations, enabling her to place on both her father's and Tom's graves the bluebells she had found sheltering from the west wind beside the drystone wall surrounding the steadfast church.

While she had been aboard the *Eagle*, her escort had rode along the cliffs within sight of the refitted merchantman. Following her short, coastal voyage, the well-protected journey through the wild peace of the moorland had brought to mind those she had taken in the company of Shadiz.

Returning to the old, ramshackle Lodge, Catherine had found Mary in floods of tears. Between sobs that had racked her thin body, the girl had explained about her friend having been found ravished and strangled. Although they saw each other only rarely nowadays, Mary and the unfortunate girl had been the best of friends since childhood. According to Mary, both of them had been devastated when the Throup family had moved away from Glaisdale to set up an ale house in the coastal hamlet of Boggle Hole.

While she had been comforting her little maid, the men who accompanied their leader to Saltersgate had returned, led by Richard. She had been relieved to welcome him back to the Lodge, but was hard-pressed to conceal her dismay at Shadiz's absence. The tidings that Junno had remained with his cousin had only served to heighten her concern for Shadiz's welfare.

369

After she had attended to the minor injuries a few of the men had sustained while corralling the Fylingdales men-at-arms in Saltersgate barn, Richard had hung around the stillroom and probed her withdrawn manner. At first she had been evasive, but when he had pressed her, she had admitted to being worried about Shadiz. In response, he had berated her for bestowing any kind thought upon her unworthy guardian. She had been in no mood to placate him. Especially when she was plagued by the memory of his half-brother taking the enormous risk of swallowing Mamma Petra's addictive brew in order to respond in person to Lynette's challenge. Her defence of Shadiz in the face of Richard's deep-seated bias had led to their exchanges becoming stormy.

Richard's suspicions about her feelings for his notorious half-brother had deepened the scowl on his thin face. When a fit of coughing had gripped him, maddened by his condemnation, Catherine had simply walked away from him.

An hour or so later, Benjamin had sought her out and asked her to attend to Richard.

Her grudging consent had given way to contrition upon entering his chamber. Danny Murphy and Bill Todd, once again her temporary bodyguards, remained watchful in the doorway while she had hurried to Richard's bedside. Benjamin had explained on their way back to the Lodge that the Master's men had rode through a torrential downpour. Always susceptible to such conditions, it was clear Richard had developed a fever.

By the time his malady had begun to respond to the herbs she had diligently administered, he had apologised to Catherine for his harsh words, and blamed his tiresome indisposition for his ill-temper. Both had avoided the thorny topic of Shadiz.

Yet once Richard had become strong enough to rise from his bed and sit draped in blankets before the glowing hearth, he had been unable to stop himself from probing her spirited defence of his half-brother. When she had maintained her loyalty to Shadiz, he had appeared crestfallen.

"I had a sister," he had told her, abruptly, "Elizabeth." After taking a fortifying breath, he continued, "She was two years younger than myself. Before his death, my father used to call her his little fairy. She was so sweet, gentle and beautiful. When she was twelve, she was allowed to journey to York to visit our aunt. She never arrived. Despite a large escort my mother thought prudent, she was raped and murdered."

"Oh, no!" Catherine had exclaimed in horror. Realising the effort it had taken him to relate the tragedy, she had covered his hand with hers in a gesture of sympathy.

He had responded by gripping her hand in a determined manner. "The bastards who massacred her escort were led by Shadiz."

Stung by his words, Catherine had frozen.

"But it wasn't any of the brutes who raped and then strangled Elizabeth." His voice had shook with pure enmity as he added, "It was Shadiz."

It took a few moments for her to get her breath back, even then her chest had been painfully tight.

"He must have known she was a half-sister," Richard had persisted.

Catherine had struggled to free herself from the brutal grip of his words. Not wishing to believe Richard, or her own intuitive quality. "If Shadiz had committed such an horrendous deed, how is it you are at the Lodge? I will not listen to you pour more scorn on him."

She had not given him the opportunity to respond, quitting his bedchamber forthwith.

A despairing rage flaring in her cheeks, knowing she could not escape herself, she had run down the stone staircase. To find Junno standing in the hallway. In an instance all else had vanished, and hope had flared. It had died just as quickly. Even in the gloom, she had seen the big man's desolate expression.

Catherine came to herself. Sitting tensely on the windowseat, her hand trembling, she finally broke the seal to the missive Shadiz had sent her by way of his big cousin.

371

Kore,

I am impelled to state there has been an improvement in my health, for I am mindful of your concern for all those who are fortunate to come under your most diligent auspices. Even the wretch who by his own hand fell foul of an avenging angel. Nor do I wish to visit the field of plenty. The fair jewel I wear close to my heart tells me it's unwise to trade one failing for another. Therefore, be assured, the serpent is in its lair.

Cast me, if you see fit, into the hitherto unknown regard of a coward. And try, if you can find it in your bountiful heart, to forgive my desertion from your life. I do so while all the *Hounds of Hell* gloat at my poor aspiration to good intent.

Turning to those motives that others would have us believe are in our best interest. I am informed you were regaled with the true history of the manner of your recovery when you were ill at twelve-years-old.

You will recall journeying with your father to France. There to take your ease and to restore your health at the chateau of one of his acquaintances. Shannlarrey was where he conveyed you. My 'Sanctum'.

I would have you journey there again. For your safekeeping, which is of paramount importance to me, as it was to your father. With you I will dispatch Junno and the necessary company. You are no longer safe at the Lodge from those who would use you against me. Moreover. I want you away from this war-torn land. Worse is to come. When we spoke of matters, you were astute in your assessment of the Scots. Since the weather has shown a marked improvement, Newcastle has deemed it prudent to abandon his province and to remove himself and his force to York. This will undoubtedly bring down the marauding Scots and their English allies Lords Manchester and Fairfax upon Yorkshire. Rupert will endeavour to stem the tide. His success might be confirmed if only he can first stem the ridiculous vacillation of that cretin his uncle, the so-called king. One future is assured. Yorkshire will become a battlefield.

Do not think too badly of me. I desire only the safest place for you before all hell breaks loose too close for your comfort. I understand the wrench such a move will entail. I pray you don't look upon it as a banishment. Be assured, I'll continue to watch over Nafferton Garth in your absence.

If you have any kindness for me, forgive me,
Shadiz.

Catherine stared down at the parchment for several long minutes, digesting its import. Then very deliberately, she tore up the letter. Rising abruptly and walking briskly across the library to the hearth, she flung the crumpled shreds into the fire. Rigid from head to toe, she stood and watched them shrivel and burn. Yet she knew she could not rid her life so easily of Shadiz's decree.

Wanting to scream in frustration, tense yet shaking, angry with herself for shedding the rebellious tears, she marched out of the library.

Junno was waiting in the hallway. He took one look at her young, set, tear-stained face as she passed him and then wordlessly followed her out of the Lodge. In the sunny rear pasture, she gazed down at the sprouting plants in her herb garden, totally oblivious to the everyday life going on around her; the children playing around the kitchen door, the buzz of female chatter drifting from within, the Master's men honing their skills with a variety of weapons, the horses loose in the fenced off part of the large pasture.

Standing beside her, defying anyone to interfere, Junno said, "Will y' come for a walk wi' me, Rauni?"

Catherine gave him a sidelong glance. "You are aware of the contents of his decree?"

Junno slowly nodded his smooth, bald head. "Gist o' it."

Without another word, they passed beneath the crooked archway, its grey stones nudged out of place by age and smothered in layers of big-leafed ivy. Upon entering the forest, they strolled beneath the mildly stirring canopy of dappled foliage. The seemingly endless colonnades of tree trunks closed about them. In silence, they followed a narrow, winding path, flanked by lacy ferns, tall grasses and demurely nodding daises, buttercups and bluebells.

Catherine was oblivious to the sentries perched in the ancient, close-knit trees diligently marking hers and Junno's passing. Cast down, she felt no thrill about being let loose in the forest. But, gradually, being away from the Lodge, where Shadiz's unique presence was manifest in every corner, the leafy seclusion of nature, disturbed only by the chatter of the birds, poured a measure of salve on her potent hurts.

In due course their subdued path led them to a clearing bounded by ancient oaks Catherine recognised. They had come across it from a different direction to when Shadiz had brought her. On this occasion, she encountered the crumbling remains of what was surely the first, ill-fated attempt to construct a hunting lodge in Stillingfleet. With one accord, Catherine and Junno came to a halt and viewed how the forest's verdant life had crept upon abandonment.

Catherine glimpsed the Crystal Pool by peripheral vision alone. Yet, she found it impossible to stem the deep-felt presence of the mystic water in the midst of the clearing. Junno shied away from giving the pool even one quick glance. He was soon taking hold of her elbow and urging her away between the mighty oaks that guarded the sacred clearing.

Once more wandering along a forest track made by foraging animals, with the grit of the past haunting her, Catherine's thoughts turned to the renovated Lodge, standing resolute against time in a different part of Stillingfleet. Very soon it would be a memory. And its Master?

She came to a halt, fighting the tears. The big man saw her struggle. His own expression transparent, he too stopped and, moving closer to her, put a comforting arm around her despondent shoulders.

"What will the Lodge look like in a few hundred years, I wonder? Will someone come along and sense the echoes of our presence in the forest?"

"All things've an end, Rauni," Junno pointed out, soothingly.

"Well," said Catherine, sadly, "my time here in Stillingfleet would seem to have come to an end." She sighed, confused and dispirited. "I don't understand. He acts warmly to me and then pushes me away." She lifted her head and looked up at Junno. "Am I simply an amusement?"

"No, Rauni. Never," he stated, emphatically.

They were silent for a short while. Eventually, Catherine said, "Just before you came, Richard was telling me about what happened to his sister, Elizabeth."

"Y' shouldn't believe 'alf o' what 'e says," Junno responded, a harsh note in his deep tone.

Nevertheless, she went on, "He maintained that Shadiz raped and strangled her."

Junno's stance had become rigid and his expression distinctly uncomfortable. "I know nowt o' such a thing," he muttered, not making eye contact with her.

Catherine wished with all her heart that she could believe him.

"He would have done the same to Lucinda, wouldn't he, if you had not intervened?" she persisted, shakily.

While Junno writhed in a vice of her making, an horrendous thought occurred to Catherine.

"The girl, Mary's friend … was it *him*?"

Junno looked even more perturbed. "Rauni, please."

"Do not torment loyalty, Luna May."

Both Catherine and Junno turned to find Garan a few feet away. At his side was the large boar.

The Druid smiled at them as he walked forward, holding his staff. His green robes seemed to shimmer in the sunlight pouring through the gently stirring leaves.

By the time he reached them, Junno had stepped protectively a couple of paces in front of Catherine.

"And see, he would seek to keep you from harm at all costs." Garan switched from Catherine to Junno. "And the cost to you be high, is it not?"

"What do you want?" demanded the big man.

"To simply offer up reassurance against the storm," replied Garan, remaining serenely calm. "To make plain, the renegade's salvation lies within her enchantment." His ancient wisdom became centred upon Catherine. His left hand rose and gently cupped her cheek. She gestured to Junno that she felt safe. Through Garan's light touch, she experienced great warmth and peaceful strength. His quiet words seemed to take root within her. "To draw him forth from the bridle of sorcery, you must strengthen your love against dismay. When the time comes, as it will, your irresistible pull will shatter the spell."

Trembling, Catherine half-smiled and nodded, though she did not fully understand the Druid's prophetic words.

"You will, Luna May," he murmured, as if he had read her thoughts.

CHAPTER NINE

Leave-Taking

Shadiz had been correct. It would be a wrench to leave the Lodge. At least he had some idea of how she was feeling. Damn him.

Having become familiar with his ruthless efficiency, Catherine had fully expected to be whisked away to France with barely enough time to fold up a couple of shifts. As it was, she was given ample time to pack her possessions, most of which Shadiz had brought from Nafferton Garth earlier in the year. She was unable to decide whether such an opportunity was a blessing or a curse.

The day Junno had returned to the Lodge, Keeble disappeared without a word. She had been concerned about the little man until Junno informed her he had been sent on a mission by the Master, with Danny Murphy. Both men reappeared almost three weeks later looking suspiciously bronzed. Neither man was forthcoming about where they had been, not surprising where Danny Murphy was concerned, but certainly unusual for Keeble, who liked to gossip about the least little thing.

Mary kept bursting into tears, which was proving irritating. Catherine had thought about asking the young girl from Glaisdale to accompany her to France, and then thought better of it. Mary was better off on home soil, anywhere else and she would undoubtedly wilt. To bolster her fragile spirit, Catherine kept praising the efforts Mary made to learn all the herbal remedies she had helped her to prepare. She was making good progress with her reading, too. She had blushed profusely beneath Benjamin's kindly, handsome gaze while he promised to continue her lessons. Catherine knew he would do so in a way that would put the shy moorland girl at ease. This meant that Mary, with Benjamin's help, would be able to consult the journal she had kept, in which she had recorded the herbs she had administered for a variety of ailments, injuries and wounds.

Bessie was a worry. When she had first learned that Catherine was to leave the Lodge, her old nurse had spoken adamantly about her intention to accompany her to France. Yet it was obvious her advanced age and increasing frailty meant it would be nigh on impossible for her to make the journey back to Nafferton Garth let alone travel overseas. In the end, Mary's widowed mother, Alice, offered a solution. However, it had taken a lot of persuasion on Catherine's part to have Bessie finally agree to remain behind and live with Alice and Mary at Glaisdale, the moorland village on the north-west edge of Stillingfleet Forest. Catherine's promise to return as soon as she was able won over the old woman, but left her wondering just when that might be.

The day before she was due to leave, when her chamber was nearly as bare as when she had first arrived at the Lodge, and her possessions were stored on the wagons, to her surprise Lucinda and Peter appeared with neat bundles. Even more surprising was the tidings that they would be accompanying her and Junno to France. She was glad for Junno's sake. Being one who did not harbour grudges, Catherine resumed her friendship with the unassuming Romany girl. Not least because she was of the opinion that Lucinda would be hard-pressed to do anyone harm, including Shadiz, unless she herself had been hard-pressed. Catherine did wonder if Junno's swift glance at his grandmother when Lucinda had confessed to poisoning Shadiz could be a clue. But while the mystery remained to perplex her, her usual friendly attitude brought relief to both Lucinda and Junno.

The women from Glaisdale, who served the Master's men, gave her a good send off. As did the Master's men.

Unbeknown to her, the women prepared a special meal in her honour. Her last evening at the Lodge was reminiscent of the one that had marked Tom's passing. The meal was served outdoors in the courtyard, where a warming blaze had been lit on the cobblestones to banish the chilly air of late April. Both the Glaisdale women and their youngsters, the Master's men and those Romanies under Junno's command partook of chicken and fresh spring vegetables from the kitchen garden, followed by steaming apples pies; the fruit having been picked from the orchards of Glaisdale the previous autumn, before Catherine had any knowledge of the Lodge.

She realised that someone must have given permission for the festivities. She was unable to stop herself from repeatedly glancing around the merry throng in the hope she might catch sight of Shadiz. But as time went by that hope seemed forlorn and, despite her smiles, her heart was heavy.

The urge to visit the library proved irresistible. Standing in the midst of the chamber, she yearned for his presence. But the darkness, lit by external flames, was filled only by the bitter-sweet memories of the night Tom had been honoured.

When the door opened, her heart suddenly began to pound. She spun round. Although the figure in the doorway was tall, it was not the one she longed to see.

"Rauni, they're lookin' for y'," Junno told her, kindly. "They've summat for y'."

"Oh, right, " Catherine responded, stifling her despair.

In the hallway, passing flickering torchlight, Junno put his arm around her shoulders. He had, with an aching heart, known where to find her. "Y' be well?"

She nodded, smiling wistfully up at him. "I just wondered. Silly really."

"Nay, Rauni."

She was greatly touched by the gifts she was given, which made it even harder to mask her inner turmoil. Fortunately her leaky emotions could be blamed on her enforced departure from the Lodge by the people surrounding her.

From the regretful women she received a delicate woven basket full of flowers and herbs and a shawl embroidered with the fauna of moorland and forest. And, awkwardly, from the Master's men, pearl earrings, kid gloves and kerchiefs edged with lace, all of which their grinning, feet-shuffling spokesman, Bill Todd, assured her were purchased honestly. Even the reserved Romanies presented her with a gift, a set of exquisitely carved forest creatures. In thanking them all, she tried not to be disloyal to her guardian.

Only when she was abed, and Bessie and Mary were asleep, did the dam burst silently upon her pillow.

★ ★ ★

Junno followed Tomas out of the courtyard. All was quiet now. Only the dying embers of the fire upon the cobbles remained of the evening's wistful jollity. The big man glanced over his shoulder, wondering when next he would see the ramshackle, stone-built Lodge after tomorrow. He gave a regretful sigh as he and the young Romany were swallowed up by the night shrouded forest.

Tomas's somewhat fearful explanation puzzled Junno. "What d' y' mean?" he began, and then broke off, having caught sight of two pairs of eyes gleaming in the night between the trees. A chill ran down his spine. He halted. The young Romany followed suit.

Amber slits hovered in the background while a pair of gemlike orbs, gleaming in a thread of moonlight, approached the two men. A ragged shadow made itself known to Junno. The mastiff bound away a few paces and then retraced its footsteps to him.

"Reckon it wants y' t' follow," said Tomas, apprehensively.

"Aye," responded Junno, with a notable lack of enthusiasm.

He set off alone, much to Tomas's relief. The mastiff padded softly on the uneven ground just ahead of him. He soon came to realise the dog was being guided by the other shadow, vague enough to make him suspect it was a figment of his imagination. Man and dog were set upon an invisible path, woven through the nebulous trunks of trees. While the mastiff remained a few, inviting paces in front of him, only just discernable within the forest's darkness, Junno's footsteps faltered only once upon him hearing the eerie mimicry of a hunting owl.

Having felt as if he had just been led through a nocturnal existence that defied time and humankind, at length the bulk of trees gave grudging scope for the vagaries of moonlight. Up ahead, he caught sight of an earthly glow. A beacon of normality, it drew him into a broad clearing. Although he felt sure his suspicions were about to be confirmed, he remained cautious. As he approached the fire, the grey-coated mastiff was defined, as was the great brown boar. It halted and turned its pale, scimitar-like tusks in his direction. He could have sworn there was a glint of amusement in its beady, amber eyes.

At first he thought only the Druid was present, sitting on a log by the fire. Then he spotted his cousin. A creature of darkness shunning the strong firelight, Shadiz was leaning against the broad girth of an oak, one of several ringing the clearing.

The Druid was watching Junno. "The merry-making was an appropriate send-off."

"Aye. Rauni enjoyed 'ersen," responded Junno, his attention on his silent cousin. "As best she could."

The mastiff trotted over to Shadiz, tail wagging. He sank down onto his haunches. Ignoring the two men, he playfully ruffled the dog's shaggy coat by way of praise for completing its task successfully.

When the Druid turned in his direction, the firelight shone upon his long white hair and was reflected in his grey eyes, set deep within his dignified face. "He is worthy of your decision."

★ ★ ★

Swept on by the remorseless march of time, the day dawned brisk and fresh. Catherine said her goodbyes with brittle fortitude. She left the Lodge and rode through Stillingfleet Forest, praying that it would not be the last time she set eyes on both.

From the time he had learned that his half-brother was sending her away to his chateau in France, Richard had been consumed by an impotent anger. He had recovered from the fever, but not from the tidings of her destination.

He stood beside Benjamin in the middle of the courtyard and watched as Catherine passed from sight. The twin emotions of fury and anguish were stamped upon his thin, pale face and infused every fibre of his being. His plight was made worse by Shadiz's decree that he was to remain at the Lodge and not accompany Catherine to Whitby where she was due to take ship to France. The final insult galled him beyond measure.

Rigid from head to toe, he marched back into the Lodge. The rusty hinges complained when he flung open the door of the library. Having reached the crackling fire in several brisk strides, Richard stood breathing furiously. Unable to remain still for long, he spun round and marched across to the long table in the middle of the chamber. For a couple of moments he rested his fists on the battered wood. His thunderous expression was reminiscent of the one that often rested upon the dark countenance of his half-brother. In one angry movement, he swept off the few items left on the table from Catherine's last meal at the Lodge, which he had shared with her. Mugs and pewter dishes they had used to break their fast landed with a loud crash on the floor.

Benjamin closed the door quietly behind him. He remained close to it, watching as Richard paced the library. "Is it not better for Miss Catherine to be away from here and safe in France?" he pointed out, in a calm manner. "I thought you would be relieved to see her gone from the Master? You have spoken of that desire often enough."

"Do you take me for a fool!" Richard snapped, kicking the scattered utensils away from his irate path. He rounded on Benjamin. "What of that bastard?" he rasped, jabbing a stiff finger at the glassless window. "Where is he?"

Benjamin waited until the other man had recovered from a sudden fit of coughing, most certainly brought on by his agitation, before replying to what in truth sounded like desperation, "I'm sure the Master will return to the Lodge, ere long."

"You believe so, do you," retorted Richard, hoarsely, "God's blood, man. She is going to *his* chateau."

"For her own safety," persisted Benjamin, patiently.

"For her own safety," repeated Richard, with bitter mockery. He shook his head. "I tried to make matters plain to her. To no avail. I fear this journey of hers will lead to…." he paused, and then with terrible emphasis, added, "her violation and death."

Benjamin frowned. His expression made it plain he was unconvinced by the other man's passionate argument. "The Master would not harm her."

"Hell's teeth!" exclaimed Richard. He expelled a ragged breath of pure frustration. "Have you not heard what befell that girl from Boggle Hole? Why won't anyone understand of what he is capable?" Before he could continue, bubbles of chronic air once more rose up within him.

Without a word, Benjamin crossed to the table. Bending, he picked up a fallen mug and then poured water into it from the stone jug which had escaped Richard's wrath. "Take a drink," he urged.

After Richard had done his bidding, Benjamin, concerned for his friend, persuaded him to sit in one of the rough chairs set haphazardly around the table. Trembling, staring into the middle distance, Richard tried to recover his breath and his composure. Above all, he felt impelled to try and make Benjamin understand.

"Shadiz not only murdered my father. His father. I have told you what he did to Elizabeth, his half-sister," he said, looking at Benjamin. The other man grimly nodded. "It was common knowledge she was to visit our aunt in York. She was so excited, she told everyone she met prior to her going."

Although he had heard the tragic details before, Benjamin remained silent. Folding his arms, he leant against the table, studying Richard.

"My mother and Francois between them decided upon a substantial escort to safeguard her first journey alone. Unbelievably, she was less than an hour away from the Hall when the bastard struck. In Long Hollows." He saw Benjamin's reaction. "How do you think he knew where to hit Francois when he had waylaid Catherine? The dip is close enough to Fylingdales Hall to give the allusion of safety and yet out of sight for hostile purposes. After slaughtering the escort, Shadiz and his mongrel scum took everything of value, raped and then murdered the women. But it was Shadiz who stripped and took Elizabeth. And then strangled her."

"It is possible one of his men?" began Benjamin.

Richard sharply interrupted him, "I've made it plain before. It was Shadiz. The only survivor told us so."

For a couple of moments, the two men were silent, lost in the murk of their respective thoughts.

"I brought you here to support me. I expected your understanding," said Richard, getting to his feet suddenly, wiping a brutal hand across his sparkling eyes. "Yet you would seem to have gone the way of all the rest and become ensnared in the bastard's black web."

Benjamin frowned. Empathy with the other man's pain at the murder of his father and sibling gave way to a demand. "What do you mean … brought me here?"

Richard exhaled impatiently. "You know very well, I am here at this godforsaken place to try in anyway I can to bring down Shadiz. And if that means assisting those who have wronged me, so be it. I've had to wait a long time after that old fool Tom Wright arranged Shadiz's escape from Scarborough Castle. I thought with your help, I could bring my hopes to fruition. I arranged with Francois for the troopers to waylay you, and made sure we were in the area." He shrugged, apologetically. "When you put up such a good defence, they went a little too far. They were only supposed to make your indisposition bad enough to warrant a few days recuperation at the Lodge."

"What then did you intend?" asked Benjamin. He had straightened, and looked far from pleased at being manipulated.

"Oh, come now," retaliated Richard, "you have ample justification to stand with my family, such as it is, and demand retribution."

"I have told you on more than one occasion," said Benjamin, brusquely, "I do not know whether it was Shadiz or Nick Condor who killed my father and brothers on their homeward voyage from Malta."

"Shadiz or Nick Condor, what does it matter? They both hail from the same cesspit."

CHAPTER TEN

Til Death Do Us Part

Catherine's memory of her last visit to Whitby vied with the reason for her present one. Both were strenuous in their uniquely different demands upon her emotions. Even if she ventured a look into the future, the thought of banishment to France, to Shannlarrey, the elegant, white-stone chateau overlooking the Mediterranean Sea, served only to deepen the despondency that had dragged at her spirit while riding over the moors in sight of the sea. The two wild, volatile elements had defined who she was leaving behind, with, she doubted, any leave taking.

The large cavalcade had come under scrutiny even before entering Whitby. It consisted of Junno and his family, Keeble and an impressive number of the Master's men and Romanies. A mixture of both were due to sail with Catherine. Clearly, Shadiz was not taking any chances with her safety even in the peace of France.

His kind heart aching for Catherine, apprehensive about the next hour or so, Junno held himself tensely while leading the way into Church Street.

Those people obliged to stand back against the rough stone frontages of cottages, shops and taverns, watched with collective interest and a shrewd idea why the heavily armed riders, the wagons and the young girl, about whom there had been a certain amount of gossip, had arrived in Whitby. The answer lay in the harbour.

At the end of the sunny street where it swung sharply upwards to Haggerlythe, the wagons loaded with Catherine's possessions were driven in the opposite direction down the granite slope leading to Tate Pier. Expecting to continue into Haggerlythe to say her farewells to Laura and her daughters, Junno surprised her by leading the escort to the right, up the steep Donkey Trail.

"I believe we have made a wrong turning?" Catherine pointed out.

"There be no mistake, Rauni," Junno answered with a guilty smile.

"Be adventure!" exclaimed Peter, merrily. He was being held against his father's broad chest. Both were astride the powerful Clydesdale.

Lucinda was riding a dappled pony beside Catherine's mare Twilight. She appeared troubled, but seemed to take comfort in her husband's solicitous glance.

While their mounts climbed the rocky incline, bewildered, Catherine asked, "I do not understand. Why are we going this way?"

Junno's large, round face betrayed a mixture of emotions.

A lightning bolt of understanding shot through her. "Oh, I see," she murmured.

Henceforth, the motionless children staring wide-eyed at the big man on the big horse and the lucky boy riding with him, the clucking hens fleeing from the horses, the dogs barking at both and the women who had broken off from gossiping around their irregular cottages, all were a blur to Catherine, such was her painfully heightened expectation. Upon reaching the windy heights of the Abbey Plain, she scanned the gaunt ruins of the ancient Abbey of Streonshalh. Yet, she cared little for the shattered glories of yesteryear. All that concerned her was what existed in the vital presence.

It soon became apparent that the Abbey was not their destination. Instead, Junno led them a little distance further on, to where the Church of St. Mary had offered lofty blessings to the port since the twelfth century.

By the time Bill Todd helped Catherine to dismount in the cool shadow of the church precinct, she was trembling with anticipation. She sensed his concern but was too involved in looking about her to give him more than an absent-minded smile.

After issuing a command that ensured everyone remained with

the horses, Junno took Catherine's arm and guided her forwards. Sharing a tense, expectant silence, they took the stony path close to the jagged cliff edge. It meandered past gravestones, some so weathered their inscriptions had become illegible. Catherine's heart marked their progress by beating excessively against her contracted ribs. She was barely conscious of Junno's light, guiding touch, and knew nothing of his burdened expression.

There were no shadows on the cliff top. The late April sunshine gave warm radiance to what stood within its lofty domain. Upon setting eyes on the tall, unmistakable figure, Catherine caught her breath. She walked on without realising Junno had halted. Her entire being focused on Shadiz, she advanced slowly towards him.

While riding up Donkey Trail, she had resolved to confront him about his blackened past that had reached into her disrupted life, threatening to tear her heart out. Yet, knowing what he was capable of, what he had more than likely committed recently, upon him fulfilling her secret hope, she found it impossible to withstand the irresistible draw he exerted upon her. For all her caring of the living, what did that say about her?

Shadiz watched her while the distance between them diminished until only a few feet separated them. A tableau of constraint, a long look passed between them.

Eventually, he asked, "Y' well?"

Striving for calmness beneath his piercing, jet-black scrutiny, she drew a shaky breath. "Under the circumstances." Modifying her tone after seeing him darkly wince, she asked, "And yourself? You appear much improved."

"Aye," he responded.

Despite his affirmative response and his declaration of abstinence in the missive that Junno had delivered to her at the Lodge, Catherine sought any sign of lingering malaise, especially from the usage of Mamma Petra's habit forming potion. Thankfully, she could find none, while he endured her scrutiny. The tautness in his dark-skinned, barbarous face she attributed to their meeting. His neatness surprised her. Gone was his usual rough attire. His breeches and tall boots were both immaculate. He wore a fine cambric shirt beneath a long, linen jacket. There was no weeklong stubble about his jaw, as was usually the case. His long black hair had been combed and tied back with a thin strip of leather. Even more unusual, he wore neither the broadsword he carried on his back nor the curving scimitar usually at his hip.

Traitors to her cause, her eyes betrayed her curiosity. If it had been anyone else, she would have credited the withdrawal to shyness. He turned without speaking and looked down at the harbour. After a moment, Catherine followed his example. Upon doing so, she was astonished by what she had previously missed due to her preoccupation with him.

Below them, the cottages of the tightly-knit community, interwoven with yards and wynds, descended in a bewildering array down the cliff's craggy slope to the harbour. The full measure of the River Esk, glinting as the sun smote its rippling bronze surface, divided the populated east side of Whitby from the more rural west side.

Accustomed to the features of the port, especially those east of the stout, wooden bridge linking the two halves of Whitby, Catherine's attention rested on the two ships berthed in the harbour. Compounding her startling discovery, she realised she had not only seen one of them before, but had sailed aboard the larger of the two.

The impressive ship was moored alongside Tate Quay, overshadowing the surrounding trading vessels including the *Eagle*. Almost her equal, the other newcomer was tied up beside Fish Landing, dwarfing the bobbing fishing boats. Catherine got the disturbing impression of two sleek, arrogant warriors, having sailed from a very different world. Their numerous sails were neatly furled on soaring masts, resembling the folded wings of sea eagles whose talons were the gun ports that lined their tall sides. Their towering forecastles and poop decks dominated the nearby rooftops of warehouses and huddled cottages.

Catherine pointed to Tate Pier and the ship that, surely, was the one aboard which her father and herself had sailed to and from France when she was twelve and had been recovering from the illness Mamma Petra had cured. "That is ... it *is* the *Sea Witch*?"

"Aye," murmured Shadiz.

She turned back to him, blue eyes expanded. "The *Sea Witch* is your ship?"

"Aye."

In spite of her surprise, Catherine noticed his unguarded expression of a captain's pride.

"The *San Juan* is berthed at Fish Landing."

"They are both yours?"

He shrugged. "They're part o' fleet."

"I see," muttered Catherine, thoughtfully. Looking more closely at the activities below them on the quayside, she saw her possessions were being unloaded from the wagons and taken aboard the *Sea Witch*. She had arrived at Whitby expecting to voyage to France on the *Eagle*. The presence of the two ships explained why she had been given ample time to pack up her life at the Lodge. It also explained why Keeble and Danny Murphy had disappeared. Little wonder Shadiz had issued the order that Richard should remain at the Lodge. She could just imagine his reaction to her sailing from Whitby aboard a corsair, certainly not one his dangerous half-brother would have tolerated.

"I am to sail on your ship," Catherine stated.

Shadiz did not look at her. "Aye."

"Will you be captain?" she asked, unable to stem a valiant hope.

Eventually, in a whispery tone, "No."

The heady moment passed. The passionate outburst, which threatened to choke her, would have sharpened words and only served to make their parting even more difficult. Recognising the futility of hope, Catherine looked away from Shadiz's guarded features. In silence, both of them studied the harbour below their lofty vantage point. She half-listened to the windborne snatches of conversations from women concerned with domestic matters, children playing pirates and men commenting on the two powerful ships. The thought of sailing away on the flooding tide caused her to take an intake of air, appropriately filled with the tang of the sea. Her forlorn gaze strayed to the beach to the north of Whitby, glistening in the sunlight. She would have given anything to walk with Shadiz upon the golden thread beside surf-laced waves. And settle matters.

Shadiz swung away from the cliff edge. "We need t' go in," he stated, abruptly.

"Go in where?" Catherine asked, perplexed. She followed the direction of his stern gaze to the weathered, grey-stoned Church of St Mary's. "Oh, in there."

"Aye," he answered, looking down at her with a fierce expression, as if awaiting a challenge.

Seeing he was serious, she thought he had suddenly gone all religious on her and wished to have her forthcoming voyage blessed. She quickly dismissed the ridiculous notion. Another took its place. "You're not going to marry me off to Richard, are you?" she exclaimed in alarm, glancing around the cliff top graveyard, half expecting his half-brother to suddenly appear from behind a headstone.

"O' course not," rasped Shadiz.

Catherine frowned, puzzled. "Then, why must we?"

"Develesko Mush." There was more than a hint of desperation in his whispery tone. "Y' ain't off into Med wi' 'em reckonin' y'r me ratvalo."

"Ratvalo?"

"Me ... wh ... mistress."

Her long hair was being tossed over her shoulder by the strong breeze. She brushed fair-white strands away from her face impatiently. She dismissed his declaration in the same vein. Whoever was in the Mediterranean would simply consider their pairing incongruous, for surely they would realise he would give her only a passing glance. Despite all she had been told recently, she sort another motive. "If it is not to marry me off to Richard or have my banishment blessed, then why?"

He looked elsewhere, anywhere but at her. "Fer what it's worth, I don't want 'em thinkin' bad o' y'. I ain't 'avin' 'em gettin' notion y'r me whore," he growled. "Mistress," he added, quickly.

"You've made that quite plain. The simple response, refrain from banishing me."

He gave her a pained scowl. And prowled a few paces away from her. When he turned back to her, his black eyes rested upon her young, mystified face for no more than a few seconds before shifting to the church. "Y'r father once said 'e wouldn't voice any objections. I'm sure 'e'd want y' treated wi' respect wherever y' went."

"Objections to what?" she demanded. He must consider her thick as two short planks, for she had no idea what he was talking about, and was becoming irritated.

He drew in a long breath. With an expression of extreme wariness in his black eyes, he turned his attention directly to her. "We need t' go in t' be ... romered."

No wiser, Catherine emitted a frustrated sigh.

After several moments of obvious hesitation, he gave her a stilted translation. "Married."

She simply stood and stared at him, immersed in jaw-dropping incredulity.

"I ain't 'avin' 'em makin' out y'r me whore," he rasped, defensively. "Mistress."

"So you keep saying," she replied, shakily.

"Y' ain't t' worry," he assured her, with rapid awkwardness. "I'll not make ... demands on y'." He shrugged. "An' when this be all over ... well."

"*Oh, no*! *Ye Gods and Little Fishes*! Oh, no you do not," Catherine exclaimed. "Don't you dare!"

She glimpsed the stir of guilt within darkness before the veil was hastily dropped. "You have to promise me, here and now, if we are to be wed this day, the only way our marriage will end, if it has to, is by an annulment. Promise me, or you'll have to cart me off kicking and screaming."

"What'd y' 'ave me say, for Christ Sake," he growled, like a man thwarted.

Catherine made as if to answer, then pressed her lips together in a determined manner. Her sudden resolve caught him off guard. She stepped forward, hastily closing the gap between them. He tried to retreat, but she moved with him, forcing him to a cautious halt on the edge of the grassy cliff. Standing on her tiptoes, she pulled the pendant from beneath his fine cambric shirt. The large, milky white stone encased in silver rested warmly in her hand for a second before she grasped his hand and, raising it up, closed his unresisting fingers about the stone.

"I want your pledge you will not make me a widow," she challenged.

They were very close because of her purposeful action. She felt his swift, light breath on her face as he continued to look down at her. Felt the brisk rise and fall of his chest beneath her left hand. Continuing to balance on her tiptoes, she swayed. His arm went immediately around her waist, steadying her.

At last. "I swear I'll keep you a wife. Till 'ell freezes over."

"I would break the bitter ice," Catherine informed him, tenderly. She prayed, she was doing just that.

Shadiz's expression softened. The bone deep tension left him in a sigh. "Kore." His other arm went around her. Meeting her expressive gaze, in a gentle manner, he asked, "Do I 'ave y'r acceptance?"

She put her heart into her smile. "Aye." *For better or for worse.* The words echoed in her mind of their own accord. Soon, it would seem, she would pledge herself to them.

He kept an arm around her when they turned away from the cliff edge and the sight of the waiting ships below in the harbour.

Although he had seen enough, Junno watched Shadiz and Catherine for a little longer before turning back to the people outside the church. He would have given anything for the day to be one of rejoicing. To have the bells of St. Mary's ring out for a true union.

Lucinda was waiting for Shadiz and Catherine beneath the high pitched roof of St. Mary's Norman porch. Catherine got the impression Shadiz was already aware that his men had presented her with the pearl earrings Lucinda gave her to wear. When she removed her cloak, the young Romany woman placed the embroidered shawl around her shoulders. Its fresh spring colours went well with her blue silk gown. Finally Lucinda handed over the pretty wicker basket, filled with violets and bluebells. It had also been given to her by the women from Glaisdale, little knowing it would become her bridal bouquet.

Catherine thanked Lucinda for her help, noting that her quick smile was somewhat forced and her dark eyes were cautious. She had not glanced once in Shadiz's direction. Even when she curtsied to him, she kept her eyes downcast. As she hurried away to join her husband and son in the main body of the church, Catherine wondered how many people had known of Shadiz's intention, but decided it mattered little.

His black scrutiny rested upon her. She swallowed nervously as he gave her a slightly anxious smile while taking her hand in his in a formal manner. His tall presence beside her gave reassurance and a wealth of other emotions.

When they started to walk together down the narrow aisle, the few people occupying the boxlike pews got to their feet. The cool, faintly musty atmosphere was charged with tension. Apart from Junno and his family, Laura and Bob Andrew and their two daughters were present. Also Keeble and Bill Todd. And the Romany, Imre Panin. Catherine sensed the spirits of those sadly missed also hovered close.

Parson Skinner received Shadiz and Catherine where the white-stone Cholmley Pew spanned the chancel arch, obscuring its ancient grandeur. A man of about forty, he was tall and thin with wispy grey hair and a sharp ruddy face. Confronted by Shadiz, he appeared devoid of his usual assurance in his pastoral duties.

After a noticeable hesitation, beneath Shadiz's instigating glower, Skinner embarked on the marriage ceremony. His nervousness became more pronounced when it was incumbent upon him to inquire, "If anyone knows of any just cause why this man and his woman should not be joined in holy matrimony, speak now or forever hold their peace."

For a notable few moments, Shadiz's rigid stance gave mute testimony to his reaction to the traditional challenge. Glancing sideward, Catherine was not surprised to see his expression had become significantly fierce. The memory of Richard waving her farewell at the Lodge filled her with a momentary qualm. She breathed a discreet sigh of relief when Parson Skinner judged it prudent to move on in haste with the alarming ceremony he had been called upon to perform. Having overcome the thorny pause, he proceeded with a little more confidence.

Whatever the motive for their utterance, the marriage vows were exchanged with quiet sincerity within the peaceful simplicity of the church.

Those present looked on with mixed feelings as Parson Skinner led the newly married couple up to the high altar. The heathen darkness of the husband was in striking contrast to the youthful fairness of his new wife. Together, they knelt to receive the ritual blessing before the Elizabethan Communion Table. Sentinels of the Light, long slender candles in golden candlesticks shone upon the velvet hammer cloth. They added silvery light to the rainbow hues cascading through the stained glass window depicting Saint Peter and a host of angels watching over a storm-tossed ship. A large gold cross, the most precious artefact of the isolated port's congregation, emitted a radiant glow between the flickering candles.

Upon completion of the ceremony, Skinner, struck by the demeanour of the bride and the groom, forgot to whom he spoke, "You may kiss your bride."

Shadiz scowled down at the shrinking parson until Catherine put pressure on the arm that had guided her from the high altar. Upon him responding to her, she gave a slight shake of her head in an attempt to convey her understanding of his reticence. Shadiz's expression altered. The small congregation was beginning to recognise the smile that was for her alone. They watched, intrigued, as he took her left hand. He raised it to his lips and kissed the gold band that minutes before he had placed upon her finger. Catherine felt shy suddenly, and unable to halt the attractive blush within her cheeks.

Parson Skinner cleared his throat. In an hesitant manner, he was duty bound to ask, "Who stands witness to this marriage?"

Catherine and Shadiz were once again in the shadow of the Cholmley Pew, half-turned towards the few people gathered in the evocative atmosphere of the church. Shadiz ended the brief pause by looking first at Junno and then at Bob. Both men moved to do the Master's bidding.

When all the formalities had been performed, man and wife stepped out into the warm sunshine where the Master's men continued to stand guard. He was handed his weapons by Danny Murphy. And appeared to tolerate the congratulatory bows Bill Todd and the rest of his men gave Catherine.

CHAPTER ELEVEN

A Far Better Deed

The breezy heights of Abbey Plain on the east cliff of Whitby, where the Church of St. Mary's stood close to the ruins of the Abbey, was left behind. Ahead was Tate Pier, where the full measure of the River Esk lapped against the *Sea Witch*. The distance between the two was diminishing far quicker than Catherine would have liked. She believed it to be the last time she would ride her mare Twilight for the foreseeable future. Her regretful supposition proved incorrect.

Riding alongside her on the black stallion, Shadiz offered her a choice. "Y' can tak y'r mare wi' y' t' France. Or I'll deliver 'er back t' Nafferton Garth. Tis up t' y'."

While speaking, his gaze roamed over the steep, narrow path they were descending, the dwellings that bordered Donkey Trail to the left and the bushes growing thickly along the drystone wall to their right. Whereas before the progress of the well-armed escort up the cliff path had been viewed with open interest, upon its return down to the harbour the curiosity of various bystanders was tempered to a noticeable degree by wariness because of the Master's presence.

When her indecision caused her to remain silent, he gave her a sidelong look. "She'll not be only mount aboard. They fare better than y'd expect."

Heartened by his experience in such matters, Catherine nodded enthusiastically. "Her company in France would be most welcome. Thank you."

Although Lucinda had given her the kid gloves, presented to her by the Master's men, upon leaving the church, she had not put them on. Not for the first time, she looked at her wedding ring.

"The wongustrin were 'onestly come by," Shadiz said, watching her.

"I never thought otherwise. I was simply admiring it. And ... feeling proud to be wearing your ring."

Upon meeting his gaze, Catherine found a reflection of her own profound emotion. An affirmation underlying the politics of the day. By the time they reached Tate Pier an air of tension had developed between them.

His barbarous face strictly impassive, Shadiz dismounted and then lifted Catherine down onto the blunt, stone-built quay protruding out into the River Esk. Bounding forward to answer his terse command, Keeble led her mare away towards the steep gangway of the *Sea Witch*. The little man soothed the nervous horse with idle chatter while his eager gaze rested on the fighting ship so familiar to him.

Viewed at close quarters, both the *San Juan* and particularly the *Sea Witch* appeared even more impressive, the height of their bulwarks even more imposing than when seen from afar. From the harbour, their tall masts appeared to reach up into the cloudless sky. The abundance of furled sails gave a strong impression of predatory knots through any kind of sea, and their gun ports close-mouthed death.

Churning within, Catherine focused on the hive of activity taking place around her upon the quay. Her attempt to take her mind off the forthcoming departure only resulted in her experiencing disconcerting qualms about the cosmopolitan atmosphere that had descended on the Yorkshire port. It made her apprehensive about the immediate future. She realised just how secure she had come to feel at the Lodge, with Shadiz.

Movement on the opposite quay, at the other side of the river deluged foreshore, caught her eye. Men of different races were loosening the thick ropes holding the *San Juan* fast against Fish Landing. Soon afterwards her gangway was raised and she began to be manoeuvred from her berth by her fleet of jolly boats. Before long, in mid-river, the freshening wind was filling her canvas, unfurled by sure-footed sailors on her lofty yardarms.

As she glided past Tate Pier, heading for the wide mouth of the sun-glinting estuary, Catherine was not the only one to admire the impressive corsair. The inhabitants of Whitby looked on from various locations, safe in the knowledge that the ominous visitors had not posed any threat because of the Master's authority.

Shadiz returned to her side after speaking briefly to Junno. Following her admiring gaze, he informed her, "She'll tak up station offshore until *Sea Witch* sails."

"H'm," responded Catherine, quietly. She noticed several of the gun ports of the *San Juan* were being opened.

"She'll act as escort t' France."

His low-pitched words brought back the cruel reality of leave-taking. With a heavy heart, she turned and located Laura and her daughters. They were standing on Mussel Beach below their cottage, waiting to wave her off. They were not alone. The narrow stretch of sand above the high water mark abounded with adult spectators, playful children and fascinated youths who were worrying their mothers.

All too soon the commands being issued on the *Sea Witch* vied with the raucous cries of the scavenging herring gulls. Shading her eyes against the glare of the sun, Catherine saw movement aloft. Experiencing a desperation she did not realise was reflected on her upturned features, she watched the seamen begin to unfurl canvas upon the main and mizzen masts. Too fast. Too soon.

The time came for Lucinda and Peter to board the *Sea Witch*. The tall, sturdy youngster had viewed all the alien bustle with wide-eyed wonder, holding onto his mother's hand. She appeared noticeably ill-at-ease. Nevertheless, she obeyed her husband and went with the two-man Romany escort. A robed figure stood politely aside at the head of the gangway in order for Junno's family to set foot on the main deck, then proceeded down to the quay.

Bob Andrew and members of his crew, standing in the shadow of the *Eagle*, considered with suspicion the Moor's flowing white robes. The gems set within the hilt of the huge, curving scimitar at his hip glinted in the sun with each brisk stride he took.

Halting before Shadiz, he salaamed. He spoke in Arabic to Shadiz, who answered him in the same language.

To Catherine, Shadiz said, "Sayid is my commander o' *Sea Witch*." Turning back to the Moor before she could offer any kind of greeting, he continued in cold, crisp English, "This is my wife, the Lady Catherine, who will be your most valuable passenger."

The Moor's dark eyes, set in his aquiline face, widened briefly. Recovering swiftly, he salaamed to her. "I am most honoured to meet your beautiful wife, and shall guard her with my life, hakim," he responded in heavily accented English.

The Master gave a curt nod to indicate his satisfaction. After bowing, the Moor withdrew to where Junno waited.

Shadiz had chosen well. Catherine viewed bitterly how their farewell was destined to be as public as his poisonous, self-loathing rage had been; vented upon the muddy foreshore between the two stone quays. She did not require a sixth sense to inform her that inquisitive eyes were focused upon them from all directions. Through dint of comradeship, Bob Andrew had engaged those men with him on the quayside in some sort of discussion in an effort to turn their backs upon her and the Master. It worked only in so far as the backward glances were surreptitious.

Despite their sunlit exposure, Shadiz stood immobile, looking down at Catherine. She was reminded of their first encounter in Colonel Page's tent, a lifetime ago it now seemed, when his manner had possessed a similar involuntary reaction. And she wondered briefly if the circle had been completed. If he was trapped within. Leaving her without.

His tribal-dark countenance gave the impression of someone thrust freshly from a cherished dream by his own vindictive hand. Seeing this unmistakable consequence of their parting, Catherine dared to take heart. In spite of the lengths Shadiz had gone to in securing her safe departure, she pinned her hopes upon one last entreaty to remain if not as his wife then to continue as his ward.

But no last minute reprieve was forthcoming. In response to her mute, heartfelt plea, he slowly shook his head, as one might who is pursued by a fiendish persecutor.

Cast down by his painful refusal, her blue eyes filled with tears she could not stem. They rolled unchecked down her pale, unhappy face. "You have kept me safe thus far. What has changed that I must sacrifice this present life in which you are central?" She pressed on, knowing what he was about to say in mitigation. "I don't believe my going is just about the developments in the war. Or the threat Fylingdales poses." She saw her words tormented him yet her own sorrow stopped her from being prudent. She whispered brokenly, "Please, do not send me away. *Please*."

His tortured stillness was shattered by a ragged breath. "Kore, I ain't able t' keep y' safe ... from mesen," he rasped with a viciousness that was not directed at her.

The forlorn wind had gone from the sails of her argument. "I don't understand?"

A light touch on her shoulder startled Catherine. Twisting around she found herself in Junno's towering shadow. His arrival was certainly due to his knowledge of the sting of their parting. The lingering touch on her shoulder was the big man's attempt to persuade her to be the one to end the poignant moment. A brave act she found impossible. She turned back to Shadiz, bewilderment plain upon her creased brow.

It was as if he stood apart from himself, to be a harsh critic. "D'y reckon 'is zeal t' guard y'r chamber door at night stemmed from simply a desire t' serve?"

"I did it wi' 'onor," put in Junno. He regarded Shadiz over the top of Catherine's head, silently willing his cousin to desist, and even to be gone.

Shadiz ignored him. "D'y reckon Lynette'd find ways t' come on mincin' tiptoes in the night. Or, in 'is stead, 'is bloody whinin' nephew?"

Struck by a staggering revelation, Catherine switched from Shadiz's bitter honesty to Junno's grim misery and then back again to her new husband. In a breathless rush, she declared, "He was guarding me against ... *you*?"

Shadiz gave a sour laugh. "An' now, y' get gist o' it." He checked himself. His black, magnetic eyes roamed over the river and the sea while he continued in a more reserved tone, "Tis more than six years gone, I returned to Nafferton Garth on a whim t' repay y'r father for the 'orseflesh I'd taken as a lad. I'd just saved Billy's scrawny neck from bein' stretched for thievin'. It put me in mind o' when Roger prevented me from swingin' from the nearest tree. On me way t' 'im, I stumbled upon the fairest scene, an' decided at the time the ale played me false. But the image o' a young girl playin' in fields wi' a wolf-hound 'aunted me an' drove me back. I found the ale weren't t' blame."

There was a lengthy pause. Catherine stood rigid, willing more to come, marvelling at what had gone already, though it threatened to break her heart.

Shadiz sighed, staring at the *Sea Witch*. "Roger was no Demeter, though I ain't casting no slight upon 'im. 'e just didn't comprehend what manner o' beast 'e would bestow 'e's daughter upon. Events went ill for 'im. An' me. But I must keep faith wi' 'im. For 'is daughter's sake." His anguished jet gaze finally came to rest upon Catherine. "These passed months, while the earth was cold an' desolate, y've lived within my lair, Kore. Now's come time fer y' t' take y'r fairness from my nether world. I can go no further than the north bank of the Styx. My ferryman'll sail y' across t' a safe haven."

Catherine was trembling uncontrollably. "Allow me to light the darkness in you that has driven you to foul deeds. To Elizabeth's destruction." Weeping softly, she added, "To Lucinda's violation. Mary's friend's demise. And … others?"

He flinched. "*Want* desires y' t' keep safe," he managed, in a harrowing, painful whisper. "The single light within the Serpent's eternal night is that you are its soul. Kore."

Scrutinising her as if etching her forever in his memory, Shadiz took one backward step, then another, then another. Then, with the greatest difficulty imaginable, he turned and walked away, leaving Catherine to stare after his tall, unforgettable figure as he made his way down the pier to the tethered stallion. Too soon, he disappeared from the waterfront and her despairing sight.

CHAPTER TWELVE

Kore

The stallion cropped the tough grass on the cliff top. Not far away, the mastiff lay with its head resting upon its big paws, watching seagulls soar on the brisk air above the North Sea.

Oblivious to all else, the tall man stood and watched the two ships sail away to a safe haven.

You've gone! I stood and watched your ship
Glide slowly up the sound,
Lost the hull, the sails, the mast;
Then lonely, I turned round,
And found your Spirit everywhere
On seas, in heavens, Sweetheart,
On hills, trees, flowers and birds, and shall
Till Time and I do part.